CROSSING THE LINE

"*Crossing the Line* is entertaining, touching, and insightful. Laura Castoro is a welcome new voice in women's fiction."
—Susan Elizabeth Phillips,
New York Times bestselling author

"*Crossing the Line* is warm and insightful, exploring the many ways our perceptions of love and identity need to be reinvented. A timely and enjoyable *must* read."
—Sandra Kitt, author of *Close Encounters,*
Between Friends, and *Family Affairs*

"Fascinating . . . undercurrents of suspense and buried secrets kept me turning pages in anticipation . . . the impact of crossing the color line is explored in its many aspects . . . a graceful handling of the social complexities of race and color. . . ."
—Carol Spencer, DIASPORA BOOKS,
Sag Harbor, New York

"*Crossing the Line* is wonderful! It captures the essence of our pain and our struggle to work through that pain. The characters are vivid and real. I wish more authors would write with as much authenticity of the world in which we live. You spoke to my heart. God Bless!"
—Joseph E. Washington, Pastor
Brooks Memorial United Methodist Church
Jamaica, NY

CROSSING
THE LINE

LAURA CASTORO

BERKLEY BOOKS, NEW YORK

This is a work of fiction. Names, characters, places, and incidents either are the product of the author's imagination or are used fictitiously, and any resemblance to actual persons, living or dead, business establishments, events, or locales is entirely coincidental.

CROSSING THE LINE

A Berkley Book / published by arrangement with
the author

PRINTING HISTORY
Berkley edition / August 2002

Copyright © 2002 by Laura Castoro.
Cover art by Franco Accornero.
Interior text design by Julie Rogers.

All rights reserved.
This book, or parts thereof, may not be reproduced in
any form without permission.
For information address: The Berkley Publishing Group,
a division of Penguin Putnam Inc.,
375 Hudson Street, New York, New York 10014.

Visit our website at
www.penguinputnam.com

ISBN: 0-425-18575-3

BERKLEY®
Berkley Books are published by The Berkley Publishing Group,
a division of Penguin Putnam Inc.,
375 Hudson Street, New York, New York 10014.
BERKLEY and the "B" design
are trademarks belonging to Penguin Putnam Inc.

PRINTED IN THE UNITED STATES OF AMERICA

10 9 8 7 6 5 4 3 2 1

acknowledgments

THIS BOOK MADE it into print because of the abundance of good people in my life. Below are only a few of those I wish to thank.

Rhonda, Mike, and Polly, the generous owners of Mountain Thyme B&B Inn in Jessieville, Arkansas, where, during a writing retreat, the characters of Xavier and Thea were born.

Reverend Joseph E. Washington and Dr. Dode Washington, who, out of friendship, opened their home to me and acted as advisers on church matters.

The "Bracelet Girls" Gwen Terry, Aundrie Botts, and Frances Griffin Brown, for their profound belief in me. No sisters could be better loved.

Gus Granger, who listened to my tales of writing woe and then always answered, "Get busy!"

Denise Marcil, my wonderful literary agent, who believed in this work when I was ready to throw in the towel.

Allison McCabe, my brilliant editor, whose clear vision allowed me to tell the story I wanted to tell.

Theresa, Anthony, and Christopher, my children, who have successfully navigated many of the issues brought up in this book.

Chris, my husband, who set out with me on this journey many years ago when the ways of the world were much less forgiving.

Dr. David E. and Mary Dell Parker, my parents, who instilled within me the pride, strength, and positive outlook to "know who you are and what you're up against, and then go out and do it anyway!"

To each and every one, I say: God bless.

prologue

THEA MORGAN COULDN'T quite believe the transatlantic conversation she had just had with her daughter. Six weeks ago, allowing Jesse to study French at the Sorbonne with other honors high school students had seemed a perfect opportunity. Instead, her daughter had gone to Europe and lost her mind!

And I lost my cool!

Could she stay over a week to backpack around France with a twenty-year-old college student named Emil? Who was that child trying to kid?

No almost-sixteen-year-old child of hers was going to go off to do God and she both knew what with some man she'd just met in a bistro!

You're booked for a flight home tomorrow, Jessica Darnell Morgan. Be on it!

She took a deep breath that ended in a little gasp of nerves. This panic. The fear and the hurt. Where had it all come from?

No way this time to have Evan's agreement in the matter. Tethered by careers that kept them traveling, she and her husband often had their most intense parenting conversations long-distance.

Thea shook her head. At least she had stopped reaching for the phone.

Jesse could be every bit as stubborn as her father. Her arguments, though sometimes flawed, were devastatingly effective. She might have lost the war but not without a final volley that left her mother's victory feeling hollow.

"I didn't expect you to be reasonable, *Mother. Fine.* I'll come *home,* but you can *forget* about me going to any stupid wedding! The way Aunt Selma keeps marrying, she'll have more exes than Exxon."

Too true.

Though she didn't admit it to Jesse, she hadn't made up her mind about attending her sister's third wedding until Aunt Della had put it this way: "Selma can be the most thoughtless creature God ever made. Be that as it may. As the eldest, it's up to you to take the higher ground. The least we can do is present a united family front at the ceremony. It's the Christian thing to do."

Christian duty. That was the heavy artillery.

Aunt Della was right. There was no sense in holding her sister responsible for her every irrational act. So what if they weren't close? She could play the magnanimous big sister for one afternoon. But this wouldn't be a lovefest. She wouldn't even stick a toothbrush in her purse. No way was she going to get trapped into staying overnight in case things soured.

No baggage. No worries. Easily done in one long-ass day.

She'd already called her sister with a cover story. *"Sorry, but I can't stay overnight, Selma. A shipment is due to arrive in Jubail—Jubail? That's a seaport in Saudi Arabia. You know I manage worldwide. Yes, girl, I've done well."*

Selma believed her. Only Aunt Della would know it wasn't true. But her aunt wouldn't blow her cover. That's what counted.

As she turned away from the phone, she sighed as she remembered another thing Della had said.

"Theadora, you haven't been home since your mother passed. Don't you think it's time?"

Unlike Jesse, I have a good reason for not wanting to go home.

Everybody had something to live up to—or live down—in

her hometown. She had both, and leaving Grambling at sixteen was the best thing that could have happened to her. Or was it? All these years later, she still couldn't decide. Nothing about this weekend was likely to answer that question.

Relax, Thea. You can do this, go home again.

one

"YOU HATE IT."

Thea couldn't keep the disappointment out of her voice. This welcome home surprise wasn't going as she had imagined it. They'd already had words about Emil on the drive in from the airport, a not-quite-a-fight that left the air humming.

"I watched that video over and over, trying to get it right."

"You got it right." Jesse let her duffel bag slide from her shoulder to the floor as she studied her bedroom, a blaze of magenta and gold walls. "It's fine. Really."

"But?"

The sulk Jesse had brought with her off the flight was still in place. "It's just that I now realize . . . well, it's *gauche. De trop.*" She turned to her mother. "Too much, you know?"

"I know what gauche means." She winced at the bite in her voice. "If you really hate it, change it. But you pick the colors *and* do the painting this time, okay?"

"I know you worked hard, Mom." Jesse's smile had only half an effort behind it. "It's just that I've seen so much, experienced so much. Developed my critical eye."

Her critical eye! Thea hid her smile and put her arms about her daughter, who topped her by three full inches. "Then I got my money's worth."

She swallowed. She was not going to cry. Evan always teased her about being sentimental. But right now, all she wanted to do was hug her child and keep on hugging her. Jesse was home! She rubbed a hand up and down her daughter's back before letting go. "You've lost weight."

"Isn't it great?" As Jesse pushed a swatch of pale blond hair from her eyes, Thea noted blue nail polish on display. The old Jesse did not wear nail polish.

Nor had she recognized the tiny tank top that bared her daughter's midriff or the hip huggers riding so low her navel was fully on view. The old Jesse had been a more conservative dresser. Her stomach did a flip-flop. *My baby's changing.*

Even so, Jesse remained so much like her father, from her hair to her beautifully blue eyes. The day Thea brought Jesse home from the hospital, her Aunt Della had peeked into her blanket and shook her head, saying, "You better do that again, Theadora, 'cause you sure didn't get any of this baby." Sadly, she and Evan never got around to that second dip into their gene pools.

Jesse seemed to notice the lapse in conversation, for she quickly said, "I forgot how major hot Dallas is in August. I need a shower."

"You should be jet-lagged. Why don't you stretch out after your shower while I make your favorite coffee ice cream float?" This was more of the homecoming that she had imagined.

Jesse wrinkled her nose. "No thanks, Mom. All that fat and sugar are bad for the skin and the teeth. I'll have spring water. With gas, if you have it."

With gas? Oh, bubbles.

"I'll have to check." She had gone to two stores to find Jesse's favorite brand of coffee ice cream. "We may have club soda. With lime?"

"Whatever." Jesse peeled off her hip huggers, revealing a black lace thong. She seemed both curvier and more slender. Only the strong muscles in her legs were familiar.

"Jesse, before I forget. Mrs. Franklin called. Soccer practice starts next Monday. I've been drafted for the committee to choose new uniforms."

"Oh, I gotta call Harper!" Jesse stripped off her top, leaving on a new lacy black bra. American Express charges from Paris were beginning to add up in Thea's mind. "She's going to have a cow when she finds out about Emil!"

"Call your grandparents first. They made me promise."

Jesse stopped short of reaching for the phone, her mouth pushing into another pout. "What's with this family togetherness all of a sudden?"

Thea smiled. "Could it be we missed you?"

Jesse shrugged. "But the only reason you made me come home was because you don't trust me."

"It wasn't you I didn't trust."

Jesse plopped down on her bed. "It was so embarrassing! Having to tell Emil I had to go home because my *mother* said so. But then why should I expect you to allow me to practice the language you *sent* me there to *study?*"

Thea didn't rise to the bait, but it was hard.

Jesse began picking at her nail polish. "You know, I could have been doing anything I wanted anytime I wanted these last six weeks."

You remember fifteen, don't you, Thea?

Did she really want to know? "Don't you have phone calls to make?"

" THEADORA? THIS IS Aunt Della from N'awlins."

Her father's elder sister always identified herself with her city, as if she didn't trust her niece to remember the woman she'd lived with during her last two years of high school. "Why aren't you in Grambling yet? More to the point, why aren't you Selma's matron of honor? That's what I want to know."

Mouthing a cussword, she put down a glass containing Jesse's soda with lime. She should have checked her caller ID before she picked up. Better tackle the least arguable point first.

"Now, Aunt Della, we had this discussion when Selma sent out her invitations. She'd already asked her business partner to be her maid of honor."

The last time they spoke, Selma freely admitted that the big wedding was a throw-down to entertain her fiancé's business connections. She nearly asked why, if it were a business gesture, the wedding wasn't being held where Selma lived, in that Godiva of chocolate cities, Atlanta. But she could guess the answer. After two bad marriages, Baby Sister had finally found a man she could brag about back home.

Aunt Della clucked her tongue. "I know you've had provocation. It's the gospel truth, Selma says and does things to provoke a saint. But blood is thicker than water, Theadora. Now, what's this about you not arriving in Grambling until Saturday?"

So much for her excuse not being questioned. "Business, Aunt Della. I do work for a living."

The huff on the other end of the line was too ladylike to be called a snort. "Listen to your Aunt Della, Thea. Family's all you got. Everybody else is just acquaintances. You turn your back on family, then you're really alone."

"I promise, I'll be in Grambling first thing Saturday."

"That's my girl! Now, wear something feminine. Something that brings out the color of your eyes and shows off your pretty legs. When a woman reaches a certain age, she has to make the most of her remaining assets. 'Bye now, sugar."

"This weekend had better be worth the aggravation," Thea muttered as she hung up the phone and picked up the glass to resume her errand. Just then, Jesse walked into the kitchen. She had changed into black biker shorts and a baby doll pink cropped tee. "I thought you were going to rest?"

"Harper and Cassandra are coming by to take me out." Jesse waved off the glass her mother tried to hand her. "So then, you're serious about going to Aunt Selma's wedding?"

Eavesdropping? "Very."

Jesse shot her a skeptical glance. "Why? It's not like you're all that close."

"All the more reason I should go." Thea took a sip of the refused club soda.

But, truly, she was busted. She and Selma weren't close. They went months without speaking. After a few five-cents-a-minutes' worth of how's Jesse, how's work, and how's life, they had little more to invest in conversation.

"That means I'll be alone this weekend."

You wish! "Actually, I'll be home Saturday night, late."

"Why?" Jesse blinked. "Don't you even trust me at home now?"

"Strange as it may seem, my plans have nothing to do with you." *And everything to do with my own comfort level.*

Jesse folded her arms across her chest and jutted out a hip. "One thing I never expected was that you'd be a hypocrite."

Thea very deliberately set her glass aside before raising her gaze to meet her daughter's. "I don't care how long you've been gone or what kind of critical judgment you've developed. You don't get to talk to me like that."

Jesse ducked her head, chin tucked protectively against her neck. "You think just because I don't say anything, I don't know." She lifted her chin. "I know plenty. Like the fact Aunt Selma didn't like Daddy."

"What are you talking about?"

"I heard you and Daddy talk sometimes. I know Aunt Selma walked out on your wedding, even though she was your maid of honor. And it was because of Daddy!"

The glint of triumph in Jesse's gaze confirmed that her mother had failed to keep the surprise she felt out of her expression.

Thea made a helpless gesture. "Okay. When she was young, Selma sometimes said and did things she shouldn't. But she's changed."

"What I don't get is why you've changed. When Daddy died, you told Aunt Della that you'd never forgive Aunt Selma because she couldn't be bothered with showing up for the funeral."

Guilt jolted Thea. She had said that. Only later did she learn that Selma was in the hospital with a miscarriage. "I was wrong. I didn't know she was ill then."

"Whatever."

Jesse almost never mentioned her father's death, much less his funeral. She had to be upset. Groping for the right response, she came up with a pitiful, "We need to talk, Jesse."

"No, we don't." Jesse straightened up, as if daring her mother to contradict her. "You go and be happy for her, if you want. Maybe it's easy for you because Daddy's dead. But I won't be a hypocrite!"

The sudden beeping of a horn sounded outside.

"That's Harper." She headed for the door. "We'll be back, late."

"Midnight, Jesse. Not one second later."

The door slammed.

"Damn!" Thea stared at the closed door for several seconds. Then she carefully sat down and leaned her head against the kitchen tabletop, the joy of the day gone completely. In its place was the creeping certainty that she could have handled things better. From the get-go.

She had had no idea that Jesse held a real grudge against Selma. Sure, she'd let her impatience with her self-indulgent sister spill over into general conversation from time to time. But she always saved her real grievances for late-night conversations in bed. How much did Jesse know, and what had she simply guessed at? Clearly, enough to be wounded and resentful but not enough to get it right.

She and Evan had tried so hard. They were so careful to shield Jesse from any and all family unpleasantness. And, really, there had been so little of it after the first couple of years of the marriage. Maybe they had handled it wrong. Maybe she should have explained to Jesse the real source of her estrangement with Selma a long time ago. But trying to explain her family's relationships was like playing Pick Up Sticks. You could hardly ever pick out one thing without touching on half a dozen others.

For instance, the last big fight she'd had with Selma, the one that cost them the home they grew up in.

She had been potbellied with Jesse. Selma had driven in from her junior year at Spelman College to attend their mother's funeral. Selma must have felt as cheated as she did by the sudden departure of their last parent from their lives. Where was the grandmother Thea's baby was going to need? Where was the mother to tell her how to be one? And who would be Selma's steadying influence in a world that offered too much temptation to a girl with a lot of imagination? Two other sisters would have pulled together, made closer by their mutual pain. But their frightening loss erupted in the only energizing emotion they had left: anger.

They had a catfight over their parents' possessions. Damn the will! They both knew without saying so that this was really about who loved who best. Evan tried to convince her that she was making a mistake. She didn't speak to him for three days. In the end, they sold what they could not snatch out of each other's hands. Even the house. To this day, she had not touched a cent of the money from the sale. It seemed like blood money: the price of sisterhood.

Sisterhood. Strangers seldom realized they were sisters. Selma had their father's coloring, that soft Halle Berry shade between ginger and pecan. She inherited their mom's remarkably fair Creole skin. Selma's hair was a thick, deeply waved mahogany, while hers was a lighter, straighter version of their father's sandy brown. Selma never let her forget the difference.

"Just because you look white and marrying white, don't make you white!" Selma had shouted just before she walked out on the wedding.

Thea gave her head a quick shake against old resentments too familiar to make her really angry anymore. Selma's nineteen and her twenty-four were a lot of years ago. In that time, Selma had mellowed. Even Evan would have agreed. But the changes still did not make loving her easy.

After this wedding, she would have to find a way to make Jesse understand that sisters could love one another and still need every mile between Atlanta and Dallas in order to keep the peace.

But first she had to go home and face down some ghosts of her own.

two

HOT ASPHALT SUCKED at her heels and breathed suggestively up her skirt as Thea crossed the parking lot of Saint Luke's AME Church. Heat shimmered and sheared off in waves from the metal surfaces of the cars she passed. Six P.M. might be the evening hour for a formal wedding, but August had yet to yield its triple-digit hold on the day.

A bead of perspiration slid down one cheek as she approached the entrance. She was late. "Operating on CP time," Aunt Della would say in disapproval. This was Jesse's fault. She had returned an hour late from her sleepover at Harper's, mumbling something about a failed alarm. Furthermore, she had informed Thea, the French regarded Americans' mania for being on time as a further indication of gaucherie. This new Gallic attitude was wearing very thin.

So she was late and hot *and* there was no place to park within two square blocks. The line of white limos drawn up at curbside before the low-roofed brick church amazed her. Six? The scale of the wedding altered in her mind as she hurried toward the entrance.

Balancing her gift in one arm, she swung open one of the

great paneled doors to the vestibule and came to a full stop. A blur of saffron and ivory and penguin suits met her eye. The wedding party was ready to march down the aisle. She stepped back and let the door go before she could be recognized. The last thing she wanted to do was make a spectacle of herself seconds before Selma walked down the aisle. She needed time to compose herself before she faced all those people.

She found the side door and an usher in white stationed there. He took her gift and handed her a program embossed with a gold-stamped magnolia. This might be Selma's third marriage, but it was her first wedding. The distinction was beginning to dawn. The realization reached full potency when she stepped into the church.

No pew was left unbowed or flourish furled. It was the kind of bash that would be photo opped in *Jet* and *Ebony*. The sanctuary looked like a floral shop: flowers everywhere the eye could see. Brilliant yellow and pale gold blossoms cascaded from tall pedestals stationed along both walls. The altar overflowed with tiers of waxy magnolias, delicate branches of orchids, and sweet trumpets of stephanotis. Their perfume enfolded her as she moved forward. Even as she appreciated their effect, she could not help thinking that the allergic among the guests must be frantic.

Clearly, Baby Sister had called in every favor of her professional interior decorating life. Or Elkeri Yoruba, the groom, had some serious money. Selma always wanted to marry serious money.

From the far side of the altar, the first notes of Vivaldi swelled from an organ announcing the procession, forcing her into the first unoccupied space, which happened to be a pew on the groom's side of the aisle. She smiled at everyone whose eye she attracted and received polite nods in return. It had been drilled into her from toddler age. Respect in "the community" was measured in syllables, a tone, a glance. "Always speak, Theadora. Don't want to seem stuck-up."

She had forgotten how Southerners, especially her people, like to dress for weddings. Most men wore tuxes, while the women wore beads and sequins.

They better have that air cranked up to full, she thought and began fanning herself with the gold-embossed program. There were not enough perspiration shields in the world to save all the silk and lace and chiffon packed into this church.

Finally, the music changed, signaling the bride, and the crowd rose to an accompanying chorus of aahs and oohs, while dozens of camera flashes lit up the sanctuary like the sudden arrival of a Louisiana thunderstorm. From her vantage point, Thea could not see a thing. Selma was almost at the altar before she glimpsed her sister through the forest of people. Then she understood the reaction.

Arriving unescorted, Selma wore a long-sleeved, open lacework, gold-beaded tunic that clung with runway precision to her slim body. She didn't carry a bouquet. She didn't need one. Attached to her upswept dark hair was a single large magnolia blossom from which sprang a veil of exotic feathers that curled up, over, and back, to end below her nape. The effect was dramatic. Exotic. Very Selma.

"Go on, Baby Sister!" she murmured in admiration. Give it to Selma, she knew how to create a moment. In fact, Selma was her own best creation.

Though barely five foot two, people inevitably remembered her as tall. Credit the impact of her personality and the fact she seldom stepped out of staggering heels. A sultry beauty packaged in a petite size four. Most women felt the urge to clutch their men a little tighter when Selma Broussard walked into a room.

The groom, who moved forward and reached for Selma's hand as she arrived at the altar, did not look as she expected an Elkeri Yoruba would look. No dreads or Kente cloth. Instead, he wore a flowing white silk suit with a gold vest. In place of a bow tie, he wore a short gold ribbon crossed and studded by a diamond with enough *wink* to reach the back pews. Selma's touch?

How different from my wedding, thought Thea. Evan had a job waiting at a Philadelphia law firm as soon as he passed the state boards, so they planned for a quick civil ceremony in D.C. right after his graduation. But her father wanted to be certain it was "legal with God." He insisted a minister should conduct the service in a church. The compromise was a lawn service at the

Morgan home in Philadelphia, with the Morgan family minister officiating. A child of the seventies, she bought a dress from a vintage shop in Georgetown. Evan, who the day before the ceremony cut off his mustache and shoulder-length hair, opted for a tuxedo shirt and black trousers. Her bouquet had been picked right from the Morgans' greenhouse. It would have been strictly a family affair if not for a "few close family friends" Shirley and Richard invited to their son's wedding. The Morgans were *the* Morgans of Philadelphia banking. The few friends numbered over a hundred, and the wedding gifts included enough silver, crystal, and china to serve a dozen.

"Did your in-laws forget that you're black?" Selma declared after glimpsing the early arrival gifts. "Because you just know these people don't envision a bunch of Negroes eating collard greens and sipping malt liquor out of all this Tiffany china and Baccarat crystal."

Thea shook her head at the memory. In those days, Selma liked to pretend that she was not advantaged growing up. Loved to tell the story that she had once regaled a roomful of liberal whites with tales of her youth in the cotton fields. Truth was, of course, that not only had they grown up in a house with china and silver, but it was Selma who demanded most of it when their mother died.

She did not spare a glance for the officiating minister until he stepped forward beyond the cascade of altar flowers with uplifted hands. "Dearly Beloved, Brothers and Sisters, we are gathered here today in the sight of God . . ."

Thea caught her breath. The shock that ran through her did not thrill. It stunned. She was prepared to tough out many things today. This was not one of them. It couldn't possibly be! There on the altar was the man who had been the first and worst mistake of her life.

"Oh, Jesus!" She started breathing again.

"Amen!" murmured the elderly woman next to her appreciatively.

Thea looked at her, startled. Then she blinked, eyes itching from perspiration. Maybe she was wrong. With all the hats and heads between her and the altar, she could not see well from this distance. Maybe it only looked like him. As the guests re-seated themselves, she snatched open her wedding program. Beside the designation "Officiating Minister" was a name engraved in shiny black: **Xavier Templeton Thornton, Pastor Saint James's AME Church, Atlanta, GA.**

Xavier. No mistake.

The black letters danced before her eyes. Why had Selma not warned her?

Get a grip, Thea. Nobody knows.

She inhaled a steadier breath. No one had ever known about Xavier. Not Selma nor their parents. Not even Aunt Della.

The woman next to her pointed to his name. "You do know who that is?"

She nodded. She knew what anyone who bothered to pick up a sports section, fanzine, or even a tabloid during the past twenty-five years knew. Some of the headlines she could recite by heart. "The 'X' Factor: New Tight End Sensation." " 'X' Pro Tackles Hollywood." " 'X'It Hollywood—'X'celling on Wall Street." "Entrepreneur 'X'changes Shares for Souls."

As if given encouragement, the woman whispered knowingly, "Women came to this wedding I *know* weren't even invited." Disapproval puckered her lips. "They just want to see the 'X' Factor."

Thea did not need to be reminded that Xavier was once the target of romantic and erotic fantasies for women worldwide. She fell mad-bad in love with Xavier long before "X" was a factor in his life. Once she had spun endless daydreams about how it would be if she saw him again, what she would say, what he would say. Now that the moment had arrived, she felt numb.

"Who gives this woman . . . ?" She quickly lifted her gaze to the altar.

"I do." Della Broussard Wilson Bennett St. Claire came forward to the altar, her short, plump figure dressed in eye-catching chartreuse from picture hat to pointed heels. Their father's eldest sibling, she was standing in as proxy parent.

Thea could see Xavier's lips moving, but she could not hear what he was saying. Her mind was racing. Thank God Jesse was late this morning! If she had gotten here on time, she would be sitting in the front pew with the family, as visible to Xavier as he was to her. From this distance, it was safe to stare. He was still worth staring at.

The imposing muscular breadth of a onetime professional athlete filled out his clerical robes. Tight black curls and modified Vandyke beard framed a broad, bittersweet chocolate face that was pure-D handsome without a trace of pretty. That face and physique, combined with a genuine intelligence, had propelled him from pro football through a minor stint in Hollywood and on into the corporate boardroom with a lot of gossip-producing stops in between. He had succeeded, she suspected, even beyond his own outsized expectations. And now he was a minister. That was still hard to believe, but she'd read about it in the papers. And he was here, of all places, at Selma's wedding.

His voice was the same, a deep baritone that resonated with the rapid rhythm of his Chicago minister father combined with the drummed-in diction of his high school English teacher mother. "An educated black voice: one of God's gifts to sound," Aunt Della liked to say.

Thea looked away. By the time she reached the reception, she would have some perspective on seeing him. Until then, she decided, she was *not* going to sit here staring at him like he was the prize behind door number three.

She had plenty of other things to occupy her thoughts, and she willed her mind to consider them.

Jesse had shut down on the subject of family. In fact, had avoided all day yesterday any discussion even casually related to Thea's family or Selma. She was going to have to do something about that, as soon as she figured out what "that" was. Maybe she should talk to Aunt Della about it. If only her parents were alive, there would have been some continuity of her family in Jesse's life. . . .

She snapped back to attention as Xavier said, "Repeat after me. I, Eugene Yearly, take thee . . ."

Eugene? She pinched off a smile. That must be the groom's legal name. Then Elkeri Yoruba was a cultural affectation. Eugene! That was more like it. Even from a distance, he had the pampered, complacent look of someone whose doting mama named him Eugene.

"I, Selma Montgomery Broussard, take thee . . ."

Thea's mind wandered to her sister's other two attempts at marriage. The spring after their mother died, Selma eloped with an exchange student from Senegal who claimed he was a tribal prince and would one day make her a queen. Six weeks later, she discovered he was already married to the niece of the real king. Bigamy was a crime, U.S. Immigration told her. It invalidated not only their marriage but also his visa, and he was shipped home faster than you could say, "Word to the motherland, brother!"

Her second husband was a pro basketball player. They had been vacationing in the Caribbean and, as Selma later admitted, smoking some serious ganja when the mood struck Mr. Pro Bro. He popped the question, bought the license, and said, "I do" in front of a Rastafarian minister all in the same weekend. Aunt Della worried if the marriage was even legal. Validity was not the problem, fidelity was. He was a playa, all right. Continued making slam-dunks in other women's baskets for two long, miserable years. When Selma stopped forgiving and giving out, he filed for divorce, claiming desertion.

Thea jerked her attention back to the present in time to listen to the exchange of vows that included Selma's personally worded pledge to "Love, honor, and cherish my noble African American prince." Anyone who knew Selma understood that "obey" would not even come into it.

"I hope Selma's third time is the charm," Thea murmured. "I truly do."

Finally, the music swelled again, backed this time by a full gospel choir that filed out from the wings and rocked the rafters of the old building. The big kiss, drawing laughter and applause. Jump the broom, and it was over. A syncopated reggae shuffle provided the recessional.

She came to her feet slowly as the other guests boogied their way out of the pews. Twenty-five minutes. She hoped Selma thought it was worth the effort and the money. Now, if she could get out of the church without being seen—that would be priceless.

three

"WHERE IS THE wedding party?" Aunt Della's sugar praline drawl had a vinegary snap. They stood near the entrance to the hotel ballroom, all but swallowed up in a sea of evening dresses and tuxes. The air was thick with Egoiste and Poison and half a dozen other perfumes and colognes.

"All these nice folk standing around starving." Della clucked her tongue.

Thea decided not to comment. Those nice starving folk were clustered around bright saffron-skirted tables piled high with the latest fashionable cocktail tidbits. Others were gathered around the displays of African and Caribbean art that served as the theme of the reception. For better or for worse, Xavier was not among either group. Could he be too busy to attend the reception? Was that good or bad? She couldn't decide. She did know she was in need of a stiff drink, and she made her move toward the bar.

"Now, where are you going?" asked Della, catching Thea's arm in a surprisingly firm grip. "The least we can do while we wait for Selma is present a united family front. You stand with me. You won't remember everybody, of course, but we all know you cope beautifully under pressure."

For forty-five minutes, she helped her aunt welcome the wedding guests, a full dozen of them she had never before met—relatives through marriages. Della and Selma had that much in common: three husbands each. Unlike Selma, who found divorce expedient, Della always buried one husband before acquiring another. At age seventy-eight, she was still open to the possibility of number four.

"Now I'm going to get myself a drink," Thea said when the flow of arriving guests finally slowed. "Can I bring you anything?"

"Oh, sugar, yes. I'd like a Sazerac."

Maybe she wasn't the only one feeling the strain, after all.

Thea hadn't moved five steps before Della stopped her. "Thea, wait, you must meet Mr. and Mrs. Shephard. They came all the way from Washington, D.C. Selma's decorating their place in Sag Harbor."

Smiling what she hoped looked like a pleasant smile, Thea waited for the introduction.

"This is my neice, Thea Morgan. She works in Dallas, for Petro Chem."

Thea shook hands, recognizing Representative Marge Shephard at once. Her face had become familiar a few years earlier as one of the early backers of the Clintons' ill-fated health reform bill.

"Everything is so lovely. I see Selma's touch everywhere." Mrs. Shephard smiled at her husband. "Hasn't she done a splendid job, Ed?"

"It's different," Ed replied noncommittally.

"Ed's old-fashioned when it comes to decor," his wife continued smoothly. "If it's not Colonial or knotty pine, he thinks it's avant-garde."

"I can speak for myself," he muttered as he stared at the colorfully painted carved piece that stood in the center of the bridal registry table. "What do you call that?"

"It's part of Selma's collection of African artifacts," Aunt Della answered. "That's her specialty, finding one-of-a-kind items for her clients."

"Is that right?" Ed said mildly. "What is its purpose? They

all have a purpose, don't they? Some sort of voodoo hex maker, perhaps?"

Caught short, Della glanced at Thea.

"It's an elephant kissing mask used for wedding celebrations," she answered smoothly. That bit of African culture owed itself to a trip she had taken with Jesse's art class last fall to the Dallas Museum of African-American Art. "The elephant represents long life in many African cultures. Sorry, but I don't know which tribe this piece is from. Selma would be able to tell you."

Ed nodded philosophically. "African's good enough for me."

As the couple moved on, Della took Thea's wrist. "Don't look now, but you are attracting admiration."

She hoped her face did not change color. Had Xavier come in while her back was turned? She glanced in the direction of her aunt's subtle nod and met the frankly flirtatious smiles of two men standing together, chatting. She smiled but looked quickly away, not wanting to give them encouragement. At least the last-minute shopping yesterday at Neiman Marcus now seemed worth it. The salesperson had assured her that the smoke-gray cocktail dress was a "steal" at $348 and the $249 red strap sandals with black spike heels provided the necessary punch.

"Didn't I say wear something pretty? You never know you who might meet."

An awful suspicion struck her. "Aunt Della, you didn't tell people I'm in the market for a man?"

Della shrugged her small shoulders. "A little encouragement never hurts. Don't pucker up, child. Men don't like a lady . . ."

She tuned out the rest of this well-worn lecture. New Orleans born and bred, Della came of age when a lady had one purpose in life: to preside graciously over the home of a worshipful man with the good taste and money to keep his wife in style.

"It's such a shame Jessica couldn't be here," Della continued. "Playing soccer's all very well for modern young women, but it's time she witnessed the expectations of a lady."

"Hm," Thea hummed noncommittally. She had told her aunt that Jesse had stayed behind to participate in her team's first practice of the season, which was true. She wasn't about to spoil her aunt's enjoyment of the day by explaining the real reason Jesse wasn't with her.

"Did I tell you little Jolene has made a catch for herself?"

"I don't think I know her." Though they produced no children, Della's marriages had added at least fifty assorted in-laws to the family.

"But of course you do. She's Viola's eldest girl. You must remember Viola, my Sy's sister's youngest child? You sat together at his funeral. She's a divorcée. A good bit older than you, and showing every year, I might add. That hasn't stopped her from finding a new beau. Surely you—"

More than ready to end this line of conversation, Thea looked toward the doorway. "Isn't that the wedding party?"

The scarf of her aunt's hat whipped across Thea's bare arm as Della turned her head. "Oh, yes. There they are!" She hurried toward the bridal couple at a pace that belied her age.

Applause greeted the wedding party. Selma was laughing and hugging her husband's arm while the happy chatter of bridesmaids and the heavier male laughter of the groomsmen floated across the room.

Thea spied Xavier lagging behind the rest. As he entered, the excitement level in the room soared. He had shed his robes. Dressed in a cut-to-the-body expensive pearl-gray silk suit, he looked like the celebrity he had once been rather than a Georgia preacher. His confident stride drew all eyes.

She pivoted on her heel and headed for the nearest bar station. She needed to stop staring at him. Definitely.

As the receiving line formed, people hurried past her, jockeying to be among the first, which would also put them at the head of the dinner buffet line. Not at all eager to see and be seen, she hung back, sipping her well-earned drink. Her gaze swung briefly to where Xavier had joined the receiving line. No way was she going anywhere near it. She would wait and greet Selma at the head table. She avoided Aunt Della's eye. At sixteen, she would have done anything to please this woman. Now, she pretended not to notice her. She was past tired of coping beautifully.

She ignored Aunt Della's warbled *"Yoo-hoo"* from the other side of the hall. But then she made a strategic mistake. She looked up. No mistaking the imperial signal of that chartreuse-gloved hand. She took another substantial gulp and placed her half-finished cocktail on the tray of a passing waiter. Sixteen again, after all.

She joined the receiving line. Xavier was an appointment she could no longer avoid.

She smiled and mumbled her way past Elkeri's parents, keeping in mind that no one really listens to what you say under these circumstances. Just smile, and shake hands, and you'll make a good impression. Of course, the fact that she had begun to sweat didn't seem the best way to do that. It struck her then that that's what she wanted to do: make a good impression on an old boyfriend.

Selma squealed when she saw her. "Hey, Big Sis!" She reached out and hugged Thea quickly, enveloping her in a drift of superheated Bulgari perfume and trailing feathers, then pushed her away before any serious damage could be done to her makeup.

"Sorry I was late," Thea murmured, startled but pleased by her sister's warm reception. The girl *must* be happy.

Selma rolled her eyes. "You work for some rotten company, you can't even get off until the last minute for your own sister's wedding?"

"Well, I'm here." The story about having to work was a cover in case she failed to show. "You look beautiful, as always. Now, introduce me to my new brother."

Selma grabbed and hugged her husband's arm. "Elkeri, this is my sister, Theadora."

She saw his gaze widen slightly in a way she was accustomed to, but to his credit, he recovered quickly and took her hand, covering it with both of his.

"Pleased to meet you, Theadora."

"Welcome to the family."

She gave him a brief hug. Up close, he was not particularly handsome, but he carried himself with the air of a man who had been told often that he was special. His manner was patronizing in a way that said, "Going places, doing things, making it happen! If you're lucky, I just might let you in on the ride."

Laughter drew her attention momentarily to the end of the

line where half a dozen adoring people surrounded Xavier. Her stomach muscles tightened. She needed a memorable opening line. At least a good one. Elkeri was pumping her hand and saying something about her coming to Atlanta to see his realty company.

"I'll have to take you up on that," she said, then moved toward the blur of bridesmaids. More conversation that had nothing to do with the thoughts in her head. What should she say first to Xavier? Would he remember her? Would he be as embarrassed as she was by their unexpected meeting? Or would his expansive reaction give her grief with her relatives? She smiled as she stepped at last before him, the wobble in her knees echoed as a waver in her voice.

"Good evening, Reverend Thornton. I'm Thea Morgan."

His gaze grazed hers as he gave her hand the briefest of shakes.

"Good evening, Ms. Morgan. Happy to make your acquaintance."

Before she could gather her courage to say more, he released her hand and turned toward the elderly couple behind her.

She sucked in a breath. He did not even recognize her.

An odd kind of relief made her giddy as she moved automatically away from the line. Of course he would not remember her. A lifetime of living for each of them lay between then and now. That's what she got for thinking herself too important to be forgotten! It was done. Over. Nothing to fear.

She moved toward the long line at the nearby serving table, wishing she had not given up her drink. In all her daydreams, the one thing she had never taken into account was that he might have forgotten her.

She picked up a buffet plate and noticed her pale reflection on its shiny surface. She looked a bit severe with her hair pulled back into a chignon, the only safe choice for this sultry bayou heat. A purely female thought crept into her mind. Did she suffer by comparison to what his memory of her might have been? Of course she did. What woman of forty-something would stack up well against a snapshot memory of sweet sixteen? Woman of a certain age, indeed!

Something was creeping into her relief, an emotion that felt too much like embarrassment with a chaser of regret. He didn't remember her. Nothing to do about it.

There was one consolation. She would not have to answer any uncomfortable questions from members of her family about how she knew Xavier Thornton.

For the next hour, the reception followed the traditional pattern. Eating, more greeting, conversations about children, jobs, and remember-whens. She gave out business cards, fumbled a few names of distantly familiar faces, and then found a seat far from the head table. Even though he hadn't recognized her, she was uncomfortably aware of Xavier's presence. It seemed he could not move without drawing a crowd of jocular men and twittering women. After the cake was cut, and the first dance danced by the newlyweds, she checked her watch and wondered if she could now slip out. She was more tired than she would have expected. The six-hour drive back to Dallas waited.

"Theadora Broussard! Is that you?"

Hat brims as wide as lampshades shaded a pair of faces powdered and lipsticked to perfection. Something in those faces, gazes expectantly alert, was familiar. But no names would fall into the vacuum of her discomfort. Thea stood up and widened her smile. "Well, hey!"

"You don't remember me?" The speaker's expression cooled.

"Johnny Rae . . . Wilson." Relief was in her voice. Was it on her face?

"*Grrrl*, it has been forever!" This time Johnny Rae hugged her. "I didn't even recognize that was you until Yvonne pointed you out. Sitting over here by yourself."

"Johnny Rae thought you were a white woman." Yvonne nodded, shaking the brim of her enormous hat.

Thea grimaced. That joke was stale by the time she was twelve.

"Wait till Harold Pelman hears you're home," Johnny Rae said.

Yvonne nodded. "People are always asking about the Broussard sisters. We haven't seen either of you since your mother's funeral. That must be twelve or thirteen—"

"Sixteen years."

"Sixteen years?" Johnny Rae cocked her head forward. "You

should come home more often. People want to see you, see how you're doing."

"Evening, ladies."

She stiffened at the sound of that voice. *Not now . . . not after . . .*

She turned to find Xavier standing beside her. This time, he looked right at her.

"How are you all on this fine evening?"

"Just fine, Reverend Thornton. We're so honored to have a personage of your stature here today!" Johnny Rae gushed. "Aren't we, Theadora?"

She did not answer. Her graceful departure had been train wrecked. What came next was anybody's guess.

"I surely do appreciate that sentiment." He took Johnny Rae's hand and patted it. Yvonne gazed at him adoringly. "Now, if you ladies will kindly excuse us, Ms. Morgan and I have some catching up to do." A pair of dimples backed the unmistakable tone of dismissal.

"Catching up?" Yvonne's gaze now ping-ponged curiously between him and Thea. "So then, we'll see you later, Theadora?"

"Hm." Better than a lie.

Xavier turned fully to her, his dark gaze taking her in whole. "Hello, Theadora."

"Hello, *again,* Reverend Thornton." She held out her hand out of habit.

He took it. No polite handshake this time but a grip of recognition she no longer wanted. "You think I didn't recognize you before?" It was a direct question meant to disarm.

"Did you?"

"At first? *Nawgh.*" In his deep voice, the single word combined chagrin, apology, and humor.

He squeezed her hand. "Green eyes. Now how could I ever forget those green eyes?" The slow smile that followed seemed much too sexy for a minister. This was an "X" smile.

"You might have remembered me sooner if you'd really looked at me back on the receiving line."

His brows lifted at her chastisement. "You're right. That was rude."

She rethought her attitude. No point in being equally rude or revealing how much his snub hurt her.

"Quite a coincidence, bumping into one another in Grambling, after all this time. It's been what, twenty-six years?" So much for a memorable opening line.

"Twenty-six years." He sounded surprised by the number. "That is a long time."

This conversation was so ordinary, not the way she had ever imagined their reunion. But really, what else was there to say?

The stretch from nineteen to forty-six had left marks on him she had been too rattled to notice before. A few threads of silver commingled with the black curls at his temples. The smile lines pleating his eyes were deeper. Truth was, she was already familiar with the changes. Over the years, in spite of herself, she had read any article about him she came across. His face was as familiar as Michael Jordan's or Jesse Jackson's.

Yet there was one thing the pictures failed to capture. That got-to-get-me-a-piece-of-the-world intensity was gone from his gaze. Was that because he had succeeded even beyond his own outsized expectations? Or was it because he had given it all up? "X" was now a reverend.

She slipped her hand free of his possessive grasp, hoping no one had noticed how long he had held it.

"I was about to leave. I left a weekend's worth of work unattended." She looked away. Why was she offering excuses?

He touched her elbow to draw her attention back. "I was hoping we might have a little chat."

She swallowed her surprise. "Oh?"

"Yes, I—" He paused to reach into his pocket and checked the pager he withdrew. When he looked up, a frown marked his brow. "I'm sorry, Theadora, but duty calls." He touched her again, the weight of three fingers impressed on her bare arm. "It's really good to see you again. In fact—" He hesitated, then seemed to shrug off a thought. "I just wish we had more time."

"Me, too." She said it the way people do, especially if they do not mean it.

But he seemed to think she did. The frown lifted from his brow. "In that case . . ." He pocketed his pager. "Walk with me to the door?"

She felt dozens of eyes on her as they headed for the exit. There would be a need for explanations, after all.

As they entered the lobby, she saw through plate glass windows a black Mercedes pull in alongside the white bridal party limos parked at the hotel entrance. The rear door opened, and a young man in a *Men in Black*–type suit emerged. He scanned the lobby until he saw Xavier and then gave him a curt nod.

Xavier lifted his hand in acknowledgment, then turned to her. He squeezed her elbow before releasing it. "It's been good to see you. Good."

Good for whom? she wanted to ask. It had not helped her in any way. She backed up a step and offered him an impersonal smile. "Have a pleasant journey, Reverend Thornton."

Something like disappointment registered for a second in his expression. Did he think she was going to fall on him with hugs and promises of keeping in touch? His disappointment pleased her, but that was all. Too little too late.

As he exited the hotel, the young man moved in quickly to intercept two young women who were making a beeline for him. Xavier nodded but never broke stride until he reached the car. At the last second, he paused and looked back over his shoulder directly at her, as if there was something he needed to memorize about her before he stepped in. A moment later, the younger man followed him.

A surge of emotion warmed her skin as she turned back to the ballroom. She felt exposed—and cheated. What did they say about first loves? One never got over the first.

Nineteen seventy-three. A summer Jack and Jill social. Just sixteen, she had gone with her second choice of date, the one who asked her instead of her first desire with his too-cool-to-move self. Then Xavier Thornton showed up, and she forgot both boys existed. Down from Chicago, he had a summer gig in Grambling in his uncle's law office. Later, her parents said that a nineteen-year-old college student did not belong at a high-school-age dance.

But there he was, drafted to escort his wallflower rising-senior cousin. Already attracting print as a football player for Michigan State, his appearance was as radical as his speech. In a community where conformity in appearance was still measured in quarters of an inch, his full-blown Afro rivaled a pasha's turban. While other young men struggled with starched collars and string ties, he hung loose in a dashiki and Fu Manchu mustache. For most of evening, he stood apart, watching with lazy-lidded eyes or chatting with the worshipful boys who dared approach. Finally, he moved and asked *her* to dance.

They shared one slow drag with all the world and their dates watching. Within the circle of each other's arms, they were absolutely alone for as long as the music lasted. She could not remember exactly what he said to her, only his warm breath carrying the husky murmur of an uptown brother who knew how to rap. Then there came the nibble of full lips at the curve of her ear, the prickle of whiskers as his hot cheek pressed hers. And lower down, the hard pressure brushing her abdomen to remind her that he had the means to back it up if she were naive enough to listen. Before the summer was over, he had taken her heart, and a whole lot more.

Memories of their last night together came back to her in powerful waves of sensation so real her skin tingled. The steamy heat of that August night plastering her Black Power tee to her back . . . the sour-sweet taste of beer on his soft, soft lips . . . the incredible feel of his heavy, hot body lying under her hands and over her skin . . .

Thea tossed off the memory with a tiny shake of her head. Forgive and forget. She had done both.

four

"I SEE WHAT you're aiming for but . . ." Joe Ortega frowned thoughtfully. "Run the strategy past me one more time."

"It's not brain surgery, Joe."

Thea drummed her pen impatiently on her desktop as she repeated the points of the proposal. Ortega, her best planning analyst, was usually a quick study.

It was only Monday, and she felt like she had put in a full week. That was because she'd received a tip late in the day last Friday that the new owner of ABC Barge was looking for a major customer to cement his vulnerable market position. She knew if she moved quickly, she could score big for Petro Chem. So she kissed good-bye her plans to spend a lazy weekend at Lake Texhoma with friends.

At least things had settled with Jesse. A week back in the old routine of school had done wonders. Jesse had even offered an unprompted apology for blowing up over Selma's wedding, claiming it was jet lag that made her edgy. Teens. Who knew when they were truly upset and when it was just hormonal overload?

"Forty-eight hours, and the deal's off the table," she concluded.

Joe cocked a brow. "Won't Worrell realize he's giving away the candy store with this deal?"

"He may wince, but he knows he's got to pay to play with the big guys. If you set the right tone, the negotiation phase should be a nonstarter."

"Me? This is your baby."

"My idea, but your responsibility. If I pitch it, Worrell will think we want this badly enough to bargain. Send in a lieutenant, and he gets the idea we're interested but not that interested."

"Nice!" He grinned. "That's why you're the boss and I'm the hired help." He picked up his copy of the proposal. "Give me the afternoon to prepare, and I'll be ready for them in the morning."

"You better be." She needed a quick and dirty victory to lift her spirits. It had been a difficult summer for the company. July was the worst, beginning with the loss of a barge to a freak storm in the Caribbean, and then finding the product they shipped to Jubail to be off-test. August had seemed a good time to turn things around. The calendar gave her one more week before a turn of a page to September put a period to that hope.

She looked up. Joe was still standing there. "Something else on your mind?"

He nodded sheepishly. "What about Holland?"

She tried to look thoughtful, though there was nothing to contemplate. She had pretty much promised to send him to the ship-naming ceremony in Rotterdam if she declined. As much as she didn't want to leave Jesse right now, there was every possibility the ship owner would feel slighted if she sent an underling. "Bring me this deal with Worrell, and then we'll talk about your attempt to usurp my position."

The stricken look on his face surprised her.

"I'm kidding. I'll let you know about Holland tomorrow, Joe."

"Okay, sure." He was still nodding as he closed the door.

She propped her chin in her hands and closed her eyes. An exhausted feeling crept up on her. Must be the heat. The golden fields and leafless trees visible beyond her office reflected the same source of exhaustion. Drought seemed a permanent feature of north Texas summers. Copper smog rimmed the sky, and the air smelled stale even laundered through central air-conditioning. What she wouldn't give for a weekend at the Morgan cabin in the Alleghenies. She didn't doubt she could have it with a phone call. Of course, that would obligate her to her in-laws.

She was fond of Richard and Shirley, certainly, but always felt the need to assert her independence around them. The Morgans absorbed people into their circle. The first year of her marriage, when she and Evan still lived in Philly, she felt like a planet in their orbit, a distant one. Pluto. That changed when Jesse came along. No star ever shone brighter in their universe than their only grandchild.

Of course, they had not taken Evan's announcement of the decision to move to Dallas very well. He had made it clear that he wanted to move so that she could work for Petro Chem. It was a terrific opportunity for her, for *them,* he insisted. Though they never said so, she suspected Evan's parents thought she deliberately engineered the separation. "Unlike my day, you young women will not be denied," Shirley did say once. Enough to plant Evan squarely in the middle. So they agreed that Dallas would be a three-year deal. Time enough for her to aim a few strategic blows at the glass ceiling of corporate upper management and then return "home." The three years were up this past June. Shirley had already called twice to remind her.

That thought tightened the cords in her neck, tension that too easily built these days into a headache by the end of the workday. What the Morgans failed to realize was that while Philly was home to Evan, she had no real ties there. She had no real ties to anyplace anymore.

Going home nine days ago proved that.

She rubbed the back of her neck a little harder. Her mistake, thinking that she had not taken any old baggage with her. Seeing Xavier brought it all back, every bitter, humiliating scrap.

"Forget that." She shook away the thought. Yesterday's news, and she meant to keep it that way. As for leaving Dallas, she wasn't ready. Even if she were getting tired of the corporate life, she didn't have a clue as to what else she might do. Besides, Jesse was a junior, a critical year for all college-bound students. It would be two more years at least before she could even consider changing locations or jobs. In this market, she was damn lucky to have security. She wouldn't jeopardize it by moving to please her in-laws.

The phone rang. "Petro Chem. Theadora Morgan speaking."

"Hi, gorgeous."

The seductive tone of the male voice threw her. "Who is this?"

"Ouch! She doesn't remember." Humor laced the words. "And after all we've meant to one another."

"Phillip!" Phillip Campbell was Evan's best friend from childhood and the closest thing either of them had to a brother. "It's been a while."

"At least that. How are you?"

"Never better. And you?"

"Fine. God, it's good to hear your voice. I should call more often."

"True. I don't have a phone, so I couldn't possibly call you." She cupped the phone a little closer as a colleague passed her open door. "So, what prompts this call?"

"I woke up this morning thinking about you."

"That, and what else?"

"You're supposed to be pleased by that gallant remark."

"I'm pleased. It's just that it's been four months since I crossed your mind, so I'm not *that* impressed."

"You always were hard to please."

"Maybe other women are just too easy."

"Jealousy? This sounds promising."

She chuckled.

"How's Jesse?"

"More beautiful with every day."

"Of course. Still straight A?"

"Of course. How are your folks?"

"The same, only more so. Dad's got this idea that he and Mom should see the rain forest before it's all gone. Whatever that means. Anyway, he's booked this amazing tour, three weeks in South America by boat and Land Rover. All the remote places tourists never see. I reminded him that he hates going places that don't have air-conditioning, endless ice, and color TV. But two of his former business colleagues had heart attacks this year, and he's feeling mortal. I figure they won't make it past week one. The flies alone will make him rethink just how alive he wants to feel."

"I forgot how much you love the sound of your own voice."

"You do miss me! Then you'll be pleased to know I've hopped a plane to Dallas."

"Today?" So the hollow sound of the connection was not caused by cell phone but in-flight service.

"I was thinking dinner tonight, if that's good for you."

His earnest tone took her aback. She glanced at the calendar to check it for previous engagements and frowned when she noticed the date, August 24. No, this might be just what she needed. "Well, sure. Why not?"

"Such enthusiasm."

"No, I mean it's great. I'm just feeling the effects of a hectic weekend."

"What's his name?"

"What?" An image of Xavier flashed in her mind. *Where did that come from?* "Oh no, nothing like that." It was time to change that subject. "Guess what? Selma's married again. This time, I even went to the wedding."

"And the church walls still stand?"

She chuckled. Phillip stood up with Evan when they wed, so he had witnessed firsthand her relationship with her sister in ways she could never explain to strangers. "Perhaps we've finally outgrown this squabbling tendency we have."

"Is that what you call it? I think of you as Cain and Abel in drag."

"Oh please!"

"So, about tonight. Cool with you?"

She smiled at the old slang. "Cool with me." She quickly jotted down his information. As she hung up the phone, a message popped on to her computer:

**Meeting with the department vice president in
five minutes.**

WELL INTO HIS fifties, Ron Cullum retained a big-kid face and spoke in an easygoing Texas twang. But he was shrewd and forward thinking, and had championed Thea's hiring at Petro Chem when there were no other women in a comparable position.

Today he waved her in without fanfare.

"Come on in, Thea. I hear you have Worrell in your sights. Going to hand him his oysters on a platter and make him thank you for it."

A small shock of annoyance ran through her. How did Ron know about her strategy when she had just told Ortega? She did not like her pending deals talked around, even in-house. "We try, Ron."

He waited until she sat down before continuing. "You're aware the company's considering reorganizing? Marketing. Sales. Traffic. Purchasing. Transportation. The whole ball of wax."

"Considering, yes." The rumor mill had been working over-time since the midyear report showed a decline for the second straight quarter.

He reared back in his chair and steepled his fingers before his chest in his let's-get-personal mode, the last thing she wanted today. "We've hired some boys from Ernst & Young to look into things."

"I see." Consultants meant only one thing: downsizing. She sat forward. "We run a lean machine, Ron. But I'll see if I can bring a new eye to the design." That she did not choke on the words was a miracle.

She saw his gaze shift to the door she had left ajar. "In light of this situation, how do you see the next year playing out for you?"

The next year? Evaluation period was months away. She sat back but squelched the impulse to cross her legs. "I see myself getting the job done."

"Don't have to tell you this market climate breeds fierce com-petition." He tapped his fingertips together. "Aggressiveness is the set piece of your job description. You knew that going in and made a damn fine job of it, too."

Made. Past tense. She set her jaw. He had encouraged her to cut back on her business travel after Evan's death. Now he was reprimanding her for it? She knew better than to jump in with a defense, but it was a physical struggle not to.

"We both know what you can do when you put your mind to it. That Pacific Rim contract you negotiated for us two years ago was nothing short of innovative. You must have logged fifty thousand miles in Asia. The barge deal with Worrell is more in line with the kind of effort I expect from you."

But not as spectacular as previous years' work, she silently finished his unspoken thought. She shifted slightly.

"Any other concerns about my performance, Ron?"

He waved away her question. "Just wondering if you might be feeling in need of a change of scenery. You've heard Jake Tucker is retiring from Purchasing in December? What with Jesse still at home and all, well . . . The position involves less travel. You might wanna give it some thought."

He's thinking of moving me out.

Feeling as if the oxygen level in the room had suddenly dropped, she stood.

"For the record, I'm happy with the way things are."

She did not wait for him to reassure her that he was only making a suggestion. At this point, it would be stretching credibility.

"If there's nothing else?"

She kept her head down as she navigated her way back toward her office.

Move me out! He could do that. He couldn't fire her, could he? No, not without more ammunition. He could not cite her situation as a single mother as cause for removing her from her position. That would set the company up for a discrimination suit. No, at worst, he was just laying the first plank of a lower-performance pattern he would have to cite if he decided to oust her.

A sick feeling jelled her middle. Why was Ron taking her to task now? Had someone complained that she wasn't carrying her share?

As she passed his closed door, her gaze snagged on the name-plate: Joseph Ortega. Was that why he hadn't laughed at her joke about usurping her job? He didn't yet have the experience to replace her, but that didn't mean he might not be trying. He certainly seemed preoccupied this morning.

Anger bubbled up through the edginess that had dogged her

for days. She knew how to cripple a rival. And she would give fair warning. She knocked on his door and entered.

"Joe, is your passport up to date?"

He looked up from his computer screen. "Am I going to Holland?"

"*We* are going to Holland. Have Marcia make the arrangements."

His smile was radiant. "Thanks, Thea."

She waved off his thanks. "You earned it." She turned toward the door and then angled her head back. "Why did you go to Ron about our barge deal?"

He looked surprised. "I didn't. He stopped me in hall to ask about it."

"Why would he do that?"

He looked embarrassed. "He overheard me telling Marcia about it."

She had caught the vibes of an office romance but had let it slide.

"You know better than to discuss business in the hallway." Her tone was one she might use to rebuke Jesse.

He turned scalded red. "I think I know how to conduct myself."

She smiled, turning the screws just a bit more. "I like to think so, too. It's why you have this job."

five

THEA GLANCED AT the reflection of herself in a mirror in the hotel lobby where Phillip was staying and adjusted the line of her black linen sundress. She had gone home to change clothes and considered canceling. After all, Phillip had said he'd be in town for several days. But Jesse was studying with friends, and she didn't really want to be alone with her thoughts tonight. And how often in the last two years did she get to talk with someone who really knew Evan when? Maybe this was Phillip's tactful way of helping without mentioning the subject.

She pushed a fallen spaghetti strap back up her arm, wondering if she should have worn something less revealing.

Why was she feeling so self-conscious? They were old friends. She met Phillip before she met Evan's parents. It must be the excitement of seeing an old friend after a long time. Somebody who remembered how it had once been. Those connections were nearly impossible to make these days. Phillip was her oldest link to Evan. Tonight, she needed that connection. She picked up the house phone and rang his room.

He was the first person off the elevator. Dressed in chinos and a navy sports coat over an open collar, he exem-

plified the exclusive quality often mimicked in Ralph Lauren
ads. Phillip Aristotle Campbell was the real thing. Prep school
education, moneyed, socially prestigious background. And then
there were his looks. The Scottish surname was a mere techni-
cality. He had inherited every striking gene in his Greek
mother's pool, including thick black hair and skin tanned that
deep bronze only olive-toned people can achieve. Over the
years, she thoroughly enjoyed watching women react to him.
Even men often gave him a second glance, assuming that he
must be somebody. She felt like a kid sister, ever eager to sling
mud on big brother Adonis.

"Welcome to Big D, *y'all.*" She lifted her arms in welcome.

He enfolded her in his embrace and pressed hard against her
as he rocked her with him. "God, it's good to see you!"

The warmth in his voice against her ear pricked tears. She
swallowed back the ridiculous urge to weep. Or did he feel as
she did? That, for that moment, they each held on to a little
piece of the lost past?

When he released her, he kept possession of both of her
hands. "You look great!"

She expelled a shaky chuckle. "You don't look too shabby
yourself."

"And at your disposal."

"Where to?"

"Nothing fancy. A good steak, a bottle of good wine, and
thou."

"Can do." As she turned to lead him toward the exit, he slung
his free arm about her shoulders and pulled her close to kiss the
side of her head.

Just like old times. The agitation of the day eased.

PAPPAS BROS. WAS busy, but they didn't have to wait for
a table as soon as the hostess recognized Thea, a regular business client.

Phillip took a sip of the $140 bottle of Bordeaux he had
ordered, then smiled at her, glass lifted. "To you."

"To old times." She touched her glass to his and started to
laugh.

"What?"

"I was just thinking about all those bottles of cheap wine we drank while you and Evan were in law school."

He began to chuckle. "All wines before their time."

"I don't think they had a time. Evan swore they sold half to poor grad students and the other half for paint thinner. Oh! Remember the time he . . . ?" As she continued, she saw Phillip's expression cloud, but it cleared almost instantly, and she decided it was just her imagination.

They sailed through half the main course on a series of remember-whens, mostly on her side. Phillip smiled but didn't contribute much. After a while, she realized she was rattling on and decided to dedicate herself to the porterhouse steak before her.

Finally, Phillip looked up at her. "You are past this, aren't you?"

"Past? In a way yes, in a way no."

"Good." He nodded to himself, then met her gaze again. "You should know you're the reason I'm in Dallas."

She smiled. "Oh right, me and the several-million-dollar deal for your consulting firm." On the drive over, he'd told her that he was considering moving temporarily to Dallas to oversee a project for his firm.

"The timing's simply fortuitous." He leaned toward her. "I gave you a year to ask for help. Since you haven't come home after two, I've decided to come to you."

"Why, Phillip, that's sweet. And I do appreciate the thought that someone wants to look after me. But believe me, I'm doing fine."

He nodded, serious now. "I know you can take care of yourself. That's why I left it this long, that and what they call a decent interval." He leaned in closer, raising his arm and draping his wrist over her shoulder so that they were enclosed in a space for two. "But now I'm here. Okay?"

The heat and pressure of him were too much. She moved back. "What are you talking about?"

"You and me." He moved a hand back and forth between them.

She backed up again, jostling the waiter, who was reaching

for her water glass. "Sorry," she murmured. Was she nuts or had her husband's best friend just come on to her? When she looked at him again, she saw the flirtatious smile and remembered. Charm was second nature to Phillip. Only a fool would think it was meant just for her.

"Why aren't you married yet?" She nudged a potato slice with her fork. "There was definitely a fiancée with you at Evan's funeral. In a wide-brimmed black straw hat with a gold buckle." The woman was a blank. The hat was memorable.

He popped a bite of roll in his mouth and nodded. "Over. Mistake."

"I can see how you make them." He had been engaged to one woman or another as long as she had known him. It was marriage he seemed allergic to. "So, what, you're between engagements?"

He smiled. "I know, this is scary for you. I completely understand that. Completely. But the idea of *us* will grow on you."

Her laughter had an edge. "Phillip, you don't know how to be in a relationship."

"You're right. I've never been able to make the final commitment." He grinned and reached for her hand. "That's your fault, you know. I watched you and Evan and envied what you had."

"You can't have what we had." *Not with me,* she just kept from adding as she slipped her hand free. Determined to keep it light, she said, "I'm not some kind of prefab kit, add a man and make an instant couple."

He actually blushed. "I can see it's never crossed your mind before. That kind of takes the wind out of my sails. But if you think about it, it makes perfect sense. You always planned to come back to Philly. I've seen Dallas. No offense, but the weather? The cuisine? The culture? What am I saying? This is about us."

She just stared at him.

Another man might have sulked or just given up. He regrouped on an instant and flashed a killer smile. "I'm wild about Jesse. She seems to like me."

Thea smiled, begrudgingly impressed. "You spoiled her so much when she was little, you have her affections for life."

"See, you're beginning to see the possibilities. Even the Morgans like me. What's the harm in us at least exploring the possibilities?"

She laid her knife and fork aside. "Phillip, you do remember my background?"

He looked nonplussed for a full two seconds. "Oh that. Come on, you've come a long way from your past. It's not an issue."

She wasn't about to get into how shallow and presumptuous his answer was. The fact he'd said it meant he didn't have a clue. "You don't know me, Phillip."

"Sure I do." He sat back with his glass of wine. "Ask me anything."

"Who's my favorite singer?"

"That's easy. Bruce Springsteen."

"That was Evan's favorite."

"Yeah, but you guys liked all the same things. That's what I so envied. You two could browse a ten-page menu and still order the exact same dishes. You were in sync." He started slightly and then reached into his pants pocket and pulled out a phone. "Hate the vibration mode." Glancing at it he said, "Please excuse me a sec, I need to make a quick call."

As Phillip turned toward the bar, Thea stared at her plate, feeling like a practical joke had been played on her. Phillip was in her world through his relationship with her husband. She never before looked for hidden truths in his outrageous remarks. She even accepted with good grace Evan's occasional ribbing after Phillip once remarked, following a few too many, that Evan had married the only woman that he could ever love. It was easy flattery. No chance he'd ever have to ante up on the emotion. The Playboy of the Western World now genuinely interested in her? Even if he were half serious, she wasn't up for the game. She had wanted to share memories of Evan with Phillip for an evening. She did *not* want to share a future.

"Al Green," she murmured. "Love and Happiness" was her favorite tune.

AS SHE PULLED up into the drive of the hotel, she resisted the urge to slap away the hand that fiddled with a strand of hair at her nape. The evening was almost over. She might still get out of this without saying something she would regret.

When they pulled up in front, he turned to her. "It's early. Come in for a drink. Or better yet, let's go to my room and call room service."

"I don't think so."

"I'm not expecting anything." He ran a finger down her arm, his voice quieter than before. "I just want to be with you a little longer."

She didn't even try to answer that. She reached for the door lock and popped it open. He might be an attorney, but he wasn't in Evan's league when it came to persuasion. "Thanks for the evening, Phillip. Wish I'd been better company for you."

He frowned as she leaned away from his intended kiss. "You're adamant about this staying a friendship, aren't you?"

"Yes."

He raked a hand through his hair. "I won't say you didn't play it straight. It's just that things change, Thea. I couldn't speak until now, but I really care for you."

"You're a really good friend. But I can't—" Not with Evan's best friend. Why couldn't he see that? "I'm not ready. Good night."

"Wait." He took her by the upper arm as if he thought she wouldn't listen otherwise. "I know your life with Evan was perfect. I even admire your loyalty to his memory. But you've got to move on. Take a few chances. Make some mistakes, if need be. You've got to take what you want from life, Thea."

She shrugged off his touch. "I have everything I need."

He released her. "For God's sake, you know what I mean. Evan's been dead two years."

"That's right." She was so angry she could hardly speak. "Two years. To the day."

"Jesus!" The look that came over his face made her feel sorry for him. "Why didn't you say something? God knows, I wouldn't have pushed you tonight. Look, I'm sorry. I didn't—"

Pride made her cut off his apology. "Good night, Phillip."

She gave herself credit for not burning rubber in front of the hotel. She hated this day. Hated it. And it had gone from bad to worse than she could have expected. Ron had treated her like a truant. Joe was definitely hiding something. Now Phillip had turned into Casanova. What the hell was wrong with everyone in her life, anyway? In the silence of the traffic, she noticed the streetlights had grown auras.

Damn! Migraine!

She drove home as far above the speed limit as she thought she could reasonably get away with. Once inside, she headed for the bar built into one corner of the family room and poured herself a shot of twenty-year-old single malt. She'd discovered a long time ago that scotch sometimes worked as well against the pain as any prescription drug . . . sometimes better. She fumbled in the dark until she found the under-counter ice maker, opened it, and popped two cubes into her glass. She pressed a second handful of ice to her neck right behind her left ear and slumped onto a barstool, eyes shut.

So? Maybe she had just burnt a bridge she might later regret torching. Phillip shouldn't have mentioned her perfect marriage!

Don't think! Don't think about anything! Breathe. Slow. Let the Macallan work its magic.

She had taken three tiny sips when the air conditioner compressor rumbled to life. Refrigerated air spiked the chill of melting ice running between her fingers, down her neck and back. One spaghetti strap of her dress was soaked, but she didn't care.

When her glass was empty, she dumped the remaining slivers of ice into the bar sink and headed to bed, feeling slightly better but shaky.

She picked up the framed picture of Evan she kept by her side of the bed. He would always remain as the casual shot showed him, a man with an easy grin and shock of dead straight blond hair. It wasn't a perfect marriage, but it was hers, and she would just as soon have kept it.

The familiar pain caught at her with unexpected intensity. Within seconds, tears were streaming down her cheeks.

A weak artery in the brain. Silent. Unknowable. It had ruptured one morning in his office exactly two years ago. No warning that forty-one years was the limit of Evan Morgan's life.

Phillip thought allegiance to Evan's memory kept her from wanting him. He was wrong. She was as needy as the next. But she didn't believe occupying any man's bed was a remedy for loneliness. She was waiting for that indefinable sensation that happens when a woman knows, sometimes at the first encounter, that this is the man for her—maybe not forever, maybe not for long, but most definitely for now. Twice she had paid a price for following that feeling.

"The stories I could tell!" She could almost hear her grandmother's voice full of punctuated drama as she tantalized her granddaughters with tales of her life that would never be uttered. Now she understood. She had a few of her own.

Without bothering to undress, she stretched out on the bed and turned her face into the pillow, Evan's picture pressed to her chest.

six

"JESSE? I'M HOME!" No reply.

"Want to go out for Chinese?"

Nothing.

Thea dumped her briefcase and purse on the kitchen table with a sigh of relief. Yesterday had been hell, but today made up for it. Just hours after Joe presented it, ABC Barge had called to accept her deal with very few modifications. She decided to stay late, make the preliminary contract changes, and fax them over before they could reconsider. Now she was ready to celebrate with pot stickers and Moo Shu Pork.

"Jesse?"

The house was unusually quiet. No TV or radio noises.

Jesse had been peeved when Thea called home to say she was working late, but the silent treatment was not her daughter's style. In fact, she was very vocal about wanting to go with her girlfriends to a Wednesday-night sneak-peek movie preview. Thea had said no, holding the line about no social activities on a school night. Had Jesse disobeyed her?

"Jesse!"

Flipping light switches as she went, she hurried through the downstairs. She could feel her anger rising. Dammit! What had gotten into the girl since Paris?

A hand laid on the newel of the stairway in the front hall immediately put her mind at ease. The stairway pulsated with a syncopated bass line. Jesse had her disc player cranked up to deafening decibels. She might be sulking, but she was home.

The sound of the doorbell stopped her halfway up the stairs.

A tall, good-looking young man in a suit and tie stood at her door. He was much too formally dressed for a summer evening. A sales pitch for sure.

"Yes?" Let him try to get past the reservation she laced in her voice.

He did not smile wide and toothy as most eager beavers trying to work their way through night school, trade school, or partnership-for-at-risk-rehabilitation-for-something-or-other usually did. This serious young brother looked like someone who had made a big mistake.

"I—uh, Mrs. Morgan?"

"Yes?" Curiosity replaced her reservation

He stared at her as if she had a second head. "Theadora Broussard Morgan?"

"So they tell me."

"My name's David Greer. I—" He glanced down, seemed to recover himself, and then lifted his gaze. "I think we may be related." His expression retained a hint of doubt.

"Really?" She looked him over more carefully but saw nothing readily familiar. Aunt Della usually alerted her if she had encouraged a family member visiting Dallas to drop by.

"Exactly who gave you my name and address?"

He watched her with equal attention as he said, "I'm Sylvester Bennett's grandnephew. My mother was his niece, one of the Biloxi Bennetts. My parents said they met you at your sister's wedding last month."

"I'm afraid I don't remember them." But she did remember Aunt Della telling everyone, "Thea keeps such a gracious home. She'd be delighted to have you drop by whenever you're visiting Dallas." It seemed someone had actually taken her aunt up on it. Another family duty to fulfill.

She smiled reluctantly as her stomach growled in protest. "Do come in."

His gaze widened as it swept round her entry. She had forgotten how impressive the eighteen-foot ceilings and curving staircase of her two-story house must seem to strangers. "It's humble, but I call it home."

He started, as if he had been caught peeking in her checkbook. "It's very . . . nice."

"Thank you." She glanced up the staircase but decided not to call for Jesse. David Greer looked nervous enough without adding a sullen teenager to the mix.

"Come on back to the kitchen, and let's talk."

"Okay." He still stared at her as if he was not certain she was the right person. She'd seen this look many times as people meeting her for the first time tried to reconcile what they'd been expecting with what they were looking at.

She chuckled. Maybe she should just wear a lapel badge. "HELLO: I'm light, bright, damn near white!"

In the kitchen, she went straight to the refrigerator. "Would you like ice tea? I have Coke and juice, too. Are you hungry?" She sure was. "I have chips. Pretzels?"

"Just tea. Thank you." He glanced out the bay window at the lighted swimming pool in the back. "You have a very nice home, Mrs. Morgan."

"Thank you." They had just covered this subject in the entry. He needed to broaden his topics of small talk.

She brought him one of the glasses she had poured. "What brings you to Dallas?"

"Job interviewing." He was standing by the bar, shifting his weight from one foot to the other. "I just graduated from Michigan State, summer semester."

"Congratulations." She waved him toward the breakfast set. "Have a seat."

He sat and chugged his tea. He did look hot in that jacket and tie.

"So you're in town for an interview?" she prodded when he set down the empty glass. "What was your major?"

"Computer engineering." That might be an answer to her question, but it barely qualified as conversation. He didn't seem to want to chat. He showed inordinate interest in the pool, staring at it out the window.

"How were your grades?"

His gaze came back to her, and she could swear he blushed, a hint of maroon under his nut-brown skin tone. "I graduated cum laude."

"Impressive." He was smart and cute, if a little shy. Too bad Jesse was a bit young for him. She smiled at him encouragingly. "I know how awkward it can be to have to make duty calls on perfect strangers. Aunt Della, bless her, thinks family members should be instantly at ease."

If he had a smile, he must be holding on to it for another occasion. His formality reminded her of someone. . . . This conversation had to get easier!

"I hope I'm not interrupting your evening, Mrs. Morgan."

"Not at all. I just got home from a late day at the office." There. That was a big fat softball of an easy opening for the standard follow-up of "What do you do?"

He looked away. "You have children?"

"One." Not what she expected, but an attempt at conversation. Good.

She went over to the shelf and brought back a picture to hand to him. "This is Jesse. She's almost sixteen. At the moment, she's upstairs cleaning out her ears with quadraphonic sound."

He looked long at it. It was one of Jesse's jock pictures. Her uniform was sweaty from a game and her blond hair hung from a crooked ponytail. A soccer ball tucked under one arm, she sported Band-Aids on both knees. Finally, he handed it back.

"Would you like to meet her?"

"No." His cheeks darkened a second time. "I mean, don't bother her on my account." He picked up his glass, noticed it was empty, and set it down again. "I guess I've taken up enough of your time."

"Not at all. Have another glass of tea."

"No, really—" He stood up. "I had just a short time. Thanks for the tea." He turned and began tracing his steps toward the entry. She followed him.

This had to be the record for a short visit. Maybe it was just nerves. He was fresh out of school and seriously job hunting for the first time. She could sympathize.

"I wish you well with the interviews. I threw up before my first."

He didn't even nod in answer.

He did pause to stare at the family portrait that hung on the wall beneath the stairs. When he turned to look at her again, the emotion behind his light eyes was one she could not guess at. He had the bewildered, lost look of a child who realized he had wandered too far away from his parents.

Feeling sorry for him, she reached out and touched his jacket sleeve above the elbow. "If you decide you want a job here in Dallas, I'd be happy to write a letter of reference for you."

He looked taken aback. "Why would you do that? You don't know me."

"You're family, and you graduated cum laude. Isn't that enough?" She knew she sounded abrupt, but really! If he had bothered to ask what she did for a living, he'd know how much a letter from someone in her position might help him. She softened it with, "Come see me again. I'll make dinner, and you can meet Jesse."

He shifted away from her touch. "No thanks."

The rebuff surprised her. Was it something she said, or did not say? Maybe, being family, he thought she should have asked him to stay for dinner tonight? Her Southern hospitality was a bit rusty.

He shook her hand stiffly at the door. "Thank you for your time."

When he had gone, she shook her head and turned back toward the stairs. What was that about? Weird. That was just weird. She'd have to mention his visit to Aunt Della next time they spoke. Her stomach gurgled loudly. But not now.

"Jesse!"

seven

"AT THIS POINT, all I care about is making a decision before I'm ready to collect social security!" Beryl Moore looked from Thea to Erica Peters for comment. The three of them comprised their daughters' Soccer Team Uniform Committee, and had quickly organized this impromptu Saturday-morning meeting at Starbucks when the girls decided to do a little after-game schmoozing at a teammate's house.

"Harper wants a mostly white uniform because of the heat." Erica crumbled the piece she broke off from her uneaten chocolate chip muffin. "Being a natural redhead like her mother, her skin's so sensitive. Your girls are so lucky not to have that problem."

Rolling her eyes, Beryl pointed at Erica's muffin and changed the subject. "Why do you waste the money?"

Erica dusted her fingers free of crumbs. "They look so good, I can't resist buying one. Then I think about how many laps I'll have to run to burn off the calories, and I can't eat it."

"You could take it home."

"And increase the temptation? That's why I demolish it."

Beryl looked at Thea and shook her head. "Can we wrap this

up?" She ran a hand up her nape to where a long salt-and-pepper ponytail bushed from its scrunchie. "I've got a million things to do before Harold leaves tomorrow morning."

"Where is he going?"

"To play golf at Hilton Head. The Urban League Duffers are holding their annual golf tournament there. Last year, they played one of the old segregation-era Negro courses in New York."

Erica looked surprised. "There were once courses for blacks only?"

Thea's lips twitched. "You're Dallas born, Erica. Didn't you know the first public Negro golf course in the country was built here? My dad used to play it in his college days."

"I had no idea." Erica's gaze shyly met Thea's. "I've never asked, but now that you've brought it up. Are you like Jesse?"

"What?"

"With one black parent and one white one?"

"No, both my parents were black."

Erica looked doubtful. "But how does that work? I mean, how do two black people produce a white child?"

Thea smiled. "They don't."

"Uh-huh." Erica's gaze slid away. Clearly out of her depth with the turn their conversation had taken, she fluffed her salon-colored red bangs and turned to Beryl, who was glancing over a *National Enquirer* that someone had left at the table. "You're so lucky Harold's retired. My Spencer says HMOs are destroying most doctors' abilities to earn a decent living. Thank goodness he went into sports medicine. He's not stuck using cost-managed treatments."

"Not everybody has a sports contract," Beryl said, pushing the magazine away, "but everybody gets sick."

"Oh, Beryl, you know what I mean."

"I do. Exactly."

As Erica's look got defensive, Thea decided to jump in. "*I* say we go with the teal spandex shorts and the white cotton jerseys with matching trim." She tilted her head toward Erica. "Any objections?"

"I suppose not."

"Beryl?"

"Fine by me."

Silence at the table until, finally, Erica looked at her watch. "Oh! I've got a bikini wax in five minutes. Amber's so inflexible. If I'm the teeniest bit late, she won't finish me." She stood and wriggled her fingers at them. "Got to fly!"

Thea and Beryl exchanged smiles of amusement as she left.

"White women. I'd like to see that Amber person try and leave me half waxed!" Beryl shook her head, her ponytail bouncing. "Why do we bother?"

Thea didn't have to guess the topic. "Erica means well."

"Waste of time trying to educate her about black people. What do Texans say? She's not the brightest bulb on the porch." She pinched off an untouched portion of Erica's muffin and stuck it in her mouth. "Now that that's done, we can really talk. Haven't heard from you all week. So, how'd your date with the old friend from Philly go the other night?"

Thea shrugged off the reminder of her dinner with Phillip. "Like you might expect."

Beryl reared back on her stool. "Go on, *Miss Thang!*"

"Let me rephrase that." She briefly outlined the evening, and how it had gone so wrong. "On the one hand, I feel bad. He is Evan's oldest friend." She shook her head. "But that's part of the reason I could never think of him as anything else."

"Just as well. Of course, you know more about that than I would. It wasn't the thing when I came along."

"The *thing* being interracial dating?"

"Did boyfriend even know he was doing that?" Beryl gave her a meaningful up-and-down glance. "The package says white bread."

She grinned. "But the filling is chocolate."

"Philip didn't get a taste, did he? Want proof? Next time you're together—don't roll your eyes at me! He's gonna call again as soon as he can forget the fool he made of himself the other night. When he does, ask him to name Gladys's Pips."

"Come on. I can't name them."

"Exactly. But I bet you dinner at The Mansion that he'll assume knowing the answer is a black thing, like a secret handshake, and get all defensive."

"What if he knows the answer?"

"Make that lunch at The Mansion, and I'll invite him to come, too."

"If only it were that simple."

Beryl's gaze became considering. "I didn't know Evan, but from what you say, it sounds like it was a good marriage. Still, you've got to know you crossed a line when you married him. And we both know how some of the brothers and sisters feel about that. So maybe you know what you're doing, sticking to the brand you bought before."

She laughed. "So then, solve my problem. Find me a black man to date."

Beryl cocked her head forward. "Don't think I can't . . . if that's what you really want. You know what they say, all work and no play makes a woman a B-I-Zitch!"

She glanced down to where Beryl's smooth brown arm lay next to her lightly tanned one on the tabletop. "Beryl, do Cassandra and her friends consider Jesse different because she's half black?"

"Don't think it's ever come up. Why? Little Miss Morgan giving you grief?"

"She's just different since the summer. Maybe I made a mistake letting her go so far from home."

Beryl put hand on her shoulder. "You didn't make a mistake. She's different because she's growing up. She was going to do that right here. Cassandra hasn't been anywhere, but she pays about as much attention to me as a canary does a dog. Harold says it's because she's the caboose. The things that girl won't dare! Caught her and that Aikens kid dry humping on the sofa when I came home early from work a few weeks ago. She said they were only messing around, but I took her to my doctor to be certain."

"What did Harold say?"

Beryl's head jerked back on her neck. "I didn't tell her daddy! Are you crazy? He'd have chopped Aikens's skinny weenie right off, and there are few enough young black men in the area. But I haven't seen his narrow-head self around my house since."

Laughing, Thea slung an arm about her friend's neck. "You do me good. But Jesse has no father to intimidate the boys."

"So then you be mother, father, and wrath of God all at once.

We do what we have to. Now I really got to go." She wiggled her fingers in imitation of Erica. "Got to fly!"

"Wait. You're forgetting something." Thea pointed to a package next to the chair Beryl had just vacated.

"Harold's book!" Beryl retraced her steps and picked up the small bag. "After all the trouble I went to this morning to get this book signed, you'd think I'd remember it."

"What is it?"

"*Grrrl,* let me show you!" She pulled a slim volume from the sack entitled *The Black Man's Book of Prayer.* Above the title was a full-color picture of Xavier Thornton. "Signed this very morning by the man himself!"

Xavier was in Dallas! Thea's pulse took off at a quick jog. She hoped it did not show in her expression.

"Still the celebrity, I see."

"With his too-fine self! Dark as molasses and twice as sweet! And hanging loose! The way he smiled when he shook my hand! Girlfriend, if I wasn't married . . . !"

Annoyed, Thea snapped, "Beryl, you're talking about a minister."

"I'm talking about an M-A-N. Time you remembered you were a woman with needs." Beryl waggled the picture before her face. "What do you see in this picture you wouldn't want a taste of?"

Thea felt a blush climb her cheeks. What would her friend's reaction be if she admitted she had already had a taste? "You win, dish him up with a spoon."

"That's what I'm talking about." Beryl tapped the book jacket. "Black men satisfy."

"Oh, excuse me. I didn't know we were playing Name That Stereotype."

"*Touch-ee!*" Beryl slipped the book back into the sack. "Girlfriend, lighten up. We're just women talking. A fine man is a fine man. That George Clooney? You ask me, there's a fine white boy! Now I really got to track. Call me!"

Thea stared at the few grounds in her cup. Xavier was in town. For how long?

"Oh no," she murmured under her breath as she glanced at her own watch and collected her things. Her days of keeping track of Xavier Thornton were too over. She had enough on her plate without distracting thoughts of an old boyfriend. For instance, Jesse should be back home by now. She needed to pick her up so they could make a trip to Home Depot and buy new paint for her bedroom.

> *Mom,*
> *Cassandra came by and we went to the mall. You can*
> *start without me. I know what I want. A sort of Monet-*
> *ish watercolor yellow.*
>
> *J*

Thea sighed and propped the note back against the flour canister in the kitchen where Jesse had left it for her. Her too-full Saturday now had a big fat hole in it. She didn't know whether she was more annoyed or hurt. Nothing she said or planned with her daughter these days was as important as what Jesse's friends might think of in the meantime. Annoyed won out.

She dialed Beryl's house on the off chance that the girls had stopped there before heading out. When Beryl heard the reason for her call, her whoop was entirely unsympathetic. "You think you're lonely now? Jesse's going to be headed for college in less than two years. Girlfriend, get a life!"

She hung up, feeling a bit embarrassed. Had she become so pathetic that she couldn't think of anything to fill up a Saturday that didn't involve her daughter? Surprisingly, Jesse had taken the news that she was going to Holland for several days very well, which was a 180 from her usual attitude. Since her father died, Jesse hated it when business travel took her mother away for more than one night. Thea suspected the change had something to do with the boy who had begun calling nearly every day. Jesse professed to loathe dating—she only went out in groups—but she wasn't thrilled to learn she wouldn't be allowed to stay home alone.

"Fat chance!" Thea had told her. Beryl and Erica took turns looking out for Jesse when she traveled. This time, it was Erica's turn.

*   *   *

THAT'S WHY I don't go to the doctor with every little pain. If they can't find anything wrong, they keep looking till they do," Aunt Della said with a mixture of dismissal and disgust. "I'm sure it's a fuss over nothing. My heart just bumps funny once in a while."

Heart pumping, Thea set down with a thud the can of sealant she had been carrying in from the garage when the phone rang. "How serious is it? Do you need me to come down there?"

"No, child. Dr. Leonard said it's probably nothing, but I should have tests done as a precaution. Which is why I'm calling. My Bertram—God rest his soul—has a granddaughter Lakeisha who married a heart doctor over there in Dallas. She's insisting I come there for tests."

"Then, of course, you'll come. You can even stay with me and Jesse."

"Oh, sugar, could I? That would be so nice. Make a visit of it instead of just a medical necessary."

"There is one catch." She hated to mention it but . . . "I'm scheduled to go to Holland on business next week. Can the tests wait until the following week?"

She heard her aunt fretting on the other end of the line. "I'm not even sure I want to waste the insurance money. Not to mention the trouble it's going to put me to."

"That's what insurance is for, Aunt Della. Now, if the tests can't wait, I'll cancel my trip." *Ron will love that!*

"Dr. Campbell said September twelfth and thirteenth would be fine."

She looked at the receiver before bringing it in close again to say, "Aunt Della, why didn't you tell me they'd already been scheduled?"

"I didn't want to put you on the spot, in case you were too busy to have me."

Thea took a deep breath. She had learned at sixteen that patience was a major requirement in dealings with her aunt. Sometimes Della came at you so fast, you felt the need to duck. Other times, she was as roundabout as a pretzel. This was one of those times. "Wherever you will be most comfortable is where you should be."

"I knew I could count on you, Theadora."

She gazed out at her pool after she had hung up, feeling shaken. Aunt Della was getting up in years, but such a dynamo that she never thought about the fact she would one day lose her. A new thought struck her and made her catch her breath. When her aunt was gone, she would be the eldest member of the family. She wasn't nearly ready to step up as the matriarch of the Broussards.

She reached for the phone to call Selma. She would never hear the end of it if something serious was wrong with Aunt Della and her sister was the last to know. It wasn't until she got the answering service that she remembered that her sister was still on her monthlong honeymoon cruise up the east coast of Africa. Some people knew how to make the most of life. With Selma, it was an art form.

She picked up the sealant and headed for her daughter's room.

WITH PAINT WHEEL in hand, she studied the gold leaf star on the fuchsia wall of Jesse's room. "Loud. It is loud," she murmured.

She had narrowed down the new color choice to three shades, but she was not about to be stung a second time by guessing wrong. Once she made her choice, Jesse would just have to figure out a way to get to the store to buy the paint. However, those shocking colors had to be sealed so they would not bleed through. Since she had nothing better to do, she would do that much.

She reached for a screwdriver to pry open the can of sealant.

The doorbell did a double ring as she stepped up on a footstool, brush in hand. That was Jesse's special signal! The girl could remember all the declensions of irregular French verbs but was forever forgetting her keys.

"Okay, okay!" She quickly put the brush on top of the open can, smiling in spite of herself. This would be a Morgan girls project after all! The doorbell rang again as she finished wiping her hands on her paint cloth and reached for the front doorknob.

"Jesse . . . Oh!"

eight

"REVEREND THORNTON." THE words were a whisper punched out of her by surprise.

For the second time in a month, the sight of Xavier Thornton caught her totally unprepared. This time, however, there was no opaque stare in his dark gaze.

"Hello, Theadora. I'd like to talk with you, if you're not busy." His tone was quiet, his expression pleasant.

She could not reciprocate. It was difficult to say anything at all when her defenses were crying, *Shut the door, Run,* and *Shit!* all at the same time. She never cursed. She must really be freaked, but she couldn't at this second sort out the reasons why. Finally, she managed, "How did you know how to find me?"

"Your sister was kind enough to give me your address. I hope I'm not inconveniencing you."

"I'm painting." Now that was clever. Would she never come up with a good line in front of this man?

His gaze skimmed her painting clothes as if seeking confirmation. "I can come back another time." His smile was polite, but something told her that he wasn't happy with the thought of being put off.

"No." The only thing worse than him standing here now was the threat that he might come back at some other unspecified time. Her adrenaline rush ebbed as she dragged back the door. "I've got a few minutes." That would be about as long as she could keep her objectivity.

As he moved past her, she could not help but notice how big he was. Taller than she remembered. Maybe it was just that she wore heels to the wedding and sneakers now. Or maybe her mind was playing those old tapes again, comparing him to her memory of the not-quite-grown man he had been when she knew him. Compared to that, this man was a stranger.

He took his time looking around the entry. His gaze paused for a moment on a Gullah basket of dried hydrangeas on the hall console, then moved on. Did the baby grand in the living room, easily glimpsed from the entry, seem ostentatious? Was he pricing her purchases, reviewing her taste, looking for insight into what her life was like? If he'd rolled up to her door to snoop into her life, he was fresh outta luck. The most important things were not here. Evan and Jesse. Or had he seen something in her gaze at Selma's wedding that made him think he would be welcome here?

That's when it hit her. She was angry—no, furious. The kind that made heads spin and smoke come out of ears. He had been a memory for more than half her life. Now he was back, and she could feel herself responding in ways that had nothing to do with reason and everything to do with shame and regret and fear. What could he want from her after all this time? Whatever it was, he wasn't going to get it.

His gaze came back to her. "You've done all right for yourself."

"I work hard." She made herself breathe through her nose. No need for him to know how rattled she was. She pointed to the living room. "Have a seat, Reverend. I'll just wash up."

"No need. I won't be keeping you long."

He had that right.

"Very well, Reverend." His lids flickered at her repeated use of his title, but it made her feel better. "I left a can of paint open. If you don't mind breathing fumes, you can come upstairs with me."

It took only a split second for her to be sorry she had invited him up. Much as she wanted to deny it, he had a way of looking at her that made her feel sixteen again. As he followed her up the stairs, she wished she had made a more concerted effort to lose those extra ten—okay fifteen—pounds she'd been accommodating the last year.

A memory flashed to mind, the first time she'd been alone with him. They had dragged their feet after choir practice by offering to put the hymnals away. She didn't know why he offered. She did because he did. His shoulder bumped hers, and she fumbled a book. He caught it, his hand grazing her breast. He held it there a full second longer than necessary. It was the first time she knew that he noticed her as a woman, not a kid. The hair stirred on her nape just thinking about how little it took to ignite sexual feelings when one was sixteen. At midage it should be a little harder. *Old tapes.*

Nearly every piece of furniture had been moved out of Jesse's room. Drop cloths covered the rest. The only place for him to sit was on a wicker dressing table stool. She pointed to it doubtfully. "Have a seat."

He looked at the fragile piece of furniture and raised a brow. "I'll stand, thank you."

Not knowing what to say to him, she crossed the room and picked up her brush. He had come to her. Let him start the conversation. He said nothing, just crossed his arms and leaned a shoulder against the doorjamb. Some silences are pregnant pauses, others echoes of the unsaid. This one was a test of wills.

Thea dunked her brush in the can and began stroking sealant over the gold star. Who knew brush strokes had a sound?

He sighed. Not hard enough to be impatience.

By her foot, the tinny sounds of Luther seeped from the headphones she had been wearing.

He shifted shoulders to lean against the opposite side.

She was breathing through her nose so strongly she could feel her nasal walls collapse inward with each intake of air.

"You do all your own decorating?"

She smiled to herself. First point was hers.

"It keeps me off the streets."

"It's kinda loud, don't you think?"

"Not at all," she lied. As close as she was, the gold seemed to dance a psychedelic tango with the fuchsia. She turned to look at him. "Life is about being bold."

"I hear that." He smiled for the first time.

She turned away. Her reaction to that smile should not be advertised.

"I hear you married?" The question was more of a statement.

"Evan died two years ago."

From the edge of her vision, she saw him nod solemnly. "I was saddened to hear that."

Was sorry, not am sorry. Her even brushwork faltered. *Selma must have told him about Evan.* What else had her sister told him?

At least he did not spout the usual ministerial slogans, "He's with the Lord now," or "He's in a better place." Not even a "Shall we pray for him?" If he had tried the last, she would have lost it.

"You have children?"

She might be in a mood to tell him to go directly to Hell without passing Go, but she did not see the need to lie. "A daughter, Jessica. We call her Jesse."

"Two years on your own with a child. You have my admiration. The burden of single mothers is often a hard one."

She whipped her head toward him. "I'm not a single mother. I'm a widow with a child."

He nodded. "I appreciate the distinction. I'd like to meet your daughter."

"She's not home now." She stopped painting and turned to him. "Why are you here?"

"Making arrangements to lead a weeklong men's retreat here next winter."

That wasn't what she meant, and he knew it.

"Why Dallas?"

"There's a lot of good work to be done here. Too many of my black brethren are still struggling with the effects of racism. Got to get right in their souls so they may take their rightful places in their families and community."

The seventies rhetoric was the first familiar thing about him.

Xavier Thornton had been a real radical in his youth. A "radical after the fact," her father would have called him—that's what he had called anyone who succeeded the nonviolent movement of the sixties.

She yanked up her thoughts. That wasn't true. Xavier wasn't among the hotheads who denigrated the work of their fathers' generation. Not at all. She was just looking for an excuse to resent him.

He surveyed Jesse's collection of soccer trophies, Odyssey of the Mind medals, and orchestra ribbons. Finally he moved and picked up a gold-framed family portrait from one shelf. He stared at it a long time. When he turned, there was an expression of incredulity on his face.

"This was your husband? You married white?"

She felt herself go stiff in a way that her mother said made her look like someone had stuck a broomstick up her back. So Selma had *not* told him everything.

"Is there a problem with that?"

He shook his head but continued to stare at her as if he expected her to say more. Too bad, because she had nothing to add except, *It's none of your goddamn business!*

She should have said it. She was not afraid to say those words to a preacher with his holier-than-thou attitude. How dare he! Someone she'd known briefly two dozen or so years ago. How dare he criticize her life!

"Was there another reason you dropped by, Reverend?" This time there was no disguising her hostility.

His weight shifted from one foot to the other, yet his gaze stayed on her. "I came to apologize."

"For cutting me dead at the wedding?" She hoped her tone said, *You can't possibly think it mattered to me.* She bent and dipped her brush so she would not have to continue trading stares. "No need."

He waited until she stood upright again. It was a major lull in the conversation.

"I'm talking about twenty-six years ago."

Her heart kicked her in the sternum. *Oh Lord! Not now.* She was not ready for this, had just discovered right this very second that maybe she was never going to be ready to talk about their past.

Amazing what you don't know about yourself until it's on you.

He put his hand on her shoulder. A gesture of shared emotion, or a weight to keep her still for his words?

"I need you to hear me out, and I suspect you need to hear it."

She considered the sincerity in his eyes. It didn't matter a damn. This was about her own protection.

"I can't do this. Not here." Was that a maybe in her voice?

Must have been, for his face lit up. "Anywhere you say."

Don't be found out! Someplace private. Mustn't be caught. Strange how patterns repeat themselves with the same people. She backed away, forcing him to release her shoulder.

"You can't come here again." Jesse would be home soon. She did not want her daughter, or, for that matter, anyone else in her life, to know that she knew him. "I'll meet you. Somewhere public." *Don't want to be misunderstood.*

"I'm staying at the Anatole. Have dinner with me."

"Make it coffee."

"Seven at the Nana Grill?"

"Fine." Was that Jesse's voice below? "Now I have to ask you to leave."

But he did not move. He just stood there, a half smile on his mouth. "I seem to recall you being kinda hardheaded about some things. If you stand me up, I'm gonna just keep calling on you until you hear me out. So, save us both the aggravation, and show up. Please."

nine

THE NANA GRILL was on the twenty-seventh floor. Carpet-to-ceiling glass panels provided a skyscraper view. A live jazz set was in progress, the tune "Mood Indigo." An apology did not seem to require this much background. But at least it was public.

Thea looked around with a deliberately bland expression. Now that her shock at his intrusion into her life had worn off, she was fully prepared to be pleasant, for an evening.

He sat in a wing chair on the far right side dressed in a navy blue suit. The room was crowded, noisy, yet he seemed marooned in an oasis of solitude. His expression was very serious. Whatever was on his mind, the ambiance of the setting could not supplant it. Was he pondering a new sermon . . . or wondering if he had made a mistake in inviting her here?

Don't even try to put that on him!

She saw him check his watch. Yeah, she was late. Surprisingly, he didn't glance toward the door, or he would have known she had arrived.

She took a deep breath all the same. She had thought about standing him up. But then she didn't doubt that he would return to her door. The will not to be denied had gotten him where he was today. If he met Jesse and began talking about how he'd known her mother back in the day, there would be even more questions than the ones she was prepared to answer tonight.

Yet, it was payback for Thea to be able to tell Jesse that instead of going to the movies together as they planned after *they* repainted her room, she had a better offer. Jesse's expression said she got the point.

While stuck in traffic on I-35, Thea decided she would keep the conversation superficial. She could pretend that they were adults who vaguely remembered being boyfriend and girlfriend. Bittersweet reminisence. She didn't owe him anything more. Not even that.

She moved quickly toward him before second thoughts could overrule her. "I hope I haven't kept you waiting. Traffic." Had to say something about being twenty minutes late.

"Not at all. I do appreciate you taking the time to meet with me." Something in his smile. An acknowledgment of the effort she had put him through to get her to come?

He indicated that she should sit opposite him. As she did so, his hand lightly cupped her elbow. The contact was warm but not possessive. Was it old-fashioned manners or the gesture of a man accustomed to making himself a physical presence in every sense? She couldn't decide. She did notice a half-finished drink on the small table before his chair. It wasn't coffee.

She was surprised the waitress appeared so quickly. The place was packed. Then she saw the smile the young woman offered Xavier.

"Would you like a refill or anything, Mr. Thornton?" Her tone was practically worshipful, and not the gospel-loving sort.

"No. Thanks." His gaze singled Thea out. "What would you like?"

"Alizé over ice." *Why not?*

The waitress gave Xavier another sidelong glance as she laid down a fresh napkin for his drink. "I'll have to check on the availability of that."

"Alizé, huh?" Xavier's eyes crinkled in the corners.

She answered him with a sly smile. Alizé was not a typical north Dallas kind of drink. Beryl had introduced her to the cognac and passion fruit liquor, the drink of the moment among her Delta sisters.

"You didn't mention this afternoon that you're an author." Let him talk about himself a bit, she thought, while she would wait for the calming effect of her drink.

He nodded. "I have that distinction. I haven't asked what you do for a living."

He tossed the ball right back to her! Amazing! She was sure he would want to boast a little. The Xavier she had known was never reluctant to talk about himself.

"I'm the manager of international transportation for Petro Chem."

"Impressive title. You travel much?"

"Did. Since my husband's death, I try to keep it to a minimum."

He nudged a bowl on the cocktail table toward her. "Nuts?" When she shook her head, he took a handful with the wide-palmed long-fingered hand that had snatched many a pigskin out of the stratosphere. She had a thing for men's hands. His were well manicured, nails buffed but not polished.

"So, tell me about your husband."

She had not forgotten the expression on his face when he saw Evan's picture. Her stomach muscles clenched.

"Why?" She tried to keep her voice neutral.

He funneled a few nuts through his fist into his mouth and chewed them before he said, "Seems like two old friends should do a little catching up."

We aren't old friends. We were a hot lick of a summer romance.

"Why don't you go first." She smiled. She was not going to spend the night defending *her* life.

"Fine." He leaned back, dusted the salt off his hands, and crossed his legs. Hand-sewn Italian shoes. He was not suffering on a minister's salary.

"Ask me anything. Knock yourself out."

"Tell me about your wife."

This was one of the few areas of his life the media did not cover.

His shrug did not mar the line of his jacket. That was custom tailoring for you. "It was a typical marriage between two people who need a prenuptial just to feel safe in one another's keeping." No hint of bitterness in his voice. "She was a Harvard Business School graduate. I had just left pro ball with the kind of bank I didn't know how to manage. We incorporated. Business was all we had in common. When we both realized it wasn't enough, we split."

That could have meant any of a dozen things. His expression was not giving any clues.

"And now you preach the gospel." She sounded snide, but she couldn't help it.

"Yeah." His head bobbed an easy rhythm. "Like you predicted."

"I did?" Her scalp tingled with surprise.

"You said a man with a calling is blessed. No matter how much I fought it, I would eventually come to understand that. You were right. Believe that."

She smiled. She did remember saying that. It was part of the first real conversation they ever had.

SEVERAL WEEKS AFTER the Jack and Jill social, she found him sitting alone on the brick steps outside Saint James's AME Church after vesper service. As pianist for the youth choir, she had stayed behind to put away the choral music. There he sat, looking so serious, almost haunted. His dejected expression gave her the courage to ask if something was wrong. His answer surprised her. He said he felt the Spirit moving in him sometimes, like tonight during the service, and it scared the bejesus out of him. He had not told anyone before because Xavier Templeton Thornton had other plans. He wanted the money, the fame, and all the trimmings that came with being a professional athlete. No way he was going to give it up. God better knock on another brother's door.

Something in his eyes that night. Something solemn yet soulful. She believed him. No—more—felt as if he had let her in on the truest, deepest secret of his life. And like a fool, she thought they had made a for-all-time connection.

*   *   *

"NEXT QUESTION." HIS voice snapped her back to the present. "Children?" she heard herself say, still seeing him as he was in her memory.

"I'm told I have a son."

The hair rose on her arms. "You're told?"

He looked at her with the well-documented stare that had shielded him from prying eyes all his public life. "I'm not the first to get jaded about the whole thing. After the third paternity suit—"

"Third?"

"They weren't mine." He must have seen something in her expression, because he added, "I've shocked you."

"No." She could not stop blinking.

"I *have* shocked you." A wide grin spread across his face, lifting his mustache to reveal beautifully even white teeth. "You were expecting I'd been a better man. Let me assure you, from the time I was fifteen, my pop was on my butt about not getting a girl pregnant. Even in my wildest days, I always took care of business."

That was not quite how she remembered it.

She reached for a cashew she did not really want. "How can you resist wanting to know for certain?"

"You make it sound simple."

"It's as easy as a trip to a lab."

"Not until recently." He shook his head. "And look what happened to an upstanding brother like Bill Cosby. Trying to do for years for a child he understood was not even his. Then she ups and stabs him in the back with the threat of blackmail. On the very day, some lowlife murdered his son! How's a man supposed to do right behind that?"

"I don't know."

The waitress reappeared. "We had Alizé." She placed a pale gold drink before Thea, then gave Xavier another inviting look. "Is there anything else you need?"

Thea saw him notice what else the waitress had just put on the table. He looked away, his jaw clenched. "No. Thanks all the same."

She could not resist raising an eyebrow toward the phone number on the cocktail napkin as she reached for her drink. "Subtle."

He shrugged, embarrassed, and waited until she had taken a sip before he said, "Now it's my turn. I want to know about your husband."

She took another sip and held his eye. "We met when I was an undergraduate at Georgetown."

His brows lifted. "What happened to your plans for Howard?"

"Affirmative action."

She could still hear Aunt Della's adamant opinion on the subject of college. "Why settle, Theadora, for a Negro education when you're going to need a white one in order to compete in a desegregated world?" That sentiment had echoed through middle-class black households nationwide in the seventies. The merit of it was still in debate.

"Evan was in law school. We fell in love and got married. Oh, and yes, Evan was white."

"And nobody raised hell over that?" He tucked in his chin. "Your daddy? Evan's folks?"

"Sorry. No cliché family outrage." *Except Selma.*

But if Selma hadn't told her pastor her attitude about her sister's marriage, she certainly wasn't about to enlighten him. Or favor him with some inside joke about her uptight and superwhite in-laws. Shirley and Richard might not have fallen on her in joy but they adored their only child, and anything Evan did was A-OK by them. Too late, she realized Xavier was staring at her.

"Losing him must have been especially hard," he finally offered.

"Why *especially*?"

"You loved him so much you can't bring yourself to talk about him two years after his death."

Busted! Yet, not for the reasons he thought. Talking about Evan wasn't painful anymore. She just knew she could never make him real for Xavier. Anything she might say now would sound trite or self-serving.

You let me love you, and I thought that ruined me for all other men . . . until Evan came along.

That was as close to the truth as she could get, but she wouldn't have uttered those words had he offered her a free pass into Heaven.

She shrugged. "We had what we had."

"So, no regrets."

"Sure." She was on safer ground talking about her regrets. "Evan died without warning. Walked out the door one morning, like every other morning, but he didn't come back. An aneurysm ruptured while he was at work. Nothing could be done. No time to prepare for it or even say good-bye."

She took a deep breath, ready to leave it there, yet she found herself continuing. Looking away, letting her words follow her thoughts. "It's amazing how memories can be edited by guilt. For about three months, he was a saint. And then I started to recall all the things he had done and said that I didn't like. For the next three months, I was furious with him. I replayed in my head every fight we'd ever had, every small or mean thing I'd done and said over the years."

Embarrassed by this revelation she'd not shared with anyone else, her gaze swung back to Xavier to judge his reaction.

He sat absolutely still, listening. "Where are you now?"

She shrugged again. "I've settled a couple of things. I loved him. He loved me. However the rest divides out, that much will always be true."

"Your husband was a lucky man."

"Mr. Thornton? 'X' Savior Thornton?"

Startled, they looked up at a big man in a burnt orange TU sport coat who seemed to have materialized beside their table. How long had he been there?

He was smiling broadly at Xavier. "You are the former wide receiver, right?"

Xavier stood. "That's right."

"I knew it!" The man motioned to three people staring at them from the bar. "It's him! Come on!" He pumped Xavier's arm as if he expected to strike oil. "I'm Dwayne Yardley. And you are one of my heroes."

Smiling, Xavier sized him up. "I bet you played ball, too."

Dwayne's ruddy complexion deepened. "Some, in high school. Nothing like you. Man, you were beautiful to watch."

He stretched out his arm to encompass the woman who led the trio over to them. "This is my wife, Sue. Sue, this is about the best football player God ever made."

"You might get a few quarrels with that statement." Xavier's chuckle was polite, friendly, the professional meeting his fans.

"Say, weren't you in the movies?" Sue asked.

"Sure enough was," Dwayne said. "He was in the original *Shaft.*"

"That was a little before my time," Xavier answered smoothly. "And those days are long behind me. I'm a minister now. I pastor Saint James's African Methodist Episcopal Church in Atlanta." He slid a card into her hand. "If you're ever in town, I'd welcome your attendance on a Sunday."

"Well, don't that beat all. A man of God! Nothing left but to repent, huh?"

Sue shoved an elbow into his middle. *"D—waayne!"*

Xavier patted his shoulder. "Now, you have a nice a evening."

Though this seemed a dismissal, Thea noticed he remained standing long enough to shake every hand and accept accolades from other people who walked up to meet him until the group was satisfied and turned away.

Despite the curious glances aimed her way, Xavier did not introduce her, which was a relief. The fact that he attracted so much attention was not something she had fully considered when she insisted on meeting him in a public place. She was foremost a private person. She would hate these kinds of intrusions. She hated it now.

"Sorry about that," he said when they were once again alone. *"Shaft!"* His head wagged in amusement before he caught himself. "Where were we?"

She had had a moment to think, and the thinking made her realize she'd already said way too much.

"You were about to tell me the reason for this meeting."

He nodded. "All right."

He moved to the edge of his seat, leaning toward her until she could see each of his curly lashes separately. "Seeing you last month, after all that time . . ." His voice dropped in volume and pitch. "I've prayed about it every day since, and now I understand that it was God's will."

"God's will?" She always got a little uncomfortable when people started talking about knowing what God wanted. Even if they were a minister.

"There is a purpose in everything He does, Theadora. He knows what we cannot. I truly thought I'd cleansed my soul of past iniquities some years ago, but I hadn't owned up to my first act of wickedness." He spread his hands wide. "But seeing you again? Struck me dumb with shame."

He took her hand and spoke in a hushed tone only she could hear. "I need to ask your forgiveness. You put your trust in a self-serving brother who took advantage of your honesty and your innocence."

She jerked her hand back. "No need to talk about that."

"All right." His fingers drummed the table for a moment. "As long as you know I accept that all that happened that last night as my fault."

Was it? She was mad bad in love with him. Her parents never knew she sneaked out to see him. All summer he had treated her like a kid sister willing to listen to him expound on everything from the Black Panthers to Vietnam to the Bible. Then when she thought he would never take her seriously, she reached for that first kiss . . . and the second.

She stared at his mouth, those tender, full lips, and wondered how she had dared.

The recall was there in his gaze, too. An intimacy they scarcely had time to experience and never really admitted to. And then he was gone.

Why didn't you call, Xavier?

She could not ask. She would not ask. Not now, not when the answer no longer mattered. And there were things he had no right to read in her expression, things that were not his concern.

"All things work for the common good," her mama used to say when something went wrong. And things had worked out. For both of them. He'd had the dazzling career he coveted. And she'd made a good life with Evan and Jesse.

From the corner of her eye, she saw the waitress again heading toward them. The waitress leaned in low to whisper something to Xavier.

Thea's gaze followed his to a group of men standing just inside the bar. She might not know their names, but she recognized members of the Cowboys' defensive line when she saw them.

He looked embarrassed as he turned back to her. "Please excuse me."

Less than a minute later, he rejoined her, his mouth tight at the corners. "I'm sorry, Theodora, but when you said just coffee, I accepted another dinner engagement. I didn't expect them so soon."

"No problem." She stood up so abruptly she had to make a grab for her purse.

Son of a B! He had planned a backdoor strategy! So much for his sincere interest in setting the record straight. Was he afraid she might be a bore or cause a scene, or was he just entertaining himself until something better came along? She didn't know him anymore. She couldn't read him. But she did know an exit line when she heard one.

She offered her hand but looked past him, already out the door in her mind. "Good night, Reverend."

"I'll walk you to your car."

"No need." She moved purposefully toward the exit.

She did not realize he had followed her until he tapped her on the shoulder as she paused before the elevators. His grin was as provoking as it was wide. "Giving me attitude? It's the first sister thing I've seen about you."

"Don't hurt yourself looking."

"I'll be back in town in a few weeks. I'd like to call you."

"Why? We talked. I accept your apology." She looked past him. "Your dinner companions are waiting."

His smile faded. When he tried to touch her, she backed up a step. She saw his expression change. He was now simply a man who didn't like being handed his walking papers. "Expect to hear from me. Soon." He held out his card.

She ignored it.

"Theodora . . ."

She did not care that she was being rude. She'd never see him again. She stepped into the opening elevator with a murmured, "Good-bye, Reverend Thornton."

She wasn't even out of the parking lot before she realized her real mistake. Forget about agreeing to meet him. It was talking to Xavier as though she knew him! Knew him well enough to question his private life. Why did she do it? Was that the attraction, the sense of instant familiarity that he evoked for her? Or was it something else?

She stared into the fiery blaze of the dying sunset. Her hands were sweaty on the steering wheel. The hollow feeling in her stomach had nothing to do with the fact that she had not eaten since those French fries at noon.

The trouble with youthful memories is that they are so simple and vivid, like Crayola drawings. And just as difficult to get rid of.

We were kids doing what kids often do, believing that nothing bad could ever happen to us . . . because we were smart . . . in love . . . special.

Nobody acting a fool was ever that smart . . . that true . . . or that special.

"Stupid! Stupid!"

She punched the radio to blank out her thoughts. The car filled with KRNB's alternative to a bubble bath by candlelight, The Quiet Storm. It was only seven thirty-seven, yet an around-midnight mood came through in the instrumental intro of Luther Vandross's rendition of "Creeping."

"Love comes from the soul. . . . And everyone feels the need . . . to be loved."

The voice-over was DJ Rudy V's. Deep. Quietly modulated. Pitched in that Barry White octave that made a woman want to slip off more than her shoes. She recognized this as a lead-in to a reading of one of his trademark self-penned love poems.

She reached out and silenced the seductive voice invading her thoughts.

"Expect to hear from me. Soon."

He had said those exact words to her twenty-six years ago. This time, she would not hold her breath. Could not afford to even hope.

That's a slippery slope to Hell.

ten

"WHO'S OPRAH WRINGING out today?"

She looked up from the spreadsheet she had opened out on the breakfast table to find her aunt standing in the kitchen archway in her dressing gown. "I'm sorry, Aunt Della. What did you say?"

Della pointed a freshly manicured fingernail at the eleven-inch TV set perched on the kitchen bar. "Somebody's crying on *Oprah*. You wouldn't think there'd be so many tears left in the world, much as she keeps wringing them out of people."

"Oh—right." She looked away before she completely lost her concentration. With any luck, her aunt would notice how busy she was and go back to dressing for her dinner with her step-granddaughter's family.

"I can't abide some of those other talk shows," Della continued as she approached. "They turn up some of the most broke-down no-account folk. Trashy people with trashy lives, parading it around like it was God-given. Not a speck of decency among them."

"*Umm.*" She just needed five—ten minutes at most—to finish checking the numbers. Then she'd planned a quick escape to the gym to burn off a week's worth of tension before she took Jesse to her Friday-evening game.

Della squinted at the TV. "Theodora, I don't know how you can see something so tiny. And how can you enjoy the show when the sound's so *low?*"

"If you'd like to watch *Oprah*, I'd be happy to turn on the set in the family room for you." *Hint, hint!*

A muscle twitched by Thea's left eye as the *thwang* of wailing guitars filtered in from the direction of the master bedroom. She'd only turned the TV on in self-defense. A little hard of hearing, Della kept her radio volume at levels only *she* considered low. Who had the heart to complain to an elderly woman who had just undergone a weeklong series of nerve-racking tests? But—honest to God! Did her aunt have to be the only black woman she knew with a passion for Willie Nelson?

"*Tsk, tsk, tsk!* Now look at that! Didn't that girl's mother ever tell her it's ugly to cry with her mouth wide open?"

Thea laid down her pen in defeat. Her aunt's clucking tongue meant that she was worked up about something other than the lack of good manners in a TV audience.

"What's wrong, Aunt Della?"

Della picked an imaginary speck from one satin lapel of her turquoise silk wrapper, her thin lips pursing into a coral lipstick rose before she spoke. "Now, I didn't want to disturb you, and I can see I have."

"Not at all," she lied. No point in making both of them miserable.

"In that case, I can't lay my hands on my Dr. Scholl's foot powder. And you know I can't abide sweaty feet."

Glancing down at her aunt's size fives shod in gold lamé mules, she seriously doubted those elegant little feet had ever been allowed to perspire. "Would you like me to look?"

"Sugar, would you?" The spot of rouge on each of her aunt's cheeks brightened. "I get all turned around when I'm upset. And what with all these tests I've been having . . . I think I must be getting senile."

"No problem." Thea shook off the fog of number crunching and stood up to follow her aunt. She'd just been played by a pro of old-school feminism.

Some said it was the privilege of the elderly to be immune to the desires of others, but the truth was, Aunt Della had never operated in any other manner. Bewilderment and helplessness were her tools. "Sugar, would you?" could be her middle name, along with "I'd be so grateful if you'd . . ." and "As long as you're . . ." No wonder her face was unlined by worries and care. Someone else had looked after her all her life.

Guilt pricked her. Aunt Della was Aunt Della, and she was not going to change after all these years. But that didn't mean she couldn't be annoyed with her from time to time. All this togetherness was beginning to chafe.

Della had arrived in Dallas last Sunday, barely twenty-four hours after Thea had returned from Holland. Today, Friday, was the only day of the week she had been able to take off. Della's stepgranddaughter, Lakeisha, had taken care of her during the other days. Then Jesse took over aunt-sitting duty from after school until her mother arrived home from work. Each evening, Jesse met her mother at the garage door with a big sigh of relief. At least she did not complain—much. There was the business about the debutante ball Jesse didn't want any part of and the fact Della thought Jesse's crop tops exposed too much flesh for a "lady" and that her grandniece ate "junk." From Aunt Della's point of view, of course, the two of them were "getting along famously."

She, on the other hand, couldn't report that work was going famously. Everyone was sweating the news that the hired guns were due to begin their work-process study on Monday. Consultants invariably equaled layoffs.

Then there was Joe. Conversations during their trip eased her suspicion that he was after her job, but something was definitely eating him. He was all but hostile since their return to Dallas. She didn't think it politic to grill him. Could be something personal. Yet, if she didn't know better—

"I hope you have better sense than to frequent one of those co-ed establishments."

"I beg your pardon?"

"You mentioned earlier you were going to a gym. A lady should never admit what her beauty costs her."

"Aunt Della, men today *like* to watch women sweat."

Della sniffed delicately. "As I've been telling Jesse, in my day, we had different beauty standards."

She um-hummed that topic. Since age sixteen, she'd heard all about those different standards. They emphasized feminine mystique and ageless, effortless beauty above all.

For example, Della claimed Broussard women did not gray. The solution into which she dipped her faded ebony hair twice a week, made from strong tea and coffee grounds, simply helped to "keep the shine." To this day, her sugar praline façade attracted male admirers. Few ever suspected it covered a will of steel until they tried to cross her. Like in the matter of the girdle visible even now beneath the drape of her housecoat.

"Didn't you tell me that your doctor said you should give up girdles because they encourage osteoporosis of the spine?"

Della sniffed again. "That young man is about five minutes older than the poached egg I had for breakfast. What does he know?"

Thea smothered her laughter in her hand.

"I hear that sniggling." Della squared her shoulders. "A lady doesn't jiggle. It's not dignified."

"Yes, ma'am. Now, where do you think I should look for your powder?"

"I believe the can may have fallen under the bed."

She moved to begin her search near the head.

"No, no, try the foot," Della advised without a hint of embarrassment.

Thea shifted down to the foot and lifted the dust ruffle without comment. Clearly, her aunt had dropped the can. Rather than admit that—girdle-bound as she was—she could not bend and pick it up, she had simply kicked it under the bed. The ploy was standard Della Broussard operating procedure.

"What do you know!" Thea exclaimed, dryly. "Here it is."

Della clutched the tin can to her bosom like a long-lost friend. "Thank you, sugar. Everything here is so gracious." She favored her niece with a smile of approval. "I do so regret that I was unable to visit your lovely home more often . . . in happier times."

Before Evan died, Thea finished in her thought. Though she had buried three husbands, Aunt Della still tiptoed around death as if it were a taboo subject. Evan had fondly referred to her as "Miss Manners."

"I know I'm a nuisance, I know it," Della confided with a coquettish smile. "But I just couldn't abide the thought of recuperating at the Campbells, even though Lakeisha is disappointed, since her husband is my doctor. I tell her she's done enough, carrying me to the hospital and back every day for the tests."

"I'll do something nice for her to show how much I appreciate her help."

"She is a dear. But, mercy, when she and her little family came to visit me at Mardi Gras last year, I thought I'd about lose my mind. Those children! Playing that hip-hop all hours and sassing their parents." Della's gaze flew heavenward. "The youngest, the daughter thank goodness, has the only pretense to prettiness. But her mother lets her go about with her head wrapped like somebody called Erica Bad-something."

"Erykah Badu. She's a popular singer from Dallas."

"Can't abide those jumped-up sounding names. And you'd think Lakeisha's daughter was a Zulu, the way she dresses."

Sometimes her aunt's attitude was as outdated as Jim Crow. *Different generation,* she reminded herself. "I hope you won't bring that up at dinner, Aunt Della. You know how sensitive people can be."

"Just like your father. He always was one to tell me what I shouldn't say," Della answered in an unruffled tone. "But I say there's no shame in the truth."

She sat down on the bed and slipped her right foot out of her slipper. "I will say this for Lakeisha. She made a nice catch for herself. I don't know his people, but Dr. Campbell's offices reflect great prosperity. There are pictures on the walls of him posing with Dallas Cowboys, Mavericks, even your new black mayor." She paused to give Thea a significant look. "I don't suppose he's single?"

"Married." Time to steer this conversation another way. "Dr. Campbell certainly has taken good care of you. Without him, I doubt you would have gotten to see all those specialists in the same week."

Della gave a delicate shudder. "They turned me every way

but loose and didn't find a *thing*. Which I could have *told* them, before times. I'm only too glad to be celebrating the end of this ordeal."

"You deserve it."

"I truly do." Della bent forward slightly and extended her arm to sprinkle powder on her foot. A good bit of it fell onto the carpet. "Lakeisha says the celebration was Dr. Campbell's idea. And I'm told The Rivera has quite good food, considering." Her way of saying no restaurant outside New Orleans was really worth the money. "I do wish you and Jesse were able to join us for dinner. But Jesse says she can't miss a single game if she wants remain a beginner."

"Starter," she corrected. Jesse's game was her excuse, too, to duck out on the dinner. "Jesse hopes to get a soccer scholarship to college."

"She's such a clever young lady. And pretty. I told her to be careful of incurring injuries. Men don't like scars." Della applied powder to her left foot with equal vigor, the shape of her right foot now clearly outlined on the rug. "I still say you should have allowed me to put a notice of her trip abroad in the *Times-Picayune*. One of our babies, studying at the Sorbonne! We'll just have to save it for her debutante notice."

Thea made a neutral sound and reached for the can of Dr. Scholl's before she had to vacuum the full contents off the rug. "Is there anything else I can do for you?"

Della stood up and moved to the foot of the bed. "If you will just set up the ironing board, I'll press a few of these wrinkles out of my suit." She ran a hand over the ice-blue garment with rhinestone buttons lying on the bed. "I told Oleatha to pack it in extra tissue paper, but she's getting on in years and doesn't hear well anymore."

"I'll drop it off at my cleaners on the way to the gym. They do rush orders."

"And waste money on something I can do?"

"I make good money, Aunt Della."

"And spend it, too." Della cast her gaze around the bedroom and lowered her voice. "You realize you shouldn't keep this much house, now that you're a widow?"

"Evan had life insurance on the mortgage. It's paid for."

Della drew her upper lip down over her teeth. "I hope that's not common knowledge. A widow can't afford to look too prosperous, or she might attract the wrong sort of attention. Any decent man will want to feel he can meet the needs of the lady he cares for out of his own purse."

This, from a widow who inherited three houses!

"Aunt Della, you know you love bragging about your niece's 'Dallas Palace.' That reminds me! I've been meaning to ask you about a young man you sent to see me a few weeks ago. He says we're related, through you. David Gray. No, Greer."

"Really?" Della reached for the bed and sat down a little heavily. "Why yes, I know the child. But I certainly would never have occasion to send him here. Young people have no manners today." She began to fuss with her lapel, her expression one of distaste. "Presuming on so slight an acquaintance!"

"It's not important." She had not really given the young man much thought since his visit had been quickly overshadowed by Xavier's arrival.

The reminder clenched her jaw. Two weeks, and not one word from Xavier. Damn, but she had been right about him!

"You really shouldn't allow strangers in your home, dear. Especially not strange *men*. You're a woman alone."

"I don't think that's going to be a problem." *Why had he bothered to show up the first time?*

Della perked up. "Why, have you met someone?"

"No. And I really do need to get going." Yet her aunt's manner disturbed her. There was a quiver in her voice. Although she claimed to feel fine, Della looked suddenly weary. Those medical tests had worn her out, even if she was too vain to admit it. Her color was definitely sallow.

"Would you like me to wait until Jesse gets home from school before leaving for the gym? I don't mind." *Please say no.*

"Oh no, sugar. You go on and do what you need to do." Della gave her a vague smile. "Go on now."

"Well, if you're sure?" Thoughts of Xavier had given her an additional annoyance to work off. "Jesse will be home at four-thirty. Tell her I'll be back in time to take her to her soccer game. Oh, and give me that suit. No arguments!"

*   *   *

SHE EMERGED FROM the gym dripping sweat and relief. The workout never got any easier. The only good part was the "over" part. That, and the tension relief, which was a luxury these days. The downside was the sweaty ride home. That was something she just had to deal with because she never showered at the club.

One thing she and Aunt Della shared was a sense of modesty that was considered outdated. But in her case, the need for privacy was deep-seated in a shyness she'd never fully outgrown.

THE LOCKER ROOM showers in junior high school were without stalls or curtains. Too shy to even peek at any of the other girls, each day she turned to the wall and tried to make her body take up as small a space as possible. Her classmates laughed and joked and teased each other about the varying sizes and shapes of breasts and butts and thighs. Usually Mrs. Gilroy, the gym teacher, kept an eye on things, but one day, the teacher was called to her office. Patricia Ann, the first among the girls to get her period, strutted about, her ample breasts topped by shiny Raisinet nipples, ragging on the slow to grow. Hoping to escape Pat's radar, Thea showered quickly and wrapped herself in a too-small towel. But a hawk can always spot a chicken.

"What you got so special you got to hide it?" Pat called out and snatched away her towel.

She found herself quickly surrounded by curious girls with skin shades from banana to raisin. All of them had cocoa-tipped nipples—all but her. Pat wasn't shy about pointing this out. "Look, she got white girl's nipples! They're pink! You ain't no kinda colored girl at all!"

Devastated, she ran out of the showers and cried all the way home.

"There's always one who's bound to act a fool over something different," her mother tried by way of consolation to explain the unwelcome curiosity.

*   *   *

DIFFERENT! THE THOUGHT jolted her back to the present. It was never easy to be different, her mother had that right.

She'd once asked Jesse about how she felt about stripping down in gym class. It was no big deal, Jesse said. Of course, she wished her waist was smaller, but at least she had better legs than Harper, with her cottage-cheese thighs.

Her daughter was a jock. Thea had been too intimidated to try out for any sport. But life was different when she was growing up.

Until she had met Evan, she'd never considered that calling herself black could be perceived as a deliberate *choice*. Different for her than for Selma.

"With my dark eyes and hair, ain't nobody ever going to mistake me for anything but some kind of brown baby," Selma once proudly said.

Yet one day not long after they began dating, Evan stood her before a mirror and told her to look at herself and see not what she knew to be *true* but only what the mirror *reflected*: a pale face, light eyes, hair that curled but did not kink. The mirror reflected a white woman.

The shock that went through her lasted for days after she stepped away from the image. All her life, she had been looking at herself through tinted lenses. Light, yes, but everyone could tell the difference, right? When the shades came off, it left her feeling very exposed, just like that day in the girls' shower.

But mirrors do lie.

She dabbed at her brow and then toweled her wet neck before sliding sticky thighs across another towel that protected the leather seat.

Who's the fairest of them all? As she slid behind the wheel, she caught her reflection in the car window and grinned. *It ain't me, babe!*

She turned on the ignition and leaned into the blast of air that came from the vents, a bit warm at first and then sweat-freezing cold.

The world was different now. Maybe Jesse did not need to see things her way. There was only so much control any parent had at this age. As Beryl had reminded her, in less than two years, Jesse would be going away to college.

What then, Thea?

eleven

OUT OF HABIT, Thea punched on the TV as she passed through her bedroom. Aunt Della was still out at dinner with the Campbells. Jesse had gone upstairs to shower after the game, and Thea was headed to the Jacuzzi for a good long soak. Her muscles were protesting the extra-long workout she'd put them through.

When she emerged from the bathroom thirty minutes later, she heard a voice: deep . . . resonant . . . familiar. She flipped back the ends of the towel wrapped about her wet hair and glanced quickly around. She was alone, save for the TV. As she moved toward it, Xavier Thornton's face suddenly appeared.

"We've become a culture of numbers, of statistics. Polls! Surveys! Tabulations! Demographics!" He punctuated each word with italics of tone. "We love our numbers! Yes we do! You know we do!"

Intrigued, she sat at the foot of her bed. In all the years of following Xavier's career, she had never heard him preach. She did not even know he had a spiritual program on—she glanced at the channel—BET. Aunt Della must have been watching earlier. She despised rap, the videos in particular, but had evidently found something on the channel of which she approved.

". . . Every night we hear the crime rate! The Dow Jones Average! The latest public opinion polls measure everything from the popularity of a TV show to what brand of detergent we buy!"

The perspective changed, and a wide-angle shot from another camera showed a gold-robed choir made up of a hundred or more men flanking him. On every lap was an open Bible.

"We like numbers, like to quote them. Numbers make us feel wise, learned, secure in our views." His tone was conversational. "The man on the street can quote the birth rate, the crime rate, and especially the odds and averages of his favorite sports teams." This was met by appreciative chuckles. "We've come to believe if you can quantify it, you can control it." He reached out and grabbed a handful of air. "We slot it, order it, file it—and forget it." His hand opened in a gesture of tossing something away.

"We discount others' troubles because the *odds* are statistically probable. The crime rate is up? 'It's gonna happen,' we say. The welfare numbers are growing? We shake our heads and we quote the Bible." He patted the book before him. "Matthew: chapter twenty-six, verse eleven. Jesus himself said, 'Ye have the poor always with you . . .' " He looked up with a smile. "Must be His plan. Who am I to meddle with His plan? We take *comfort* in our helplessness. We take *cover* in it! But we don't sit so easy when *we* become a statistic."

He moved from behind the podium, mike in hand, and descended the low, wide steps toward his audience as he spoke.

"You want to hear the four most reviled words in the world today?" His voice rose into falsetto: " 'Can you hold, please?' *Click!*"

He nodded slowly, smiling, until the telling laughter ebbed.

"It's the *click* that gets us, isn't it? Like a *smack* in the face. We've been put on hold, relegated to a number in line. Our needs have been shoved into the orderly column of statistical management." Again he mimicked a self-important voice. " 'Your call will be processed in the order in which it was received.' Doesn't it make you mad?"

His voice swelled with righteous indignation as he worked the congregation.

"Not *me!* I *know* you didn't put *me* on hold! Don't you know who *I* am? I'm *somebody!* My business is important. Why?" He thumped his chest. "'Cause it's *mine!*"

The audience of perhaps a thousand erupted in laughter and applause.

She smiled along with them. He was good.

"But you can be *fooled* by numbers. Ask any math teacher. There's a *thousand* ways to add up data to get the answer you want. Statisticians call it 'massaging the numbers.'"

He chuckled as he imitated the motion. "Massaging. Sounds good, doesn't it? Feels good, too. All the ache and worry rubbed right out. Only you got to know that when something can be worked around that easy, there's every chance no good can come of it."

He sobered and dropped his hands. "That's why there's only *one* way of computing that counts in this life. On Judgment Day *only* the *truth* will be used as a measure. And that's the *gospel* truth! The real deal!" He pointed skyward. "Check it out with Numero Uno!"

"Amen, Pastor!" said a voice off camera.

"*God* didn't set our lives by statistics. Statistics are numbers that are gathered *after* the fact, *after* the act. They show us where we've been—*not* where we're going. Are you with me? Are you? I hope so. Because, beginning tonight, my brethren, I'm challenging you to make a *change!*"

"Mom?"

"Yes?" She muted the sound without considering why.

Jesse hung in the doorway. "Who's Reverend Thornton?"

How long had Jesse been standing there?

"A minister in Atlanta."

"So why is he calling here?"

She tried to keep the surprise out of her voice. "He called? When?"

"While you were in the Jacuzzi."

Her gaze shifted to the silent screen. She hadn't given him her number. And she'd just written him off while pedaling like a madwoman on the stationary bike at the gym. "Did he leave a message?"

"He said to tell you he's looking forward to seeing you again." Jesse's eyes held a question she did not put into words.

She avoided her daughter's gaze. "Reverend Thornton is a old family friend. He officiated at your Aunt Selma's wedding. It must be a courtesy call."

Jesse rolled her eyes. "Mom. Give me some credit. I saw the flowers."

That emptied the last drop out of Thea's bottle of nonchalance.

"What flowers?"

"In the living room. Aunt Della said the delivery came while I was changing for my game."

"Why didn't you say something before?" She stood up and headed for the door.

Jesse followed her mother out of the bedroom. "I thought you'd seen them."

Sure enough, a vase with two dozen long-stemmed yellow roses stood in the middle of the living room coffee table. She took a deep breath and crossed over to them.

"Aunt Della says you have a male admirer. They're from him, right?"

"Let me open the card, okay?" She could limit the possible name of the sender to two. The card was typed.

> *If a potion tastes bitter,*
> *And yet brings relief,*
> *Would you give it up?*

She did not recognize the quote nor could she guess its meaning. Was she the bitter potion?

"Well?"

She looked up. "It's not signed."

"So?" Jesse's expression was far too shrewd for her comfort.

She glanced again at the flowers. Phillip would never pass up an opportunity to take credit for his own cleverness.

"I suppose they could be from Reverend Thornton." *How much truth should I reveal?* "He was in Dallas a few weekends ago. We met for a drink. To talk about old times."

Jesse's gaze rose to a spot on the ceiling. "It's okay, Mom, if you want to see men. It's time. Everybody says so. Holly's mother was dating three months after her divorce." Her gaze lowered. "It's just . . . you will tell me, won't you?"

Dating? Her stomach jumped. She and Jesse had not had this particular conversation before. "Meeting with Reverend Thornton was not a date, Jesse. Even so, let's keep his phone call to ourselves, okay? You know how Aunt Della can magnify things all out of proportion."

Jesse gave an exaggerated sigh. "Boy, do I!"

She breathed relief. At least she and Jesse were united on that front. "And I promise I'll talk it over with you *when* I'm ready to date. Okay?"

Jesse's brows arched just like her father's had when he was up to mischief. "Do I get to set the curfew?"

She chuckled. "Don't get too carried away."

Jesse came toward her, holding out a sticky note. "Here's his number. Oh and, Mom, can I borrow your Visa card? Harper and I want to shop for homecoming right after school tomorrow."

"Homecoming? That's not for another month."

"Yeah, but the dresses arrived in the stores this week. We have to choose before all the good ones are gone. Mine's got to be the bomb."

"Oh? You already have a date for the dance?"

"Not yet. But . . ."

She recognized that break in her child's voice. The universal fear of every young woman that no one will ask her to the big dance. Had the girl not looked in the mirror lately? "I predict more than one guy will ask."

Jesse's expression soured. "Mom, why do you always have to overcompensate? I've got homework to do." She turned and walked out.

Thea stared after Jesse until she disappeared up the stairs. Was she really in favor of her mother dating? Maybe the only reason she didn't already know that was because she wasn't certain *she* was ready.

She turned back to the flowers and leaned in to breathe

deeply. They smelled so good! Only the expensive ones had that kind of scent. Yellow roses. A reference to the legendary Yellow Rose of Texas? She was a light-skinned Black woman. Phillip wouldn't know that story. But Xavier might.

She looked at the phone number in her hand. There was a room number beside it. Xavier had called from the road. To see if his flowers arrived? The "bitter potion": Was that supposed to be chastisement because she walked out on him? If the man was annoyed, then why was he sending roses two weeks behind the fact? And more to the point, why was she smiling?

She walked back into her bedroom and pushed the Mute button on the TV remote.

". . . Too easy!" Xavier's face was now slick with perspiration, his features taut with emotion. His voice fell into a whisper. "Too easy!"

He laid a hand on the podium to steady himself. "Are you with me? Are you? Because God has a master plan! Every one of you is meant to be a *some*body!"

Shouts from the audience were louder now, deep voices were cheering him on, but he did not follow up on their fervor. His voice dropped into little more than a whisper into the mike in his hand.

"But you've got to *earn* it!"

His tone turned solemn. "I'm gonna talk to the brothers now. Men, where are your children? You know what I'm talking about. Are they in the statistics?" He started counting on his fingers. "Babies born to so many unwed mothers, per capita, per year. So many casualties to lust, poverty, ignorance, and indifference! Who's watching over *your* child? If the answer is your baby's mama, *all by herself*—then that's a shame! Hear me, brothers! It's not about what you *got*. It's about what you *keep!*"

He lowered his head and took a deep breath. When he lifted it again, she noticed that he looked exhausted. Watching him work that congregation, she realized that he had traded one kind of celebrity for another. But this was more important and more difficult.

"Our time is up for tonight. The Black Man's Master Plan Crusade will continue next week. For those of you who are with us tonight from the vantage point of your homes, I invite you to bow your heads and join us . . ."

She pushed the Off button and reached for the phone.

"Beryl, have you ever heard the phrase, 'If a potion tastes bitter, / And yet brings relief, / Would you give it up?'"

"What is it? Part of a poem?"

"That's what I was wondering."

"You know, there is something familiar . . . Hold on!"

Beryl was gone so long, she was about to hang up, when the receiver was picked up again. *"Grrrl,* I'm good! I found it the first time."

"Found what?"

"My book of African love poems."

She swallowed carefully. "You think it's a love poem?"

"Let's see. Ah now, listen to this, 'A flash of lightning does not quench my thirst: / What good does it do me / If I just see you from afar?' Here's another. 'My heart is single and cannot be divided, / And it is fastened on a single hope; / On you, who might be the moon!' *Uh-huh,* that's some Masai Mack Daddy macking, you just know it. *Hm . . .*"

She could hear pages of a book turning.

"All right, I found it! It's a bit from a Somali love poem. 'Until I die, I shall not give up love-songs. / Oh God, forgive me my shortcomings! / If a potion tastes bitter, / And yet brings relief, / Would you give it up?' There you go. Now, why do you need to know the source?"

"Something for Jesse's AP English class. Thanks. Talk to you later."

Xavier sent me a love poem!

She still didn't know what the quote was supposed to signify. And, of course, she'd have to make up some plausible explanation to give Aunt Della for the flowers. With any luck, she would be home in New Orleans before Xavier called again.

She caught a reflection of herself in the mirror, and what she saw was big fat grin of anticipation.

"Too easy!" The words from his sermon dropped back into her mind, this time with the weight of prophecy. Encouraging his renewed interest in her, whatever the reason, would be all too easy.

But she could not afford to be flattered by his attention unless she was willing to deal with the past and all that came attached. What was it her mother used to say about stirring up a nest of vipers?

Her smile evaporated. She needed to leave well enough alone. She crumpled the note and tossed it into the wastebasket.

twelve

"AT LEAST LET me drive home, Mom."

"We'll see." Thea tapped her foot impatiently. She hadn't slept well, and getting her aunt ready to leave this morning had become a major production. Della didn't travel easily.

Even though planes were equipped with lavatories, her aunt still subscribed to the idea that it was best to "go" before you boarded any form of transportation. She had gone to the "powder room" three times before getting in the car. Now she and Jesse stood outside the ladies' lavatory at DFW Airport terminal C waiting for Della to emerge.

Jesse walked her fingers playfully down her mother's sleeve to the hand holding the car keys. "I'll be sixteen in November. How am I going to get my driver's license if you won't let me practice?"

"LBJ Freeway's no place to practice." Driving with Aunt Della had been enough of an adventure on the trip to the airport without having a child behind the wheel on the way home. Della said freeways reminded her of a billiards table with the cars like so many balls in play. She yelped and shut her eyes each time her niece changed lanes, certain they were going to be smacked and sent careening into some giant side pocket.

Jesse made a grab for the keys and snatched them from her mother's hand with a hoot of glee. "Now, about the car you're going to get me . . ."

"Have you ever heard the words 'car for your sixteenth birthday' come out of my mouth?"

Jesse swung the car keys before her mother's face as a tease. "Daddy promised. Besides, everybody gets one. Harper's Jeep is the bomb."

Hoping to soothe the headache that had not succumbed to aspirin, she reached up and rubbed the bridge of her nose. "Harper has a daddy who's in sports medicine. He can afford it."

Jesse's grin dissolved. "You're saying I can't have a car because Daddy's dead?"

Thea twitched like she had been stung. When had Jesse decided a car was a necessity in her life? "I'm saying Daddy and I never promised you a car."

"He did."

"I think I'd remember that."

Jesse puckered up. "Why can't I ever have an opinion about what Daddy said about things? He wasn't your exclusive property!"

"That's enough, Jesse."

"Oh, right!" Jesse backed up a step into the passengers' walkway area. "So now I can't even *talk* about Daddy."

"I didn't say that."

"You did, too."

"Can we talk about this somewhere else?"

"Never mind." Jesse flung up a hand in exasperation. "You always pull rank on me. But Daddy said I could have a car. You're trying to weasel out of his promise, just because Daddy's dead!" Jesse's final words drew the curious glances of passersby.

Thea stared at her daughter. Jesse hadn't pulled a tantrum in public since she was five. She itched to grab her by the arm and snatch her back beside her. But Jesse topped her by three inches. They would look ridiculous.

No need to sink to her daughter's level. She was the adult here. "If you're done, I suggest you give me back my keys."

Jesse cocked an eyebrow at her mother. "Fine." She slapped the keys into her mother's outstretched palm.

"Thank you." Anger nicked the words. "Now, if you still want to, you can drive once we get back to Preston Road."

"Fine." Jesse folded her arms and leaned against the wall with a hip jutted out in a manner she knew her mother hated. The slut on the corner pose, she called it.

Too angry to issue a normal reprimand, she said, "Aunt Della's been in there a while. Why don't you step in and see if she needs help."

"Right. Like I can help in there." Jesse smacked her lips in disgust but moved to do her mother's bidding.

"Little *grrrl,*" Thea muttered under her breath. She had better have minded. Trying to put a guilt trip on her mother because her father was dead. That was a new one. She never used Evan as the stamp of approval for her own opinions and decisions. She—

She winced as several recent examples came to mind in rapid succession. Okay, Jesse had a point. Evan and she had not been of perfect minds about all things when he was alive. Unfair to make it seem so now that he was gone. But that didn't give their daughter the right to use Evan as a weapon against her. They had equal rights to his memory, as long as they respected it.

She leaned back against the wall and adjusted the straps on her shoulders, one for her purse and one for Aunt Della's. Della always carried "a few necessities" in case she was stranded overnight at a "strange" airport. Thea tried and failed to persuade her that this was unlikely, considering the flight from Dallas to New Orleans was nonstop.

Her stomach growled as the aroma of warm cinnamon invaded her nostrils. After dealing with the ties that bind all morning, didn't she deserve a treat? Yes, she did.

She looked around to find the origin of the heavenly smell. She glanced toward the food stalls—and her gaze stopped dead.

There at the TCBY yogurt counter stood two very well dressed men. The shorter, slighter one paid, while the taller one reached for a waffle cone. She did not have to look twice to recognize his profile.

What was *he* doing here?

Her mind raced. Had he called last night to tell her that he would be in Dallas today? The flowers meant to smooth his path? Crap! She had hoped to avoid all contact with him as long as Aunt Della was still in town.

She resisted the urge to duck into the lavatory. That would be ridiculous! All she had to do was look away, and there was every chance he would not notice her. She looked back. They were both coming toward her.

Xavier stopped short when he saw her. Then he turned and said something to the man beside him. The young man nodded and moved on, taking both cones. Xavier turned toward her.

She could not read in his expression whether or not he was glad to see her. Despite very good reasons to the contrary, she was not entirely unhappy to see him. But he mustn't know that. For twenty-six years, nothing. Now he was showing up in her life at two-week intervals? What was his game? She meant to find out.

She leaned away from the wall to meet him. "Hello, Reverend Thornton. What are you doing here?"

He looked slowly right and left before looking back at her. "At the airport or in Dallas or standing in front of you?"

All of the above. "I didn't expect to see you again."

"So you said before." His expression was one of studied disinterest. "Want to tell me why?"

She did not. Instead, she smiled and indicated his upper lip. "Yogurt."

He gave a quick sideways glance of embarrassment and quickly wiped his mouth with a palmed napkin.

She smiled smugly. For the first time, she had gotten the upper hand. "You've got to admit the coincidence factor is pretty high."

"Not as high as you might think. All the traveling I do, I'm through DFW sometimes twice a week."

"Really?" So he wasn't going to admit he had hoped to see her. Feeling the perverse need to one-up him again, she couldn't resist saying, "Given my own travel schedule, I'm surprised we haven't run into each other long before now."

"That so?" He looked away, as if seeking an escape. "My

assistant is signaling for me." He back-stepped smoothly. "I have a flight to catch."

She should just let him go, make this the most painless meeting of all. "Have a safe trip. Oh, and thank you for the flowers."

His gaze came back to her with interest this time. "You got them?"

"Mom?"

She turned to see Jesse and Aunt Della coming toward her. Oh Lord! She knew she should have just let him go. Nothing to do now but pass the moment off as lightly as possible.

She reached out to bring Jesse close. Jesse's expression soured, but she didn't pull away. "Reverend Thornton, I'd like you to meet my daughter Jesse. Jesse, this is Reverend Thornton, a family friend."

Xavier held out his hand to Jesse. "Hello, Miss Morgan. I believe we spoke on the phone last night."

Looking like thunder, Jesse took his hand for the briefest of moments while mumbling, "Gladtomeetyousir."

She motioned to her aunt, who was busy tucking a tissue into her sleeve, and hoped she hadn't heard that exchange. "And of course, you remember my aunt, Mrs. St. Claire."

"Of course." He offered the tiny woman a warm smile, something he had not offered her. "Good afternoon, Mrs. St. Claire. You're doing well, I trust."

"Well enough, Reverend, though I don't much care for flying. It doesn't suit my years, being hurtled through the air like a lawn dart."

He leaned down to her. "Don't tell on me, but I don't much like it, either. Yet there are blessings that come with the ease of air travel."

"That's a fact." Della nodded and smiled. "I've so much enjoyed my time with Theadora's family. Of course, I do worry about her, being a widow with a child to look after. You know a woman alone can't be too careful—"

"Aunt Della," Thea interjected quickly, "Reverend Thornton doesn't need to hear about that."

Xavier took the elderly woman's hand and kissed it. "Much blessings for a safe trip, Mrs. St. Claire." He nodded to Thea, looking slightly uncertain.

She nodded back curtly, relieved to let him go. "Perhaps we'll run into each other again." Now why had she said that?

She caught the glint in his eyes a split second before he said, "I trust the roses were satisfactory?"

"You sent that lovely bouquet, Reverend?" Della's tone carried an implicit reprimand as she turned to her niece. "Theadora, you said you didn't know who sent them."

"I didn't." She looked at Xavier's smug expression and wanted to kick him in the shins. She ignored Della's coo of delight. "That was quite extravagant of you, Reverend Thornton."

The look he gave her had caused men twice her size pause on the gridiron. "You think I sent them just to impress you?"

She lifted her chin. "Didn't you?"

His brows rose. "Were you?"

She had not expected a direct challenge with her family as witness. "They are lovely."

She saw his lips' slight curve beneath the edge of his mustache. "I'm speaking at a celebrity sports banquet here in Dallas in two weeks. Perhaps you'll be there."

"I stay pretty busy." Jesse had wiggled free of her grasp, and the look she was giving her mother was anything but pleased. "But I'm sure you'll be well received. You're a dynamic speaker."

"You've heard me?" He seemed genuinely surprised.

"Saw you preach. On TV."

"What did you think?"

Give the man his propers. "You are very persuasive, very charismatic."

He shrugged off the compliment, but his smile reached all the way up through his eyes. "Then perhaps, if your schedule permits, we could have dinner."

"Perhaps . . . if *your* schedule permits." It was much too late to pretend anymore.

His smile widened, or maybe it only relaxed. Was it that important to him? Something inside her relaxed, too. Avoiding him had been a strain.

His next glance took in the group. "Good day, ladies. And

again, God's blessing for a safe trip, Mrs. St. Claire." He turned and walked away.

"Theadora, you sly thing!" Della patted her arm. "When did all this come about? Don't tell me! Selma introduced you two at her wedding. I told her to be on the lookout for a proper suitor for you. But I must say, this is fast work." Della turned and nudged Jesse. "Do you know who that was?"

Her grandniece shook her head.

"That's a genuine superstar, sugar-pie. He's a self-made man with the brains and character to go with the talent and the money. You can live a lot of years and never meet that in *any* color skin."

Thea ignored the significant look her aunt gave her behind Jesse's back. "They're calling your flight, Aunt Della. Come on, you'll get first seating because you need assistance." It was way too late to put this puss back in the bag. She saw that Jesse continued to watch, one brow lifted in speculation, as Xavier walked away.

"YOU DIDN'T SAY he was black." Jesse sat in the passenger seat, scowling.

"Since when is that a necessary factor in describing someone?"

Jesse shrugged. "You might have warned me, that's all." She knotted her arms across her chest. "What part of that story you told me about him being an old family friend was true?"

"All of it. And don't use that tone with me."

"What about the flowers?"

"I told you, the note wasn't signed."

Jesse gazed at her mother from beneath lowered lids. "So why would a *preacher* be interested in *you?*"

"Because I'm an *old* friend?" she suggested lightly.

"You're not that old." Jesse stared straight out the window. "Aunt Della says a widow's position in the community is a vulnerable one. There are men who would take advantage."

"Aunt Della gave me the same lecture, and I'll tell you what I told her: I'm not that naive or vulnerable."

She saw Jesse smirk. "He spent a lot of money on those roses. He must expect something."

She opened her mouth and closed it. Her daughter sounded much more sophisticated about such things than she was comfortable with.

"So? Is he going to be coming by the house?"

"Why?" The edge in her daughter's voice did not deserve a civil reply.

Jesse hunched a shoulder. "No reason. When is it my turn to drive?"

"Preston Road. We already discussed this." Realizing that maybe she owed her daughter more of an explanation, she tried again.

"Jesse?"

"What?" The word snapped like a whip.

She gripped the wheel a little tighter. "Nothing."

thirteen

THEA SET HER jaw in annoyance as she surveyed the room. Jesse sprawled on the sofa in front of the TV, an empty microwave popcorn bag and two apple cores parked on the coffee table beside her, along with three empty soda cans. The Parisian-born craze for bottled water had worn off long ago.

"How many times do I have to ask you to clean up behind yourself, Jesse? Jesse?"

No response.

"Jesse!"

"I heard you," Jesse muttered. "I'm not done yet. When I'm *done,* I'll clean up."

You're working on my last nerve, child. "Did anyone call?"

Her daughter sulked a moment before saying, "Yeah, Harper. She got asked to homecoming."

It had been a week since the girls went on a dress-buying spree. Since Aunt Della's departure, she and Jesse had been in détente, not openly hostile but barely polite and covering no potentially hazardous territory. Could a mother safely ask? "By the way, you never said who your date is."

Jesse sat up. "Why? Does he have to meet your standards?"

Definitely, my last nerve. "We'll talk later. I've got to get dressed."

"Yeah. For *your* big date. Only you didn't ask me first, like you promised."

That unraveling nerve snapped. She took a step back into the room. "Do you *want* to be grounded for homecoming, Jessica Darnell Morgan?"

Her daughter's eyes bucked with alarm like a six-year-old who discovered the limit only after she was way past it.

Satisfied the rebellion was squashed for the moment, Thea walked away, shaking her head. What was wrong with her? Nagging Jesse over trivia, working herself up into a royal rage . . . Was that the phone?

She sat down on the edge of her bed and breathed deeply. If that was Aunt Della, she wasn't certain she could be polite about one more word of advice concerning Xavier. At least she had been able to persuade her aunt that Selma had nothing to do with her knowing Reverend Thornton and that she—and he— wanted to keep it that way. Even Della could see reason in that.

"Selma couldn't keep a rash to herself. And men of Reverend Thornton's standing require discretion in their private lives. Now, Theadora, don't run him off with one of your serious sulks . . . more flies with honey than vinegar . . ."

She picked up before the message service could kick in.

"Hello?"

"Mrs. Morgan? This is Je-*ro*-ome Weeks. Reverend *Thorn*-ton's personal assistant." He spoke in self-important tones that exaggerated words. "I'm calling to confirm your appointment with Reverend *Thorn*-ton at seven-thirty this *e-ve*-ning."

"Yes, I'm expecting him. Thank you."

She hung up, feeling mad over again. This time she knew it had nothing to do with Jesse. She was nervous about this date. And now Xavier couldn't be bothered to make his own calls. Had some high-rump personal assistant do it. Was he so accustomed to star-tripping that he did not employ the personal touch except when it suited his needs?

So, maybe she should be nervous. Maybe she *was* being played, for old times' sake. Why? That was easy. Because he could. And because she was foolish enough to let him.

"Okay," she said aloud. "You've admitted it. You are scared." Nothing to do now but get ready.

An hour later, she emerged from her bedroom, feeling more like herself. She snapped on her favorite earrings, pearls encircled with rhinestones that matched the buttons on her black silk cocktail suit. He had said dinner, and she did not think it would be too forward to expect it would be a very nice meal.

The doorbell brought her up short in the hallway. He was not due for half an hour.

"I'll get it!" she called in case there was the remote possibility that Jesse was thinking of moving her butt off of the sofa.

Beryl burst into the entry the moment she opened the door. "Girl, can I talk to you?"

"Sure, what's up?"

"The jig, that's what!" Panting as if she had run the full two blocks between their homes, she pinned Thea with a stare that showed the white all around her dark irises.

"I've never seen Harold like this! I thought he might *slap* me!"

"Oh, Beryl." Harold was the gentlest soul on earth. She reached out to her friend. "Tell me what happened."

"What happened is this." Beryl pointed to the gold-ribbon crocheted cloche that hugged her head like a ski cap. "I don't know what came over me. I was just sitting in the chair talking to Simon, my hairdresser, like usual, when I said I wanted a change. I'm tired of sweating out all this hair three times a week in my dance classes. So then he said I'd look good with it short."

"You cut your hair?"

"I know it was a wild idea." Though she smiled, Beryl looked astonishingly close to tears. "I haven't worn my hair short since I married the man. But it's my head, right?"

"Last time I checked. You look great in that hat. Short hair should look good on you."

Beryl shook her head. "I knew better. My mama didn't raise no fools. I did know better."

"Better than what? What did you do? You didn't shave your head?"

Beryl looked away.

"You *did* shave your head!"

Beryl reached up and snatched off her hat. Not a shaved head, but not much hair left. What was there was bleached a pale champagne shade.

"You're blond!"

Beryl patted her brief locks. "And I look *good!*"

"You do. The color really sets off your eyes and cheekbones. I like it."

"Then you go over to 1347 Grapevine and tell that rabid man who calls himself my husband that he better not keep packing his bags unless he's intending to put a period to this marriage."

"He's packing? Over a haircut?"

Beryl nodded, and the first fat tear splashed onto one of those prominent cheekbones. "Said he didn't intend to be married to a woman with just a little bit of yellow chicken fuzz for hair."

She knew she should not laugh. But she could not help it.

Beryl cocked her head forward. "This is your version of sympathy?"

"Oh Beryl . . . It's just . . . chicken fuzz—" She had to gulp back another outburst. "He'll get over the shock. Then he'll notice how good you look."

"I feel sort of naked." Beryl rubbed her hand self-consciously up her nape. "All that heavy hair hanging back there for so long. But it's my hair. I told him. My head. My business. That's when he said—" She bit her lip and tossed her head as if to fling off her emotions.

"Why don't you come in the kitchen and let me get you a drink. Coffee? Soda?"

"Make that a real drink, and you got a deal. Hey, what are you dressed up for?"

"I have a date."

"Girlfriend! And I didn't even know about it?"

For a fleeting moment, she considered telling her. If she were going to tell anyone about Xavier, Beryl would be it. But she could not say a little without saying a lot. Until she was sure what she was doing, her history with him was better off a secret. She really would prefer Beryl not even be here, but she couldn't very well show a distraught friend the door.

"It's really just an old friend of the family. I've got a few minutes. I want to hear all about what it took to turn you into a blond."

Five minutes into the discussion, Jesse appeared, holding a phone. "There's a call for you, Mrs. Moore." She held out the receiver to Beryl. "It's Cassandra."

"What's that girl want now?" Beryl reluctantly put down her drink and reached for the phone. "What do you need, Cassandra?"

Jesse moved quickly to her mother and whispered, "Something's wrong, Mom. Cassandra's crying!"

The stricken expression on Beryl's face said it all.

"Did you call nine-one-one? I'll be right home! Cassandra? Get some aspirin from the medicine cabinet and make certain your daddy swallows at least two. I know, baby, I know. But you have to. Cassandra, do it! . . . I'm coming. . . . I'll be right there. . . . It's going to be all right!"

Beryl slammed down the phone. "It's Harold. He—"

"Collapsed?"

Beryl nodded tightly, her face spasming as she fought for control.

"Oh, my God, Beryl!"

"That man is my life. I can't lose him now. I got to go!"

"I'll come with you."

Jesse reached for her mother's arm. "Can I come, too, Mom?"

"No, honey, you stay here." She grabbed her purse. "If Reverend Thornton arrives before I get back, explain the situation and tell him I'll call him later."

"But, Mom—"

"No arguing!"

Jesse nodded, but her lips were bloodless.

She pulled her in for a quick squeeze. "It's going to be okay. I'll be back as fast as I can."

As they hurried out the front door, she felt sick in the pit of her stomach. This was how it began for her. A phone call. Evan had collapsed at work. They were taking him to the hospital. She rushed to meet him there. Only there was no *there* to go to. He was already dead.

"Please God, please God!" she whispered as she cut across the neighbors' grass in Beryl's wake.

fourteen

THE CARDIAC WAITING Room was an unearthly quiet place full of drawn faces and furtive whispers, as if the occupants feared they might attract Death's attention by speaking too loudly.

"If I've killed him!"

"*Shh*, Beryl. Don't be silly." Thea held Beryl by the shoulders as they sat huddled on a sofa. "You did no such thing."

"You didn't see his face. Harold's slow to anger. But tonight—"

Beryl's body began to rock back and forth. "I did it. I did. I know he loved my hair. The shock. It's my fault. Yes it is."

Thea did not contradict her a second time. It was good that Beryl was talking. Letting out the misery. Occupying her thoughts with something while they waited.

"My fault. *Umm-huh*. I've killed him with my foolishness!"

Beryl kept rocking, even as Thea hugged her tight.

Harold had been brought in with what the medics said could be cardiac distress. *At least he is still alive.* A doctor who spoke too briefly with them said he would not know the cause until they stabilized Harold and ran a few tests. But the symptoms were consistent with a myocardial infarction.

Anguish pushed at her. *Why didn't they just say heart attack anymore? Simple language that spoke directly to the matter.*

She had driven Beryl's car to the hospital, insisting that Beryl ride in the ambulance. She also dropped Cassandra off to wait for news with Jesse. Beryl was emphatic that Cassandra not be subjected to the trauma of a long wait at the hospital. Thea decided that staying with Jesse was a better option than leaving the poor child home alone. How grown-up Jesse had sounded when Thea had called from Beryl's to say she was bringing Cassandra over. Jesse said she thought it was a good idea, too. That she had already rented videos. That they would call out for pizza. That they would be fine.

Thea checked her watch. That was half an hour ago. She should call again just to make sure the girls were still okay, but she did not want leave Beryl alone just yet. Adamant about carrying the burden herself, Beryl refused to call her out-of-town children until she knew what they were dealing with. She had made Cassandra promise not to call even her eldest brother in Chicago.

She didn't agree with Beryl's thinking, but she did not have the heart to push her at the moment.

At the edge of her vision, she saw a tall, dark figure striding toward them, but because it did not wear hospital white or surgical blue, she did not look up until the pair of navy blue trousers and mirror-bright men's shoes paused before her.

"Xav—Reverend Thornton?"

His face was grim. "Hello, Theadora. I hope you don't mind that I've come."

"Mind? I don't mind." Her brain was working in slow motion. She should say something more. But he was way ahead of her.

He moved to stand before Beryl. "Good evening, Mrs. Moore. How are you doing?"

Beryl was gazing up at him in vague surprise. "Reverend Thornton?"

He nodded and reached for her hand. "Have you heard anything yet?"

She took his hand with both of hers and hung on.

"No. All they've got to say is we have to wait until Harold's stabilized. But I just know he'd be doing better if I was in there with him. But they say I can't!" She turned a teary face to Thea. "I'm not ready to lose him, Thea. He can't go like this. Not with anger in his heart against me."

"Hush, Beryl," she said softly. "You know Harold adores you."

Xavier bent down to her. "Mrs. Moore." His voice was calm but direct. "You need to conserve your strength until you can be useful to your husband."

"That's true." A ghost of a smile crossed her face as she struggled for composure. "Harold so enjoyed meeting you at the banquet last night, Reverend. He's a great admirer of yours. I told Thea she shouldn't have missed it—" She frowned. "I'm sorry. I'm going on and on, while you must have other business here at the hospital."

Xavier glanced at Thea.

"He's here to see me, Beryl."

"This is the old friend you're going out with? I see." Beryl's expression said she saw all the way down the block, around the corner, and far too deeply into things for comfort. "Then you two go on and have a nice evening. I'll be fine. And Harold will be, too. Yes, he will."

"I'm not going anywhere, Beryl. But let me speak privately with Reverend Thornton for a moment." She stood up. "I'll be right back. Promise."

"All right then." Beryl looked grateful.

"Let's talk out there." Thea pointed toward the corridor and began walking. When they found an unoccupied spot, she stopped and turned to him. "I didn't expect to see you here."

The frown lines on his brow tensed. "I was concerned about you."

She stared at him a moment, trying to understand. "About me?"

He nodded. "You're going through an ordeal. It can help to have someone with a little distance from the situation to lean on."

He was right; she could use a shoulder to lean on at this moment. She put a hand to her cheek and found it icy cold. There had been no one to go with her when she rushed from work to the hospital. No one to turn to when the news collapsed her like a lawn chair. At least Beryl would not be alone, no matter what happened tonight.

He touched her shoulder. "Theodora, are you all right?"

Feeling overwhelmed but determined to hold it together, she nodded. "I'm really sorry I have to cancel our plans. But it all happened so quickly, and Beryl is a close friend. I can't leave her here alone."

"Of course not." He smiled. "I wouldn't expect anything else of you. However, when I told your daughter I was coming here, she said to ask you to call her." His hand tightened briefly on her shoulder. "You should do that now."

She glanced back down the hall at Beryl.

"I'll sit with Mrs. Moore."

She was not prepared for Jesse's outburst of tears as soon as she realized her mother was on the line. Had Xavier walked in on two hysterical girls? Suddenly she felt like a very poor excuse for a mother. She should have thought of it before. Just as she was feeling it, Dr. Moore's collapse had brought back for Jesse the trauma of her own father's sudden death. Maybe two girls alone was not such a good idea.

In her most patient and motherly voice, she reassured first Jesse and then Cassandra that everything that could be done was being done for Dr. Moore. As soon as the girls calmed down, she said, "Jesse, I want you to call Harper's mother. Tell her what's happened and ask if you and Cassandra can come and stay until I get home. It might be late. Use the other line. I'll wait."

Finally, Jesse's voice was back on, saying it was okay.

"Good. Now don't forget to lock up. . . . I don't know how long I'll be. . . . I'll call as soon as we get news. . . . I promise. Dr. Moore is in good hands. . . . I love you, too, Jesse."

She walked back quickly to the waiting room, feeling a little less rattled. In reassuring Jesse, she had soothed her own fears.

She stopped short when she saw Beryl and Xavier huddled together. He was speaking in a low, measured tone. She hung back as she saw them bow their heads in what she knew must be prayer. She was not particularly good at public displays of devotion, yet Xavier was perfectly at ease. When they lifted their heads, she put a smile on her face and approached.

"The girls are fine. Erica has agreed to keep them until we get back."

"Thank you so much." Beryl tried to smile. "Reverend Thornton was just helping me pull myself together. I have to think of Harold now. Not myself." Beryl squeezed Xavier's hand as she gazed at him with grateful thanks. "Harold will be so pleased when he hears that you were here to offer a prayer for him."

Xavier nodded. "I'm glad I could be of service to you. You remain strong in God, Mrs. Moore. Harold's going to need your strength." He rose and looked at Thea. "I'll get you both something to drink. It may be a while yet."

She stared at his retreating back. He was not going anywhere. Except for coffee. She could have hugged him.

FIFTEEN MINUTES MORE passed, though it felt like hours. Finally, a white coat came striding toward them. Beryl shot up from her chair.

"How's my husband?"

The doctor smiled. "Dr. Moore is resting comfortably, Mrs. Moore. We've established that he didn't suffer an MI. We suspect extreme gastric distress accompanied by a spike in his blood pressure."

There was a pause, as Beryl absorbed his words. "You mean heartburn laid him out?"

"In a manner of speaking. We don't expect any other events in the next twenty-four hours but, as a precaution, we're going to keep him overnight. We're waiting for the gastroenterologist. Once he reviews the test results, he will determine how to proceed. You can see your husband before we take him up. And then I recommend that you go home and get some rest."

"Heartburn!" Beryl laughed, even as tears streamed down her face.

At that moment, Xavier returned with cups of coffee. Thea gave him a thumbs-up sign.

Beryl picked up her purse and turned to Thea. "I need to call my children. But I want to see their daddy first. So I can tell them I've seen him with my own eyes and know he's going to be okay."

"I'll be here when you get back."

Beryl looked from her to Xavier and paused before them. "If you're sure?"

"We'll both be here," he answered.

XAVIER FOLLOWED THEM home in his rental car. They stopped to pick up Cassandra on the way, but Jesse decided she wanted to sleep at Harper's. After the earlier fit of weeping, Thea was reluctant to force the issue, though she would rather have had Jesse come home so she could be certain she was okay.

As she pulled away from Harper's house with Beryl and Cassandra huddled together in the backseat, she tried not to feel rejected . . . or hurt . . . or jealous. She had been relegated to teddy bear status. Jesse might still cling to her for reassurance in the dark hours, but that need was no longer something she readily admitted to in her daily life.

There were hugs and tears all around at Beryl's front door. But she didn't prolong the moment. Now that it was over, she felt the need to escape.

As she walked back down the Moores' sidewalk, she recalled fleetingly the day she buried Evan. The cocoon of comfort and compassion offered by their friends did not touch her. They meant well. Of course they did. But she could read in their eyes the secret relief that they were spared what she was going through. They felt lucky. They did not mean to feel that way, but they couldn't help it. Beryl was lucky, too. She both envied and shared her joy in that.

She paused at the end of Beryl's sidewalk to face Xavier, who stood beside her. "Thanks for everything. I can walk from here."

He didn't even argue, just reached out and swung open the door on the passenger side of his car. "Get in."

When he drove past her street without even slowing down, she looked over at him with suspicion. "Where are we going?"

He grinned. "What do you care? You're dressed for anything."

Had been dressed for anything. Now she was wrinkled and

crumpled and dog tired. "I'm sorry, but I won't make good company tonight."

"I'm not asking that of you. But answer me this. Have you eaten?"

"No."

"Then you've got to eat, right?"

"I suppose. But I'm not up for a major dining experience."

"So then we'll go someplace where the food is good and the service is quick."

"DENNY'S?" SHE STARED out the window at the yellow, green, and red sign.

"They've come a long way. Watch and see if we don't get a smile."

Dressed up as they were, they got a few looks when they entered. It was the usual mix of teenagers, truck drivers, after-movie-munchies crowd, and those who did not have anything better to do or anywhere better to do it.

While she slipped into one side of a booth, Xavier did the other, grinning like a kid playing hooky. "What do you want?" He leaned back and spread his arms across the top of the booth. "I'm a Grand Slam man. That or the Chicken Fried Steak with white gravy."

"Where'd you learn to eat Texan?"

He chuckled. "My experiences are varied and extensive."

When the waitress arrived, she ordered without even glancing at the menu

"Belgian waffle, no butter, strawberries on the side." She caught his look of surprise. "I'm well-traveled, too."

"Coffee?" the waitress asked.

"Decaf—no, make that a hot chocolate."

"You, sir?" Her eyes suddenly widened. "Say, aren't you—?"

"No." Xavier cut her off with a wag of his head and a grin. "I get that all the time. Kind of embarrassing."

"I don't wonder." She eyed him suspiciously. "You sure look like him."

"Not really," Thea said, joining the joke. "He's much better-looking, don't you think?"

The waitress grinned. "Absolutely. Now, what will you have, sir?"

"Grand Slam. Eggs scrambled. And make that two hot chocolates." Xavier winked at Thea. "You like marshmallows?"

"We don't have marshmallows," the waitress interjected.

"Then put some whipped cream on top." He leaned forward on crossed arms. "I prefer ladies with a little meat on them."

The waitress cocked her eyes toward Thea. "Is he for real?"

She smiled. "I was wondering the same thing."

"Well, if he is, honey, you got a keeper."

Xavier grinned at her. "See what I mean? Denny's has a new attitude."

fifteen

"MAKE YOURSELF AT home. I'll be right with you!"

She slipped off the jacket of her cocktail suit, stepped out of her heels, and unfastened her skirt. Something comfortable was in order, but not too comfortable.

She was pleased Xavier had taken her up on her offer to come in. Though, if she had not suggested it, she suspected he would have. He had planned an evening for them, had no doubt taken valuable time out of his busy schedule, and gotten shortchanged by the evening's events. Besides, she just didn't want to be alone yet, without Jesse in the house.

She heard the faint sounds coming from the kitchen and smiled as she reached for jeans and a loosely crocheted cotton sweater. She'd enjoyed Denny's, and more, Xavier's company. While they ate, he entertained her with a recount of his recent appearance before a House subcommittee on funding for small and enterprise-zone businesses. She was astonished to hear that *The Black Man's Book of Prayer* was the first of a two-book deal for $1.5 million. His interests may have changed but not his infectious enthusiasm for what he was doing.

She checked her messages before coming back downstairs.

Beryl had not called during the half hour they'd been out. That was good news.

Xavier had shed his coat and loosened his tie and was sitting on the sofa in the living room. He rose the moment he saw her.

"I hope you don't mind." He held out a can of soda. "I helped myself."

"Let me get you a glass for that." She headed into the kitchen.

He rose and followed her. "You have a very nice home, very comfortable"

"Thank you." The comment surprised her. Xavier had seen her home before, and he wasn't one for small talk. Or was he feeling awkward because he'd had time to think about the possible implications of her inviting him. *Oops!* Maybe she'd been wrong about his desire to come in. She hoped she hadn't embarrassed him.

She took down two crystal tumblers reserved for special occasions, searching for something witty to say. "Aunt Della says I shouldn't keep a big house. It scares off potential suitors."

"You have many suitors?"

"Dozens of them. Living large, as I do."

Xavier chuckled as she turned to the fridge for ice. Good, he sounded at ease.

"So your aunt thinks any man who shows interest must only be about the Benjamins?"

Keep it light, Thea. "And my so-so looks." She opened the ice machine and scooped out some cubes and distributed them between two glasses. "Aunt Della says that a woman *my age* must make the best of her remaining assets."

"Ouch! I'm older than you are. I'd hate to hear what she would say about me."

She gave him a sly glance. "Believe me, you don't want to know." Aunt Della had them walking down the aisle by Easter.

"Ah, I see." He took another drink from the can. "Hasn't there been anyone since Evan?"

She made a face and handed him one of the glasses, thinking of Phillip. "One man showed interest. It didn't go anywhere. He didn't see the real me."

"Oh? What was he missing?"

She reached into the refrigerator for a soda. "Now you're asking personal questions."

"Are they off limits?"

"Let's just say I just don't feel the need to talk over my social life with a minister."

"Good, because I have no interest in being your minister."

"Now, that sounds like you're flirting with me." The moment she said them, she wanted the words back. When she was too tired or keyed up, things came out of her that she didn't mean to let escape. "Diarrhea of the mouth," Jesse so indelicately put it.

Smiling in embarrassment, she glanced at him to see how he had taken it.

He was grinning. "I thought you'd never notice."

That sobered her. "Why would you want to flirt with me?"

He folded his arms across his chest and sucked in his upper lip before he said, "A man could get his feelings seriously hurt around you."

"I didn't mean it quite like that. I just—"

"Wondered."

She nodded. She wondered a lot of things. Like why he had bothered to follow up on their accidental meeting at the wedding, why he had sent her flowers with a cryptic note attached. But mostly, she was wondering just exactly why she was entertaining this man when she was obviously too tired to keep her size eights out of her mouth.

"It's been a tough night for you. I think maybe we should take this up another time."

"No, I'm fine, I . . ." She was exhausted, but she was also intrigued. She popped the top on her can and poured it into her glass. "You were saying . . . ?"

He stared at her for a moment. "I have to confess something."

His expression began to make her very nervous. "Yes?"

"I agreed to come in mainly because I didn't want to leave you alone with your thoughts just yet. Your face was gray when I got to that waiting room. You only look about seventy-five percent better since you ate."

"Well, you *are* dealing with a woman of a certain age," she joked.

He shook his head, having none of that. "You've been through what Mrs. Moore thought she faced tonight: losing a husband suddenly. It took a lot of courage to stand by your friend."

"It was reflex. I couldn't not be there for Beryl."

She picked up her glass of ginger ale and moved toward the more comfortable sofa in the family room. He had just said he didn't want to be her pastor, yet here he was ministering to her. A moment before, he had been flirting. How was she supposed to respond to the cross signals?

He followed, settling into the cushions at the opposite end from her. His gaze was on her, assessing. "You all right?"

"Absolutely." She needed to lighten things up. "Denny's and soda in crystal!" She lifted her tumbler. "This isn't my usual Saturday night."

"No?" He was still looking awfully serious. "What is it like?"

"You see it." She motioned about her. Did he realize, as she suddenly did, how lonely and dark her life must seem in this quiet, empty house?

He looked away for a moment. "I'm just curious about the path you felt you needed to take to be happy. This suburban insulation is a far cry from Grambling."

"We've all come a long way from home."

"True." He seemed to consider his next question carefully before he said it. "You once told me how hard it was for you, being so light. How it made you conspicuous in your own community. Are you more comfortable here?"

Did he have to remember every inane thing she said at sixteen? "I grew up and got on with my life." She folded her arms exactly as Jesse did when she felt pushed. "Why don't we just agree to let go of the children we once were?"

He held up both hands in surrender. "Whatever you say. But a lot of good memories will go wanting."

She eased farther back into the sofa cushions, alert now against her own emotions. His brand of TLC had a way of getting too deep inside her private space for her peace of mind.

He reached back to rub his neck, looking a little worn himself. And then she remembered that his trip to Dallas was not all social. "How did your banquet speech go last night?"

He stopped rubbing to look directly at her. "Why didn't you come?"

Because I didn't want to seem too anxious to see you, that's why.

She wasn't about to say that, so she punted. "I read about it in the paper."

"Then you know." He picked up his glass and stared into it as if contemplating his disappointment at her absence.

"The mayor was quoted as saying you gave a 'straight, no-chaser speech.' "

" 'As bracing as it was provocative,' " he finished the quote. "That's some slick stuff! I set out to chastise the money changers and topple a few idols, but they refused to hear me."

She wondered what he had said. The newspaper account was vague. "I don't suppose 'X' Savior could do anything his fans wouldn't find some way to approve of."

"There was no 'X' factored into last night. Watching self-satisfied fat cats breaking an arm to pat themselves on the back?" He snorted. "For what? For giving a few middle-class kids with good reflexes free college rides! Rubs everything in me the wrong way."

She lifted a brow. "Talk about biting the hand that fed you."

"A football scholarship paid for my education. Indeed, it did." He nodded. "But, thanks to my parents staying on my behind, I could spell more than C-A-T before I arrived at Michigan State. I didn't learn squat while there. Too busy playing ball, checking out the local talent, and spending someone else's money. I told the truth last night."

"Which is?"

It seemed as though he were talking more to himself than to her. "That I was lucky. Sports gave me a living, but when the ride was over, it was good home training that sent me back to school to get it right. Too many young people end up without a career or an education. I pray no child of mine ever shows a talent for sports. Give him brains, dear Lord. That's my prayer!"

She heard conviction in his voice and understood. "I agree, absolutely. Jesse hopes to win a soccer scholarship, but it won't be the difference between a college education or not for her. And it certainly comes second to making those grades."

He smiled. "I knew she'd be smart like her mother. She's pretty, too, like her mother."

She ignored the compliment. "You were very gentle with Beryl tonight. I want to thank you again for that. It was above the call of duty. You're a natural with people."

He shook his head. "Don't believe it. That's the hardest part of my job, bringing comfort to sorrow." Exhaustion crowded into his expression. "Sometimes I have to pray hard for the courage to just walk in the door, knowing people are looking to me for answers to the hard questions of illness and death, for the right words of comfort." He took a deep breath. "I know they don't come from me. But sometimes they come *through* me. That's a humbling experience . . . for which I'm profoundly grateful."

The intimacy of his confession left her astonished. *Who,* she wondered, *did he turn to for comfort?* "Still, you came tonight when you didn't have to."

He met her gaze, nodding slowly. "I came to this purpose a bit late. Now that God has seen fit to give me a pulpit, I try to be certain I fill its demands."

She felt the weight of truth in his words all the way to her core, just as she had so long ago. "But all the needless hate and pain and sorrow, how do you deal with it?"

"It's God's will, Theadora. Inexplicable to us mortals but part of the divine plan."

She pulled back a little. "You believe that, don't you?"

He smiled slightly. "It's what gets me through each and every day. The faith that there's something more to life than the chaotic pieces of it we glimpse."

"How do you keep from wanting to know the whys of things?"

"Oh I want to know, all right. But every time I get to wanting to know too much I remember my granny saying, 'Oh, you wants to know how come, do you, Mr. Xavier? How come the world's so big, how come the sun don't shine at night. How Come ought to be your middle name. Just is, is the answer.' And she was right. I thought I deserved answers. Yet who am I to deserve anything?"

Thea laughed. "I think I would have liked your granny." She

did not share his expansive honesty or his palpable faith. At the moment, she envied him both. "I would have thought preaching is more difficult. Bringing the word to the people."

"That's different. Any minister will tell you Sunday is show time. Got to give them something they can comment on over their Sunday chicken dinner. And heaven help the church without a good choir." He shook his head and chuckled. "The real work gets done after hours, behind the scenes, on the weekdays."

She relaxed against the cushions. "So what do you do, day by day?"

"You really want to know? Let's see. I was in New York three days last week. The first day I taped a cameo appearance for a gospel video."

"You sing?"

"Depends on who you ask." In his self-deprecating smile she could see the young man he used to be. "But, yeah, I don't embarrass my congregation."

"So the preacher makes music videos. I'm impressed."

"You can't underestimate the influence of music on the young. This collaboration could bring forward a few young brothers who are in sore need of the church."

"What else?"

He reached up and held his shoulder as he rotated his arm. "Missed a day nursing an old sports injury. That's what I get for showing off. Jerome tried to stop me from shooting hoops with the boys from Promises to Keep. That's a shelter for abused women we're helping to fund. Have you heard of it?"

"No."

"A great place. They do a terrific job. So how could I say no to those kids?"

As he continued to talk, she got caught up in his enthusiasm for his new life. His public activities as a minister seemed no less high profile than his old life. He was so expansive and obviously pleased with his frantic life that she relaxed and stopped checking the clock.

Somewhere during the discussion, they slid from the sofa onto the carpet, where she sat cross-legged, hugging a sofa pillow, and he leaned back with arms spread along the cushions. It was just like that summer so long ago when she listened for hours to his grand plans for his life and believed absolutely that he could do anything he put his mind to. Mercy, but she'd been right! It gave her a sense of pride, as if she shared a tiny bit in his triumphs because she had been the first to believe in him.

"But this Thornton Foundation," he said finally. "That's my baby. And, if I'm not careful, it's gonna kick my butt."

"Why? What is it?"

"A organization of anonymous benefactors to set up security-controlled, low-rent housing centers in several urban centers. They're designed on the courtyard principle. Four main apartment buildings enclosing a full-size park and playground center. Beauty shop, pharmacy, and day care on the premises. Tenants will have passes. Guests will have to sign in and out. Our prototype is called The Macon Project."

"It sounds radical."

"It is radical. Freedom doesn't mean a thing if it doesn't include protection. Got to keep the kids in and the drugs out."

"I can see how you might have trouble raising funds for that."

He shook his head. "Funding isn't the problem. It's the requirement of anonymity placed upon the donors. The core of my ministry is aimed at young brothers, and that's a hard row to hoe. Most Sunday mornings, our congregations are filled with women."

"In your case, I can believe that."

He sent her a glowing look under his lashes. "That's another subject. But my calling is The Black Man's Master Plan Crusade. We've already attracted members of several popular rap groups. Even a very high-profile hip-hop producer, Bazz Azz, has agreed to look over the foundation's prospectus. If he comes in, the prototype Macon Project is a done deal."

She leaned forward, jolted out of her agreeable mood. "You can't approve of rap thugs thanking God for awards they got by grabbing their crotches and grinding their pelvises in the camera lens?"

He didn't blink. "I hear a reservation in that question."

"A big one. I only know Bazz Azz by rep, but it's ugly."

He nodded his head, listening.

"The antisocial rap-crap kind of music his company produces—titles like 'Do the Bitch'—makes the mother of a teen-age daughter like me shudder."

He didn't say anything, just looked at her with raised eye-brows, as if to say, *Go on.*

"I'm really surprised, that's all." She didn't care if she sounded old-fashioned or out of touch with the community. "It's just not the kind of image I'd think you'd want to associate with."

He smiled at her. "Who needs my help more than those on the freeway to perdition? You got a lot of young brothers with CDs pulling in more in a month than they thought they'd earn in a lifetime. Think the gravy train's been signed over to them. I get a fair amount of respect because I've been where they are at their age, making the bucks and getting the attention. When your profile gets large, barriers disappear. Things you wouldn't think about doing suddenly seem possible. You do them and—say what?—people you trust to look after you just smile and look the other way. So then there's this urge to push and push and keep on pushing, looking for boundaries. When they come to me, I set up a few for them. I tell them how much is expected from those to whom God has given much. So now I'm asking that they give—give big and without recognition—to the Thornton Foundation. That's how they get to do God's work. In the background."

"Do they buy that?"

His laughter was again self-deprecating. "Not many, so far. But if it can be done, I'm the man to do it. Amen!"

She smiled. "I hope you know what you're doing." He certainly thought he did.

"So far, I'm mostly talk. Wait till you see me coming with the rent."

He stood up and smoothed out his pants. "Now I really should leave you. I thank you for the—" He rotated his wrist to look at his watch. "Almost five hours that I've been in your good company."

Did he say five? She looked at the clock on the VCR. It read one-forty A.M. "I can't believe I took up so much of your time!"

"I was determined to make the time." His words came out slowly, thoughtfully, making her aware of how animated he had

been moments before. "It seemed we had unfinished business."
Another pause. "Didn't it seem that way to you?"

"Maybe."

He nodded. "That's why I wanted to see you. To figure it
out."

"And have you?"

"Not at all."

"Waste of time?"

"Not at all."

She smiled. "You still don't like to commit yourself."

He flexed shoulders that had to be stiff from sitting so long.
"I do like the comfort of options."

"That sounds a bit smug, Reverend."

"*Ouch!* But you're right. Things always came easy for me.
Made leaving them behind just as easy." He paused to make
eye contact again. "There's never been anything I couldn't walk
away from."

"And that's fair warning to me," she said quickly, not wanting
the moment to stretch out with unspoken meaning. "So, if we're
going to be friends, I should keep my mouth shut about your
business."

"*Nawgh,* you can say anything to me, Mrs. Morgan. Most
people step lightly around me. You don't."

"I don't need to."

"Why is that?"

"You don't have anything I want."

He reached for her hand. "You absolutely sure about that?"

She let him pull her to her feet. What was with her brain's
function tonight that she couldn't keep thoughts from becoming
speech?

Her head was spinning, spinning out the possibilities of other
times, other conversations they could have. When she could
stand, she let go of his hand and took a few steps away from
the sofa.

"Where are you going?" He looked hurt.

As far away as fast as she could. This was one train wreck
she could see coming. "Things are getting a little strange for
me."

"Is that bad? It might be good."

"No. I can't do this." She picked up the suit jacket that he had earlier draped over a chair and held it out.

"What do you do in your spare time?" he asked, as he put it back on.

"I don't have that much spare time." She folded her arms. "I'm pretty busy just living inconspicuously these days."

"What would happen if circumstances came along to make you conspicuous, but only in your spare time? Could you deal with that?"

"What are you talking about?"

"Seeing me." He smiled. "Because I think that's what I keep trying to get to with you."

Her mind stalled. *See him?* "I don't think that's a good idea."

"Why not?"

People will talk. "Like I said, I prefer to live quietly. Aunt Della knows about us. And now Beryl. Word would get around."

He frowned. "You're afraid of what the neighbors will say?"

She knew she sounded ridiculous, but she needed reasons to put him off. "You're a very public person. I'm a very private one. I have a daughter to think of."

"That's a legitimate concern. But I'm willing to be circumspect if that's what you need. Next objection."

She wished he wouldn't smile like that, like they were co-conspirators, when she was the only one holding back. "It's more than that." *Oh God! Please don't make me have to do this tonight!* "There are things you don't know—about me, about the past—"

He reached out and placed his fingertips on her lips. "I don't need to know about your past. There're things, lots of things, I'll probably never tell you about mine. This is about now. Either you're interested, or you're not. If you are, we go from here."

"But—"

He pressed his fingers more firmly against her mouth. "For now. Let it be, Theadora."

She stared backed at him. Only family and people from home called her Theadora. It had a powerful pull on her. He was so certain he could handle anything, anytime, anywhere. Because for him, it was always easy come, easy go.

He took her chin in his hand. "Friends trust friends. I trust you. You don't have to trust me yet. But give me a chance."

It won't be about forever with him.

That scared her because, unlike him, she had always been about forever and for always. "Okay."

His hand moved up to touch her face and then slipped behind her neck to cradle her head as he bent to her. It was a soft kiss, gentle, close-mouthed, and unpresuming. It was a kiss with a question. In the space of five heartbeats, he convinced her that she would see him again.

Not forever . . . maybe not for long . . . but most definitely for now.

He lifted his head and kissed her again, between her eyebrows, just as softly as he had her mouth. "Good night, Theadora."

sixteen

BERYL FLASHED THEA a reproachful look. "You know Xavier Thornton, and you didn't think it was worth mentioning to your best friend?"

In the two weeks since Harold came home from the hospital, fine wrinkles had appeared about Beryl's mouth and eyes. Her once stellar blond do looked today more like old-age yellow gray. Nothing wore out a person like hard times.

Beryl had been going and blowing, trying to keep up with Harold's medications and new diet restrictions and had no time to chat. An ulcer, reflux problems, major high cholesterol, and uncontrolled hypertension were a few of the ailments doctors discovered during a battery of medical tests. Major lifestyle changes were required. Now, with Harold up in Chicago visiting his eldest for a few days, she had minute to herself. The girl talk was on.

Feeling sheepish, Thea said, "I thought you'd think I was boasting."

"I'd think—!" Beryl closed her mouth to breathe deeply through her nose. "Details. I need details."

It was so tempting to unburden herself, but as she started

talking, the long practice of self-censorship took over. Beryl got the G-rated version of her relationship with Xavier, beginning with their friendship one summer as teens. How, after all this time, she'd run into him at Selma's wedding. His unexpected visit a week later didn't play as well. She stammered past that because all she could think about was the fact that he followed it up with roses and a love poem. Dinner at Denny's played much better.

"Girl, he didn't!" Beryl's snort of laughter was reassuring. "You know he still owes you a real dinner?"

"So he says." She slid a glance in Beryl's direction. "He's been calling me, wants to continue to see me."

Beryl wasn't grinning anymore. "Don't take this wrong, but why you?"

"I beg your pardon?"

"Back in the day, 'X' was one the few players who stuck all the way with Black Is Beautiful. Was always heard to exclaim, 'The darker the berry—' "

"—The sweeter the juice," Thea finished sourly.

"You see my point. Long before Iman or Tyra could even think about the cover of a magazine, our righteous brother 'X' squired about some of the most beautiful ebony-skinned African-looking women you ever saw. Never saw 'X' OJing it with white girls or being one of those brothers 'bout to break their neck double-checkin' the tan, caramel, or yellow sistas sashaying through their range of vision. I swear some of them mulatto girlfriends we see today are really white. You just know that they're washing their hair in Cheer till it kinks up like ours—mine."

She'd come to Beryl for bald honesty, but her friend was picking at scabs she'd thought were healed. "So you're asking why is Xavier interested in me? When, if he's now into white women, he could just go out and find a *real* one?"

Beryl reared back in her seat. "Now, that's you talking, not me."

All too true. But that so-called advice had been offered when she first started dating Evan. A black girlfriend had dropped on her the news that one day he'd realize he needed a *real* white woman and leave her.

"I didn't tell you everything." *Oh God, here comes the first gust of honesty.* "Xavier and I were more than friends that summer."

An I-knew-it smile spread across Beryl's face, chasing away worry lines. "So then, go for it! At least you know what you're getting into. Or should I say what has already gotten into you!"

"Beryl, we only talked."

"Talked? You're telling me you had that too-fine man in your house until the wee hours, and the only thing that got thoroughly exercised was your jaw? What? Was he hurt playing ball? He's not, you know, incapable?"

Thea choked. "What makes you think I would even know?"

Beryl reared back in her seat. "I'm just funning. But you're still frowning."

She looked down at the wedding band she was twisting about her finger. She seldom thought about the fact that she hadn't taken it off. "There's something about seeing him again . . . I can't explain it."

Her friend's chuckle was deep-down knowing. "You don't have to."

"No, it's more than that." She looked away, more embarrassed than she expected to be. "He's been calling. Sometimes we talk really late. He has so many plans, wants to do good, is doing good in the community. Concrete kinds of things. You should hear the intensity in his voice. Beryl, he moves me." No need to mention the kiss. "What do you think? Am I crazy?"

"Oh, you're crazy. Crazy like a fox."

"I'm just not sure I want to start seeing anybody regularly."

"See, as in date? Is that what you think he wants, to hold hands in the movies and share an ice cream float afterward?" Beryl gave her the fisheye. "Let me let you in on some home truth. He saw an old girlfriend, remembered on the tardy how you had a little *sumthin' sumthin'* back in the day. He's got to be wondering what it'd be like to kick it again after all this time. Still, you better get medical papers from him before you hop in the sack. A man who can make a room sweat just by entering it must bounce in a lot of beds."

Beryl's observations were uncomfortably close to her thoughts. "We're just supposed to be friends."

Beryl's long look reminded her of her mother's measuring gaze. "I don't need to remind you that some ministers do as much preying as praying?"

"He said friendship," she repeated, mostly for her own benefit.

"*Uh-huh*. Is that reason coming out of your mouth or rationalization?" Beryl's smile was now all sympathy. "You're entitled to a life, Thea. Nobody else's business who you have it with. Xavier Thornton might not be a bad place to start. You have a past together. That's enough baggage to keep it real. You just need to decide how you want it to turn out, beforehand."

"It can't be anything more than short term."

"Then I'm gonna say one more thing. You've got that hot and sweaty love-me-some-of-him look. It's in your eyes and in your voice. You can bet he's noticed, too. You best scratch that itch before you go looking for any kinda *friendship*. Otherwise, you're gonna make a mistake."

Beryl's version of cold, hard reality doused her daydream of a fine and bright platonic relationship with a man who interested and challenged her. Was a little time in the sheets with a man who knew how to make it feel real all she really needed to correct her view of the world? If Beryl was right, well, then that man could not be Xavier. That would be a huge mistake. But she wasn't yet ready to lay on Beryl the reasons why.

"I can't see myself bedding a minister." She smiled a shade too brightly. "What if it turned out that it was just a test to see if I was holy enough to be in his company?"

" 'She led me on' is as old as Adam and Eve." Beryl chuckled. "The original excuse to go with the original sin."

Thea laughed, too. "Why is it women so often get the short end of the stick in the Bible?"

" 'Cause too many men got short sticks!"

seventeen

JESSE PEERED AT the array of fish fillets and steaks on beds of crushed ice. "The tuna's been frozen." She looked up at the butcher. "Two salmon steaks, please. No, the two here in the front." She glanced back over her shoulder. "I'll fix it the way Daddy liked it, with bourbon and pecan sauce." •

"You're cooking?" What had Jesse done—or what was she about to do—that she felt this sudden urge to be productive? Not that they hadn't had a recent talk about the fact that, with the increase in her traveling schedule and her work hours stretching, it would be nice if once in a while she could come home to a cooked meal. Should she give herself a mental high five—Jesse had listened—or remain suspicious? Only time would tell.

As they steered the cart into the produce section, she did a subtle double take at the young man perusing the citrus. He wore a lightweight knit shirt that allowed the muscles beneath to be clearly seen. It was cropped above sweatpants so worn they clung to the impressive muscles of his thighs and cupped his butt like a friendly hand. North Dallas was peppered with professional athletes. Was this a new pro player in the neighborhood? When he turned around, her gaze took a dive for safety into a bin of potatoes. Oops! The too fine brother was a child!

His face had been all over the local papers in preparation for the upcoming high school homecoming game. Able to throw three consecutive eighty-yard passes, Keith Coates was drawing the attention of college scouts with passing teams like Tennessee and Florida State and UCLA. None of this might have stuck with her if not for the fact that Beryl had recently complained about how Cassandra had gotten downright stupid over her new quarterback boyfriend. She could see why Cassandra might be possessive.

She leaned over to whisper to Jesse, "Isn't that Cassandra's boyfriend over there picking out oranges?"

Jesse glanced sideways and then away. "Yeah, I suppose. Mom, can we get on with the shopping?"

"Uh, Jesse, he seems to be coming this way."

Jesse glanced up like a hare sighting a predator and murmured, "Oh *man.*"

Keith approached in a slow bop. His smooth shaved head and chiseled features beneath sable skin reminded her of singers like Seal and Tyrese. At the moment, those features were taut and his dark eyes half-lidded. He stopped a few feet away. "Hey, Jesse."

"Hi, Keith." Jesse sounded like someone had her by the throat. "This is my mom."

His gaze moved to Thea. "Afternoon, Mrs. Morgan."

"Hello, Keith. Good luck in the homecoming game on Friday."

"Thank you." For someone who looked so serious, he had an amazing smile. His gaze swung back to Jesse, and the smile spread, popping a dimple in his left cheek. "Can we talk a minute?"

Jesse looked uncertain. "I guess."

Mother knew a cue when she heard one. "I've got a few more things to pick up. See you at checkout, Jesse. Nice to meet you, Keith."

"Yes, ma'am"

Polite. The child was polite.

* * *

JESSE DID NOT catch up with her until she was wheeling the bagged groceries into the parking lot. Sunglasses hid her eyes, but her complexion was pinker than usual. She did not say a word, just started loading bags.

Thea held on to her curiosity until they had hoisted the last bag into the trunk. As she slid in behind the wheel, she said nonchalantly, "I didn't know you and Keith were friends."

Jesse shrugged, sucking hard on a piece of candy she had taken from the by-the-pound display. "We aren't, really. But, I mean, somebody had to try to smooth things over the night Cassandra kicked him to the curb."

"When did that happen?"

"The night her dad got sick. She wanted everybody to feel *sooo* sorry for her." Jesse snorted. "And all Dr. Moore had was *gas!*"

"It's a little more complicated than that." Thea put the car in reverse and backed out of the parking space. "At the time, we were all pretty upset."

Jesse shrugged. "Cassandra was okay until we got to Harper's. That's when it all hit the fan."

"Hm." Jesse could usually be counted on to continue if she did not interrupt.

"You should have heard her, going on and on about how upset *she* was when her dad collapsed before *her* eyes. She *had* to see Keith. *He* was the *only* one who would really understand. Harper's parents said to invite him over. But when she called him, he said he couldn't come right then. That's when Cassandra lost it. Started screaming on the phone. Told him she knew he was seeing someone else and that they were too over. Mom, she actually said she didn't ever want to see his black ass again. Dr. Peters gave her something to calm her down. It was so embarrassing!"

This was news. Jesse hadn't said a word at the time. Something must have motivated her to bring it up now. Could that something be Keith Coates?

"You know, when people are upset, they sometimes say and

do things they're ashamed of later. I'm sure Cassandra has apologized to Keith by now."

Jesse smirked. "It didn't do her any good. Keith has moved on."

"How do you know?"

"He just asked me to the homecoming dance."

She glanced sideways at her child. "I thought you had a date."

Jesse avoided her mother's eye. "I never said that."

"Jesse, don't get yourself into anything you can't handle."

"If this is a speech about how to take care of myself around guys, I heard it before I went to Paris. I handled Emil, and he was twenty-one."

You said twenty! "Have you told Keith about your background like you did Emil?"

Jesse hunched a shoulder. "It's not like it comes up every time."

She wanted to ask if it came up at all but decided not to make an issue of it now. "You do know girlfriends dating each other's ex-boyfriends can ruin the friendship?"

"It's not like Cassandra and I are all that close these days."

Thea hesitated. If she made more negative statements, she knew she would lose her daughter's attention. "Well, we know one thing. Keith has good taste."

Jesse's head swiveled toward her mother. "What's that supposed to mean?"

She smiled encouragingly. "He asked you to the dance."

Jesse rolled her eyes. "I was his second choice."

"So then, you didn't accept his offer?"

"Yes, I did." Jesse sounded positively smug. "I'm going to the dance with the top-ranked quarterback in the state. Harper's going with Bryan, who's only second-string quarterback. Everybody will envy me, not her."

The logic did not escape her, but that didn't mean she had to be happy about this mercenary aspect of her daughter's personality. If only Jesse would confide in her more. "You know you can talk with me about anything. Anytime. Just like always."

"Sure, Mom."

In your dreams, Mom!

"So what's with you and Reverend Thornton? He sure calls a lot. What do you talk about?"

She'd opened herself up with the offer to discuss *anything*. "His ministry mostly. He's a very busy man."

Jesse plucked another candy from her pocket. One was a sample. Two bordered on shoplifting. "So then, we won't be seeing much of him, him being so busy and all?"

"Don't you like him?"

Jesse shrugged. "Do you still miss Daddy?" She stared straight ahead. "I mean, really miss him?"

"Every day. What makes you ask?"

"I just wondered if love is different for older people. You don't have anybody to buy you things anymore. Take you places. Show you a good time."

Jesse is comparing herself to me. What to answer? "I miss those things, sure. But they aren't love. Love is about feelings, about a deep, sincere caring that can't be bought by presents or a good time."

"Have you ever loved someone who didn't love you back?"

"Yes." A funny little pain registered near her heart. "I was about your age." She reached out and pressed the back of her fingers against Jesse's cheek. "But then I met your dad."

Jesse smiled for the first time. "And he was the best?"

"The very best."

eighteen

"IF THAT ANSWERS all questions?" Thea's tone held a note of *It had better.* "Then let's break for lunch before we move on to the next report." She glanced at Joe, a cue that he should push back from the table. Everyone else quickly followed suit.

As the others filed out, Ron came down the length of the boardroom toward her. "Good meeting, Thea. I'm counting on you to be equally effective in D.C. next week. We have to have our input in Washington, or they'll legislate us right out of business."

"I'll be ready."

"Remind me to give you the address of my favorite D.C. spot, a little Portuguese place over in Georgetown. The best paella outside Lisbon."

So Ron was pleased. He'd been putting her through her paces, no two ways about it. Now her rededication to the job was paying off. In choosing her to go to D.C. as the last-minute replacement for an ailing higher-placed colleague, Ron had shown renewed confidence in her. Sitting on the congressional advisory subcommittee was a plum job. Even if it meant cramming a week's worth of studying committee reports into a weekend dominated by Jesse's social life.

She and Beryl were in agreement. The subject of Keith Coates was off limits. The girls would have to work it out themselves. She was relieved to hear from Jesse yesterday that Cassandra had a new date. An old family friend from Chicago was flying down to do the honors. Maybe that would balance things out in both their minds.

She smiled as she picked up her things. Keith had come by the night before with the biggest homecoming corsage she had ever seen. The traditional gift for every girl who had a date to the dance, it was worn to school and then the game. This one covered half of Jesse's chest, while streamers of bells, whistles, hearts, footballs, pom-poms, miniature teddies, and ribbons with their names in gold lettering reached past her knees. She could not remember the last time she'd seen a smile that big on Jesse's face. Keith had even let her borrow his letter jacket to wear to school.

Things were looking up for the Morgan women!

Joe sidled up to her and handed her a fax sheet. "Marcia said you were waiting for this. You'll be in Washington next week?"

"Yes. Meetings Tuesday through Thursday." She glanced at the fax, then smiled as she tucked it away. "And I'm taking Friday off."

Joe looked surprised. "Staying over to see the sights?"

"Something like that." She felt giddy in a way she chose not to think about just at the moment.

"What about the barge company dinner scheduled for Wednesday? We set it up to celebrate the new contract."

"They can thank you."

Joe looked far from pleased. "The way you've been covering all the bases, I'd have thought you'd want the credit."

She let the barb slide. She had been on his case. These days, she stayed on the backs of all the people who worked for her. The consultants' report was due soon, and she didn't want to make it easy to point to slackers in her department. "You did the negotiation. I just drew up the strategy."

He pushed open the door for her. "Sharing the spoils?"

"Giving credit where credit is due. Ask Ron to join you. They'll be like pigs in slop if he shows up."

"Hogs in slop." He grinned. "Luziana has hogs. You're losing touch with your roots."

A secret smile lifted her mouth. He'd be surprised to know how much in touch she was with her roots. "What's the special in the cafeteria?"

"Enchiladas, empanadas, and Spanish rice with chorizo."

"Looks like we'll be getting in touch with your roots today. Have lunch with me."

Joe grabbed his flat stomach. "*Aah,* not me. I blow up like a piñata with all that grease. I'll grab a yogurt and work at my desk." He backed off. "See you at one."

She bit off the question of what was he working on. A few months earlier, it would not even have risen.

She couldn't fault him for no longer keeping the late hours she did, not when he had started coming in early and did get the job done. But she missed having someone to share the after hours with. They used to joke how they got more done in two hours after five P.M. than in the eight-hour day they were obligated to put in. Now he wouldn't even have lunch with her.

Despite the lure of Mexican food, a favorite, she chose a salad and cup of vegetable soup. If she could not get to the gym regularly, the least she could do was eat sensibly. She reached up to check her French twist. When would she have time to get her hair done?

Xavier was serious about their friendship. During the past three weeks, he had called her as often as his schedule permitted to talk about his life and ask about hers. Each time they were ready to hang up, he mentioned the hope of seeing her again soon. But see her how? They lived almost a thousand miles apart. She had a child to rear and a job to do while he was busier than God. Could she think that way if she was seeing a minister?

"You travel. I travel. Our paths have to cross sometime," he kept saying. "When they do, we'll work out the details."

She'd had no travel plans when they last spoke. But this morning, she faxed him about her week in D.C. Tucked into her purse was his answer. He would be in D.C. Thursday evening. He would take Friday off if she could. She could.

Despite Beryl's hot and bothered take on his interest in her, she had since decided that the reason for their mutual attraction was more matter-of-fact. They reminded one another of a time before either of their lives had become complicated. They still related as teens, frank and provoking. He asked questions no one else dared. She certainly did not spare him her own observations. What a relief to speak her mind again. It could be a thrilling and heady friendship. If she was careful and remembered the rules.

Rule one: This was not a romance. No sitting by the phone or allowing herself to be hurt, disappointed, or kept waiting.

Rule two: She was along for the ride as long as it was comfortable. Nothing she could not walk away from anytime.

So why did she feel like a cheat, stealing a little fun? Because agreeing to meet him smacked the tiniest bit of tiptoeing past a cemetery. She did not owe him an explanation of her past. But it was there between them, and it always would be.

Until I tell him.

And she would, eventually. Before things went too far.

nineteen

THEA CHECKED HER watch again as she took the Frankfort exit off the Dallas North Tollway and swallowed a cussword as the traffic light ahead turned red. Lunch hour traffic was the worst.

Maybe she should have left for the airport straight from the office instead of making this detour, but she just couldn't resist going home to surprise Jesse with another good-bye in person.

A dedicated school-lunch hater from first grade, Jesse had off-campus lunch privileges, which meant she walked home to eat each day. Thea checked her watch. She might still catch her daughter at home before the airport shuttle arrived.

As the light changed to green, she yawned. The two all-nighters she'd pulled to finish the required reading for this trip to D.C. meant she and Jesse hadn't had any time together over the weekend. She really had wanted to hear about homecoming. Not that Jesse had been very forthcoming with details. But then, she could probably see how stressed her mother was.

And the first phone call of the day at the office made her doubly glad she'd given up every lost minute of sleep.

Okay, so Tom Grant from Union Carbide was not her favorite

person. They'd had professional contact in the past, and his patronizing attitude toward women in the chemical "bidness" was well-known. The fact that she had learned that he was chairing the subcommittee would not spoil the week ahead. She was prepared. Tom could be handled.

And there was something special to look forward to at the end of the week. A little thump of expectation pulsed inside her whenever she thought about seeing Xavier again.

THE FIRST THING she saw when she entered the house was Harper Peters standing in her kitchen. No visitors was a rule.

"Harper? What are you doing here?"

"Mrs. Morgan!" Harper's smile was drill team perfect. "I'm here for Jesse."

"For Jesse?" Panic nudged her. "What's wrong?"

"Something happened at school, and she got really upset and left. She's in there." Harper tossed her red hair and pointed toward the family room.

Heart thumping, Thea hurried into the room where Jesse sat hunched over on the sofa. "Jesse, what's wrong?"

Jesse's head jerked up. "Mom!" It was obvious she had been crying.

She reached a hand to Jesse's brow. "Are you sick?"

"No." Jesse looked away. "And I don't want to talk about it."

Harper, standing nearby, said, "If you need a witness, I saw everything."

"Butt out, Harper."

Harper gave Jesse a slow shake of her head and turned toward Thea. "I hope you can persuade Jesse to see reason, Mrs. Morgan. She should press charges."

That throb of righteous concern rang false. But the suggestion of the need for legal action redoubled Thea's concern to find out what the hell was going on. "I'm sure Jesse can speak for herself. If you'll excuse us, Harper?"

Harper, obviously disappointed, looked back at Jesse. "See you later, okay?"

Thea waited until she heard the front door close before she sat down next to her daughter. "Hi."

Jesse cut her gaze to the side. "Why are you here? Aren't you going to miss your plane?"

"I came to see you before I left." Fighting the urge to scream, "What's going on here?" she reached up and tucked a swathe of blond hair behind her daughter's ear. "You want to tell me what happened?"

"Nothing I can't handle."

"Okay. So tell me what you're handling, so I can go to D.C. with an easy mind."

Jesse shrugged. "Something happened at the homecoming dance."

"Saturday night? Why didn't you say something then?"

"I thought I'd handled it." Jesse's expression curdled. "Everything would've been cool if we'd been partying with the team. Everybody was so pumped because we'd won the game. Only Keith wanted to hang out with this other crowd."

"What other crowd?" Her daughter's reluctance to get to the subject was causing her to do damage to her tooth enamel.

"Some people Keith knew, but I didn't know most of them."

"You can't be expected to know everybody." Jesse's school was huge. Over three thousand students between the eleventh and twelfth grades.

Jesse shrugged. "That wasn't the problem. Some of the girls had dates from other schools."

"Oh." She did a quick recalculation. She didn't approve of the policy allowing kids from other schools to attend social functions. Maybe because they didn't feel a bond to the school, they often broke rules and generally made nuisances of themselves.

"Anyway, Keith was on this real trip. Nothing was good enough, dope. The DJ didn't know how to work it. The music was lame. So after a while he said, 'This is whacked; why don't we go somewhere else.' So I said I had this invite to Jillian's party. But it's invitation-only for two."

She nodded. She'd given Jesse permission to attend the party.

"So then Keith says, 'Let's everybody go to Jillian's.'"

"Even though they weren't invited?"

Jesse glanced up defensively. "Didn't I say that? But he said after the game he played, he and his posse would be welcome anywhere."

"Go on." But she already knew where this was going.

"So, anyway, we go there, and it's like really wild. Lots of people who weren't invited were hanging out on the lawn and in cars. Mr. Clark comes to the door looking really hassled. He said Keith and I could come in but nobody else."

Thea's anxiety level rose a notch, but she made a concentrated effort to keep her voice neutral. "That seems reasonable."

Jesse shot her a hostile look. "You weren't there. Keith got all offended! Said he wasn't going where his posse wasn't welcome. He knew where there's a better party down in Oak Cliff."

She held her tongue but liked less and less what she was hearing.

"I said I didn't have permission to go. Then a friend of his starts ragging on me about how I'm afraid to go to a real throwdown in the 'hood. I said it's not like that. So then Keith said that I look hot and he wanted to show me off to the homies. That you wouldn't know where we're going as long as he got me home on time."

She kept her expression bland as Jesse glanced sidelong for her reaction.

"I said I wasn't interested in his homies' opinion. So then this other guy got really pissed. Started talking really loud about how that's why he doesn't date white girls. They don't know how to be down with a good time."

Jesse made a sound suspiciously like Aunt Della's sniff. "So I said I sure didn't want to ruin his good time. Keith could just take me home."

Is that it?

Breathing relief, she put an arm about her daughter. "Jesse, you didn't do anything wrong. And Keith shouldn't have pressured you about the other party."

"Mom, that's not the problem!" Jesse pulled away and stood up. "It was all over the school today, about the party. Some black kids called Mr. Clark a racist, that he wouldn't let Keith's friends in because they were black. Jillian's telling everybody that I shouldn't have shown up with all those uninvited people. Like I was the only one."

Jesse bit her lip, looking for the first time a little overwhelmed by her story. "Mom, when I went to my locker before third period, someone had written 'Traitor to the Race' on it in black marker."

Every generation, the same mess! When feelings ran high in mixed company, all too often a misunderstanding degenerated into an issue of race, even if the problem initially had nothing to do with it.

She struggled to keep her own outrage out of her voice as she stood up. "You think Keith did it?"

Jesse jerked her head in the negative. "But he wouldn't talk to me today. Acted like he didn't know my name."

Something in the way Jesse would not meet her gaze made her ask, "Anything else?"

Jesse stared at the floor. "In third period, Julie Plangent said people are saying the real reason I left Jillian's was so Keith and I could go to a hotel. Then, this rumor starts about how there's this message posted on a certain web site from an eyewitness giving out all the details." Jesse clenched her jaw so hard her chin trembled. "Mom, I checked it out. It's porno! Makes me out to be a total slut!"

She pulled her daughter close, trying to absorb some of Jesse's shame and pain as she searched for something comforting to say. "My mother used to say you don't have to turn and look at every dog that barks at you, Jesse. You have to ignore the whispers and glances. They'll eventually go away."

Jesse bent her head to her mother's shoulder. "You don't understand. People believe it. Even Harper asked me what it was like . . . like to do it with a black guy."

So that's what was on Harper's devious little mind. She hugged Jesse tighter. "Okay, then you—" The sound of the doorbell cut her off.

Damn! This was the worst possible moment for the shuttle to arrive. Reluctantly, she released Jesse. "I'm going to get the door. But I'll be right back."

She snatched open the door so quickly, she startled the caller and herself.

Keith Coates stood there. "Hello, Mrs. Morgan. Is . . . ah, Jesse home?"

Indignation rippled through her. "Yes. But I doubt she wants to talk to you right now, Keith."

However, I'm ready to give you a piece of my mind!

"It's okay, Mom." Jesse had come up behind her.

"Are you sure, Jesse?"

"Yes." Despite her red eyes, Jesse looked every inch a woman scorned as her gaze narrowed in on Keith's doubtful expression. It carried over into her voice. "What do you want?"

Keith's gaze kept shifting between her and the ground, as if it had just occurred to him that maybe he did not really want to be here after all. "Can we talk somewhere?"

Jesse's right brow arched in disdain. "What about?"

"About—" He shrugged. "Whatever."

"Okay. But outside." Jesse moved past her mother so quickly that Keith had to step back to keep from being plowed into. She reached back for the door and closed it with a bang.

Thea stared at the closed door. Jesse's transformation from wounded girl to outraged woman left her stunned. At least Jesse—and Keith—knew she had backup if it became necessary.

Either you've got a lot of courage or brass balls, son!

She turned and headed to collect her bags, but her mind was on what Jesse had just confessed.

Intuition had told her that homecoming weekend held all the makings of disaster, but then it seemed to pass without a ripple. Keith had arrived with another couple, and Jesse knew this girl. Next to Keith in his custom tux, Jesse had looked great in her sapphire blue slip dress. There were undeveloped pictures of them still in her Minolta. When Jesse returned home a little before the agreed-upon one A.M. curfew, she was quiet and not anxious to talk.

But then neither was I.

Half asleep with another hour's work to complete, she'd been all too happy to let the moment pass with the promise that they would talk in the morning. She should have tried harder. Because now she was going to have to leave town, problem solved or not.

She glanced at the phone with the urge to call Jillian's parents. It wasn't Jesse's fault that uninvited people tagged along. No, maybe the principal was the appropriate person. "Traitor to the Race!" The very idea infuriated her. Using a slogan that had once ignited bloodshed to express petty jealousies and mindless animosities. Had people learned nothing?

Her fingers danced on the back of the phone. But did she really want to make an issue of it when she wouldn't be here to see things through? No, that conversation, if necessary, could wait until she returned from D.C. But what about Jesse?

Maybe I should cancel my trip.

The mother and corporate person squared off for a debate, while her emotions jerked her this way and that.

If it had been a real emergency, illness say, she'd cancel in a heartbeat, and no one would fault her.

But did she really want to give up a seat on a committee that was going to influence congressional legislation because of her daughter's boyfriend troubles?

If she hadn't come home unexpectedly, she wouldn't even have known about any of this. Jesse wasn't particularly happy that she'd showed up. She must think she could handle things.

Sure, Mom. That's why she left school.

Guilt prodded her. Despite what she said, Jesse could be hurt that she'd been too busy to notice that something was wrong.

So, stay home and prove her wrong.

Could she afford to let Ron down, just when he'd put her forward into the spotlight? When the consultants were looking for redundant employees?

If not, she had no choice but to catch that plane.

Still debating the issue, she brought her things to the front hall as the door opened. Jesse came through it, looking less haunted.

Her worry eased a bit, but the guilt remained. "How did it go?"

Jesse squared her shoulders, as if prepared to rejoin a battle. "Mom, can I come to D.C. with you?"

That was one angle she had not figured.

"Oh, Jesse, baby. I'm going to be busy day and night. You aren't even packed. Besides, you'd miss a week of school."

Hurt blunted Jesse's expression. "Never mind."

A car honked outside. That would be the shuttle.

"Look, I'll try to take you with me another time." That wasn't what Jesse was asking, and she knew it.

She put down her bags. "We already talked about how my position could be in jeopardy with the new reorganization. My job requires that I make this trip. I'm really sorry."

Jesse grabbed her mother's hand. "Mom, please don't make me stay at Harper's where she can torment me with questions. I want to stay here, alone."

The car honked again, reminding her she was not the only one with a flight to catch.

Emotional blackmail. And it was working. She felt every ounce of Jesse's mortification. It was leaning hard on the slab of guilt that had descended on her. But leave a fifteen-year-old alone for four days?

Maybe I should take her. Missing a week of school wouldn't be held against her. Not if she called the principal and told him what she thought of a school that allowed delinquents to deface lockers with racist slogans! She would have to cancel her date. Xavier would understand.

The bell rang, and someone knocked on the door. The shuttle driver was clearly losing patience.

"Okay, you can stay here." *This is crazy!*

Jesse's face lit up.

"I'll call Harper's mom from the airport and tell her I've given you my permission. But I want you in by six P.M. every night. No company. I'm going to call and check." She couldn't believe she was going to allow this!

"And I expect you to go back to school today and to be there all day every day the rest of the week." She cupped her daughter's face in her hands and looked deep into her eyes. "Is there any reason why you can't do that? Like, maybe, Keith?"

Jesse shook her head. "Keith says everything's cool. He didn't have anything to do with the—you know—web site. And if anybody bothers me again, he'll take care of it."

"I don't like the sound of that, Jesse." She didn't know Keith, didn't know whether he'd spoken as a man stepping up to do the honorable thing or a hothead chest-thumping. And why was Jesse avoiding her gaze? "I'll be home Thursday. If anything else comes up, you call me, and I'll come straight home. I promise. Jesse?"

"Sure."

Am I doing the right thing?

She pulled Jesse to her for a hard hug. "I love you. You're my bestest child."

Jesse rolled her eyes. "I'm your *only* child, Mom."

twenty

"I LOOK FORWARD to it. I'll be right down."

She waited until she was certain the caller had hung up and then slammed down the hotel room phone. Tom Grant was running true to form. After two full days of committee meetings, he had just extended an obnoxiously worded invitation to join him and a "few members of the subcommittee" for drinks at six-thirty.

"As if I'm *not* a member, the prick!"

She smiled, thinking how her acceptance had probably pissed him off. No doubt he expected she would decline. Well, he didn't know her well.

She checked her watch. Six twenty-five. It was a little early, but since she would be tied up for a while, she would try to reach Jesse.

When she'd checked in Monday night after her guilty nail-biting four-hour flight, she'd found Jesse sulky and uncommunicative. Last evening, Jesse was vaguely annoyed to be reminded about the incident at school the day before. She wanted to talk about her birthday, and a car—again. The child was learning devious ways! Because she was still feeling enough guilt about leaving her behind, she didn't issue another unilateral "No," just a "Don't count on it."

She picked up the receiver thinking, only one more day until—

"Hello?" The sound of a deep voice on the other end of a phone that had not rung made her jump.

"Xavier?"

"How're you doing, Ms. Morgan? Fine enough, I hope, to see me tonight."

"You're in D.C.? You're a day early!"

"You could sound happy about that."

"No, it's a nice surprise." If he could see the silly grin on her face, he would believe it.

"But?"

"I just wasn't expecting you." Wasn't certain she would be available tomorrow evening. It all depended on Jesse's mood tonight.

"But?"

She chuckled. "It's good to hear from you."

"You can tie a ribbon on that by saying yes to seeing me tonight."

"Oh, Xavier, I have an appointment for cocktails with business associates tonight. I'm due to meet them in five minutes."

"I'll wait."

Pure feminine vanity stuck in its oar. She'd made appointments to get her hair and nails done tomorrow, if she stayed.

"I'm really tired—" She couldn't even finish that lame excuse.

"We'll make it an early evening."

"You're not picking up on any of my polite excuses."

"You noticed."

I noticed. So much for getting a manicure. Will this man never catch me at my best?

"Where do you want me to meet you?"

"In your hotel lobby. Do you have a problem with that?"

"No." The smile on her face was clearly in her tone.

"Just checking. You put a lot of stock in your privacy." She could imagine the smile in his eyes. "Would seven-thirty work for you?"

"Make it seven." No need to let Tom cut into the real social time. She glanced at her image in the mirror hanging over the dresser. She had planned to change quickly from her suit into a white shawl-collar sweater and black slacks. Fine for cocktails in the hotel but a bit casual for a really nice dinner date. "I've been told about a good little restaurant in Georgetown. Should we try it?"

"Next time. For tonight, put yourself in my hands. All right?"

"You the man."

"Believe it! And wear something you won't mind getting sweaty. Comfortable shoes. Bring a coat. It's getting cold."

"What are we—?"

"You'll be with me. That's all I'm saying."

She hung up the phone, grinning. The man was being mysterious.

Sweaty? She had just enough time to change and pack a gym bag but not call Jesse if she didn't want Tom to think she was reluctant to join them, or worse, a woman trying to make an entrance. She'd have to catch her daughter later.

"THAT'S A SHORT-TERM view, Tom."

She leaned forward to place her soda with lime on the cocktail table. So far, the rest of the committee members were content to watch this skirmish from the sidelines. If Tom thought her vote was open to influence, he'd miscalculated. "This modification in the New Shipping Act frees us all from cookie-cutter contracts."

Tom smiled, growing an extra chin in the process.

"I respect your view of things, Mrs. Morgan." He held his hands up, as if framing a shot. "The 'big picture.' But I'm more like my dad's dinky old Kodak Brownie. It may not be part of the latest technology, but it still takes a damn good snapshot."

Well shut my mouth wide open, Cuz.

When the good old boys got folksy on her, she knew she was making headway. "Worldwide computer-generated analysis makes a snapshot view of the global economy obsolete, Tom. We already do the bulk of our day-to-day business on-line."

She tuned out Tom's reply as her gaze scanned past his shoulder to the man who had just entered the lobby. Xavier wore a buttery suede jacket over a cream turtleneck sweater she recognized as cashmere even from a distance. And those were slacks with the knife-edge creases, not jeans. What happened to dressing to sweat?

She picked up her gym bag and stood up. "If you gentlemen will excuse me, I have another engagement."

Her companions rose, turning out of curiosity to follow the direction of the broad smile she aimed at Xavier.

When he reached her side, she took his arm. "Hi."

"Hi, yourself." He pressed her hand to his side, the warmth of his smile reflecting his pleasure in her gesture.

She pushed lightly against him. "I'm ready to go."

A question entered Xavier's gaze, but then he merely acknowledged the standing men with a quick nod and started to turn away.

"Aren't you going to introduce us, Mrs. Morgan?"

Damn! She made herself smile when she turned back to Tom. "Xavier, I'd like you to meet business associates of mine, Tom Grant, Fred Dunne, and Jack Wilson."

"Evening, gentlemen." The cordial reserve of a public figure laced Xavier's tone.

Grant stuck out his hand with a grin almost too big for his face. "And you are?"

She moved quickly, leaning toward Grant as if to impart a secret. "My date." She saw his reaction of astounded surprise, too reflexive to control. "I'm sorry, but we're going to be late." She tugged Xavier's arm. "Good evening, all."

She didn't glance up to see how Xavier was taking her actions as they headed for the exit. They passed through the revolving doors together before she got up the nerve to check.

Yeah, he's mad.

He didn't say a word, just directed her with a pointing finger down past a line of cars to where a limousine waited.

They were seated in the cream leather interior of the custom limo before he did speak. He reached for her hand, his palm hot against the evening chill of hers. "Why did you do that?"

"You mean not introduce you?"

He began playing with her fingers, lifting and inspecting first one and then the others. *Tomorrow night I would have had perfect nails.* "You plan to make a habit of not introducing me to your friends?" When he finally glanced over at her, the force of his displeasure hit her like a full tackle.

Her throat all but closed over the words. "They aren't friends of mine."

"Answer the question, Theadora."

She slipped free of his stare by aiming her gaze out the window. "It was to preserve my privacy."

His hand stilled on hers. "You don't want them to know who you're seeing?"

"Something like that." Seen through the tinted window, the lighted dome of the Capitol building had a greenish halo.

His hand moved away from hers. "People usually react well when my name is mentioned."

"People lose their minds when they recognize you." She turned back to him. "Did you see Tom's face? If I'd introduced you, we would still be standing there listening to what a phenomenal athlete you are."

"Were."

"No one else makes that distinction. You're still a celebrity. People think they have a right to a piece of your time, anytime, anywhere."

His frown eased into a grin. "So, this isn't about your being embarrassed to be seen with me? This is about you wanting to keep me all to yourself?"

She kept her smile in check, but her heart pounded. "If it makes you happy to think so."

He chuckled. "Then I'm going to be a very happy man tonight." He reached for her hand again and gave it a tight squeeze. "Too bad you won't be as happy. Where we're going, most everybody knows me."

"That could be anywhere."

Shaking his head, he reached forward into a black leather portfolio at his feet and withdrew a CD. It was a new Christmas album of gospel music. Printed on a banner across one corner were the words, "Featuring Reverend 'X.' "

She smiled. "Go on, Reverend 'Rock Star' Thornton. When does it debut?"

"This week. We hope to put a bit of Christ back in Christmas. My cut of the proceeds—quite modest—will go to the Thornton Foundation."

"And to pay for a few staples of life, like renting this limo?"

"*Nawgh.* I own it. And others in Atlanta, New York, and Chicago."

She felt her smile growing, but it was from chagrin. "You own a fleet of limos?"

He leaned toward her, earnestness in the very angle of his body. "Do you know that a funeral is the most dignified service many people ever have performed for them? Even the destitute will scrape together their last dime to see a loved one buried properly. I bought into a couple of car services in cities where I have a church affiliation. That way, the local churches can provide free of charge a ride for family to accompany their loved one to their final resting place."

Her suspicious glance around the car drew his laughter. "The deceased don't ride in the car."

"I know that." What she had never known was someone with Xavier's resources or with as much imagination in how he used them.

She felt no urge to break the silence for several blocks until a question circled back through her thoughts. "How does it happen that you're in D.C. a day early?"

"Plans change."

And that is that. She supposed he wasn't accustomed to people questioning his actions. Fair enough. She did not much like it, either.

The purse on her lap vibrated with the ring of her cell phone. "Excuse me."

It was Jesse, announcing that she was back from the library. The excitement in her daughter's voice was the kind usually reserved for new clothes. Something was up.

"Have you talked with Mrs. Peters today? I know you don't want to hang around Harper, but her mother is responsible for your welfare. . . . Did you eat? . . . Oh, Jesse, that's not even close to a balanced meal. Mrs. Peters would be happy to feed you. . . . You're certain everything is okay? No more problems? . . . I love you, too. Bye."

"You sound worried," Xavier said as she slipped the phone back into her purse.

"More like guilty. I had to leave Jesse at home with a problem I couldn't solve."

"Want to tell me about it?"

She did. "Jesse went to the homecoming dance with Keith Coates. I think you must have met him at the Night of Celebrities banquet."

He reared back in his seat. "A young brother? Dating your daughter?"

"You don't have to sound that surprised."

"I'm joking. Go ahead."

"If I'd followed my instincts, I would have warned her to be more sensitive to the issues of dating Keith."

He gave her a hard look. "You're going to have to explain that statement."

"Keith used to date a good friend of Jesse's. When she dumped him, he asked Jesse to the dance. As a way of getting even, I suspect. Jesse said yes only because he's the number-one quarterback in the state. I tried to warn her about dating a girlfriend's ex *and* someone she didn't know. Something was bound to go wrong."

"What did?"

"It shouldn't have been anything to get worked up over. Jesse had an invitation to an after-dance party. It was invitation only. Keith went right ahead and invited other friends along. The party girl's father turned away the uninvited. Feelings got hurt that had nothing to do with race and everything to do with pride and embarrassment."

"So there was a racial overtone?"

She angled her body toward Xavier. "You and I both know when something has the potential to be misunderstood, especially between white and black, and we take certain steps to steer things."

He nodded. "Preventive maintenance. Jesse might have made certain Keith was cool with it being just the two of them at a mostly white party before she agreed to go."

"That's our experience, justified by the world in which we grew up."

"Segregation was more than a memory, and integration was still a novelty."

"Jesse hasn't had our experience. Neither have her friends. Yet they resorted to the same old, same old when it turned ugly."

"How ugly?"

"When she got to school on Monday, someone had scrawled 'Traitor to the Race' on her locker."

Xavier's brow rose. "Who did that?"

"I don't know. When Jesse told me, I assumed it was the kids who didn't get into Jillian's party. Now I realize it could just as easily have been some of Jillian's friends."

"White kids?"

She nodded.

He gave up a deep sigh. "I see why you're worried. Jesse obviously isn't comfortable with her mixed heritage, and you want to protect her. But step back, Mom. Race is an issue she has to learn to deal with on her own."

She concealed a ripple of disappointment. He didn't understand. She couldn't just step back. But then, he hadn't reared a child.

She turned to look out the window. This was not the way she imagined this evening would start out. "Anyway, there's nothing I can do about any of it tonight."

"I hear that. So then, can we table this discussion for another time?"

"Sure. It's not your problem."

"I'm not saying that. But this is our first real evening together." He stretched out an arm behind her head, adding the icing of a slow smile. "Can we concentrate on us?"

"I could do a better job of that if I knew what we were doing." They were skirting the Tidal Basin heading away from D.C. "Where *are* we going?"

"To Alexandria."

As passing headlights swept through the interior, she saw that he was smiling to himself.

"To have dinner with my sister."

twenty-one

"JUST HOW ANGRY are you?"

After a quick lean in to check her expression, Xavier shook his head and whistled. "All right. If you want, the driver can take you back to your hotel."

I prefer that to being kidnapped under false pretenses!

The thought echoed so loudly in her head that she was surprised he did not hear it. Meet his sister? What kind of first date was that? And what was all that about sweating? Thank God she had gone for cocktails first! Imagine if she had taken him at his word and was wearing sweats!

"You will like Cherise," he said as they pulled up outside an imposing multilevel brick home.

"More than I like you at the moment?"

He just grinned. So much for her hopes for a quiet tête-à-tête for two.

Three sets of terraced steps led up to the double-door entrance. This was the residence of people who did not count pennies. Xavier gave her a quick, reassuring smile as he rang the bell.

The young woman who opened it bore a striking resemblance

to him. Tall but not towering, she had the same fathomless black eyes and generous mouth. Yet where Xavier was broad, she was slim, with all the right feminine curves. Her relaxed hair was cut short with deep, glossy bangs combed forward from her crown. She stepped forward with a wide grin. "Javier! Looking smooth, as usual."

Javier? The Spanish aspirated *H* replaced the buzzing *Z.*

"Looking beautiful as always, Cherise." Xavier enveloped her in a hug that lifted his sister a foot off the floor.

"Put me down! Right now!" She aimed halfhearted blows at his head as he carried her back into the house.

"Still the tigress!" He set her down on the mirror-bright hardwood floor of the entry. "Makes me wonder if Harlan is doing right by you."

"I know you've got some nerve!" She reached up and tugged his chin whiskers. "Always did pick up things that didn't belong to you."

"Now, don't start telling stories. I brought a guest." He turned and motioned Thea over the threshold.

She recognized that flash of wide surprise in Cherise's eyes as she stepped into the foyer. Yeah, Xavier's brought home a paleface. *Only, she isn't.* When and how to jump that hurdle gracefully?

"Hi. I'm Thea Morgan."

It took his sister about a whole second and a half to take her extended hand.

"I'm Cherise Dickerson. Xavier's baby sister."

Brrrr! The frost was building. Poor Jesse might not be accustomed to dealing with the hostility of being seen as an outsider, but her mother had a Ph.D. in it from the school of life.

She smiled broadly and said, "I hope I'm not an imposition."

"Not at all." Cherise sent her brother a *What have you done now?* look. "Any friend of Xavier's is welcome."

"Thank you."

Xavier smiled as if their oh-so-polite introduction was a love-fest, leaned toward Cherise, and said in a loud whisper, "Theadora's embarrassed because I didn't tell her ahead of time that she was about to meet you." He turned smoothly to Thea. "Let me take your coat."

"Yes," said Cherise. "And then you can meet the family."

Family? That's plural!

Her nervousness spiked as she slipped out of her coat. She eyed Cherise's outfit of Chinese red silk and the two rows of red toenails encased in gold sandals that peeked from beneath her trousers. She could guess what this stylish woman would be thinking if she'd shown up in a running suit.

The trip down the hall solidified her impression of Cherise's taste for elegance. The walls were the color of peeled almonds, as was the deep-plush carpet. Indirect lighting and original art gave the hall the hushed quality of a gallery. She noticed in passing the name of an artist. Cherise *was* doing well.

They followed the sound of voices and the wail of Coltrane. This part of the house smelled of real cooking, the kind that required lots of pots and a warm oven instead of a catering service. She wondered if they had interrupted dinner. Perhaps by *family* Cherise meant herself, her husband, and children. That comforting thought faded away as she stepped down into a large room with a vaulted ceiling and a huge stone fireplace on the far wall. There was a party going on.

Half a dozen people stood around a pair of curving sofas that bracketed the center of the room. A quartet sat around a nearby felt-topped card table, arguing good-naturedly as they bid the cards in their hands. Gold and diamonds glittered in ears and on fingers. Cashmere sweaters, silk blouses, tab collars, and turtlenecks bespoke casual chic. Not a pair of jeans or jogging suit in sight.

"Come right on in, young lady!" A bewhiskered man seated at the bar beckoned to her with a hand.

Cherise moved ahead of her, saying, "Yes. Come and let me introduce you around."

Xavier, she noticed, had walked rapidly over to the far side of the room to begin a conversation with another man. Given no choice, she smiled at the old gentleman as she followed Cherise over to the card table.

Cherise paused behind one of the seated players. "Pearl? You and Liz must meet Javier's *guest.*"

The older, heavyset woman frowned as she looked up, rhinestone-rimmed reading glasses perched on her nose. Her gaze when it met Thea's over the top of those glasses narrowed.

"Who did you say she is, Cherise?" Her faultfinding contralto registered in a key just a little higher than Xavier's deep baritone.

"Javier's *friend.* Theadora, this is our oldest sister, Pearl."

"You mean lady friend?" The blunt question came from the other woman at the table who was slight of frame with a dash of cream in her complexion. Still, the Thornton in her could not be mistaken.

Cherise's dark irises made a meteor's arc around her sockets. "I'm sure I couldn't say, Liz."

The arrested glances and slight hesitations were familiar signals. She could read in their faces what they were too polite to say to hers.

A white woman! Better keep her hands off our men! I know that's right!

Jesse had once been terribly insulted when a black woman they knew slightly through a school activity refused to acknowledge her mother in a department store.

"She looked right through you!" Jesse had declared after her mother's wave was ignored.

Later, she tried to explain it was a leftover custom from segregation sometimes called "giving a pass." That was when a dark-skinned Negro didn't acknowledge a light-skinned Negro in public for fear of outing the one who might be passing for white.

"What about now?" her logical daughter had demanded.

Nowadays, it was used to embarrass or exclude. But tonight, she intended to be recognized.

She held out her hand to Pearl. "It's a pleasure to meet you."

A dead fish handshake. *"Um-hm.* You're welcome, I'm sure."

This was repeated with Liz.

"Now, this is Liz's husband, Al." Cherise affectionately patted the shoulder of the man she stood behind. "Over there, that's Pearl's husband, Jarvis."

Both men nodded and smiled a considerably warmer greeting. That was enough to set Pearl in action.

"Where are you from, Theadora?"

The opening I need.

"Originally, Louisiana. My parents were professors at Grambling State University."

"Grambling?" Jarvis asked in amazement.

"Yes. You know it?"

He grinned. "I guess so. I graduated from there."

Eyes shifted left and right as the first recalculations took place around the table. White folks at a black institution?

"Liberal do-gooders," Pearl murmured in disapproval under her breath.

She didn't give Pearl a chance to expound, for she had spied the small pink and green enamel ivy leaf pin surrounded by pearls on Liz's lapel.

"You're Alpha Kappa Alpha."

"Yes!" Liz touched her pin.

"Mother was an AKA, too. She pledged at Fisk. Daddy crossed the burning sands to Alphaland at Howard." She smiled. "I'm the only non-Greek in the family."

Two parents. Both black. Slam dunk!

"I didn't pledge, either." Cherise offered her the first genuine smile. "What would you like to drink?"

"I've taken care of that. Your Alizé with ice." Xavier handed her a tall, frosted glass.

"Thank you." She smiled at him, though he did not deserve it. The Buffalo Soldier branch of the cavalry was a bit late to the rescue.

A moment later, his hand was on the small of her back, propelling her into another encounter with yet more strangers. Why hadn't he warned his family before she came in? Or was he unaware of the assumptions what would be made about her?

"I hope they weren't too hard on you."

He knew!

Had she passed some sort of Thornton family initiation? If so, she wasn't at all certain she was pleased about it.

"Nothing I couldn't handle." Unlike with her daughter, it was absolutely true.

"That's what I figured." He grinned. "Come meet a fine old gentleman by the name of Uncle Way."

Uncle Way was the small man seated at the bar, the only one who'd bothered to greet her when she first entered. He rose from his stool, short white whiskers framing a chocolate Santa smile.

"All right, nephew!" He patted Xavier on the back, although he had to reach up to do so. "About time you showed up for one of Cherise's soirees. You been sorely missed!" His deep amber gaze slid approvingly over Thea. "And had the good sense to bring with you a lady of quality!"

"Ain't you ever gonna grow, Uncle Runt?" Xavier bent down to kiss the much shorter man on his balding head.

Uncle Way swatted him playfully. "Git off me, nephew!"

Xavier laughed. "Uncle Way, this is Theadora Morgan. Theadora, this is my dad's brother, William Thornton."

"Good evening, Mr. Thornton."

"That's Uncle Way, to you." He winked and patted her hand. "I knew you were one of us the moment you walked in." His voice rose to include the room. "Some Negroes can't recognize their own anymore. I know that's right!" he added when the card players glanced around. Still holding her hand, he slipped his free arm about her shoulders and leaned in close. "You stay over here with Uncle Way and ignore these uppity boojies!"

She laughed. "I'd be honored."

Her instant liking of him increased when he looked up at Xavier and said, "What're you standing there for? Ms. Morgan's with me now."

"Oh, it's that way. You better watch out, Theadora. Don't hurt yourself, old man." Grinning, Xavier backed away.

Uncle Way was an outrageous flirt, holding on to her as though she was his new girlfriend. He also proved to be one of the best interrogators she had ever encountered. Within half an hour he had finessed more personal history from her than many of her friends knew. Then he escorted her round to meet the other guests.

She met Harlan Dickerson, Cherise's husband, who was a banker. Joining the Thornton family evening were two of his colleagues and their spouses. Harlan explained that the Wednesday night soiree was a once-a-month event begun when the various family members found weekends inconvenient to get together. So began Third Wednesdays, for adults only. A babysitter was keeping Cherise and Harlan's three children out of sight. By the time Cherise announced that dinner was ready,

Thea was thoroughly at ease and enjoying herself.

As she tried to make choices on the buffet line, others filled their plates with jerked chicken with penne pasta, shrimp curry, spinach-stuffed pork loin, sautéed string beans, and field green salad. Served along with these dishes were the traditional greens with fatback, candied sweet potatoes buried beneath a mound of browned marshmallows, macaroni and cheese, potato salad, and piles of steaming corn bread.

Not one to lose track of a good thing, Uncle Way saved a seat for her beside him at the dining room table. At the opposite end, Xavier smiled and shook his head. When the last diner was seated, Xavier said the grace.

"He's a nice boy," Uncle Way commented afterward and turned to watch her reaction. "You see much of him?"

"Not much." She stuck a forkful of string beans in her mouth so she could not be expected to say more.

Grinning to himself, Uncle Way looked around the table, choosing his next victim. "Jarvis, didn't you have an English professor down at Grambling by the name of Broussard?"

"I did!" Jarvis nodded and swiped the marshmallow clinging to his upper lip. "Students called her Madame Gator! Her freshman English class would snap you up, work all the juice outta you, then you spit out for remedial."

"Ha ha! That was Theodora's mama." Uncle Way nodded. "The apple don't fall far from the tree. You better believe it!"

Pearl, who sat directly across, looked up. "Javier's never mentioned you before, Theodora. Why is that?"

Xavier merely met her glance for help with a polite listening expression on his face.

"There's not much to tell," she began a bit nervously. *He is going to pay for this!* "We only recently ran into one another again. But we met many years ago in Grambling. The summer he worked in his uncle's law office."

"I remember that." Liz leaned in to catch her brother's eye. "You weren't happy about spending your summer there. Called it Uncle Tom Town."

"I admit I was grown before I came to appreciate Grambling's good points." Thea wasn't about to let Liz get away with that.

"I don't remember that Javier ever discovered the good

points." Pearl dabbed her lips, looking as if she had swallowed a bad bean, before she continued. "Got into some sort of scrape toward the end of the summer, but he would never talk about it." She aimed a pointed stare at Thea over the rim of her glasses.

A school principal. She would bet on it. She'd better change the subject.

"Why do you all call Xavier 'Javier'?"

"It began as a tease," Cherise replied. "His first-grade teacher wrote his name down wrong, and all year long, notes to our parents contained references to 'Javier.' " She sent her brother a fond glance. "We kept it up because he hated it."

"Didn't your parents correct the teacher?"

"Many times," Pearl replied. "But the teacher was white." That seemed sufficient explanation for all at the table. The assumption of the imponderable ways of white people was as old as miscegenation.

"Since he became famous, we use it as a family code," said Liz. "When someone calls asking for Javier, he knows it's one of us."

"I always assumed he was an only child."

"There have been times when I wished I were," Xavier responded, drawing laughter and a few derogatory comments.

"There are five of us," Cherise said. "Seven, if you count the two foster children our parents took in later in life."

"Pearl is the oldest," Xavier continued. "Followed by me, my brother Geoffrey, Liz, and Cherise, the baby."

"Geoffrey still lives in Chicago," Uncle Way put in, "with all eight of his bad kids. Yes they are. They *baaad!*" After the laughter died down, conversation flowed freely with lots of simultaneous conversations.

Xavier had a family—a big family—full of brothers and sisters and in-laws, nieces and nephews. He always seemed alone in the world. Obviously, he did not need to be.

Content to simply observe, Thea fell silent. It had been a while since she had been to a real family outing like this, the kind her parents had taken her and Selma to several times a year in New Orleans. Her favorite was always the Fourth of July picnic at Aunt Della's, where the tables in her yard groaned under tons of good food shaded by spreading oaks. Children ran and laughed and played and fell down and scraped knees and got the wind knocked out of them. Parents fed, cajoled, fanned, scolded, ate, laughed, and nursed the occasional casualty. The picnic was canceled the summer she turned sixteen. Aunt Della's third husband was on his deathbed. By the following summer, her life had been turned upside down, and she never again spent another Fourth with family too large to keep all the names straight.

A deep sense of loss caught her off guard. Through a series of life changes and missed opportunities, she had let go of contact with practically all her family. At Selma's wedding she hadn't known what to say to cousins she hadn't seen in a dozen years or more. If not for Aunt Della and Selma, she would have to say she had no real family to share with Jesse. She had wanted more children. Evan saw the advantages of being an only child. Perhaps if she had insisted . . .

Halfway through the meal, she gazed down the table at Xavier, whose head was thrown back in laughter. Suddenly, she felt like a cheat, sitting here with his family. His sisters were right. She was an outsider. She should not have come.

Uncle Way touched her arm, and the look he gave her was one of concern laced with speculation. He did not speak but patted her hand as if he had seen more in her expression than she wanted him to and knew she needed a little reassurance.

twenty-two

ONCE THE MEN were sated from trips to the kitchen for extra helpings followed by desserts of coconut cake, peach cobbler, and pecan pie, they made satisfied grunting sounds and trudged off to the basement den to watch the sports summary on cable. When the other guests left, the Thornton women retired to the kitchen to make coffee and clean up. Cherise invited Thea to join them and put a dish towel in her hand.

"Am I the only one to notice," Cherise said as she lifted a soapy platter from the sink, "that Javier hasn't answered his cell phone or pager once since he got here?"

"I expect for once he had the good sense to leave them behind." Pearl held the glass she dried up to the light for inspection. "He's working much too hard. I tell him that every chance I get."

"He needs a reason to slow down." Liz slid a sideways glance at Thea. "He needs somebody willing to look after him properly."

"He's got Je-*ro*-ome," Cherise said in perfect mimicry of the way the young man pronounced his name.

"Liz said *properly*." Pearl sniffed. "Jerome thinks he's supposed to fill up every blank hour in our brother's schedule."

Cherise chuckled. "Last time he was here, I said, 'Je-*ro*-ome, you see these three days here circled on my kitchen calendar? That's Xavier's holiday. If you put even one tiny mark in that space, I'll knock you silly!' Then I rubbed his shiny bald head 'cause I know he hates it!"

Liz chuckled. "I'd have paid to see that!"

"Xavier is lucky to have family to look after him." Thea placed a clean silver spoon back in its velvet-lined box.

"When he allows it." Pearl shook her head. "Most times, he's the one doing the giving. Always felt he had to do more than his share to make up for his success."

"I say, let him." Liz smirked. "Having a celebrity in a family can bend things out of shape for the rest. All those dollars in your brother's pocket, all those fine cars and clothes? And you sitting there watching him play ball, thinking about how that's the same nappy head you saw Daddy swat whenever he got any lip."

Cherise nodded. "It's been hard at times not to be envious."

"Of course, nobody's envious of Cherise's itty-bitty old house and dinky BMW convertible," Liz razzed and popped her sister on the hip with her dish towel.

Cherise threw a handful of suds her sister's way. "I know you're not dissing my home after you came in and ate up all my food!"

"Ladies, please!" Pearl clapped her hands for order as her younger sisters continued to trade towel snaps and suds and giggles.

Thea smiled. She and Jesse hadn't horsed around together since before Paris. She, Selma, and their mother had done much the same. A memory of her mother doing her Pearl Bailey imitation as she sashayed around the kitchen floor with a cup towel for a handkerchief provoked an emotional response halfway between a guffaw and a sob.

When she placed the last of the dry silver in its velvet-lined box, she said, "I certainly have enjoyed the evening. Does Xavier often spring uninvited guests on you, Cherise?" Okay, she was curious.

Cherise elbowed her in a friendly way. "You're the first

woman Javier ever brought across my threshold."

"She's not saying he didn't have his days as a player," Liz advised.

Cherise nodded. "Had himself a platinum card in the Playa's Club for a while."

"But he always kept us out of it." Pearl picked up another glass and peered into its depths.

"Player or no, he got hurt a couple of times. I remember one little bit—"

"Liz!" her sisters chorused in protest.

"What? You think Theadora doesn't know he's had women?" Cherise rolled her eyes. "Lots of women."

"That was a long time back." Pearl pursed her lips. "He's a righteous man of God now."

"All that pretty man going to waste!" Cherise clucked her tongue. "Time Javier was a daddy."

Liz looked Thea up and down. "How old are you?"

"What kind of talk is that, Miss *Thang*?" scolded Cherise.

Liz rolled her eyes. "I just wondered if she wants a family."

"I already have a family." She stiffened as three pairs of Thornton eyes pinned her. It was time to make her position clear. "I have a daughter, Jesse. Nearly sixteen."

"You're married?"

"I'm a widow."

"You got pictures of your daughter?" Liz asked.

"Sure."

But it was with a bit of reluctance that she went in search of her purse. Pictures would provoke a lot of questions. She flipped through her wallet until she found a snapshot of Jesse with Evan and her, the last photo taken of the three of them. He would always remain as the casual shot showed him, a blue-eyed man with an easy grin and a shock of dead straight blond hair. Across from it was a head shot of Jesse's yearbook photo. She pulled out the snapshot.

Liz practically grabbed it from her, but her sisters were just as eager, crowding in on either side as she held it up for inspection.

She saw the startled lift of three sets of eyebrows and then the doubtful speculation in the glances they raised to her.

"Evan was white." She said it with a defiance that wasn't needed. No, she needed it.

With a smack of her lips, Pearl put down her dish towel and started for the door. "Where are those men? Some of us have to work for a living in the morning."

And that was that. She had just put a period to their interest in her.

Seeking an escape of her own, she looked over at the kitchen clock. "I need to get back myself. If Xavier wants to stay on, I can take a cab."

"You just wait right here," Liz said firmly. "Thornton hospitality never requires a cab."

twenty-three

"YOU WEREN'T BORED?"

"Not at all." She leaned back into the soft leather seat of the limo. "I like your family."

"They took to you, too."

"Hm."

It had been a genuine dark chocolate evening: bittersweet with laughter and memories. Perhaps she should not have brought Evan into the mix. She had made the promise to herself when she married him to never be ashamed. But as she'd said to Xavier earlier in the evening about knowing when to steer things, perhaps she might have let that moment pass.

"If you're ashamed of it, don't bring it home," her mother always said. Xavier had brought her home. What was he thinking?

"Your family is very protective of you."

Xavier nodded. "My sisters can be a formidable hurdle."

"You want to tell me why I had to jump through their hoops?"

His gaze dipped briefly to the gym bag at her feet. "I really had planned to take you bowling until Cherise found out I was in town and called. She wouldn't take no for an answer."

"That's weak, Reverend Thornton."

He grinned like a little boy caught with his hand in the cookie jar. "All right. I was going to tell you about the change of plans when I picked you up. But then you were so busy hustling me out of the hotel, I forgot."

"Ah." The Thornton women's reactions were still churning in her. Should she tell him about the photo before his sisters gave their version? No, she had fought enough battles for one evening.

She looked out the window. "Cherise has a lovely home."

"Too formal for my taste. I prefer yours." He turned her face back toward his. "And you."

The kiss was better this time because she had just made up her mind. There wasn't going to be another moment like this between them. She didn't need his sisters' reproachful gazes to remind her how impossible a romance would be. If she'd entertained for even a second in the middle of the evening how, if things were different, she might have been part of the Thornton family, that was a little secret to be tucked away with all the others.

But now she put all the evening's awkward and unpleasant moments out of her mind and gave in to the moment. Her lids fluttered shut as heat seeped through her lips from his. The old-time connection was still alive. But different. They were different.

He did not reach for her. So she reached for him. She rested her hand briefly on his shoulder, then moved it to his cheek. Murmuring something low against her mouth, he leaned more strongly into the kiss. When her lips opened on his, his hand moved from the seat to her waist. Even through her coat, she could feel the heat of that hand pressing hard against her. Good thing she was sure it was a one-time thing. Otherwise, it would be hard to let this man go.

"Reverend. This will be the hotel."

She broke the kiss at the sound of the driver's voice. She had forgotten there was a witness.

Xavier pressed her waist briefly before releasing her and moving back. In that moment, she saw the longing in his expression that she knew must also be in hers. He seemed about to say something, but then he looked away. Amazingly, his voice sounded perfectly normal as he said, "Thank you, Floyd."

Once out of the limousine, she turned to Xavier, but her gaze stopped at his chin. "Thanks for a lovely evening, Reverend Thornton." She touched his arm above the elbow. "Really. Have a safe trip home."

Not waiting for his response, she hurried into the lobby and headed for the elevators. She punched the elevator button and stepped in as the door slid open. He was right behind her.

He had an unreadable look on his face, but he waited until the door shut on them before he said, "What's wrong?"

"Nothing." She gripped her bag like it was struggling to get away. He'd get an earful as soon as Pearl or Cherise called him.

He moved in very close to her, his presence a physical persuasion, though he did not touch her. "Talk to me, Theadora."

Wondering if his gaze would still reflect the emotions that she felt, she looked up. It did, and the sight prompted the truth from her.

"I told your sisters about Evan. They disapprove."

He blinked. "You need to make a crusade out of that?"

"No, I—" What could she say to make him understand how impossible this was? How much truth? The heat of cowardice crowded into her face. "I feel like I'm—"

"Tempting a man of God?" he supplied. The triumphant curve of his smile could not be mistaken. "Best news I've heard in a while."

She smiled but shook her head. "This is moving way too fast."

"It just seems that way. A lot of years came between our beginning and now. But you still *know* me, Theadora. I can feel it. And I feel the same about you. We made that connection a long time ago. My decision, to make that big detour. I'm late, but I'm back." He grinned. "I'm not ashamed of my game."

"Game?" Her jumbled thoughts locked on to that word. "As in 'player, play on'?"

"*Nawgh!* Those days are long over. I'm looking for something real." He was watching her, as she often suspected he did, to judge the impact his words were having. "You asked me to come to D.C. That must mean something. I want to see how it might have been. Don't you?"

Yes! It almost escaped her. *Don't start what you can't finish!*

"I have a daughter, responsibilities. I can't afford to make another mistake."

"Another?"

"*Any* mistake." Lord, did he have to catch every slip?

"Then let me make it simple." He cupped her cheek, his thumb brushing her lower lip. "Once a man knows who he is, then it's an easy matter to figure out what he wants. What's important. I bless the day that I found you again."

This is serious. He is serious!

She stepped back out of his caress, shaking her head. "You mustn't say that to me." She shut her eyes. "I know you said you didn't want to hear it, but I must tell you something. Should have said it at the beginning but I didn't think—"

His kiss was brief yet bracing. "You think too much." He reached for her left hand and brought it up between them. His thumb rubbed lightly over the simple gold wedding band on her ring finger. "When you're ready to let go of the past, all of it, I'll be happy to hear anything you have to say."

The elevator chimed, and the doors slid open. He sidestepped to let her exit. "Now shall I take this back down, or are you going to invite me in?"

She glanced down the hall, noting it was empty. Why did she always feel the need to hide when she was with him?

She looked up at him, doubt in her gaze. "You don't sound very much like a minister at the moment."

"What I am is a man who very much wants to spend a little more time with you."

She nodded, then turned and walked briskly down the hall, wondering what she was doing. Was this what she wanted? He wanted to know what might have been. Was she ready to let him find out?

HE LOOKED AROUND her suite when they had shed their coats. "I don't suppose you have a stereo system in here?"

That was a conversational leap. "As a matter of fact, I have." She opened the doors of the entertainment center of her suite's sitting room to reveal a TV, VCR, CD player, and receiver. She touched Radio.

Into the room surged the syncopated drumbeat and cymbal rattle of Marvin Gaye's, "How Sweet It Is."

"*Ah* now. That's better." He began moving in time to the beat and even to sing along. Smiling, he held out his hand. "Come, dance with me."

The suggestion so surprised her, she felt herself flush. "I don't think so."

He gave her a shame-on-you look. "Don't be like that. It's just a dance. You do still remember how to dance?"

"I remember." She took his hand, conscious of his touch in a way that made her draw in a careful breath. *I didn't know ministers danced.* She could guess his reply to that. *This one does.*

She smiled and moved in to match his rhythm. Her skills were rusty. But this song, old even when she was young, had a simple human tempo that quickly made her feel more graceful than did the less forgiving rhythms of newer music.

Caught up in the pleasure of it, too, Xavier popped his fingers and swung her wider with every turn. He twirled her once underarm, bringing her close. His free hand rested for a moment on her waist and then he spun her out and away from him, all the while keeping a lazy smile on his face.

Marvin gave way to newcomer soul singer Maxwell, who crooned a little less certainly about the possibility of getting a little "Sumthin' Sumthin'."

Still dancing, they got a little funkier in their movements. She was wrong about new music. She liked this beat even better, and so did he. Watching him navigate the floor, the evening's anxiety ebbed out of her. He was big but light on his feet and not afraid to show off a few of his better moves. The man could still throw down!

"It's good to hear you laugh," he said when he drew her close for a second.

She nodded but didn't answer. The moment did not require it. He didn't require it. They were in perfect harmony.

When the song ended, he paused, still holding her hand. "I don't get to do that much anymore."

"Dance?"

"No, let go and just enjoy myself." He released her hand. "Thank you."

"You're welcome." She decided not to add that it had been years for her, too. No more references to her former life were allowed tonight.

The breathy voice of Cherelle was next, murmuring her surprise about meeting an old boyfriend she hadn't seen in a while.

"Come on. Just one more." He stepped in close. "For old times' sake."

He didn't haul her in like he would have in the old days, so close she had to lean back to fit his embrace, yet he seemed perfectly comfortable with the fact that they met chest to chest. She, on the other hand, was very much aware of every place they touched. Palm pressed firmly to her waist, his long fingers reached almost into the indentation of her spine. The heat of his exertions came through his sweater, where her hands anchored his shoulders. That heat rose up around her, carrying the scent of his cologne. No knock-you-down bragging there, only a subtle invitation to get closer.

The space expanded with Cherelle's sweet longing, the words speaking of looking at old love through new eyes. Backed by Alexander O'Neal's earnest baritone, the intimate harmony of their blended voices gave the impression of eavesdropping on lovers' whispers in the dark.

She turned her face away from his as they rocked to a beat both slow and insistent. This was how it all started, a slow dance in a dimly lit room. Some distances didn't need to be spanned. Emotions could leap the chasm of time effortlessly. Like no one before, Xavier had stayed on her mind.

So familiar, this slide into sensation. So natural, no thought required. He rested his chin in her hair. She closed her eyes. Their movements slowed, tilt and lean replacing actual steps.

Her hands slid up higher on his shoulders until her fingers touched the crinkly hair at his nape. *So simple. So easy . . . so long since . . .*

She jerked upright in his arms. What was she doing? Getting too comfortable, that's what!

She took a step back. "I think I better sit the rest of this one out."

He gave her funny look but simply said, "All right."

She didn't know what to say now, couldn't quite make up her mind how to be casual when nothing about her emotions was even in the general vicinity of detached.

She saw him moving toward the adjoining room. *Bedroom.*

Five heartbeats, and then she followed.

He sat on the side of the bed and patted the place beside him. "Come here, Theodora."

She eyed him warily, but they were both past pretending that this was anything other than it was. She had stopped renewing her birth control pills a year after Evan died. What was the point? Besides, her system needed the rest.

"I think you ought to know I don't practice any form of birth control."

He grin was slow to catch fire. "Thank you for the information, but that's not going to be an issue tonight."

Not going . . . ? She shut down the sharp mind she was so very proud of because thinking wasn't getting her anywhere. She moved and sat down beside him.

He took her by the waist and pulled her down beside him. Then he reached out and stacked a couple of pillows at the head of the bed and leaned back, pulling her close to him. "I just want to hold you for a while. Do you mind?"

"No. It's been a long time for me, too."

He eyed her down the length of his nose. "How did you know what I was thinking?"

She shrugged, her shoulder moving against the hard weight of his arm. "I was just thinking. Sex is easy to come by, if you're not choosy. Closeness is more difficult."

"I like the way you think." He reached out and switched off the bedside lamp. "Now I'm going to hold you until you fall asleep, or I can't take it anymore. You good with that?"

"I'm good."

He leaned over and kissed her, long and slow and so thoroughly that she wondered if he was changing his mind. When he came up for air, he sighed heavily. "You're a trial to my resolve, Theodora."

"And mine."

He raised up a bit more to look at her in the gloom. "You telling me something I want to hear?"

"Not unless ministers are like Boy Scouts and always come prepared."

"Read my thoughts." As her eyes widened, he chuckled and stretched back out. "Not tonight. We'll know when we're ready."

She lay silently a long time, aware of the strength of his arm across her back and around her waist and the pressure of his heavy thigh along the length of hers. In his embrace was a sense of rightness that had been missing from her life.

That thought kept her staring at her ceiling long after he had excused himself and left.

twenty-four

"I UNDERSTAND. I do."

She swallowed her disappointment as she sat on the edge of the hotel bed and kicked off her heels. "Your responsibility is to your congregation."

"I'm only sorry I had to make this call." She could imagine the frown bars on his brow as he stood waiting to board his flight. One of his congregation's most important members had died unexpectedly during the night. Naturally, he had to go back to Atlanta.

"We never seem able to finish what we start."

"Maybe somebody's trying to tell us something." Good, she'd said that with a light touch.

The whine of a jet engine blocked out the beginning of his reply. ". . . resolve is being tested. I've been trying to see how to get us together again, but my schedule is booked solid through November. Then there's Christmas . . . the church's busiest season."

"We'll figure something out."

"All right." He sounded a little happier. "Your final session go well?"

"Absolutely." No need to mention the events following the morning's final committee session. But she couldn't quite get it out of her mind.

TOM GRANT'S PROPOSAL *died a short, ignominious death with a "no" vote of seven to three. Rather than slink out of the room, he cornered her afterward, grinning like a practical joker who could not wait to sucker in his victim.*

"Did you enjoy yourself last night, Ms. Morgan?"

"More than usual, Tom."

"Really?" He was lapping up the moment, probably devising his own porno movie behind those beer bottle brown eyes. "This is a new side of you, a side I never would have suspected."

She regarded him coolly. "And what would that be?"

"An adventurous streak. You're a sly one. Took me a while to place him. That was 'X' Savior Thornton. Way I heard it, you weren't even dating. Now, here you are seeing a black ex-jock."

Her gaze met his. "That's what black women do, Grant. Date black men."

"You're joking!" Her lifted brows made him pause. He closed his mouth, his eyes becoming two smooth stones of uncertainty. "You don't look black."

She could feel his gaze crawling over every inch of her face. It had happened before. Each time, it made her want to scratch. That gaze quested along her hairline, dove into her eyes to find the ring of tinted contacts, slid along her nose to find evidence of cosmetic surgery, something—anything—to explain her statement.

He frowned, unsatisfied. "So what? Your father was white?"

She made herself smile. "No, my mother was. Excuse me."

Mama forgive me!

LIKE A SOLDIER geared for a battle that never arrived, she was shaking with disappointment and relief as she hung up with Xavier.

I don't have to tell him!

She had built up her courage to tell him the truth today, no matter the consequences. After all that had happened last night—especially the final hours in his arms—she could not allow this to go on between them. She knew how to put a period to it. The words had been circling like vultures in her head all morning. Now her confession would have to wait, again.

She reached for her bottle of water but instead knocked it over and had to make a grab for it before it hit the floor.

"Dammit!" She glanced at the clock. It was only noon. There might be a flight available that could get her home in time to have dinner with Jesse. She needed desperately to get back to the reality of her own life.

Ten minutes later, she had an evening flight, the best they could manage on short notice. Only one snag, there was a layover in Atlanta.

Her cell phone was ringing as she hung up the room phone.

"Mom! I need to talk you. I've been invited to go to Taos this evening with Harper's family for the holiday weekend. Please say I can go."

"Holiday weekend? What holiday?"

"It's the last school day of Texas Fair tomorrow and teacher in-service on Monday."

"I thought you and Harper weren't getting along."

"That's so old news. We're talking Taos! Dr. Peters's got this time-share condo up in the mountains. Mom, *pleeee*-ase!"

Five minutes later, her consent given, she realized she now had no pressing need to go home. A quiet weekend to herself loomed ahead.

"I'M SORRY. THERE isn't a flight out of Atlanta to Dallas available until after noon tomorrow." The ticket agent gave her a sympathetic smile. "Shall I book it for you?"

"Yes. No. I'll try again when I wake up."

She turned abruptly away from the reservation desk and picked up her bags, squeezing past the line of other passengers stranded in Atlanta overnight. An early winter storm had stacked up the entire Atlantic coast. Major thunder boomers over Georgia that now closed Atlanta's airport had made the last half hour of her flight a series of abrupt elevator drops. She popped a couple of antacids in her mouth as she stood trying to make up her mind what to do.

She was never airsick. She could not quite believe it when the final approach sent her digging frantically in her seat pocket for a barf bag. She'd piled off the plane and into the nearby ladies' room to rinse her mouth and splash water on her face.

Nothing to do now but find a hotel room for the night. Or she could call Selma. Her left eye twitched. Onset of migraine? She'd spent too much time aboard the plane contemplating regrets and might-have-beens. She needed comfort and sanctuary. She needed family.

She headed for the bank of phones with a promise to herself to keep the peace with Selma, no matter the provocation.

"Thea, is that you?" Be-there-around-midnight Selma sounded sleepy.

"Yes. Guess where I am?"

"Girl, you don't mean Atlanta?"

"You got it. My flight was canceled. I'm stuck overnight."

"Oh. So, what? You need a place to stay?"

Talk about enthusiastic invitation. "If it won't inconvenience you."

"No but . . ." She heard the sounds of voices muffled by a hand over the receiver. "Could you get a cab? It's kind of late. Elkeri and I were just going to bed."

Thea checked her watch. Nine-thirty P.M. *Newlyweds.*

Forty-five minutes later, the crack and blast of thunder rolled through the cab as it pulled up in front of a tall office building to let her out. Toad-strangling weather, her father called this kind of deluge.

When the elevator doors opened at the penthouse floor, Selma stood in the entrance hall dressed in a coral peignoir edged in marabou feathers and matching feather-toed heels. "Thea, girl, you look awful!"

Trust Selma to state the obvious. "At least one Broussard sister is doing the family proud."

"Careful now." Selma forestalled her hug by clasping her by the upper arms and bent forward carefully to bestow a lipstick imprint on each cheek.

Then she glanced down at her sister's feet. "You're going to have to leave those here in the hall. They'll ruin my floors."

Thea stepped out of her soaked shoes and pushed them to one side. Most likely they were ruined anyway.

"Oh lord!" Klieg-light brilliance speared the blackness above their heads.

"Impressive, isn't it?" Selma smiled and pointed upward. "It was Elkeri's idea to put in a glass dome in the foyer. He's like that, full of innovative ideas. His company is handling the building. This space was originally zoned commercial. It was his idea to use the upper floors for residences. We may even put in a pool on the rooftop patio."

"Very nice." She stifled a weary sigh. Selma was selling what did not need a pitch.

"Forgive the mess. I haven't had time to do a thing since the wedding."

She followed Selma around a curving partition into a huge open area, where she paused, eyes widening. Two hand-carved Ompe drums from Ghana supported a glass top that served as a coffee table. Zebra skins upholstered two side chairs. Colorful Kente cloth throw pillows flanked the U-shaped sofa of nubby gold fabric. An array of museum-quality African figurines stood on the sofa table set before floor-to-ceiling windows that looked out upon a panoramic view of Atlanta. This was Selma's idea of unfinished?

Silent lightning at eye level turned the room milk white for an instant. She flinched again. She was not getting a headache. She had one.

Selma pushed a button on a console set in a nearby wall. A moment later, the dull hum of machinery accompanied the *shrrrr* sound of draperies rolling smoothly closed over the view. "Better?"

"Yes, thanks."

"You look beat down, girl." Selma raised a perfectly manicured hand to adjust the tortoiseshell comb in her hair. "How about a drink?"

"Just water." She sat on the sofa and scrunched the plush carpet with her stockinged toes. *Two hundred dollars a yard retail, easily.* "Where's Elkeri?"

"Asleep." Selma's voice carried from around the corner where she had disappeared. "His business keeps him constantly in demand. Then there are his civic responsibilities. Everyone calls on a man like Elkeri, even the mayor. He says he didn't know the meaning of relaxed until he met me."

Selma was smiling as she reappeared with a Waterford crystal tumbler in one hand and an old-fashioned glass full of what looked like cranberry juice in the other. "I make it my business to see that his every need is met. Tonight, he's too weak to move."

"Don't let me keep you up." She absently rubbed her left temple. Something seemed to have hold of her left optic nerve and was tugging at it. "Just point me to a bed, and I'll be fine."

"Just like that?" Selma perched on the slender arm of one of the chairs and crossed her legs, revealing the perfect curvature of slender calves. "You never visit and now don't have anything to say to me?"

Thea hurriedly swallowed a sip of water as lightning flared through the foyer's dome followed by a cannon blast of sound. How long could one storm last?

Okay, I can be the good guest.

She dug in her purse for the Imitrex. "You're right. We might as well catch up."

Selma's head jerked back on her neck. "You must have been through Atlanta sometime in the past three years. Why didn't you ever come to see me before?"

"And you could have come to Dallas, but you didn't."

"You know I didn't miss Evan's funeral on purpose." Selma's gaze engaged Thea's for a moment and then darted away. "You over the loss yet?"

Thea took the pill before answering. "I loved Evan. I'll always miss him."

"As Tina says, what's love got to do with it? I loved Rashid, but I don't miss him. The bastard would hump a fork in a tree."

Tiny pains spiked through her vision each time she blinked, making it hard to concentrate on the conversation. "I'm sorry."

"Why? You told me not to marry Rashid."

Everybody who knew you more than ten minutes told you not to marry that basketball-playing fool.

She took a count-to-ten breath. "The important thing is now you've found the right man."

"You got that right!" Selma swung out her arm, making the ice cubes in her glass tinkle. "This is just the beginning. So you can just go back to Dallas and relax. Baby Sister hasn't messed up again."

The silence lasted longer than either of them expected before Selma said, "This juice is begging for vodka." She headed for the bar.

Thea sank back in the sofa and closed her eyes. Neon rickrack danced behind her lids. Bed, she needed to lie down in darkness and peace.

"It's not like I disliked Evan." Selma's voice came from nearby. "He did right by you. Nice job. Nice money. Nice house. White men do seem to get that part of it right."

"I really don't want to talk about this."

"Come to that, when are you going to give up that mausoleum to white flight Aunt Della's forever talking about?"

Thea opened an eye. "Didn't you hear? The neighborhood went Rainbow Coalition years ago. A brother owns the biggest house. We've got Asians, Hispanics, East Indians. A family from Ghana lives just across the street."

Selma appeared again, her drink a few shades paler. "Boojies and third world émigrés chasing the white man's dream."

"No, we're just not stuck with that minority-as-victim attitude."

"How would you know? You married yourself right out of minority status."

You knew it! You saw it. And still you stepped in this pile!

She reached for her purse. "I can still get a hotel room. In fact, I think I'd better."

Selma gave her a sour look. "Like Dad always said, if you're ashamed of your situation, don't bring it home."

"Mama said that." She stood up. "But neither Mama nor Daddy ever said anything against Evan to me."

"Daddy was too proud. That first time you brought Evan home, the folks didn't know where to look. Didn't tell anyone you were dating a white man, just dropped him in on us." Selma eyed her over the rim of her glass. "You always got your way, didn't you? No matter who it hurt. Mama cried for weeks after you left for New Orleans."

Pain pushed tears into Thea's eyes. "How many times do I have to tell you it wasn't my idea to go to New Orleans?"

"You didn't say no." Selma twisted her lips. "Aunt Della picked you because she's always been partial to white meat. Didn't ask me down to New Orleans when I turned sixteen, not even for the summer. That's because I couldn't pass her paper bag test. Only Theadora was good enough."

"I was pregnant."

"What?"

"I was *pregnant!*"

twenty-five

THE WORDS WERE out! Words she had prepared for Xavier. She sat back down, defeated.

Selma gaped at her sister, her glass tilting in her hand until a stream of vodka and cranberry juice soaked the carpet. "I can't even believe that!"

She looked up at Selma, hoping against hope to see in her sister's expression the understanding she knew she did not deserve from Xavier. "Daddy and Mama sent me to Aunt Della's to have the baby. You were only eleven. They wanted to shield you."

"Shield, hell!" Selma set down her glass, ignoring the stain at her feet. "When I think—! All those times they held you up as an example! You'd have thought you were the Virgin Mary while I was Mary Magdalene."

A particularly bold strike lit the room. An instant later, the room vibrated with thunder.

"*Humph! Humph! Humph!* My perfect older sister wasn't so perfect after all." Her gaze flicked Thea's way. "And I thought you got all the breaks! Leaving for the Big Easy . . ."

Caught between pain and shock at her own admission after

so many years of silence, Thea could only shake her head.

Selma sat back and stared at her. "Lord! Theadora! How the hell did you get knocked up?"

"The usual way." She pressed a hand to her eye. Stainless steel tongs gripped her head, the kind that left a metallic taste in her mouth.

Selma leaned toward her. "Who's the daddy? Not Harold Pelman?"

"No."

"Because I happen to know he turned out gay."

Focus. She needed to focus before her sister's ramblings woke Elkeri. If Xavier found out this way! "Selma, I have to ask a favor of you."

Selma's brows shot up. "What would that be?"

"To keep this to yourself, even from Elkeri."

Selma buffed her nails on the fabric covering her thigh. "Why should I?"

"Because I never even told the father about the child."

Selma laughed suddenly. "Did Evan know you had a black man's child? Or did he think you saved it for him? Just how many black men have you slept with?"

"Go to the devil!"

"Yeah now! I've come up in the world. Baby Sister's not the black sheep anymore. Black Sheep, you get it?"

Thea stood up. "This conversation is over." If she did not lie down in a dark room soon, she would be sick all over her sister's outrageously priced carpet.

"No skin off my nose. I'll show you to your room." Selma stood up. "Pregnant! Miss Perfect! Ain't that something!"

Thea followed her sister down what seemed like an endless, curving hallway, or maybe it was just that she was feeling queasy again. Finally, a doorway loomed like Alice's rabbit hole. The first thing she saw when she entered was Great-grandmother Estelle's mango wood Art Nouveau armoire. "I see you're taking good care of my armoire."

Selma's eyes narrowed. "You mean my armoire."

"We both know Mama left it to me. You took it out of the house while I was away."

Selma threw up a hand. "I can't even believe this! Gonna dog me out after you come to my home seeking shelter! You're something else!" She turned and walked out.

What the hell have I done?

Anger throbbed with the tempo of her headache, sending pulses of acute pain along her optic nerve. Why in the name of heaven had she blurted out to the one person who might, just out of spite, expose her long-held secret?

Because I had to tell someone. The confession she'd spent the night dreading could no longer be contained.

After taking a second heavy-duty sedative, she lay down fully clothed, needing to put the last minutes behind her and sleep. But, like the storm outside, her emotions had yet to wear themselves out. Numbed by pain, she was at the mercy of her thoughts.

THE DECISION THAT she be sent to her father's sister in New Orleans to have her baby was her parents'. She didn't fight them. How could she when the hurt and bewilderment stamping their faces was her fault? Once her father stopped raising the roof over her refusal to name the father, he withdrew. She could still recall the sick clammy feeling that stole over her whenever she walked into a room where he was. He could barely look at her. She was a shame and a disgrace. He did not say so. He did not have to.

Then there was Selma to consider. What kind of example would she be setting for a younger sister if she swelled up like a balloon with a fatherless child? The Broussards had a reputation at Grambling College. People talked in those days. Reputations suffered from gossip.

They drove her down to the Crescent City the day after Christmas. She had pretended to her friends and sister that she was too glad her Aunt Della had chosen to "give me this boss opportunity to attend a really tough school in the city." She was going to be an A student where it counted. Everyone believed her.

Aunt Della made only one reference to her "unfortunate error in judgment," then told her she would be expected to enroll in school in January. Nothing must be allowed to derail her education.

Nothing did. After she became too big to hide her condition from the counselors in her new high school, Aunt Della arranged for private tutoring, which Thea's father paid for. Thanks to her aunt's arm-twisting, string-pulling, and favor-collecting, she was allowed to take her finals in the teacher's lounge after school.

Her baby was born in late May, the experience little more than a cloudy memory of pain, antiseptic smells, and then a wail from a wrinkled sepia face wrapped in blankets whisked from her body and her life forever. Her mother was there. Her father was not.

Until the baby was born, every hour of every day of every month she waited and hoped that Xavier would call or write or come to her because he would just know she needed him.

After her son was born and taken away, she stopped expecting anything.

By the time her "blue devils" passed, as Aunt Della called her slide into deep sorrow, school was open again, and she was a senior with new friends and a determination never to make a mistake again. She could not bring herself to go home, and her parents did not insist.

Aunt Della never answered any of her questions about the child she had given up for adoption. "It was for the best," she would say, her lips pursed with purpose.

The last time she inquired, she had come to tell her aunt that she was in love with a man named Evan Morgan. She needed to know, for the sake of any other child she might have in the future, what became of her son. Aunt Della answered, "You have a chance at a new life, a good life, child. Can't take old ways into new things."

SHE SOBBED SOFTLY in the darkness. That was her mistake with Xavier, thinking she could even for short while live in her past.

It took several seconds for the beeping of her cell phone to register through the web of sorrow and sedated pain pressing in on her. She groped for it in the dark.

"Theadora, where have you been?" The man on the other end did not sound friendly. She was not feeling any friendlier.

"I'm fine, Reverend Thornton. Why? Is something wrong?"

"I called your hotel in D.C., but they said you'd checked out early. Been calling Dallas all evening, but no one's home. Finally, I remembered I had your cell phone number. Lady, where are you?"

"I missed a connecting flight home." No need to tell him she was on his doorstep. She rolled slowly onto her side. "I'm a grown woman. I can take care of myself."

"It's time you remembered you shouldn't always have to. Someone is ready to look out for you again."

The prick of tears. *Someone . . . but not you.* "Thanks."

"You sound upset."

She rubbed her brow. "I had a fight with my sister." Damn, now why did she go and admit that?

"You two fight long distance?"

"Cheap thrills."

He was silent for a moment. "You want to talk about it?"

"No."

"I care, Theadora."

"Comes with your job description, doesn't it, Reverend?" He was silent long enough for her to suspect she had hurt his feelings. "I need some time and space, Xavier. You weren't in my plans."

"How much time and space?" When she did not respond, he said heavily, "I know I sprung a lot on you last night. Take some time, Theadora. But not too much."

"THERE YOU ARE! We were about to put out an APB for you." Selma carried a tray of wineglasses as she met Thea in the foyer. "Some folks! Sleeping past noon!"

"The medication I took last night put me under."

"You take sleeping pills?" Selma shook her head. "Now, you know those drugs are no good for you. I've got some herbs in my cabinet will set you right."

"Thanks. It was migraine medication. And I just need coffee." She waited to see if Selma would say anything about the night before, but her sister continued along with her tray.

No "Let's make up"? No "I'm sorry about last night"? Why should she expect it? Selma never apologized. Her style was to pretend that bad things never happened.

She noticed that half a dozen tables now stood in the living space. "What's going on?"

"Elkeri and I are having a little dinner party. You're welcome to join us."

"Thanks, but I just booked an afternoon flight."

"I didn't say anything to Elkeri, if that's what's bothering you."

"I didn't think you would." She wondered if that would remain true.

Selma gave her a funny look. "I didn't ask last night." Her voice lowered to a whisper. "But where is your child? I mean the one you didn't keep."

Trust Selma to touch the sorest point. "Adopted."

Surprise spread across Selma's face. "That must have hurt. Being sent away and then losing the child."

"Yes." The night before had been enough to convince her— once again—that there were some conversations she and Selma should not even try to have.

Selma ran a French-manicured nail along the edge of one table setting. "So that's why you never threw it back in my face before, all those times I ragged on you about being Miss Perfect."

"You're the only one who's ever been in that one-sided contest, Selma."

Selma looked down and rearranged a wineglass. "You'll have to excuse me. When you're networking for the church, things have to be letter perfect. Elkeri's on the board of the Thornton Foundation. Of course, you have no idea what a coup that is. Reverend Thornton is a comer. Jesse Jackson better look out!" Selma glanced at her. "I would invite you, if you were going to be here."

And face Xavier after last night? Head that off! "About that coffee?"

Selma waved her toward the unseen kitchen. "Ask Naomi. But you really need some wheat germ and fresh-squeezed OJ. Tell her to put it in the blender with my special Power Powder. She'll know."

twenty-six

"FINALLY YOU'RE HERE!" Jesse met her mother at the front door with her wireless phone in her hand. "Gramma and PopPop are going on a Thanksgiving cruise next week. And they want me to come. Isn't that awesome?"

Thea didn't comment on the lack of greeting from her daughter. She had just returned from yet another overnight business trip, the fifth in four weeks, this time to Cleveland. So tired her eyes kept crossing if she didn't concentrate, she put down her suitcase with a thud, shut the front door with her hip, and then took the phone.

"Hello, Shirley. Hi, Richard." She hoped she sounded sufficiently pleasant. "How's Philly?"

There was an etiquette to conversation with the Morgans that included the weather, the condition of mutual family members and friends, and, of course, the perpetual "When are you coming back to us?" question. Jesse was picking threads off the stair carpet by the time Shirley worked around to the main topic.

"We planned this cruise with another couple, but they've had to cancel. So we thought, wouldn't it be perfect, since we have two extra tickets . . ."

Spending time on a cruise with her in-laws would be a mixed blessing. It was sure to be first-class, and relaxing, but . . .

"We're inviting Jesse and a friend along as her birthday present," Richard put in. "After all, she'll be sixteen and old enough for such things."

"Quite the young lady," Shirley added.

She paused for a moment replaying what she had just heard. Two extra tickets, but for Jesse and *a friend?* She made sure her tone was solicitous. "That's very generous of you both. But Jesse and I have birthday plans."

"No, we don't!"

She turned toward her daughter, who smirked as if to say, *Now try to stop me!*

"Shirley, I've just gotten back from a business trip this minute." She gave Jesse a hard stare. "Can I call you back with a decision in a day or two?"

"I suppose." The Morgans were not accustomed to their ideas being questioned.

"We'll have to swallow that deposit if it's a no," Richard put in testily.

"We have until tomorrow," Shirley added.

"Good. I'll call first thing in the morning."

"That will be fine, dear. Love and kisses to you both."

She punched the Off button. "You want to tell me why you did that?"

"What?" Jesse was all wide-eyed innocence. "We don't have any real plans."

"But we always do something together for your birthday. You vetoed the party idea. So on the plane—and thanks for your warm welcome home, by the way—I was thinking, how about the two of us go to New Orleans? We could stay in the French Quarter in one of those funky old hotels. Shop and eat the weekend away."

Jesse shrugged.

"What would you like to do?"

"Go on a Caribbean cruise."

For a full second, she thought about booking a cruise for the two of them, but she couldn't justify blowing the budget at this time. "It's Thanksgiving weekend, Jesse. We've never spent a major holiday apart."

Jesse didn't respond.

"Who would you invite on this cruise?"

"I dunno. If I can't think of anybody, PopPop can return the other ticket."

Don't be hurt. She just did not think of it. And neither did Shirley or Richard. None of them thought to ask me.

She handed her daughter the phone. "Tell your grandparents it's a go."

Jesse threw her arms about her mother. "Oh, Mom! You're the best!" After a second hug, she pulled back. "But what about you? What are you going to do for Thanksgiving?"

The unprompted question made her feel better than she cared to admit. "Oh, I don't know. A five-day weekend to myself?" She rested her chin in her hand. "I might go to New Orleans alone. I could get myself a wide-brimmed hat with a silk scarf and cigarette holder and play the mysterious wealthy widow to some gorgeous young gigolo."

"Mom, sometimes you are insane!"

"Most probably." She reached for her bag. "How were you while I was gone?"

"Fine. I like being on my own. Only next time, we need to shop first. There wasn't any ice cream." She grabbed her mother's suitcase. "I'll take this. Oh, you got a couple of phone messages from your *friend.*"

Thea didn't dignify the swipe by asking if she meant Xavier. But a sudden dry-mouthed feeling made her head for the kitchen for a drink of water.

She had been ducking his calls for a month. Well, only the last two weeks. He had given her two solid weeks of peace, but now he was getting impatient. He was on a speaking tour, a different location every night, and couldn't be reached by return call. Which was fine.

I have nothing to say.

She filled a glass with a shaking hand, then downed the water in quick gulps.

After confessing to Selma, she found she'd exhausted her ability to tell that particular truth. Selma was keeping her word.

But how long would that last? She'd given her sister some powerful ammunition. And she couldn't even explain to herself why.

Xavier was another matter. She needed to tell him, straight up, that she didn't want to see him again. She didn't feel what he felt. Or, even if she did, that it wasn't anything she wanted to deal with right now.

"Uh-uh. That's a conditional *no,"* she murmured to herself. A man like Xavier would see it as a challenge to be overcome. Worse, he would see the lie in her eyes.

Bad to worse, her nights had become a sweaty tussle that no amount of self-pleasuring was going to appease. Despite what the women's magazines touted as a form of empowerment, that kind of thing seemed to her an ice milk, oleo, artificially sweet relief. A mighty poor substitute for the rich, creamy, honeyed pleasure of body-to-body contact. Doing without made one better appreciate the real thing when it came along.

If she could feel this way about Xavier, any man after Evan, then surely there was someone else out there for her. And if not?

She drew in a long shaky breath.

twenty-seven

TO JUDGE BY the stunned looks ringing the table at the weekly Monday meeting of department heads, Thea was not the only one imploding under corporate news. Copies of the consultants' preliminary recommendations lay nicely bound before each of them.

Ron tapped his copy. "This appears at first glance to be a bonus for our department. All of rail, trucking, barge, and marine will come under one head."

As he expounded on the corporate decision in positive speak, her brain shunted off track for a quick recap. Merging her position with two, maybe three, others meant one thing: one job where there had been four. Three would be transferred or demoted or downsized into the street.

". . . Decisions on the final restructuring will be announced the first week in December."

When they were done, the department heads walked out in near silence. No one bought the spin. Ron signaled for her to remain. Once alone, he looked at her over the top of his reading glasses. "This isn't personal, Thea."

She stared at him. Any time a person's job was threatened, it was personal. "Will I be considered for the new position?"

He nodded so slowly, she wondered if he had to resist shaking his head in the negative. "I'll make every effort on your behalf."

She made her way back to her office on autopilot. What Ron had not said was patently clear. That impromptu summer review could come back to bite her in the ass when she made a bid for the higher position.

Marine plus barge, rail, and trucking. Barge was a cinch. She had experience from her previous job. What she knew about the last two would fit in her shoe. She could study. Crash course. Maybe.

She stood for a moment looking out of her window at the Dallas skyline. The first day she set foot in this space, she knew she had made it. Her outer office had a full block of windows. She had salaried people under her and a package that tied her to bonuses. The pay was great and the perks even better. And at the end of every year, she knew she had earned both. She saw more of the world her first year here than during the previous combined years of her life.

What would she do if she lost out at Petro Chem? A year ago, her Rolodex bulged with numbers of corporate headhunters looking for a woman with her expertise in the basic chemicals industry. Now she couldn't recall the last time her phone had rung with a prospective job offer. Jobs were scarce, and the competition for the remaining ones was fierce.

Even if she made it, she couldn't count on keeping her staff. Layoffs in December! Joe, Lois, Marcia . . . ?

She scooped up her purse, computer bag, and jacket and headed out the door. It was early, but she needed to get out of here before she said or did something she'd regret. Besides, she had an errand to run before going home.

She gave a brisk wave to the secretaries helping to decorate the United Way/Make-A-Wish angel Christmas tree in the building's main lobby. Was it that time of year already?

She had few fixed beliefs about the targets of God's vengeance. But she was pretty certain He had it in for corporate honchos who announced major layoffs just before the holidays.

*   *   *

THE FIRST SPLATTER of rain from the lead-gray comforter drawn over the Dallas sky thudded against the windshield of her car as she pulled out of the jeweler's parking lot. The radio forecaster gleefully trumpeted the arrival of an early blue norther.

Thea shivered. She had gone to work this morning in cotton knit. She would need her all-weather coat for tomorrow's morning rush-hour drive. At least the rough weather would have passed by the time she had to put Jesse on tomorrow's evening flight to Miami, where her grandparents were meeting her to start their cruise.

She'd almost gotten over the fact that she wasn't going to be part of it.

Girls didn't have sweet sixteen parties anymore. They had events. In north Dallas, the events came with all the trappings of a society debutante's bash. Harper's sixteenth, last spring, had begun with a rented limo that picked up a group of girls and took them to a private party at Planet Hollywood in Dallas's West End and then a sleepover in a luxury suite at the Adolphous Hotel. She didn't know until later that champagne had been part of the suite's amenities. Jesse was sick as a dog the next day, so sick Thea hadn't had to give a lecture about alcohol. She did call Erica, who laughed off the incident with the observation that at least the girls weren't drinking *and* driving.

Jesse's friends thought a birthday cruise was cool, even if her grandparents were going, too. But she was sticking with a tried-and-true tradition.

Thea patted the jeweler's box tied with a pink bow lying next to her on the seat. In the beribboned box was a cleaned and polished pearl ring surrounded by half a dozen very small diamonds. Her mother had given it to her when she turned sixteen, a gift from her mother's mother at that age. Jesse would be the third generation to receive the ring. One day, God willing, she would pass it on to her own daughter.

She couldn't wait to see Jesse's face when she opened it.

SHE DIDN'T FIND Jesse parked in front of the TV in the family room. Instead, she followed the sound of voices into the living room, gift in hand. What she saw as she entered sent a charge through her.

Jesse was on the sofa, lip-locked in a hot and heavy embrace with Keith Coates. Thea hadn't even known Jesse was still seeing him; she hadn't mentioned him since homecoming. Obviously, she was doing more than that. As she watched, Jesse crawled into Keith's lap, straddling him.

"Excuse me." Her voice was too loud.

Keith was in her line of vision. The moment he saw her, he popped up from the sofa like bread from a toaster, almost dumping Jesse to the floor. Chagrin sharpened his broad cheekbones. And his mouth looked a little too swollen for her peace of mind.

They've been at this a while!

Jesse stood up more slowly, her head hanging forward, her loose hair shading her face like a veil of modesty. "You're early."

"I doubt that." *Clothes on, buttoned, and zipped.*

"We were studying," Jesse mumbled.

She noticed the book lying open and forgotten on the cocktail table. "Then I suggest you take the studying to the kitchen table. And, Jesse? That's enough with the anatomy lessons."

She turned away, as embarrassed as the pair slipping off toward the kitchen. On the one hand, she didn't expect Jesse to reach sweet sixteen and never been kissed. But she didn't really want to be confronted with the details. Then again, if Jesse were that attracted to someone, she needed to know. And the young man needed to know that she knew so that . . . What had Beryl said? She could be mother, father, and the wrath of God, if necessary.

But even the best parents couldn't know everything.

What had been going on each time she was out of town?

Oh Lord!

That thought stopped her in the entry hall with the irrational desire to chase Keith out with a broom.

No wonder some parents kept their children on lockdown like felons before they had a chance to stray. Others, like Erica, laughed, shrugged, and looked the other way, hoping the odds were in their favor. A reasoning parent was caught between extremes.

Through the glass panels of the front door, she noticed the headlights of a car pulling up at her curb. She moved in for a closer look. In the light reflected off the rain-splattered street, she saw a man get out. He closed the door, braced both hands against the edge of the car roof, and stood in the cold drizzle, staring at her house. After a few seconds, she recognized him. It was David Greer.

What on earth was he doing here again?

twenty-eight

AS SHE WATCHED, he suddenly pushed back from the car and moved briskly around it, some decision made.

She waited to see if he would actually ring the bell. Aunt Della said she knew this young man. But she wasn't in the mood for another stilted visit, family or no. Not after the day she'd had. She would make an excuse not to invite him in this time.

She reached for the door as he lifted a hand to the bell, a businesslike smile on her face. "Well, hello. David. This is a surprise."

"Hello, Mrs. Morgan." His gaze grazed her left shoulder. No eye contact. A few drops of rain slicked his lean face. He shifted from foot to foot like he half expected a punch to come his way. "I . . . I need to talk to you."

"I'm sorry, but we have company tonight." She made her tone sharp, unanswerable. "This isn't a good time."

His lids flickered. Those light eyes could not hide emotion. "Look, I came here under false pretenses last time. I should've said something then, only I was . . . surprised."

She didn't mistake his evasive manner for shyness this time. He was trying to get up the courage to say something. A chill wind blew through the half open door. She could feel herself tensing. Something in his tone.

"What do you want, David?"

He slicked the raindrops from his face, closed his eyes, and inhaled deeply. "I told you I was reared in Biloxi, but I was born in New Orleans." He said the last words slowly, as·if he were speaking in code.

Finally, he looked directly at her. "Lena and Marcus Greer aren't my birth parents."

She slipped outside herself, watching two other people standing in a doorway on a rainy November night.

"I think we may be related." That was what he said the first time.

He reached into the pocket of his leather jacket and pulled out a sheet of paper folded three times. He bit his lip, a childish gesture for so serious a young man. "This is a copy of my birth certificate."

Her gaze shifted to the unfolded paper he held up before her, and she saw her maiden name typed in the space marked: Mother.

The sense of being an observer vanished. She was suddenly sucked deep inside her thoughts, no longer even part of her arms and legs and torso but a mere awareness behind her eyes.

He has my eyes. How could she not have noticed before? Light eyes, green flecked with gold. Mama called them Nile eyes. My eyes, but Xavier's smile.

My son. It had been her secret. Now it wasn't.

The slide back into her fully conscious body came as a flush of release. "Yes, you are my son."

He stood straighter with an expression of relief. Of course, he must have thought there was a good chance she would deny it, deny him.

"I haven't come here to mess up your life or embarrass you." He glanced beyond her toward the hallway, no doubt alert to the voices coming from the kitchen. "I'm sure you had your reasons for giving me up."

He hadn't said *good* reasons, just her reasons.

"Come in." She moved out of the space of the open door to allow him in.

"No!" He licked his lips twice and then again looked fully into her eyes. "Just answer one question, and I'll leave you alone." He held out the paper again. "There's something missing: My father's name."

It was the one question she had never answered. The question asked of her over and over the autumn of 1973. By her father, her mother, their minister, and Aunt Della. *Who is the father? Who is the father? Who is the father?*

"I can't tell you that."

The color drained from his face. "It wasn't . . . rape?"

That whisper raked her spine. Lord, how much courage it must have taken for him to come here, hoping yet not knowing what he might hear.

"No. It's just that I never told your father I was pregnant."

He looked suddenly like he was going to cry. She knew he was trying to gauge if she were telling him the truth. "Why not?"

"We were no longer in touch." The simple truth hid so many complications. She had never told anyone the full story. David couldn't be the first to hear it. She put a hand on his arm. "But I'm glad you came back."

He jerked away from her touch. Her belated wave of motherly love repelled him. She could read it in his eyes.

His face spasmed. "After I came here that first time, I could see why I wasn't ever a part of your life's plan." Hurt cracked the educated veneer in his voice, and anger pumped up the volume. "My father's black, isn't he? Darker than me?"

She stiffened, sensing where this was going. "Yes."

He smiled, but it held no joy. "Is that why my daddy was a secret? 'Cause his skin didn't match up to your family's high-yellow standards?"

The accusation didn't surprise her, but it hurt all the same. "That's not the reason." How calm she sounded when everything in her was screaming, *Why is this happening now?*

"We were just kids. I was only sixteen. He was about to enter his junior year in college—"

"My daddy's got a college education?" He grunted, bouncing now on the balls of his feet. "That's something."

"He's something," she replied before she could stop herself.

David stiffened. "You kept up with him?"

She looked away for the first time. "In a way."

"Is he married?"

"Divorced."

The guard went back up behind those Nile eyes. "Has he got other kids?"

"No."

He nodded, as if having gained some sense of satisfaction from her answer. He backed up a step, rolled his shoulders twice, and then recomposed every muscle in his face, pulling himself together with supreme effort. "Look. I'm going to leave you alone. I swear. I just want my father's name."

Her head began shaking before her words came out. "I can't give it to you."

His serenity evaporated. He took a step toward her and grabbed her arm. Hurt, impatience, and frustration bunched up his features into a threat that stalled her heart. "I want to know who my father is!"

She flinched, afraid for the first time as his long, strong fingers—his father's fingers—dug into her arm. "Just let me—"

She reached out to grip his wrist.

He yanked away from her grasp, freeing her. "Who the hell are you protecting, *Mother?*" His voice crackled with anger. "Him or yourself?"

When she did not answer, he threw up his hand with an explosive "Shit!" Then he turned and started walking away.

Halfway down the sidewalk, he spun on his heel, his expression as willful as any child's. "I will be back!"

She nodded. "I hope so." It was a whisper she knew didn't reach him.

She didn't close the door until after his taillights disappeared. When she turned around, Jesse and Keith were standing in the hallway.

Her daughter's face was ashen. "I heard you." The voice carrying the accusation did not sound at all like Jesse's. "Is it true?"

"Jesse, I—"

"I can't believe it! I can't believe you did this to me!"

The look of utter revulsion in her daughter's eyes slipped into her as quietly as a knife blade, up to the hilt before she could register the cut. With a wail, Jesse sprang for the stairs.

"Jesse, wait!"

"Go away!"

"Jesse, please. I can explain. There're things—"

But Jesse ran up the stairs to her room, slamming the door with a bang that seemed to shake the house.

"I . . . uh, gotta be somewhere."

She turned a shocked gaze to Keith.

He ducked his head and shoved his hands in his pockets.

"I'll tell Jesse. See you later, Keith."

She was surprised she could be polite. Surprised she could even function. When he was through the door, she took the stairs two at a time.

twenty-nine

AS SOON AS boarding began for Southwest Airlines, Jesse pushed ahead in line. Seating was strictly first come first serve, and she moved as quickly as she could, plopping down into the middle seat between an executive and a young woman with a baby.

"There're available seats together in the back."

Jesse did not acknowledge her mother by so much as a glance.

Thea moved on until she found a vacant seat on the aisle. Let Jesse be ugly, at least she was on the plane. She wasn't about to leave her behind while she went to New Orleans, even if it was a school day.

She checked her watch. The before-dawn flight should give her enough time to do what she had to in New Orleans and still get Jesse back in time for her flight to Miami. But Jesse wasn't going to set foot on that plane for Miami until they had a talk, even if that meant Jesse missed school.

Her *daughter* had not spoken since her *son* left.

She clenched her teeth as she buckled her seat belt. She'd been up half the night, sitting on the floor outside Jesse's closed door, trying to get her to come out and talk. Pain tapped her left temple, and the tendons in her neck were tight enough to hold up a suspension bridge.

Your mom was an unwed mother at sixteen. Had a boy.

What Jesse overheard couldn't be taken back. And Keith had witnessed the whole thing going down!

She didn't even try to factor that complication into the what-am-I-going-to-do-now equation. She needed help, an ally. There was only one other living person who could fulfill that role. That was Aunt Della.

"Aunt Della? I'll be in New Orleans in the morning. You be ready to tell me what I need to know about David Greer."

It was the only call she'd made last night. She accepted none. Not even when Xavier's number came up on her caller ID for the third time. This morning, she'd left a carefully worded message with his answering service. She was unexpectedly called away for work. She couldn't be reached. She would be in touch when she could.

Dear Lord! She now had to face Xavier with the truth. Soon. No, sooner than soon. As soon as she knew all she needed to about David Greer.

My son.

She moved aside to allow a stout woman with a shopping bag from Grapevine Mills Outlet Mall to take the window seat. After that, she ignored those who paused to consider the empty seat between them. The only thing worse than a migraine was the queasy morning-after hangover feeling that came with it. She needed breathing room. The flight was not full; she had asked. Let them make a few more tracks down the aisle. Last time she checked, the back end arrived at the same time as the front.

SOME THINGS DON'T change.

She surveyed the house as she pulled up at the curb. For as long as she could remember, two elderly weeping willows draped Aunt Della's front yard in deep shade, leaving only the sliver of sidewalk leading up to the front porch uncovered. Daddy used to call them Della's Shady Ladies. The way they flirted with the breeze and shook their lacy green fringe reminded him of hoochie-coochie dancers down on Bourbon Street. The ladies had lost their shimmy on this November morning, but they were still there, their long, mostly bare-branch streamers rustling in the autumn air.

"We're here, Jesse."

"I thought you said I didn't have to come in?"

And I thought you weren't speaking.

She put the rental car into Park before turning to her daughter. "What I said was you didn't have to be *company*. That's not an excuse to be rude to your aunt. Now, dust that powdered sugar off your jacket and put a pleasant expression on your face."

Jesse gazed into the greasy paper bag she held. "I want to finish my beignets while they're hot."

"You can get another batch at the airport on the way home."

"You're paying."

She heaved an inward sigh. At least they were talking, even if fried dough was the topic.

The front door opened before they reached the porch, and Aunt Della stood there dressed in a form-fitting lilac dress with a lace collar.

"Isn't this a lovely surprise? Jessica! Can that be my sweet, precious girl? You've grown since I saw you last!"

"I don't think so, Aunt Della." Jesse bent down and submitted to the small woman's hugs and kisses.

"My, you just keep getting prettier and prettier. Doesn't she, Theodora Maxine?"

Theodora Maxine? Aunt Della was pulling rank early. Anyone who grew up in the South knew when your first and second names were called, you were either being warned or reminded of your lower rank in the family, or both.

"Come right on in. I've had Oleatha make us a nice lunch." Aunt Della took the girl's arm, though she didn't need the anchor. "You still like gumbo, don't you, Jessica?"

"You didn't have to go to any trouble."

Della waved away Thea's remark and said to Jesse, "When your mother was just a bitty little thing, she always insisted on eating the same number of bowls of Oleatha's gumbo as your grandfather, who was a large-size gentleman. To keep her from popping we served her portions in an ice cream dish." She offered Thea a fond smile. "I always take care of my children. See they get what they need in the right amount."

Definitely pulling rank.

Thea was able to eat very little of the splendid meal. When Oleatha came to remove her nearly full soup plate, she ducked her head like a child to prevent meeting the housekeeper's reproachful gaze.

Luckily, Aunt Della didn't seem to notice. The role of fragile, elderly lady had been supplanted by that of reigning matriarch.

At one point, Della got up and dusted off the glass of an old pewter frame with a handkerchief and brought it to the table to hand to Jesse. "Did I ever show you this picture of your great-great-grandmother? She was half Indian."

"You mean Native American, Aunt Della," Jesse responded.

"Do I? Well, her father was a full-blood Seminole. How's that? After the Civil War, those bloodthirsty Reb boys turned their rage for our people to clearing out those unfortunate Indi— Native Americans. So her father signed his children up in the census as colored to keep them from being robbed of their land and sent to the reservation."

"There was a time when it was better to be black than Indian?" Jesse's expression reflected her amazement.

"Sugar, it's always been a good time to be us. It's the ignorance of other folk that's been at the back of all our troubles. We are a proud people with a good history. If you came to see me more often, I could tell you all the old stories."

Della favored Thea with a reassuring smile. "Did your mother ever tell you about your Great-great-great-great-uncle Cleobis? He was an educated gentleman before Louisiana was even a part of these United States. An accomplished musician, he trained in a Paris conservatory during the reign of Emperor Napoleon. Your attendance at the Sorbonne was actually keeping up the family tradition."

Jesse finally turned to her mother. "Is that true?"

"It's the family lore," she answered neutrally.

"Speaking of family, I believe someone has a birthday on Friday."

"Yes." Jesse smiled like her old self for the first time that day.

"Then it's a good thing I laid by a little something for you." She signaled to Oleatha, who brought out a small package wrapped in a lavender silk scarf and placed it before Jesse.

Thea thought about the pink-ribboned box in her purse and decided to leave it there a little longer.

Inside the scarf lay a delicate gold filigree necklace with small, dark-red stones.

"It's so pretty," Jesse said, fingering the necklace as if it might break by just touching it. "Are those rubies?"

"They're called pigeon's blood garnets. The necklace belonged to my mother, your great-grandmother. I've always thought of your mother as my own daughter." Della spared Thea a warm smile. "So I'm giving this to her daughter."

"Thank you, Aunt Della!"

"You're very welcome, sugar." With that, Aunt Della pushed back her chair and rose. "Now, your mother and I are going to retire to the front room to drink a little sherry and chat. Oleatha's going to take you down to the Quarter for a dish of bread pudding."

Jesse's gaze met her mother's for a moment, and then she shrugged. "Okay."

ONCE THEY WERE alone, Thea could not hold back.

"How could you lie to me, Aunt Della? When I mentioned David Greer back in September, you never said a word."

"Have a seat, Theadora. My carpet's too old for your pacing."

She paused but didn't sit. "I want to know about my son."

"So I gathered from your call." Della poured a golden stream of sherry into each of two stemmed cordial glasses from the decanter on the table beside her chair. "What is it you wish to know?"

"How you knew who he was, for starters. Adoption agencies don't usually inform the person giving up the child who adopted him."

"He wasn't adopted through an agency." Della held out a glass of sherry to her, but she shook her head. Della took a sip before she set it aside. "As it happens, David was taken in by the married niece of my second husband's sister. She was barren."

"David's been in the family all this time?" She could not quite catch her breath. "How could you not tell me?"

Della folded her hands together in her lap. "It was a necessary lie to spare us all. I went to great pains to make certain that the boy's new parents did not know whose child he was. I told them he was the natural child of a relative from New York City who came to New Orleans to give him up. One can never been too careful in such matters."

"You had no right to just give my baby away like that!"

"I had every right." Della reached for the sherry again, but when she noticed that her hand was shaking, she abandoned the attempt. "Your father asked me to take care of the matter as I saw fit. But once I saw the baby, I couldn't put him out for adoption. He was family. I couldn't give away blood."

"Yet you let me think *I* did!"

Della looked away, her mouth primed in that familiar way that said if her niece was going to shout at her, she had nothing more to say.

Thea pressed her fingers to her eyelids, pulses of anger making her tremble. "I'm sorry, Aunt Della. But this is just such a mess!"

"How did you find out, Theadora?"

"David has his birth certificate."

"His parents needed that for identification purposes." Della looked vexed. "It's difficult to block every avenue of inquiry."

No answer to that.

"I did call the parents soon after you told me David had been to see you. I was careful, as always, with my inquiries. They didn't know a thing. He had told them years ago that when he was grown, he wanted to locate his birth parents. Since he never mentioned it again, they thought he'd changed his mind. I suppose it was after they mentioned that they'd been to Selma's wedding and met a relative named Theadora that he began putting the pieces together."

"You might have warned me."

Della lifted her chin. "I didn't see any purpose in that. When he didn't say anything to you, I hoped that he would let the matter drop."

"You hoped! You've never once let me make a decision concerning my child."

She could not keep still, and her frustration made her want to shout and throw things. She walked the length of the floral rug and back before stopping by her aunt's armchair. "I wanted to keep the baby. *You* talked me out of it."

"I did, indeed." There was no hint of repentance in Della's expression or voice. "It was painfully obvious to your parents when you wouldn't name the father that the matter was repugnant to you. That, perhaps, you were. . . ." Della pushed the final word out through stiff lips. "Forced."

"You mean raped?" *That's what David had thought, too!* Her mind tripped back over the years. No one had ever asked that question. "Is that what everyone thought? My God! It wasn't like that at all."

Della's sharp eyes held her. "You can tell me the truth, now, Theadora. There's no shame in it."

"The truth is, I thought I . . . we were in love." Bitter, the thought was still bitter to her after all this time. Even though Xavier—no! She couldn't think about him. Not yet.

Exhausted, she sat down heavily in a nearby chair. All this time, David was part of her extended family, and she never suspected a thing! "Did Mama and Daddy know about your arrangements for David?"

"I thought it would be better for all if I kept the details to myself." Della's voice once again held a note of calm finality.

Thea closed her eyes. Della's answers were hard to hear. "And my parents never asked what that best might be?"

Della looked off into the middle distance. "After your father's cancer had spread, he asked if I knew what had become of the boy. I told him what I'd done and why. I also told him how I saw to it that his grandson had his name. He . . . wept." Della's chin quivered, but she pressed her lips together until it passed.

"Then not even David's name is a coincidence?"

"Of course not. I told you, I took care of things. My brother deserved that his name be passed on. After he entered the hospital that final time, we talked about David quite a bit. I even brought him pictures of the boy. I told him I saw the child at least once a year. Knew how good his parents were to him. Sent him little gifts for Christmas and his birthday. He was grateful." Her lips quivered again, but nothing close to tears clouded her direct gaze.

"And Mama, did she know?"

Della shrugged. "Perhaps he told her. I didn't ask. Some truth is hard to share."

The truth.

The bare bones of painful truth strangled her with so many emotions she couldn't speak for several seconds. "Daddy never forgave me for bringing shame on the family."

Della looked startled. "Child, no. It wasn't you he couldn't forgive. He was stewing in his own remorse."

She reached for her aunt's hand where it lay on the armrest. "You don't need to protect me anymore. Daddy thought I deserted him. Selma told me a long time ago that he saw my marriage to Evan as the final insult."

"Selma never did have sense to suit a fly! I remember one afternoon in particular. Your mother had gone home from the hospital to change and rest, and I was keeping the vigil. Your father talked about your wedding. How proud he'd been. How grown-up and poised you were, walking down the aisle on his arm. He said he didn't deserve any of the credit for the woman you'd become. . . ." Della cleared her throat. "He'd sent you away in your hour of need."

Thea gave up trying to hold back her tears. "Why couldn't he tell me that?"

"The question, Theadora, is why didn't you ever ask for his forgiveness?"

She caught back a sob as tears flowed freely over her lashes. "I was sorry, but I was never ashamed of what I did." As she said the words aloud, she realized she meant them. Still meant them. "I thought he wouldn't forgive me for not being ashamed."

Della gave a single jerk of her head. "Stubborn! Just like him! I told him that. That's why you could go on. He'd given you the stubbornness to survive."

That stubbornness cost us both too much!

She reached for her glass of sherry. It tasted much too sweet and burned as it went down, but she needed to swallow that big fat lump in her throat.

"Before we married, Evan said he would help me look for my child. But I knew I couldn't take a six-year-old from the only parents he'd ever known. All these years, I've had to hope there was nothing I could do for him that he didn't already have."

"Wise thinking, child. Now, what about Jesse? How will you tell her?"

She winced as regret jabbed that fresh wound. "She knows. She eavesdropped on my conversation with David."

"Lord deliver us!" Della lifted her eyes heavenward. "That poor, sweet thing!"

For a short while, the women sat in silence, with only the faded gold of the afternoon sun filtering through ornate lace curtains and the tinkling sounds of Della's collection of glass wind chimes to keep them company.

Finally, Della rallied enough to ask, "So then, child, what will you do now?"

"David found me for a reason. He wants to know who his father is."

Della leaned forward to place a wrinkled hand on Thea's knee. "Did you never tell the father about your condition?"

"No."

"Would you even know how to reach him?"

"Yes." *We've been in touch recently.*

Della sat back with a sigh. "Then you have a lot to think about, don't you?"

thirty

"YOU GOT PREGNANT at sixteen. My age! I can't believe it!"

Okay, at least Jesse's talking, getting her anger out. They were pulling into the DFW Airport for Jesse to catch her Miami-bound flight. The flight back from New Orleans had been as silent as the flight out, Jesse having opted to sit between two elderly women. But Thea needed to talk, even if Jesse didn't, before they were parted for four days.

"I never held myself up as paragon of virtue, Jesse. I just want you to be wiser and more careful than I was."

"I'm too smart to get pregnant."

"What does that mean? Jesse, you aren't—?"

"Leave me alone!" Jesse's face swelled with indignation. "You made your mistakes. Let me make mine."

Thea gripped the wheel as she made a turn into a terminal. "You're right. I did make mistakes, several of them. What are you trying to do? Play tit for tat? Having sex with Keith won't make us even."

Jesse jerked, combative despite the tears in her eyes. "I don't know what you're talking about."

"Don't you?" She knew she'd hit a nerve. "If you like Keith, fine, date him. But, Jesse, don't use him to get even with me. Sex isn't going to solve your problems."

"I'm not having sex. Are you?"

She took a deep breath. "No, not that that's any of your business."

"Nothing seems to be my business anymore. I feel like a fool! I'm the last to know anything in this family!"

"I've told you I didn't deliberately lie to you about having another child. I just didn't know when to tell you." She shrugged helplessly. "Or how."

Jesse glared at her. "What'll my friends think when they hear that I have a black half brother I never knew about? How will it make me look, besides stupid?"

"Is this about Keith? Jesse, didn't he already know your background?"

Jesse looked down.

She shifted forward to navigate her car into a passenger drop-off spot. She couldn't reassure her daughter on that score. Keith had overheard enough to make Jesse again the center of gossip, if he told. "No one will blame you for my mistakes."

"But I have to live with them." Jesse heaved a great sigh, her eyes brimming. "I thought when Daddy died, that was the worst thing that could ever happen. But now you've forgotten all about Daddy."

"That's not true."

"Oh yeah?" She slanted a hateful look her mother's way. "You're seeing Reverend Thornton. If you wanted a black man, why didn't you just marry one the first time?"

Before she had time to realize what she was doing, Thea grabbed a handful of Jesse's jacket sleeve and jerked it hard. "Just a minute, young lady! This isn't about race."

Jesse's blue gaze veered away from her mother, but her furious expression remained. "All I know is, suddenly I'm the outsider in my own family." Her face was suddenly full of loss and confusion. "When Daddy was alive, I didn't feel strange. Now . . . Face it, Mom. I don't fit in with your son and your new boyfriend!"

"That's not true!" She released Jesse's sleeve and pulled over at the curbside space marked Passenger Pickup.

When she had put the car in Park, she turned in her seat and reached out to touch her daughter's cheek. "You're part of me, Jesse. That will never change."

Jesse jerked away. "Don't you get it? I don't want to be like you. I don't want to be black!"

She turned and shoved her door open, grabbed her bag from the backseat, and slammed the car door.

THEA STARED AT the bottom of her glass. Was that her second or third scotch? Wrinkling her brow felt funny, as if the muscles were not working together but making separate decisions about what they would do.

"I don't want to be black!"

She sucked in a breath like she had been punched in the stomach.

Jesse didn't mean it. She was just upset. She was being as nasty as she could.

She wanted to hurt me.

Her fingers felt numb as she reached for the caller ID beside the ringing phone. The number was local but unfamiliar. She didn't really want to talk to anyone. Except Jesse.

"Hello?"

"How's my lady?"

"Xavier."

"I got your message about leaving you in peace until your work schedule let up. But a side trip brought me to Dallas for the evening."

"You're here?" Her stomach dropped.

"Just for a dinner meeting." When she did not respond, he sighed. "Maybe this call was a bad idea."

"No." She put her glass down. "No. It's good. We need to talk."

"I can be there in an hour." He sounded really happy about the prospect.

"No. I'll come to you." Neutral territory. "W-where are you?"

"At the Melrose. Ask for me at the desk." A pause. "Are you okay? You sound foggy."

"I—I'm fine. Holiday cheer. I'll be there in an hour."

"I hope you don't plan to drive?"

"No."

It took two attempts before she correctly dialed the local cab company. Sooner than soon had just arrived.

By the time the cab picked her up, she had it all worked out in her mind. How to say it. The order in which to say it. Get it over in clear, declarative sentences.

thirty-one

"YOU HAVE A SON? That's what you've been wanting to tell me about all these months?"

"Yes." She could see the next question lurking in Xavier's eyes. His face was as serious as the charcoal pin-striped suit he had on.

He leaned a shoulder against one wall of the entry to the suite where his meeting had been held. "Anything else, Theadora?"

This was as hard as she expected. The scotch wasn't helping at all. "I gave him up for adoption at birth."

"I take it he was born out of wedlock."

She nodded.

"Did you think that would matter to me? That I'd judge you?"

You will.

"I was still in high school. I went to New Orleans to have the baby."

He frowned. "Why?"

Don't answer questions. Just get through this. "Until a few days ago, I had not laid eyes on my son since the morning he was born."

"I see." For the first time, he broke eye contact. "What about the father?"

"The father never knew. I didn't tell him."

She saw him tense, the involuntary reaction of a man who had just realized he might be in jeopardy. "Why not?"

She reached deep inside to find the courage to go on. "My son recently found me. His name is David. He had his birth certificate. There's a blank. He wants to know who his father is."

Xavier's pupils went supernova. There was no need to say the words.

She glanced down at his shoes. *How did he keep that mirror shine?*

"You need time to think about this. If you decide against it, I won't tell him."

It was harder not looking at him. She looked up.

Xavier stared at her for so long, she was no longer certain he had understood her. But he had. His hands were fists. Was he feeling as she did that the ground was shifting, reopening a chasm between them, cracking and shattering and reshaping their lives in ways that could not be repaired this time?

"He's mine."

"Yes."

"Hold up! *No!*" Xavier shook his head a couple of times, like a prizefighter slinging off an extra hard punch. "You had *my* child? And you never said a word? Never even thought to pick up the phone?" Hurt and shock raked the mellow from his deep voice. "Why?"

She tasted blood. She had bitten through the skin on the inside of her lip. "I told David I never told . . . his father." She still could not say *you*. Even now, she wanted to shield him, somehow soften the betrayal. "I don't think he understood what it would mean for me to have to confront his father after all this time. That the man might not even believe—"

Xavier made a sudden violent movement with his hand. "I believe you."

He moved several paces away and then came back, as if action was all that kept him from exploding. He wiped a hand over his mouth. "Ain't this somethin'!"

Finally, he refocused on her, and she saw his pain find a

lightning rod. "Were you ever going to tell me? That is, if David hadn't shown up?"

His sarcasm pricked her pride. "I did try. More than once these last months."

His head jerked back. "When did the words *pregnant* and *your child* come up in any conversation we had before now?"

She closed her eyes as his anger hit her like a Sahara wind, rough and withering. "I told you we shouldn't begin anything. It would never work."

"You didn't say *why*, Theadora. Never once *why!*"

Her gaze shifted away from him. "You need time to think. To—"

"Shut up, Theadora!"

Startled, she looked up. His face was expressionless, leaving no place to hang an emotion or a crevasse in which to hide a hope. When he took a step toward her, she stumbled back.

Xavier's eyes widened. "What? You think I'd lay a hand on you?"

"No." She did not think that. It was only that she would risk touching him if he got close enough. He had just been hit with the shock she was still reeling from. She didn't have the right to comfort him, and she shouldn't try.

"Theadora . . ."

She trembled when he put a hand out to her, and she turned away from him toward the exit. She didn't deserve any bit of compassion he might be able to dredge up.

"I have to go, Xavier. Jesse is expecting me."

"How's Jesse taking the news of a black half brother?"

He said *black*. A distinction he did not allow Jesse. A flicker of resentment made her turn to face him. "Jesse is doing as well as can be expected."

Antagonism edged his expression. "Does *she* know I'm David's father?"

"No one knows, Xavier." Suddenly she felt too weak to argue. "I never told anyone."

His brows shot up. "Your parents?"

She shook her head.

"What did they think when they saw David? They had to know that no child of mine could belong to the light-skinned guy they *approved* of you dating. What was his name? *Harold Pelman?*" He voiced the name with contempt. "Didn't they suspect—?" His face contorted with a pain he could not hide. "Is that why you had to give him up? Because my son was too black?"

She just stared at him.

"Dammit, Theadora! Why didn't you *tell* me? All these years, I've had a son. *My* son!"

Her voice was barely a whisper. "You made that choice, Xavier."

"When?" He thrust his face into hers. "Exactly *when* did I do that?"

"When you never called me!" she yelled right back at him.

He recoiled as if she had slapped him. She felt almost sorry for him.

"Remember what you said to me not so long ago? Nothing's ever come into your life that you couldn't walk away from. I was one of those things you walked away from. That's still your choice this time."

She turned to reach for the doorknob.

He better not say one more word. Not . . . one . . . more.

thirty-two

"I DON'T WANT to argue, Theadora." All the same, Xavier sounded prepared for a fight. "I just need to know how to get in touch with my son."

This was the third time he had called since she walked in the door from their confrontation. She hadn't picked up the other two times.

"No."

"What kind of game are you running now?"

"No game." She rubbed her brow where the beginnings of a hangover were tapping. "You're not ready to talk to David. You're shocked. Angry. You haven't given this any real consideration."

"I know I want to meet *my son*. Twenty-five years late. That's enough!"

"Maybe for you. What about him? What if you meet him and then change your mind about wanting to acknowledge him?"

"Why would I do that? What's wrong with him?"

"Nothing." She collapsed onto the closest chair. "He's wonderful, Xavier. Tall and handsome and smart. He even has a computer engineering degree."

"From where?"

"From—" She felt the tailwind of the mistake she almost made.

"I'm not going to help you find him. I'm thinking about both of you. What's best for both of you. You need to do that, too."

"If this is your way to trying to punish me because I wasn't—"

"It's not."

For several seconds there was only the sound of an open line. "I need to meet my son, Theadora. *Our son.* If you won't help me, then I'll do it without you. You can't keep me from him. I've got connections you wouldn't believe. I know his first name. I know about when he was born and where. And I have his mother's name."

"I'm sure you can find him, eventually. But it will take your connections time to locate him. And while that time passes, you need to think about what it will mean to bring a grown son into your life. You can't pick him up into your world and then shake him loose when you get tired of the novelty of him."

Long, long silence. "What kind of man do you think I am?"

"A good man with a good heart." *The man I loved? Still love? No, too late for that.* "But also a man who is used to having things his way. You have so many blessings, Xavier. You don't live like the rest of us. If David finds out that his natural father is the great 'X' Savior Thornton, he's going to be dazzled. Don't expect too much of him."

"And that means?"

"I've gotten to know David, just a little. He's serious, quiet, self-contained. He's like me. He'd hate being front-page news. Will you be able to protect him? Keep him out of the gossip columns and celebrity magazines? If not, he could end up hounded, his life shattered."

Silence.

"You know I'm right."

"His address. Phone number. E-mail. Something, Theadora."

She shook her head, even though she knew he could not see her. "I don't have any of those things. And I wouldn't tell you if I did. Not until you've given this more thought. I'm sorry, Xavier. Good night."

thirty-three

"HE HAS NO business being here."

Jesse turned and walked away from the open front door, leaving David standing on the step with a brightly wrapped package in each hand.

He looked uncertainly at Thea. "If I'm going to be a problem . . ."

"You're not. I can't say the same for Jesse." She gave him a big smile as she waved him in. "Jesse and I already brought the boxes down from the attic. All we have to do is open them and start hanging. Let me take your jacket. Now, go on into the living room. I'll be right with you!"

You're talking way too much!

When she was out of sight, she hugged his jacket briefly to her chest. It represented a major achievement. Xavier wasn't talking to her. Jesse wasn't talking to her. Only David would talk, even if they were less-than-friendly exchanges.

For the last three weeks, David had made several argumentative calls that ended with some variation of, "I only want one thing from you: my father's name." In this way, her children were alike, stubborn.

Finally, last Monday, he had agreed to meet her for lunch at the Quadrangle near downtown—to talk about the circumstances of his birth. No mother ever worked harder at trying to engage her child's interest. She asked dozens of questions. He answered a few. He hadn't just graduated. He had been living and working in Dallas for more than a year. Yes, he was a computer geek. Coincidence that she lived here, too. It was only in the summer that he had gotten the papers he needed to track her down.

She told him about her work, her education, her family, and finally about himself. What brief history they shared.

She knew she had finally broken through his self-protective shell when she saw the look in his eyes after she told him about an incident during her eighth month of pregnancy. One of those God-given memories she hadn't known she remembered until she began telling it.

She had been playing bridge, or attempting to learn, with her Aunt Della and Oleatha and an elderly gentleman neighbor. As she reached across the table to play the dummy hand, her baby—he—gave her a solid jab with his foot, a kick so strong that the thump made the card table jump.

The old gentleman reared back, nearly toppling out of his chair. When he recovered his surprise, he said, "That boy's gonna be a comer!"

David looked surprised and then embarrassed, as if she had revealed something too personal for a stranger. But he wasn't a stranger. Not when she had given birth to him.

At end of their meal, she was feeling so confident of her success with him that she suggested, on the spur of the moment, that he join Jesse and her Saturday afternoon for the annual family ritual as old as her marriage, the Christmas tree-trimming party.

Jesse, whose responses since the Thanksgiving cruise consisted mostly of "Maybe," "No," and "Uh-huh," pitched a verbal fit when told about the invitation.

"He can't come here. This is Daddy's house."

*"This is **our** house, and I want David to meet his sister."*

"Well, I don't want a brother!"

*   *   *

DAVID HAD GOOD taste, she decided as she laid the suede jacket aside. Now that she thought about it, the jacket was nearly identical to the one Xavier had worn in D.C.

Xavier.

She had called him two weeks ago. *No need to mention their estranged relationship.*

She was busy at work. *No need to mention her job was in jeopardy.*

Things with Jesse were up in the air. *No need to mention she and her daughter were barely speaking.*

She had again asked him for a few weeks—until after the first of the year—and then she would call him, and they would talk about David. He agreed, but he wasn't happy about it.

Neither was she. *"A bitter potion . . ."*

She walked into the living room with a big smile and a determination to see this through. David stood by the tree, a nine-foot blue spruce she had had delivered the day before. Jesse sat on the sofa, glaring at him. If looks could kill, he would be in serious jeopardy. In the background, Nat King Cole was crooning "I'll Be Home for Christmas."

"I see you've found our target of operations, David."

"Nice tree." He moved to pick up from the coffee table one of the packages he had brought with him. "This is for you."

She opened the wintergreen velvet pouch with gold tassels to find it contained a bottle of Perrier champagne. "Oh, thank you. I love champagne."

A little less certainly, he turned to his Jesse. "I hope you like this."

He held out a cellophane-wrapped, chocolate-covered, caramel-dipped apple on a stick, one of Neiman Marcus's Christmas specialties. She looked away without taking it from him. "I don't like sweets."

"That's a first. Jesse has been a fan from birth of anything dipped in chocolate."

The look the pair of them gave her made her wish she had chosen another imagery. *Okay, so you're going to make mistakes.* "Let's begin."

"You can do this without me!" Jesse hopped to her feet.

"Look, I can go." David's expression had gone on remote setting. "I didn't really want to come."

Jesse smirked. "Yeah. Once we had a rule that no outsiders, not even real close friends, were allowed to join in the tree-trimming party." She gazed sullenly at her mother. "You said it was for family only."

"David *is* family. And he's about to see me ground my daughter, if she doesn't get a new attitude this second!"

Jesse's face took on a "You wouldn't dare" expression. Then she must have seen on her mother's face the truth behind that threat, because she shrugged and flopped down.

"That's better. Why don't you open that box marked Lights, David? You can use a socket behind that end table to test the strings to see if they still work. Jesse, you can help him. I have to check on dinner." She gave her daughter one last, meaningful glance and then walked out.

God, please don't let them trash each other!

She stood stock-still on the other side of the swinging doors that led from the dining room into the kitchen and waited for a raised voice, hiss of anger, or a thrown object. After half a minute, she had heard only a few mumbles, male and female.

She blew out her breath and decided she really should check on her meal, as long as she was in the kitchen. In fact, she found enough to occupy her so that fifteen minutes had passed before she decided to peek into the living room.

She cracked the louvered doors and saw, wonder of wonders, that the two were actually draping the tree in lights. She let the door swing shut. No need to trouble trouble.

She poured hot cider into Christmas cups and piled a plate with homemade cheese crackers and another with sugared pecans. Something to snack on until the pork roast was ready. Usually, they just ate finger foods when decorating the tree, but it was David's first visit, and she wanted him to know his mother could cook. Once he got accustomed to her, she would gradually introduce him to her friends. She might even throw a party in his honor. She wanted him to know that she wasn't ashamed of him, for him to know that he wasn't an only child, that he had a half sister. She wanted . . . so much.

The cider and snacks went down relatively smoothly, though

she did most of the talking. Jesse and David exchanged one-word directions as they finished the lights while Perry Como sang, "The weather outside is frightful." Inside it wasn't "so delightful," but it was a beginning. She hung a few ornaments before the kitchen timer went off.

She had just bent down to pull the roast out of the oven when she heard Jesse cry, "Not that box!"

She pushed through the dining room doors in time to see Jesse snatch a white gift box out of David's hands. His thumb snagged one corner of the tucked-together box, and it came open. Two mercury glass bells tumbled out of the split. Before either of them could react, they struck the floor and shattered.

Jesse's cry of distress echoed her mother's gasp. Jesse looked up at David, her face contorted in outrage.

"Look what you did! You broke Daddy's favorite ornaments! I hate you!"

Jesse hurled the box at David, who caught it, and ran from the room, her long legs taking the stairs two at a time.

David turned as Thea reached his side. The anguish in his eyes matched hers. "I didn't mean—"

"No." She put a hand on his arm "You didn't do it. Jesse's responsible." *And she knows it!*

She bent down and picked up one of the larger silver shards. The bells were a first Christmas gift from Evan's parents. They had had pride of place on every tree they had ever had. Now they were gone. Like Evan. Gone forever.

She batted back the sting of tears. *The small losses hurt as much as the big ones.*

When she looked up again, David stood in front her with a broom in one hand and a dustpan in the other. She hadn't even noticed he'd left the room. Smart of him to find just what she needed. "Thank you."

"No, I'll do it," he said when she reached for the broom. He glanced back over his shoulder. "I think I smell something that needs your attention."

"Yes."

She moved toward the kitchen, feeling a sense of unreality. He had such nice manners, just what I'd want in a son of mine.

Son of mine! Would that phrase ever become as natural as my daughter?

When he had emptied out the broken glass, David came into the kitchen with his jacket in his hands. "I think I should go."

"But I made dinner for us." She pointed out the roast sitting on the serving platter.

He looked from it to her with the resolve of someone who had to make it clear, "It's over, baby." "I'm sorry this couldn't work out the way you wanted. But it's better this way. Good night, Mrs. Morgan."

"Another time." She tried to smile again, but even she knew it was pointless. "Anytime."

He looked at her long and hard. "I don't see the point. I only need one thing from you: my father's name."

thirty-four

"HELLO, THEA. IT'S Richard Morgan."

Clutching the receiver, she rolled over to glance at her bedside clock. Red numbers swam through the early morning darkness. It was six A.M. "Hello, Richard." Her in-laws never called out of their accustomed second and fourth Sunday routine. "Is everything all right?"

"That's for you to tell me." The heartiness in his voice struck a false note, even in her state of semiconsciousness. "I hear there's been quite a ruckus going on down your way."

She sat up, pressing a hand to her forehead, for it felt like her head was going to topple off her shoulders. "I don't know what you mean."

"Now, don't be upset with her, but Jesse called us last night."

"Did she . . . ?" She didn't have enough energy to finish the sentence. She was swimming thorough a leaden fog. "What did she want?"

"I gather there've been a series of surprises at your house these last weeks."

She sipped a little of the water she kept beside her bed. She didn't know what if anything Jesse had said to her grandparents

during their cruise. Since they hadn't mentioned it before, neither had she. "You're referring to the appearance of my son."

"In part, yes."

"Is there something else?"

"You know, Thea, we've tried not to be typical in-laws.
Would never dream of interfering with how you rear Jesse. But
there are some things that I—we—feel that as her grandparents
we have a right to be concerned about."

She clenched her jaw to keep from asking again what he
meant. Let him say it in his own time.

"It seems that Jesse is unhappy with the fact that you're dating. A minister. From Atlanta? Is that correct?"

"I was seeing someone." What did that have to do with David? David's parentage was still her secret. "And, yes, he's a
minister."

"I see." She was certain that he did. No doubt Jesse had told
him all about Xavier. But Richard didn't want to ask, and she
wasn't about to volunteer.

"I'm sure I'm the last person you want to discuss your personal life with. But I will tell you that Shirley and I never expected you to wrap widowhood about you and retire from life.
We assumed that sooner or later, you would be ready to reenter
the social sphere. Given the right opportunity, you might even
marry again. We wish that for you. You do understand?"

"Of course." He was beginning to sound like a doctor who
had come to tell the patient he had discovered cancer.

"Then maybe that will make this a little easier to hear. Jesse
is just a child. She doesn't understand the world as we grown-
ups do. She's a bit traumatized by the discovery that her mother
had another child . . . before."

"Before I married her father." Why were they talking about
this before dawn?

"Exactly. It seems she never knew a thing about it. None of
us did."

Ah, that beat of indignation rang true. "Evan knew."

"Did he?" He couldn't keep the hint of doubt out of his voice.
She supposed she couldn't blame him. Still, it was none of his
business.

"Well, that does mitigate matters some."

"What matters?"

"Jesse was quite emotional when she called. We couldn't quite make heads or tails out of much of what she said. We just responded to her need."

"I'm sure you did." So Jesse had a cry on her grandparents' shoulders. "Thanks for letting me know. I'll have another talk with her. Sorry we had to bring you into this."

"There is another reason I called. Under the circumstances, Shirley and I want to propose a solution for you to consider. We'd like to bring Jesse up to Philadelphia for a while. Just until things smooth over."

She swung her feet over the side of the bed, fully awake now. "Jesse and I may be having a few problems, but we're a family. We'll tough it out."

Movement at her doorway caught her eye. She switched on her lamp. Jesse stood there, fully dressed, with a duffel bag at her feet. "I want to go, Mom."

"Hold on, Richard." She pushed the Mute button. "What do you think you're doing?"

"I'm going to Philly. Gramma and PopPop have arranged it."

She stood up and laid the phone aside. "I don't care what they've arranged."

Jesse swelled up. "You can't stop me. There's a shuttle coming to pick me up any minute. The plane ticket's waiting for me at the airport."

"That doesn't matter. You're my child, and I say you can't go."

"I don't feel like your child anymore." Jesse looked away. "I'm the last one you care about these days."

"Jesse, come on—"

Jesse snatched up her bag and turned away.

Thea picked up the phone. "I don't appreciate you making arrangements behind my back, Richard. I call that the height of interference in family matters."

"It's Shirley, dear. It's understandable that you're upset." How calm and reasonable she sounded. "But when you've had time to think, you'll see it's for the best. And it's just for a short while."

"She won't be coming, Shirley. I forbid it." She hung up.

She didn't bother to don her robe but ran through the chill rooms in her gown to find Jesse staring out through the drapes of a window in the living room.

She willed herself to be calm, to be the voice of reason. "You can't go, Jesse. You can't imagine the ramifications of what you want to do. Believe me."

Jesse looked back at her. "I don't know what to believe anymore. You're not the person I thought you were. Ever since Daddy died, nothing makes sense. I just know I don't want to be here anymore."

"What about Christmas? Jesse, it's only a week away. We are a family. We have to be together."

"I'm not the one who invited a stranger into our house to destroy things. Ask David to come back. You're more concerned about him than me, anyway." She looked away. "Your *precious* firstborn."

"Jesse, no one can replace you in my heart."

"He doesn't even have to try, does he? He came first. He's got that on me forever. Even if you did give him away." She looked at her mother from beneath her lashes. "I guess I should be glad you didn't give me away, too."

The doorbell made them both jump.

As her daughter went to pick up her bag, she tried to snatch it from her. "Jesse, no!"

"You can't stop me, Mom. When you go to work, I'll just call a cab and catch the next flight."

"Then I won't go to work."

"Not ever? Not tomorrow or the next day, or the next?" Jesse's scorn underscored the ridiculousness of her position.

She began to shiver. "Jesse, baby, listen to me. I was sent away when I was your age. I thought it was for the best, too. But it wasn't. It was never the same at home again. Never!"

"You were sent away because you were in trouble. I haven't done anything! I'm not the one who destroyed our lives! Everybody has to take a backseat to what you want. Daddy even gave up his job for you. Moved to Dallas." Her chin began to tremble. "If we hadn't left Philly, maybe he'd still be alive."

"Jesse, you know that doesn't make any sense."

The doorbell rang a second time, followed by a brisk hard rap of knuckles on the wood.

She stared at her child. In her face she saw a reflection of her own youthful defiance and vulnerable pride that had made it possible for her to leave home at sixteen. "It will change things, Jesse. You don't know."

Jesse bit her lip, tears welling up over her lashes. "I know I don't want to be here. I don't want to be with you!"

She yanked her bag, and this time, her mother let it go. She half ran, half dragged the heavy bag to the door and flung it open. "I'm ready!" she said a little desperately to the driver and pushed through the door without even a backward look.

Don't think about it! Don't think about what's happening!

After the shuttle pulled away, she headed for her bedroom. She didn't wait for the person who answered the call to speak.

"I did not give my permission for her to go. I expect you to return her to me at once. Do you hear me? If you don't, I'll take legal action."

"Before you do that, Thea, I strongly suggest you take stock of exactly what you hope to accomplish by taking this young man into your family. More than that, what you think you are doing by exposing your daughter to the reality of your bad judgment at her age."

"That's pretty judgmental, Richard."

"We're only thinking of Jesse. You need to think about what you're doing. You made certain decisions when you married Evan. You owe Jesse the life her father would have seen to it she had."

"What life is that, Richard? A lily-white one?"

"You needn't be disdainful, dear." So Shirley had picked up, too. "After all, you are the one who chose to marry into our family."

"Yes, but your son chose to marry black."

"Well. I don't—"

"You don't know me, if you think I'll allow you to take my child. I will get her back!"

She hung up and sagged onto the bed, bending her head into her lap and wrapping her arms about her knees to try to keep the sobs from escaping.

She had allowed her own family to take one child away from her, for the best. She wasn't going to lose her daughter.

"Oh God, please help me! Help me get Jesse back. Please!"

She sat up and reached for the phone. She wasn't certain the numbers she punched in were the correct ones. She wasn't good at begging. She wasn't good at admitting she couldn't cope. She didn't even know what to ask for.

But when her call was picked up on the other end, the words came. "Please help me, Xavier. They've taken Jesse!"

thirty-five

SHE COULDN'T SIT still. She had been pacing for half an hour before the arrival gate for Xavier's flight from Atlanta. She had probably drawn the attention of airport security.

She caught her reflection in the plate glass window of a shop. She fit the profile of a suspicious character. She had scraped back her hair, pulled on a bulky sweater and jeans, and come to the airport an hour early to wait. It was better than sitting in the empty house. Better than pretending to work. Better than sitting by the phone, praying that Jesse would call her.

After she had received Xavier's return call to give her his flight information, she had called in sick at work, something she had never done before. A voice coarse with tears was a pretty good imitation for a sore throat she realized when Marcia turned instantly sympathetic and began giving advice.

She stepped aside as an adjoining gate flooded the walkway with new arrivals dressed for the season, many carrying gift-wrapped packages. So many smiling faces and so much laughter, waving, and cries of delight as arms opened wide to receive a welcome. Amid the crush of happy travelers, she felt like Scrooge. She resented the joy and warmth she was being denied.

The keening of jet engines drew her attention back to the right gate.

He was first off the plane. First-class travel had its privileges. She hung back, suddenly aware of the enormity of what she had done in calling him. Dressed all in black—leather jacket, turtleneck, and slacks—and carrying his own bag, he looked big and solid and dependable. Not like a celebrity or a mover and shaker backed by the money and power to get things done. But simply a man. Someone she could lean on, depend on, trust. She needed to trust him. Needed to share some of the burden of her life, if only for a little while, with him.

He stopped short of the main aisle, his gaze swinging back and forth over the heads of the crowd until he spied her. The look of concern on his face was all the reassurance she needed.

She plowed into his arms.

His arms closed tight about her, a convulsive clinch that nearly took her breath away. "Are you all right?"

"No." She gripped handfuls of his jacket and pressed her face against his chest. "I can't lose her, Xavier. I can't lose one more thing!"

"You won't lose her, Theadora. I promise you. And I'm here for you, for as long as you need me."

She leaned back in his arms. His gaze held equal amounts of the hurt and uncertainty pent up inside her. She was prepared to receive from him the spiritual assistance of a minister. She couldn't expect more. After all, she had ended their personal relationship in a way that had left him feeling less than friendly toward her. She had seen his professional sympathy at work when he sat with Beryl that night in the hospital. That would have to be enough.

"Are you sure you can spare the time? What about your church? It's—"

"*Shh,* now. Where are your car keys?" He took them from her. "Okay. First, we're going to get you home and calm you down, and then you're going to tell me everything that's been going on. After that, we'll decide what to do."

She nodded and took her arms from about him. Yet she couldn't move. She needed to say more, make him understand what it meant to her to have him here. He deserved that much. "Thank you for coming, Xavier."

He smiled. "My pleasure."

No, that wasn't what she wanted to say.

She rested a hand on his chest just above his heart. "I thought I'd run you off."

He wagged his head. "I'm not that easy to get rid of."

THE MAN HAD a sweet tooth. Xavier made sandwiches with butter and raspberry preserves and heated cups of cocoa with marshmallows. And he ate with an appetite she did not have.

It wasn't as if Jesse was technically missing, he said on the drive to her home. They didn't need to contact the police or set up a search party. She knew where Jesse was, and with whom, and that she would be safe and well cared for. What she needed was to get her bearings, eat something with energy in it, and then talk. Talk it all out.

But she couldn't get the words out to explain how she felt about all that had occurred in the past few months, and he didn't press. When he noticed she was shivering, he went and got the throw off the foot of her bed and wrapped it around her shoulders as she sat on the family room sofa. Then he went looking and found firewood and made a fire. He put on music, an old Roberta Flack release, nothing to remind her of the holiday that stretched before her in desolation.

But first, before any of that, he sat down beside her and took her hands in his, and with heads bowed together so close they touched, he prayed with her. For her. And Jesse. And, for the first time in a long time, she felt the real possibility in prayer.

She watched him moving around her home, as much at ease as if he had been here often and knew the when and how and where of things. When he came and sat on the opposite end of the sofa, he sloughed off his shoes and ran a hand over his face as if he could rub off the weariness.

She remembered then that he told her he had caught a red-eye out of New York the night before and had just arrived in Atlanta when she called. Here it was barely noon, and he was in Dallas.

"I shouldn't have asked you to come."

He smiled at her. "Tell me about Jesse."

She started by telling him about the afternoon before, the disaster of the tree-trimming party. Jesse's anger over the broken decorations. David's embarrassment.

He stopped her once, when the mention of David brought him up short. "He lives in Dallas?"

"Yes." Only so many lies she could tell anymore.

"And he came here, to help decorate your Christmas tree. But he still doesn't know about me?"

Her nod sobered him, but he didn't say another word about that.

"Jesse is much angrier than I guessed. She must have called her grandparents after I went to bed last night. Richard's call this morning came just minutes before the shuttle arrived. Everything was planned. I couldn't stop her."

"Maybe that's not a bad thing. Jesse took the initiative. Now she will have to find a way to come back."

"I don't know that she will. She's so hurt." She drew up her legs onto the sofa and wrapped her arms about them. "I don't blame her. All these years, I could have said something. But I didn't." She glanced at him for a reaction, but he didn't respond. "And then for her to overhear David announcing that he's my son!"

"Yeah. Tough break."

"Maybe I moved too fast, trying to draw David into our lives. He's angry as well, blames me for giving him away."

"You've been punishing yourself a long time." He looked at her long and hard. "Now you're afraid that you've driven Jesse away, because you know what that feels like."

She lifted her chin from her knees. "What?"

He leaned forward and laid a hand on her stockinged foot. "I know your parents sent you away when they found out you were pregnant."

She pulled her foot in, away from his comfort. "Who told you that?"

He lifted his hand and leaned back. "I called my uncle in Ruston last night. He told me you went to live with your aunt in New Orleans that Christmas. That would have been about the time you might have started showing to anyone who was looking. Your parents couldn't afford the scandal, not in their positions on campus. I'm right, aren't I?"

She looked away. "It wasn't that dramatic. I wasn't tarred and feathered first."

"Don't even try to duck this."

"You want to know? Fine." She let her feet slide back onto the floor. "My parents tried to cover up, but people hear things. Some of the kids even suspected about you and me. I wanted to leave to stop the talk. If my parents heard enough, they'd put two and two together, until they had a pretty good idea of what had happened. You were already a college football star, destined for greater things. Getting a girl pregnant could have ruined your career."

"You should have given me a chance to do the right thing."

She nodded. "I know you would have done the honorable thing. But it wouldn't have worked. You'd made it pretty clear by your silence that you weren't interested in me. I was afraid you'd grow to resent the baby and me. I left to save everybody."

He shook his head slowly. "After the pain I've caused you, how can you even stand to be in the same room with me?"

"It wasn't about you," she answered coolly. "My life. I handled it just fine."

"Yeah, because I didn't make that phone call."

The wall was up between them again. Good. Better in the long run.

"What do the Morgans think about your other child?"

"They said that under the circumstances, they thought it best if Jesse came to stay with them for a while. Until things smooth over."

"Nothing else?"

"Jesse told them I'm dating." She glanced at him. "They say that I have an obligation to finish rearing Jesse in the world in which her father lived."

"The white world?" His question was edged in the same offense hers had been.

"I can't be certain they meant it quite that way. But, yes, I took it that way. Which is unfair to Evan's memory."

"Is it?"

She could see anger seeping into his expression. "I won't defend Evan to you. I said that at the beginning."

His gaze locked with hers. "I'm not asking you to do that. I'm just wondering if you think your husband would have accepted—be honest—the idea of us."

She shut down an automatic back-off response. He was looking at her like he really wanted to know the answer.

She smiled faintly. "I doubt that as long as he had a say, Evan would have been happy with the idea of any other man in my life. But race wouldn't have come into it. He wasn't like that."

"His parents are like that."

A straight shooter, straight to the heart of the matter.

"I know it doesn't make sense. But when did prejudice ever make sense? So why should the lack of it?"

"I hear you." He seemed to relax deeper into the sofa cushions. "So then, what about Jesse? Clearly she doesn't like the idea of me."

"She doesn't know you."

"She doesn't want to."

"She's still grieving for her father. I can't blame her for not wanting to see another man in his place."

"In his bed?" He smiled. "She's old enough to have thought of that."

She ignored that. "I can't lose her, Xavier. If that means making sacrifices, I will. I can't lose another child."

"What are you going to do about it?"

She sat up straighter. "I'm going to catch the next flight to Philadelphia and talk to her. I won't make my father's mistake."

"You're going to have to explain that."

She told him about her visit to Aunt Della and the unraveling of the mystery of David's adoption, her father's distance, and her own shame. It was only when she was done that she realized she had given him a clue to find his son. She felt stupid. "So now you know."

He nodded. "I'm going to find him just as soon as I get the chance. But this is about you." He stood up. "Come on. You need some sleep. You don't look like you've had much of that lately."

"I need to make arrangements to go to Philly."

He took her arm to steady her as she stood. "Not today. Let Jesse stew overnight. By tomorrow, she should be good and worried about what she's done."

His words surprised her. "You think she'll regret it? I've made a lot of mistakes. Said and done the wrong things. I'm not sure she'll forgive me."

He took her shoulders in his hands, holding her just close enough so that she could feel the old tug between them, the one that time and experience and distance had never quite obliterated. "You don't give yourself enough credit. I'm here, aren't I?"

Nothing to say to that.

He steered her into her bedroom, where he undressed her as impersonally as if he was handling a child. And she let him because suddenly she was too weary, too tired to be strong, do the right thing, or reserve some semblance of self-reliance. When she was buttoned up in her pajamas, she felt as chaste as a child.

He sat her down on the bed and moved in behind her to massage her shoulders. He knew all the places where the kinks were, how to press and rub and knead them loose.

She was half asleep, her head and shoulders propped against his chest, when he finally spoke again, his lips near her ear.

"You've been holding out on everybody, Theadora."

"Hm?"

"You make it hard when it doesn't have to be."

Yes. Maybe.

"The question is, how can a man get close to a woman when she doesn't even know she needs him?"

She didn't reply. *I don't have the answers anymore. Not for me. Or you. Or anyone.*

His fingers slid slowly up the sides of her neck, into her hair, behind her ears, and cupped the weight of her head. "I'm not even certain I could ever have been what you needed *but* . . . It can't be all on my head, all the risks and choices and fault, if it didn't work out between us. You have to give something, anything, admit that you needed me . . . if only that."

But I may yet have to choose between you and Jesse. If I do, it won't be you. It can't be you.

* * *

SHE DIDN'T REALIZE she had company until she heard voices in the other room. She sat up in bed. Though the door to her bedroom was closed, Xavier's deep tone could not be mistaken. But who was that he was talking to? Beryl, maybe?

She swung her legs over the side of the bed and glanced at her clock. It was nearly five P.M. How could she have slept so long? Leaving Xavier to fend for himself. And why hadn't she heard the doorbell? She'd become a superlight sleeper since Evan's death. The first and last line of defense.

She used her toothbrush and ran a comb through her hair, and started to reach for her clothes just in case her visitor was someone she would have to explain—explain what? No more defending her life. It wasn't perfect. She wasn't perfect. So what?

Join the human race, Thea.

She tied a knot in the sash of her velvet robe, put a smile on her face, and opened the door. In the space it took her to separate the voices, her sense of reality went from ready for the world to did anyone get the license of the truck that ran me down?

They were sitting on her sofa with soft drink cans in hand. The smell of popped corn mingled with woodsmoke. In the background, the canned laughter of a TV sitcom underscored their pleasant conversation.

They stood up together when they saw her, wearing identical smiles. But Xavier was clearly the more relaxed. "Come and join us, Theadora. I'm just getting to know our son."

thirty-six

THE CABBY LOOKED back over her shoulder. "Looks like a party's going on."

Thea leaned forward for a better view of the Morgan residence. Evergreen swags and twinkle lights draped the two-story Georgian façade, a tasteful yet festive holiday welcome. The welcome was, no doubt, for the occupants of the line of cars moving in and out of the semicircular drive. Shirley hadn't said a word about a party.

Suitcase in hand, she made her way past guests dressed in furs and diamonds toward the brick and stone testament to the Morgans' wealth and influence. The first time she climbed these steps, she had felt very much out of place. Until that moment, Evan's blue-blooded lineage had been a source of amusement to her. Now, once again, the enormity of that advantage stared her in the face.

Hat in hand to the big house.

Not quite. But she was up against one of the Philadelphia Brahmins. Did Jesse understand the position she had put her mother in? Possession was nine-tenths of the law, and Jesse was voluntarily beneath this roof.

"At last." Shirley Morgan stood in the foyer wearing a full-length gown of silver bugle beads and gunmetal chiffon, the perfect complement to her blunt-cut silver hair. "Jessica expected you much earlier, dear."

An accusation already? How un-Morgan-like. "The flight was delayed."

"Yes. Richard said you called. You'll have to forgive us. We're entertaining a few special friends with holiday cheer." Tiny ripples rowed up on Shirley's brow. "You're welcome to join us, if you'd like."

"Why don't I just look in on Jesse?"

"Yes, of course." Shirley seemed to realize she had not greeted her daughter-in-law with the usual hug and kisses and quickly remedied the fact. Her lips, like her cheeks, were as cool as glass. "You're always welcome, dear."

She wasn't fooled. Shirley's gaze kept flitting to her guests and back. Did she fear her daughter-in-law might make a scene?

Get ethnic on her?

A memory of the phone call she'd placed right after Jesse left flashed through her mind. She had played the forbidden race card. Now it lay in the open between them, the joker in the deck of their relationship. Was that it? For the first time, Shirley Morgan was looking at Theodora Broussard Morgan and seeing a black woman.

Richard Morgan entered the foyer. Fit and still tan from their cruise, he looked particularly like his son tonight.

Only, Evan will never grow old and distinguished.

Spurred by a sharp pang of regret, she placed a real kiss on her father-in-law's cheek, embarrassing him.

He moved back to stand beside his wife. "You're looking well." Assessing character through physical cues was second nature to a banker. "You should know we've changed our plans to fly to Paris for Christmas so that we can be here for Jessica."

"That won't be necessary." She nodded at a couple skirting them. Contrary to their fears, she wasn't about to air family laundry in public. "I'd like to see my daughter."

"Jessica's staying in the east wing," Richard said. "Sarah will show you up."

"I know the way." She turned away and headed quickly for

the staircase. No uniformed maid was going to show her up to the bedroom she and Evan had shared for the first six months of their marriage.

And what was this business about calling her daughter Jessica? She'd been called Jesse since the day she was born. Whose idea to change, Jesse's or her grandparents'?

Resentment over being managed leavened the anger she thought she had flattened before heading east. Everybody thought they knew how she should behave: Jesse, Shirley and Richard, even Xavier.

He'd left the evening of the day he arrived, happier than when he'd come. But that had nothing to do with her.

She didn't know about David's call, because Xavier had thoughtfully turned off the bedside phone while she slept. Thinking Jesse might call, he had picked up every ring. When David identified himself, he invited him over, then introduced himself as David's father. All of it before she could intercede on either behalf.

The look of amazed joy on David's face when she found them together said it all. His birth father was none other than "X" Savior Thornton, a man whose career he had followed practically from diapers. Even David's adoptive father was a fan. She couldn't have made up a better ending to his story.

Nothing for her to do, after all. Nothing to say. What happened between them was no longer her responsibility. She was right back where she started, almost.

Xavier might still be there for her, but it wasn't the same as it had been in D.C., and they both felt it.

The least of my problems!

The announcement for the restructuring of Petro Chem had been set back until after the first of the year. Rumor said corporate was still wrangling over a new position. Ron was out with the flu and couldn't be pumped for information, but instinct told her it was her position that was in doubt. Not the best time to take two personal days in the same week. She hoped to blunt her absence by hopping a train to Manhattan to meet with a ship broker after she left Philly. Unless Jesse wanted to go straight home.

The second floor was much quieter than the first. The live

string quartet playing Mozart could scarcely be heard once she turned into the east wing.

She knocked on the second door, then opened it and stuck her head in. "Hi."

"Hi." Jesse sat curled up on a love seat before a TV, which she returned to watching after a brief glance at her mother.

Okay. What did I expect? A brass band?

The large bedroom looked just as it had when she lived here: daffodil yellow walls with glossy white woodwork and bright English floral drapes and bed hangings. The "hothouse," Evan called the décor.

She was amazed to realize she was nervous. Tension stretched from her neck to her fingertips as she put down her bag.

"Your dad and I always thought this room was kind of drafty in winter. We used to roll up bath towels and put them by the doors at night."

Jesse hunched a shoulder, not looking away from the TV.

Okay, I'm talking about the wrong things. "You know why I'm here, Jesse."

Jesse twisted around on the sofa to face her mother, hugging one of the decorative pillows like a lifeline. "PopPop says I don't have to go home if I don't want to."

She clamped down on the response that came to her lips. A new sense of vulnerability made her vibrate. A parent could only push so far a child who had learned the power of independence. Even if it was only in flight to another adult.

She noticed the open physics book by Jesse's foot. "I called your counselor and told her we had a family emergency. She says that when you return, you'll have to talk to each of your teachers. If they each agree, you can take your final exams right after the holidays. If not, you'll have to repeat some classes in summer school."

Jesse's expression turned sullen. "PopPop says he can get me into private school here in the East. A really important one that will open doors to places like Harvard."

There's no place like Harvard. Richard and Shirley were playing for keeps.

She sat down beside Jesse, who drew herself in to keep from being touched. "This sounds good to you?"

Jesse looked down. "I didn't say that . . . exactly."

She took her first easy breath. "Why don't we just start over? Come home, and then you can think about what it is you do want."

Jesse leaned back and folded her arms. "What about David?"

She had made the self-promise not to make demands. "I know you're angry, and not without cause, but I need to make you understand some things, Jesse. The reasons why I can't allow you to do what I did."

Jesse smirked. "I'm not going to get pregnant."

"I'm talking about running away from your problems."

Thea fanned her hands across her face. This might be her last chance to get through to a daughter who didn't share her regrets in hindsight. That meant telling it like it was.

"My parents were what we called pillars of the community. Highly respected. It didn't mean much to me until I was about your age. That's when I found out that kind of respect was the kiss of death to guys' interest in a girl."

"They thought you were too good for them?"

"Something like that. But knowing why doesn't make a girl feel any better about sitting home."

Jesse shrugged. "So what did you do about it?"

A vision of Jesse and Keith on the sofa flashed through her thoughts. How much truth should a mother tell her hormone-laced teen? "The summer I was sixteen, this college student from Chicago came to town to work. We met at a party. He was a good dancer and very smart, what we used to call 'deep.' "

Jesse sniffed. "He sounds full of himself."

"That was part of the attraction. My parents said he was too old for me. So we just talked, and sometimes he'd tease me, saying when I grew up he might ask me out."

"Guys always say dumb stuff like that." Jesse's lips twisted. "Like that's supposed to make you feel better. So what happened?"

"A few days before he was to leave, he told me about this juke joint over near Monroe where a lot of Grambling college students went to party. I said I'd love to go. He dared me to figure out a way, and he'd take me. So I sneaked out to meet him."

"Wow!"

She could see her story was taking on an outlaw glamour for Jesse. Maybe she was remembering things a little too well. "It was dark and smelly. Full of sweating bodies, liquored-up voices, and so much cigarette smoke the air looked like gauze. At least it chased away the mosquitoes."

Xavier bought me my first beer and then we danced and danced until the stars went out, as my mother liked to say.

If we'd gone straight home it might have been all right. But I knew he was leaving. I had this ache for him, so bad it hurt. And I wanted him to kiss it away.

Strange to think about it now, think about all the consequences of what had seemed at the time *nobody's business if we do!*

"It was light enough to see the paperboy coming down the street when I slipped back through my bedroom window."

Jesse stared at her mother as though she was seeing another person. "You never talked to me like this before, like I was old enough to understand things."

"Sometimes I forget that you're almost grown. Forgive me?"

"So what happened next?"

"The next day, I learned he'd gone back to Chicago a day early."

"Without saying good-bye?"

"Yes." Telling the truth required reliving the humiliations. "Almost three months later, I realized I was pregnant."

Jesse frowned. "You really loved him, huh?"

"Yes. Love can make you feel like you are the most special person on the planet. But that won't keep you safe, Jesse. In the end, I had to face alone what I'd done."

Jesse gnawed her lip. "Were your parents mean to you?"

"No. They were angry and hurt, but they tried to protect me. Turning up pregnant without a husband in those days wasn't a feminist statement or an optional lifestyle. The shame could ruin lives. So they sent me to live with Aunt Della, then arranged for the baby to be given up for adoption."

"That's pretty cold, making you have the baby and then give it away."

"They did what they thought was best." Aunt Della's words. She shook her head. Couldn't think about that betrayal again just yet. "But it changed everything. I was ashamed of what I'd done and too proud to ask to come home. And so I stayed with Aunt Della until I went off to college. All the rest of my life since, I've wished I'd gone home."

But Jesse seemed hung up on another thought. "So, David's father never knew about him?"

The last piece of the puzzle. "Not until recently."

"You told him?" Jesse's expression darkened. "When?"

She took a deep breath. It was just as hard to tell Jesse as it has been David's father. "David's father is Xavier Thornton."

Jesse absorbed the shock with a blink. Then her emotional interest collapsed into a flat stare. The condemnation in her daughter's eyes was a terrible price for honesty.

"You lied to me! You lied to Daddy, too, didn't you?"

"No. Your father knew about David before we married. I wouldn't keep that from the man who loved me."

"You're still in love with him, aren't you?"

She felt the sting of her own unhappiness. "It's difficult to explain—"

A No Sale sign went up behind Jesse's gaze. "Mom, how can you love the man who messed up your life?"

The question deserved as good an answer as she could provide. "I messed up my life, Jesse. Xavier was the reason, not the cause."

"How long have you been seeing him?"

She didn't have to ask what Jesse meant. "Until Selma's wedding, we hadn't seen one another or spoken in twenty-six years."

Righteous indignation flashed in her just-like-Daddy's blue eyes. "What if he'd come back into your life when Daddy was alive? How would you feel?"

"I loved your dad as much as I know how to love anybody." That felt like a truth she didn't have to wrestle with.

"So then your feelings for Reverend Thornton are no big deal?"

Just say no. Xavier's a lost cause, anyway.

The temptation to lie settled over her like a familiar quilt made of a patchwork of reasonable excuses and beneficial results. Why not raise her daughter's hopes and get her to come home? But her new willingness to tell the truth, no matter the consequences, was not quite smothered.

"Relationships aren't math, Jesse. Only so much love to go round. Someone's got to be subtracted so someone can be added. Come home, and we'll talk about it."

"I'll come home if you promise not to see Reverend Thornton."

The offer on the table would alter their positions as mother and child forever.

"I have a question for you, Jesse. I want you to think about it a while, because I'm not certain you know the answer. Why don't you want me to see him? Is it because of your dad's memory? Or is this about what you said the morning you left? That you don't want people to know you're part black?"

Jesse ducked her head.

"Because if that's it, it has nothing to do with Xavier or David. It *is* a fact of your life. Nothing I do or don't do will change that."

Jesse looked cornered. "I know. I just need to think about . . . things."

"It's almost Christmas, Jesse. What about Christmas?"

She glanced sideways at her mother. "PopPop's getting me a car for Christmas."

Too angry to speak, she rose and moved to pick up her bag. "Where are you going?"

"To New York. I have a business meeting in the morning." Surprise lifted Jesse to her feet. "What about me?"

"Come with me. Right now. You don't even have to pack." Jesse shook her head. "I said I need to think."

She hoped her expression didn't reveal her desperation. "You belong with me, Jesse. I'm your mother. And I'll always love you. No matter what."

Out in the hallway, her knees begin to shake. She had pushed Jesse. Maybe too hard. Yet she hadn't said anything but the truth. If Jesse couldn't handle it, well then, maybe she did belong here in Philly.

She closed her eyes. *Please God, don't let that be the answer.*

"There she is, the one the only Ms. Morgan herself!"

She frowned at the man coming down the hallway toward her. "Phillip."

He flashed a smile as classy as his tux. "Good, you're still speaking to me."

"That depends on what you have to say." She should have suspected he'd be among the Morgans' group of friends.

He offered her a rueful glance. "I've given it some thought, and I'm now positive that last summer was my worst moment as a suitor. Ever."

"You must have a long list to choose from." Why was she just now noticing that he, like Selma, never apologized?

"I hear you didn't waste any time replacing me."

That was when she noticed it. Phillip was looking at her oddly. As if, like the Morgans, he had never really had her in Technicolor focus before. She wasn't going to apologize for that or explain.

"The party's downstairs. Why are you wandering the east wing?"

"The Morgans asked me to have a private word with you before you came down."

Like ice water in the face. "I know how to behave among the civilized, Phillip."

"Sharp-tongued as ever." He smiled. "They just need time to adjust, Thea."

"And *I* need to have my daughter home with me."

The snap in her voice cracked his *bonhomie*. "You've changed."

"No. You've just never seen me really angry before."

"About Jessica." He nodded solemnly. "I see your side, I do. But Evan's parents have needs, too. She's their only heir. They need to have contact with her. See her."

"Jesse has always been free to visit them, and they can certainly come and see her. But not without my express consent."

"They've never required your consent before."

"That was because they had my unconditional trust. They broke it by encouraging Jesse to run away."

"I don't like saying this to you, but they felt they had no

choice. Jessica was traumatized by . . . certain revelations." He paused in expectation she would now want to explain her side.

She did not.

"It isn't inconsistent with reason that in this instance they sought to put concerns for their grandchild above considerations of her mother."

That was just short of legalese. "Have they retained your services, Phillip?"

"Oh no." His smile could ice cake. "I'm acting strictly as family go-between."

But she had seen that credulous look before. Phillip might be a good attorney. Evan was better. "In case they do retain you, you should know they've told Jesse, a minor, that she doesn't have to obey her mother. They've offered her a free ride to prep school, dangled Harvard before her. Even promised her a car. A car I refused her! That's nothing short of bribery, which I doubt will play well in court." She waited a beat. "But it's not going to come to that. Is it?"

Phillip seemed about to say something but then gave a tiny shake of his head.

"And tell them her name is Jesse. That's what her father called her."

It took all she had not to turn back to Jesse's room and drag her out. Instead, she concentrated on putting one foot in front of the other until she was out the front door.

She felt a little sick. She didn't have to take legal action. The Morgans already had.

thirty-seven

"THEADORA, THIS IS Aunt Della, in N'awlins. Where are you, child? I've been calling and calling all this holiday week. Now, you phone me—no matter how late—when you get this message. I'm sure between us we'll think of something."

There was a rustling sound, then her aunt's voice, this time much fainter. "Of course, I'm certain I have the right number, Oleatha. I just hope her machine is recording." Another rustle, then she spoke directly into the mouthpiece again. "Theadora, don't forget."

She punched the button to erase the third message from her aunt. Della had been leaving messages for three days. The first two were invitations to join her aunt for Christmas in New Orleans since "You've nothing to do but ramble about in that too-big house all alone, feeling sorry for yourself."

She almost hung up on the final message, but this time, Aunt Della sounded very subdued, as though she were sick or had been crying. All she said was, "Child, child, the ways of the world are sometimes troubling. Selma needs our help. But this, too, shall pass. I promise you that."

She checked the clock. It was half an hour past her aunt's

usual bedtime. She didn't feel much like giving a repeat performance for her aunt of her failure with Jesse. And what was that about Selma? Aunt Della wasn't above a bit of subterfuge when she felt it was required. She knew that last snippet was bound to rouse curiosity. Her hand covered over the receiver. Was she being suckered in?

Be a touch more selfish, guilty as it makes you feel, and wait until tomorrow to call.

She picked up before the first ring was complete. "Hello?"

"How's my lady tonight?"

My lady! The way Xavier said it, soft and low, went all over her. "I'm fine, Xavier." *Back in love at the sound of his voice. I'm pathetic!*

"Did you go to Philly?"

"Yeah."

"That sounds like you've got a story to tell."

"It wasn't the easy victory I had hoped for." Running to Xavier with her problems was getting to be habit. A habit she couldn't afford without bankrupting her emotional life. Still, she recounted as succinctly as she could the scene that had greeted her.

"They have no legal standing," Xavier said in response to her final concern. "Grandparents don't have legal rights."

"There's always the accusation of unfit mother."

"Do you really think they'd take it that far?"

She shrugged, though she knew he couldn't see the gesture. "I can't quite believe Jesse won't be home for Christmas."

"You don't know that for certain. It's still three days off."

She leaned into the sound of his voice offering comfort in every syllable. If he were here, she'd be in his arms. Hard to remember to keep a distance. "Everybody's offering advice. They all seem to think they have a right to make demands on how I live my life."

"Is that why you live so secretly?"

"What is that supposed to mean?"

"You live undercover, Theadora. Did you ever intend to tell Evan's parents about me? Tell anybody about us?"

She looked about for something to divert her attention from the emotion welling up inside her. "We had this conversation."

"No. We were fighting. I can see why you didn't tell your parents all those years ago. You were just a scared kid. But if you had, you got to know my uncle would have come straight up the highway to Chicago with the news."

"That's why." She kicked off her shoes, watching them bounce across the carpet as she spoke. "I didn't want a man somebody had to force on me."

"What about the child? I might have wanted my child."

That was one scenario she had not thought of. Her turn to be silent as she recalled Cherise saying how their parents had adopted two children into an already full house. Surely David would have been as welcome.

"You really didn't trust me at all, did you?" Xavier sounded burdened by that realization.

"Maybe I made a mistake." *Don't let him get to you!* She leaned out to punch on the radio. "I seem to be making a lot of them lately."

"And I haven't said thank you."

She found WRR on the dial. Barber's Adagio for Strings. "For what?"

"My son." She could feel the smile in his voice curl inside her. "God is good, Theodora. David's a fine young man. Smart and respectful. And his spirit is bright! Tells me he's a youth director at his church there in Dallas. And he's got a serious lady friend. Of course you know all about that."

"No." *I don't know him.*

"He's coming to Atlanta for Christmas." He chuckled. "Now, why didn't I think of that before? You should be here, too."

"What?" She pushed her hair back from her forehead as though it was in the way of her understanding.

"We need time together. Time we figured out what we've got going here."

I don't even know what we had. So what could we have now?

"I can't." She fiddled with the latch on her watch. "Jesse may decide at the last minute to come home for Christmas."

"Okay. I see that. But we owe us another chance. Promise to come soon. Before the New Year." His voice dropped into a deep, low register. "I need you. Need to hold you. All night."

The thought occurring to her was not one she was ready to

admit to. He might forgive her, after all. *I need to hold you, too. All night.*

"I know what you're thinking, Theadora, because you think way too much for my peace of mind. So here's the deal. I'm here for you now. Let's just go on."

She looked at the clock and away from the plea in that persuasive voice. "I think that our being together now would be a mistake."

"Don't say that. I'm serious about us, lady. You know that. Serious."

The slight catch in his voice was all it took. The room emptied of distractions, the flash of clarity brilliant in its insight. Suddenly, the indecision of months was gone. She knew the answer.

She cupped the receiver with her free hand. "It's tainted, Xavier. Now that you know about David, neither of us will again ever be certain whether our feelings are mixed with belated guilt or even an attempt to do the honorable thing."

"Seems like I was courting you before I knew about David."

"We were grooving on a lot of old memories, playing on what might have been, teasing ourselves with possibilities we didn't have to make good on."

"Is that what you were doing?" Doubt made the question skip on the LP of his baritone.

"Yes." Only half a lie. "You said it not long ago. Everything in your life has been easy come, easy go."

"There was never anything easy about us. Ever."

Ain't that the beautiful truth. "It's not about us anymore."

"I don't believe that."

"Then ask your sisters to explain it to you, if they haven't tried already."

The familiar, considering silence. "I guess this conversation is over."

After he hung up, she sat on the edge of her bed, staring at the even vacuum trails on her bedroom carpet. Her brain was in neutral because she didn't even want to set in motion the emotional roller coaster waiting at the beginning of her first thought.

How many times can a woman be a fool over the same man?

Suddenly she understood all those he-done-me wrong-but-I-can't-get-over-him songs of loss. The "Stormy Weather," "Blue Monday," so-tore-down-I-can't-even-think-about-gettin'-up wallows in self-pity. More fundamental than grief, the blues had a hold of her.

She was letting go of a good man, a decent man, a man for whom love had led her to do the most dishonest things in her life. For him she had alienated her parents, left her home, traded her reputation, and given up her child. Being with him again had jeopardized the most precious thing that remained, Jesse. How could the right thing for her be so wrong for everyone else in every other way?

Yet decisions had a way of building their own scaffolding from a foundation of self-reasoning. Letting go of Xavier felt like letting go, period.

She slid the wedding band from her finger, kissed it, and rose to put it in the smaller of her jewelry boxes, the velvet-lined one that held her best gold jewelry, diamond earrings, and engagement ring.

He left me. She had to remember it that way. Otherwise, nothing she had done would ever again make sense.

But I did love him.

thirty-eight

SHE SAT STRAIGHT up in bed as the warning signal of the security alarm went off. She grabbed her robe as she heard the beeping sounds of a code being punched in. The intruder knew her code. Could it be—?

She flew into the hallway just as the light was flipped. "Jesse?"

"Oh Jesus!" Beryl spun around, a hand to her heart. "Thea, is that you?" She blew out her cheeks in relief. "Girlfriend, you about scared the fool outta me. What are you doing here in the dark? You're supposed to be in Philly."

"I didn't go." She turned away, hoping Beryl wouldn't see the crush of disappointment in her expression. *Not Jesse. Might never be Jesse coming through the door again.* "Why are you here?"

"Cassandra came in just now and said she saw a light go on and off in your window as she passed." She looked toward the dark living room where the tree stood still only half decorated and then back at Thea. "Since you're supposed to be out of town until after Christmas, I thought I'd better come over here and check."

Thea looked back, her expression as blank as she could make it. "Thanks, but I'm back."

"I can see that." Beryl folded her arms. "You want to tell me why I didn't know that?"

She didn't. Didn't want anybody to know why she was hiding out in her own home. But it was bound to come out now. "Jesse ran away."

"Uh-huh." Beryl shot her friend a doubtful glance. Thea knew she was taking in her wrinkled dressing gown and unkempt hair. "You been drinking? Girlfriend, you don't want to be slipping down that slippery slope. But *wait* a minute. I thought Jesse went to Philly to look after a sick grandparent?"

"I lied." The words were starched with shame.

Beryl's eyes bucked wide. "You mean she ran away for real? Have you called the cops?"

"No." Though there wasn't a scrap of humor in the moment, she smiled slightly. "It's a long story. You got time for a cup of coffee?"

"I got time for whatever it takes to get this story straight."

"GRRRRL! YOU'RE FULL of more surprises than a case of Cracker Jack!"

She was getting accustomed to the I-don't-know-who-you-are-anymore stare that was now Beryl's gaze.

"Now let me get this right. You had 'X' Savior's baby? Gave him away. And Daddy never knew about it until Son found you just a few weeks ago?"

She nodded.

Beryl sat back with a sigh that blew out her cheeks like Dizzy about to attack his horn. "You got to know that's a lot to take in."

"You don't believe me?"

"Oh, I believe you all right." Beryl wagged her head back and forth. "The way he looked at you the night he came to the hospital. Deeper than lust. That stuck with me, even before I knew a thing. And he didn't even know you'd had his child then?"

"No." She stirred her mostly empty cup.

"And here comes the reverend tipping back into your life, not knowing he's about to be tripped up by his past." Beryl chuckled. "I'm *too* through with soaps. I can just catch the latest episode of *As Thea's World Turns*." She turned serious on the instant. "You know, you should have told him."

"I tried, Beryl. Several times these last months, but he didn't want to hear it. Said our pasts belong where they were, behind us."

Beryl nodded. "Men. They think they can control everything. That aside, what you did, hiding it at the time, that was wrong. I can't say I blame you for not saying anything later."

"I've turned it ten ways from Sunday. I thought I was protecting everybody. Then when Jesse found out..." Thea's folded hands blossomed in a helpless gesture. "I thought I could still make things okay for everybody."

Beryl leaned forward. "What did you do?"

She continued her story, feeling a strange objectivity from the narration of the Christmas tree disaster. She finished up with, "After David left, Jesse called her grandparents, who bought her a ticket to Philly."

"I can't even believe that. I'd like to see Cassandra even try.... I'd ..." Beryl's thoughts seemed to jam together, damming up her speech for a moment. She stood up. "Get your coat! We're going to snatch that child back before they fill her head with so much trash she won't ever get straight!"

"I went. She won't come back."

Beryl stared at her for a long time before she subsided back into her chair. "You've got a real problem."

There's a time and place for family, for husbands and lovers, sisters and mothers. And then there's the kind of misery that's best shared in the arms of a girlfriend. The sister-to-sister, woman-to-brokenhearted-woman connection that's close enough to feel like blood and yet that critical step removed so that a body can wail out her misery like a banshee without fear of being misunderstood, ridiculed, or judged for letting her feelings show.

"You know it's going to be okay. You got to believe that, Thea. Pray for that." Beryl pushed her gently back into her chair and then began wiping the tears from her friend's face with her fingertips. "Enough of this pity party. You got a fight on your hands. Can Xavier help you? He's got lots of connections. Get you the best lawyer."

"No." Thea wiped her own face with the heel of a hand. "I can't ask anything of him."

"Why not? How mad is he?"

"The kind with a seal spelled C-L-O-S-U-R-E. I broke it off between us."

Beryl began to chuckle and offered her a high five, a low five, and two snaps. "Now I know you're a sister! That's fierce!" She rocked so far back in her breakfast chair that the two rear wooden legs squeaked on the tile. "Handed the man his papers. That must mean he still thought there was something worth walking worthy for. You go, girl! Make him earn it!"

She didn't even try to answer that. Every bit of fight had leaked out of her in that good long cry. She didn't believe one hang-up made an ending with a man like Xavier, either. He was angry, and angry was keeping her phone from ringing. For that she was grateful. Jesse was all she could think about.

"THEA, IS THAT you?"

"Selma?" She was sitting with a final cup of coffee after Beryl left when the phone rang. "Why are you whispering?"

"Listen, I don't have much time. I need your help."

"What's wrong? You sound sick." Call waiting beeped in.

". . . not sick, girl. Scared! Some things have been jumping off around here you wouldn't believe."

"What kind of things?"

"I—" She heard through the phone line the sound of a door opening and then Selma's husky voice rose to an F-sharp as she turned away from the receiver.

"Oh, hi, baby. Just talking to my sister. Of course, I'm serious. You want to say hi? Okay." Another beep. ". . . ready in a minute."

It sounded like Selma's chin collided with the receiver and then she said, "So you'll be here the day after Christmas? Right? I'll meet you at the airport." She added in a quick whisper, "I can't talk."

"Selma . . . Damn!"

Typical of Selma to be silent for months and then call when she was going through one of her periodic my-life-is-shit upheavals. That usually meant man trouble. Elkeri trouble?

She ticked off four months on her fingers. "If this is another divorce . . ."

She punched the flash button on her phone for a dial tone, intending to call her sister back, and got a pulsing one. She had a message. She keyed in her code.

"Mom?" For several seconds, there was just the hiss of an open line. "I . . . I just wanted to talk."

She didn't even wait to erase the message but pressed the button and then keyed in the Morgans' number.

She chewed her lip while Shirley went in search of Jesse. An hour seemed to have passed before she heard her daughter's very subdued voice say, "Hi, Mom."

"Hi, baby. I'm so glad you called. How are you?"

"Mom, I just want . . . Mom, can I come home?"

She felt her heart expand so quickly it seemed like it would burst. "Oh, Jesse, I need you to come home. You get on the first plane home, and we'll work everything else out."

"Promise?"

"Promise!"

thirty-nine

"LOOKING SO SMART. Doesn't Selma look smart?" Della encouraged, brushing her hand lightly over the arm of her niece's gray fox stroller as they emerged from the Atlanta terminal into an almost balmy day with Jesse and Thea bringing up the rear.

"Now, Aunt Della, this isn't even my good coat." Selma hugged her three closest relatives in turn. If she noticed Jesse's impersonal embrace, she didn't comment.

"You've grown up since the last pictures your mom sent!" Selma motioned her niece back with a flip of her fingertips. "Turn around, Pumpkin. Let me see you."

Frowning, Jesse did a quick, self-conscious pirouette.

"Look at those big legs." Selma pulled open Jesse's jacket. "Tits and an itty-bitty waist. Huh, huh, Miss *Thang*. The boys must be jumping off around your house."

"Not that much." Jesse aimed a pointed glance at her mother that reflected their most recent discussion. The Morgan women had agreed to swear off men for thirty days. Keith and Xavier were both off limits.

Selma's dark gaze flicked between the pair. "Your mom

knows best. A woman needs to learn how to handle herself before she goes trying to handle men."

Jesse's expression slid into sulky. "My soccer coach says if you want to get better at something, you have to practice."

Selma laughed, an unexpected earthy sound that turned heads, most of them male. "You better not be practicing anything with any boy!"

Only then did Selma turn her attention to Thea, and Thea felt her chest tighten up in what seemed an unwarranted response to sisterly perusal. Selma had enough ammunition to make this trip a miserable exercise. "Looking good, Sis. You lost some weight?"

"A pound or two." *Five, to be exact.* That was definitely an exercise in misery, too sad to eat.

It wasn't as if Thea hadn't already learned that life was unpredictable. But these days, it was downright surreal. Here on the Saturday after Christmas, she was sharing the sidewalk with the three women responsible for making her life difficult.

At least Jesse had agreed to come with her.

She had already been musing on the idea of getting Jesse out of the house, where for the past two days unanswered phone calls from Philly seem to come in on the hour. God bless the creator of caller ID!

Jesse hadn't offered a reason for her sudden change of heart, and Thea was too glad to have her daughter home to probe the reason just yet. Even so, it was clear there had been a problem. Each time the phone rang, the corners of Jesse's blue eyes tightened. Then an excuse presented itself in the form of a call from Aunt Della the day after Christmas.

"Something's wrong with Selma, Theadora, and she won't say what. I'm packing. We simply must go to Atlanta and find out."

That was no royal *we.* *It was a you and me.* After a change of flights in New Orleans to pick up Della, here they were.

She'd made a decision since the Philly debacle. From now on, Jesse would be as much a part as possible in the messy affair she called her family. That included *The Good, the Bad and the Ugly.*

She fell into step beside her sister, searching her expression for clues. "Where's Elkeri?"

"Oh, we had a fight." Selma answered quickly and began digging in her purse like it was a duffel bag. It was no bigger than a paperback.

"What kind of fight?"

"The usual kind." Selma rolled her head on her neck as she glanced back at Jesse. "Don't ever let any man disrespect you, I don't care if he is your husband. Got me so mad I had to tear up some stuff."

"Isn't that how you lost your Lladro collection?" Della questioned in concern.

Selma pursed her lips. "I'll never know why I ever dated that fool in the first place. Tripped trying to duck my shoe. Broke several thousand dollars' worth of figurines. The most expensive gash he'll ever get! Some of those pieces were signed!"

Thea looked at Jesse, wondering if her rush to *G, B and U* territory was about to swerve into regret. "Aunt Selma doesn't throw shoes anymore, though, do you?" she encouraged with a quick glance at her sister.

"You got that right. I made a vow that very day. Nothing breakable. Like Mama."

"What *are* you talking about?"

"Don't you remember? Mama only threw the soft stuff. Paper towels, oven mitts, boxes of cling wrap. Never china or crystal. The drama's just as good, and there's nothing to break. The best thing is a handful of spoons 'cause they're noisy and bounce good but won't nick up the floors. Never throw knives or forks." Selma's voice held the conviction of experience.

"Then what happened?" Jesse asked.

"Then I started on his closet. Like I was packing for him. By the time I finished tossing around underwear and shoes and ties, he was offering to clean up the mess for me. And I let him. Making me so crazy I had to do all that mess just to get his attention!"

"I take it the fight's over, and you made up?" Thea didn't like the admiring expression on Jesse's face, and this time she directed her glance toward Della.

Selma made an impressive spin on one stiletto heel in the

middle of the crossing lane. "You won't believe what that sweet man up and did for my Christmas. Bought me a new car! A silver 911 Carrera coupe! Only two years old and got less than twenty-four thousand miles rolled up on it."

An impatient honk punctuated the statement.

Undeterred, Selma pulled a pile of snapshots out of her fur coat pocket and she waved them in Jesse's direction. "Take a look, Pumpkin. My Christmas present from the finest, kindest husband in the world!"

Thea accepted the inch-thick pile of snaps one at a time from her daughter as they finished crossing. Selma had taken a dozen shots of the Porsche from all angles, including several of her stretched out across the hood. In the background of one, Elkeri could be seen smiling like a husband who knew he was about to reap one hundred ways of his wife's gratitude.

Aunt Della caught her eye and nodded as if to say, *You see?*

Thea did see, all too well. Selma had had a fight with her new husband, displaced three relatives during the holidays, and now it was over. She and Della didn't know the why of any of it. And probably never would.

"So where is it?" Thea asked when Selma led them to a Cadillac Escalade.

"Girl, you must be tripping, thinking I'd park my new car in a public lot. Elkeri loaned me his ride. Besides, there's no place for luggage in a coupe."

"WELL. WELL. WELL. Your son is in the family." Selma was propped up against the headboard of her four-poster mahogany bed in the master bedroom. "And here I am, as usual, just now hearing about it."

"It wasn't common gossip, Selma."

Right after lunch, Aunt Della had excused herself to begin her daily beauty-rest nap. In her just-short-of-a-sulk attitude, Jesse had taken a book up to the roof of the penthouse to indulge in a rare opportunity to December sunbathe. Left alone, Thea thought it was time to share a bit more about David with Selma, who would hear about it sooner or later. Listening to her now, she wished she'd chosen door number two.

Selma placed her blue bottle of water on the mud cloth covering the bedside table, then ran a hand through her new bob. Her gaze flicked Thea's way. "You going to tell me who's the daddy now?"

This deep-dive breathing was getting to be second nature. "His father is your minister."

"My *what?*" Selma's bug-eyed amazement turned sourball bitter. "Girl, you had me tripping for a second. So don't tell me. Like I could care less!"

Thea smiled slightly. It wasn't often anything flustered Selma. "Do you remember the guy from Chicago who came to work in Mr. Dickerson's law office the summer I was sixteen?"

"Not really. I was only, what, eleven?"

"Yes. Well, Mr. Dickerson's nephew is Xavier Thornton."

Selma seemed to be doing a lot of quick thinking. "You expect me to believe you could have attracted 'X' Savior in his wild days? Girl, you got a flat ass!"

"I love you, too." The who's-the-daddy conversation was over. Just as well.

Half a dozen silver bracelets tinkled as Selma pointed at the chignon at the back of her sister's head. "And when are you gonna let a real stylist do you a def do?"

Thea touched her hair defensively. "A woman in my position has to look serious to be taken seriously."

"You always did worry too much about what the man thinks. Let me call Simon. It's Saturday, but he'll work you in, as a favor to me."

"No, really, Selma—" She sighed as her sister picked up the phone.

Having one's hair done, one of the few rites of passage left a woman, had never held much appeal.

At age fourteen and against her parents' wishes, she cut her own hair in an attempt to wear an Afro. Her hair was too soft. It wouldn't hold the woolly shape required. No matter how much back-combing and pounds of Aquanet went into it, any passing breeze was enough to make huge canyons in her efforts. A friend suggested she wash her hair in Cheer to strip out all the oil. That only made it impossible to comb.

In defeat, she allowed her mother to drag her to Mrs. Saunders, her mother's beautician. True to her time, the woman tackled her frizz with the universal tamer of black hair, the hot comb. The first curl instantly fried and dropped off the iron onto the floor.

Swiping away the stench of singed hair from her nose, the astonished Mrs. Saunders had said defensively, "I just don't know, Mrs. Broussard. Though it surely curls black, your daughter's got white hair. It's too soft for grease and too fine for hot combs. Best grow it out again and keep it that way."

To this day, the smell of overheated hair made her queasy.

Selma hung up with a tiny crease between her brows. "Simon's off on a cruise for the holidays. And he didn't even tell me. Just wait until I see him!"

"I didn't come to get my hair done. You sent for me. What's wrong?"

Selma's dark gaze engaged hers for a moment, but she did not respond directly. "You're always ready with answers, aren't you? Think you know best."

Thea held her temper. "We're family. When you need help, you turn to family."

Selma went limp. "Yes, well, I hope being a family is all that. Because I forgot by a day to get my pills renewed after our honeymoon and . . ."

"You're pregnant?"

Blushing in confusion, Selma looked almost like a little girl again. "Can you believe that? I almost couldn't fit in these pants."

"Congratulations!"

"Look out, you're crushing me." She pushed her sister's hug away. "And you can just keep your congratulations. I don't know that I'll be needing them."

"Why? What does Elkeri say?"

Selma gave her a blank look.

"You haven't told him?"

Selma reached for her water bottle. "I'm not sure there'll be anything to tell."

"You can't be thinking of not having it."

Selma slanted a hard look at her. "You can't talk. You didn't keep David. Why didn't you just get rid of the baby instead of having it?"

Thea hesitated. There were several answers. Abortion wasn't legal. The illegal kind was dangerous. In either case, she was too far along by the time she understood her situation for it to have been simple. But none of that had come into it. "I never thought of it. If you're scared about the pregnancy, let's talk. I was—"

Selma held up her hand. "This wasn't supposed to happen. Not yet. I shouldn't have mentioned it."

"Is that why you called me, to ask for help in making a decision?"

"You can't fix this. And I haven't asked you to try!"

"You brought me into your business."

"Now I'm telling you to butt the hell out!"

Thea put a hand on her hip, feeling a long-ago playground attitude coming up to the surface. "So what? You're saying you're not going to keep the child of the man you married?" An ugly suspicion struck her. "Doesn't Elkeri want children?"

Selma gave her an are-you-a-fool look.

"Then I don't get it." Then a second awful thought struck her. "Selma, this *is* Elkeri's baby?"

"Not even you get to insult me with that kind of talk."

Selma always claimed not to be that fond of sex. Too messy. "So what was that big fight about the other night?"

"Nothing much." She shrugged. "We'd been to a party, and this young guy asked me to dance."

"He must have done more than that."

"So maybe he was bumping on me kinda hard."

"Something just short of fornication?"

Selma made a sound too sophisticated to be a grunt. "As if I'd be interested in some collegiate needs-a-few-fashion-tips brother with no job and a lot of loans!" Contempt reached a whole other level in Selma's black-ice gaze.

No mystery here. "You wanted to make Elkeri jealous."

"Elkeri's been like father-knows-best since we got back from the honeymoon, staying in, eating at home, watching TV. I don't want to be Suzy-stupid-homemaker. I like my good times. The truth is, I never wanted to be like you." Resentment bristled through the words. "Still don't."

"Why would you?" Thea threw her arms up. "You've got a wonderful man. A great home. Terrific job. Oh, and a Porsche. Stop looking for what you don't have, and start staring at all you do."

"And I'm not ready to grow a big-mama butt." Selma pressed her hand against the flattest abdomen in the lower forty-eight. "Once a woman's sprung with a child, it never comes back exactly the same. All the money I've dropped on this winter's wardrobe—"

"Get over yourself, Selma!" Why had she stopped fighting so long ago when it felt so damn good! "You're not Halle Berry's worst nightmare! Be glad you got pregnant so easily. Plenty of women your age—"

Selma rose to her knees on the bed and flung out a hand. "You can just stop right there and throw it in reverse. I am *not* old."

"You're not the baby of the family anymore, either, Selma. Time you passed on that damn mantle!"

SHE BROUGHT TWO lemonades up to the roof and sat down in a chair beside Jesse, handing one over. The sun had warmed Jesse's skin to pinkness beneath her tanned legs. "I appreciate you being civil to your Aunt Selma."

Jesse shrugged. "She's okay. I forgot how pretty she is."

She nodded and let the straw slide out of her mouth. "Envied her all my life."

"Why?"

"What's not to like? Skin, hair, figure, my sister's fierce."

Jesse laid her book aside. "How come she acts so black?"

"Why," not "how come." She didn't say it. Jesse was talking for the first time in a long time. Asking questions. Wanted to know.

She gazed out across the tops of downtown Atlanta to the rare crystal-blue horizon. The first answer that came to her mind was, *So she's nothing like me.* Hadn't Selma just said, "I never wanted to be like you"? But that didn't seem the whole truth, even if in her heart, she knew it was the beginning of it.

"Aunt Selma likes to live large. She's a diva in her own mind. The walk and the talk are meant to attract attention." She paused. "And people tend to adopt the pattern of the society around them."

Jesse frowned. "You didn't."

"Selma stayed in the African American community, and I didn't. What, don't you think your mother can get down?"

Jesse laughed as Thea did her best neck rotation with attitude.

"Did you ever wish you were more like Aunt Selma?" Jesse added in quiet voice. "Darker?"

Now we're getting to it. "Only on a daily basis. One summer when I was about ten, we went to the beach in Mobile. We stayed all day in the sun, trying to get the darkest tan we could in a hurry. Selma turned all dark coppery. What I got was a chest and back full of big juicy blisters and a case of sun poisoning. After that, whenever we went to the lake or shore, Mama and Daddy kept me so lathered in sunblock that I looked albino." She chuckled. "I am what I am."

"Hopeless?" Jesse suggested and then grinned.

She grinned back and flipped a straw full of lemonade in her daughter's direction.

All of a sudden, she felt tears push behind her eyes. *Little things. It's the little things that mean so much. Ordinary. Normal. Boring life things. Why do we disparage normal? Take it away, and it's all we really want. Nothing special going on.*

forty

"WE'LL TOUR YORUBA Realty after church." Elkeri met Thea's gaze in his rearview mirror. Looking clean in a sunset rose sport coat and a wide-slice smile on his face, he could have been an ad for any luxury item. He had the charm that only truly gifted salesmen possess. And he was always selling something.

"Since Reverend Xavier joined us, membership at Saint James's expands weekly. The man can preach. You're sure to enjoy the experience."

The scowl on Jesse's face was the reservoir for her opinion about that.

"We don't go to church that often," Jesse had said when the subject came up at dinner the night before.

"I wouldn't go either, if I had to listen to a dry Episcopalian sermon," Selma had replied. "Thea, just why did you let your husband talk you into converting from AME? That's African Methodist Episcopal, Jesse. That's what we are, emphasis on African!"

Aunt Della's clucking tongue silenced any further argument.

Later, alone with her mother, Jesse asked, "How come it has to be *his* church? And what about our pledge?"

"I plan to keep it," was all she could offer in consolation.

"Did Selma tell you Yoruba Realty was named one of Atlanta's top minority businesses last year?" Elkeri glanced back over his shoulder. "That's just the beginning. We're expanding outside the county next year. Now, ladies, I want to direct your attention ahead as we turn the corner. A lot of consideration went into choosing the site on which Saint James's new sanctuary is built."

As he made the turn, Thea leaned forward to get a better view through the windshield. Not that she could have missed the edifice that stood dead center at the end of the street. The pale stone building dominated the surrounding modest neighborhood. The peaked center rose several stories to a point that balanced a golden cross, while the sides of the building curved back and away.

"We call it the Jubilee Crown of Heaven," Elkeri said proudly.

Once he said that, she understood the building's unique shape. It was as an enormous tiara. The series of tall, narrow leaded glass windows along the building's upper story reflected light like jewel baguettes.

Selma twisted around to look at Thea. "Impressive, isn't it?"

"It's not the little chapel in the woods." *Why don't churches look like churches anymore?*

Selma patted her husband's arm. "Elkeri's a member of the Saint James's council and has his own parking space."

I can see why he needs it. The traffic rivaled that at AA Arena when the Mavericks played a home game.

Once parked, they joined the stream of well-dressed men and women crossing the parking lot. Laughter and affirmations accompanied the parade of parishioners. Sunday morning service at a black church was still a big hat-bag-gloves-and-heels affair.

Jesse reached for her mother's hand. "Am I dressed okay?"

She nodded and squeezed Jesse's hand. Jesse wore navy slacks and a sweater. Remembering Selma's penchant for entertaining, she had thought to bring a suit, just in case.

"Hey, hey, girlfriend!" The woman smiling and waving at Selma had stepped out of a BMW.

"Celeste!" Selma rushed up to the tall, willowy woman who

wore a snug-fitting sapphire suit and elaborate love knots all over her head. They embraced with the ritual artifice of Kabuki dancers, trying not to disturb hair or makeup.

"And here's my favorite boss!" The woman embraced Elkeri, deliberately leaving a smear of Raisin lipstick on his freckled cheek.

Elkeri said helpfully, "Celeste, meet Selma's sister, Theadora Morgan."

Celeste did a genuine double take before turning to Selma. "I know you're not just now telling me after all these years your family's biracial?"

"No. Thea's a sista," Selma snapped. "This is my Aunt Della, and that's my niece, Jesse. This is Celeste Freeman, Elkeri's top agent."

When the introductions were done, Selma said, "Join us for brunch after service?"

Celeste shook her head. "I've been goin' and blowin', girl. Too much. Mama said if I don't make Sunday dinner *today* she's going to put a notice in the want ads for a new daughter."

"What's got you wearing yourself out?"

"Reverend Xavier. Asked me to volunteer this weekend. And you know he's not a man you can easily say no to on any account." The two friends *um-hmed* in unison.

"You still got your eyes on the prize?" Elkeri asked with a chuckle.

"Better than that!"

Selma stopped fiddling with the turned-up collar of her plum suit. "Don't tell me the elusive reverend finally asked you out?"

"Not yet. But I heard from Mrs. Molette that the bishop is in town. She said he told Reverend Xavier there's a great deal of talk about his high profile in the national religious community. It'd go a long way toward dispelling certain concerns if there was a *Mrs.* Thornton at his side."

"So Miss Celeste is too ready to make her move?"

"For real! Thanks to my soul sister counselor's advice on redefining my aspirations, I have separated the boys from the men. And, *hon-ney,* Reverend Thornton graduated magna cum laude from the soul school of All True Man. I know that's right!"

Jesse elbowed Thea as Celeste and Selma exchanged a low five. She ignored it, as well as Aunt Della's questioning look. Everybody wanted in on her business. Everybody!

"Let's move along, ladies," Elkeri directed affably. "We're going to be late."

The narthex of the church was a long, curving hallway that disappeared around either flank. Most people turned right or left. Elkeri led his party confidently toward the open double doors to the main aisle.

Once inside, she recognized the sanctuary. Xavier's sermons were televised from here. Larger than it seemed on-screen, the thousand-seat auditorium sloped down toward the altar. The raised pulpit stood amid lagoon blue carpeting. Cascades of fresh flowers spilled over brass railings that separated it from the choir loft. Permanent stage lighting hung overhead. Fixed TV cameras were stationed around the room, while two cameramen down front held portables. There was even a professional soundboard midaisle of the main pew.

This wasn't church. This was theater!

As she slid into a push velvet seat, an almost forgotten memory tapped against her thoughts.

SHE WAS JUST six years old when she was sent to visit her mother's mother outside Baton Rouge while her mother dealt with barely toddling Selma. Years later, she learned her mother had had a summer pregnancy that ended in a stillbirth. Every Sunday, Ba'Mama took her to church. It was a simple barnlike whitewashed building with few amenities besides large windows raised high to entice the breeze from out of doors. Slowly rotating fans with rusty brown blades twirled in the wooden ceiling overhead. Years of the slide and rub of pious backsides had worn slight depressions in the rock-hard mahogany pews. In the back of each pew were black bound hymnals and hand fans courtesy of the local funeral home with pictures of a kind-faced, blond-haired, blue-eyed Jesus, carrying a lamb or blessing the Last Supper.

Oh, how the ladies worked those fans in crocheted gloved hands, sending waves of Chantilly and White Gardenia per-

fumes wafting through the Deep South summer air. Inevitably, though, sweat beaded up on plump brown bosoms covered by lace collars and a dusting of talc. Whenever a drop slid from under the strand of pearls clasped about Ba'Mama's ginger throat, she dabbed at it with one of her embroidered handkerchiefs.

"Be still and count your blessings, child," her grandmother would whisper whenever she began to fidget during the long sermon. "Got to count your blessings, or you won't know how much God loves you."

Yet her strongest memory of that summer was of voices backed by a tinny piano singing "Abide With Me" and "His Eye Is on the Sparrow." That was Ba'Mama's favorite. The Allen Street choir sang it and other gospel songs in a rich soul-searing harmony impossible to capture in even the best recording. That music transformed teachers and hairdressers and garbagemen and farmers into a force that made her head sweat and her stomach jump.

No one seemed to mind that the elderly gentleman behind her pew sang off-key. Or that the woman to their right chimed in a half beat behind. This was deep-down-from-the-gut singing, dredged up from a long week of thankless, hard-luck work and make-do lives where the smallest upset could become a crisis.

Though sometimes mortified that such lyric power could move adults to tears and shouts, she never left without feeling she had been lifted up out of herself in those moments to a place where she was not separate but connected at the soul to the power of every note.

SAINT JAMES'S JUBILEE Crown of Heaven seemed too modern and self-congratulatory an edifice to elicit that kind of simple faith.

No sooner were they seated than an organ, backed by a twelve-piece orchestra that included guitars, trumpets, and drums, levitated people to their feet. Voices lifted in song, the choir robed in powder blue and gold emerged from side aisles and filed up steep steps to fill the loft. From the back of the church, a procession of sisters in identical white dresses and stewards in black suits marched down the center aisle. As the final figure in the procession entered, expectation stirred the congregation.

Xavier stood head and shoulders above the elderly steward just ahead of him. Robed in black silk with three broad scarlet velvet stripes accentuating each broad shoulder, he strolled along with hymnal in hand, nodding to people on either side of the aisle.

The hair lifted on her arms as he neared her place on the fifth row, third seat from the aisle. She and Jesse were conspicuous in the sea of dark faces. Would he notice her? Oh Lord! If he noticed her she would . . .

He looked right at her and kept moving.

As she resumed her seat along with the rest, his poise in the face of the unexpected impressed her anew. He had seen her, but she would bet she was only one in the sanctuary who knew the reason for the fractional widening of his smile. She peeped sideways at Selma to be certain. Her sister was engrossed in song.

As the service proceeded, conducted for the most part by the two assistant pastors, Xavier sat almost immobile in his high-backed chair. He nodded and murmured encouragement occasionally, but she had the distinct feeling that his mind was elsewhere. The set of his head, one shoulder shifted lower than the other as he propped his chin on his fist, was a reflective one. Sometimes he closed his eyes. There was something serene in his demeanor, a peace that set him apart, even in the midst of the rousing choral moments or the prayers.

Finally with the last chords of the Hymn of Preparation echoing in the recesses of the enormous church, he rose from his chair.

Inexplicably nervous, she clasped her hands tightly in her lap. What had he said about preaching? Sunday morning in the pulpit was show time. For no good reason she could think of, she felt like the curtain was going up on an opening-night performance backed by her last dime.

He read a passage from the Gospel of Saint John, where Jesus proclaimed that he was the Light of the World. Then he set the book aside and moved out from behind the pulpit down onto the altar's expanse of blue carpet.

"When the Pharisees scoffed that His testimony could not be verified, Jesus' reply was in part, 'Even if I bear witness to myself, my witness is true, because I know where I came from and where I go. . . . You judge according to the flesh: I judge no one.'

"So powerful, that message." He nodded to himself. " 'I know where I came from and where I go.' " He repeated the phrase conversationally, as if he had a long way to go and was pacing himself.

"Many of you here today don't *walk* in the Light of the Word. No, you don't! You walk through your lives with your eyes *down*-cast! Your hearts *down*-trodden! Your spirits *down*-fallen. You tell me, 'Pastor, I just don't know. I don't feel able to measure *up* to the burdens of my time. I can't seem to stand *up* to the poverty of my place. I can't find it in me to rise *up* beyond the occasion of my life.' "

A few amens came in scattered reply.

He gazed downward for a moment, as if he could feel the wearying weight of the souls surrounding him. "I haven't come here today to chastise you. I feel the burden of your confusion. Your questions strike at my heart. They are, truly, the perplexities of human experience. In a world of plenty, we feel empty and alone. Money can't sate us. Success becomes a never-ending stair to climb. A new husband or new girlfriend only diverts us for a short while." He threw his arms wide. "We feel *lost* in the stars, as insignificant as a mustard seed."

The amens came more frequently and louder.

"There are times when I, too, feel my insignificance. Times when I see only *loneliness* and feel only the *lacks* in my life."

He's talking about himself. She looked away, uncomfortable with his private revelations in so public an arena. It seemed somehow contrived.

"Like you, I search for answers. And in doing so, I always turn to the Lord." He knelt before the pulpit, and he bent his head in the attitude of prayer.

"Mom, what's he doing?" Jesse asked in a smothered voice. *"Hush!"*

Xavier began softly. "Lord, why are your people so troubled? They say the *lamp* of *faith* grows dark. The *path* of *righteousness* is murky. *Pain* and *anger* and *frustrations* obscure their way. We cannot see the *Divine Plan* Thou hast set out for us. And so we are *afraid!*"

He lifted his head. "Always the answer is the same. We're looking in the *wrong* direction! To see and hear and know the word of *God*, you got to look *up!*"

He rose to his feet amid the swell of callbacks, his eyes on the people before him like a prophet of old.

"Are you listening? Can you hear me? Are your *ears* open? Are your *hearts* open? Are your spirits *exposed* for the blessings of God? Because I'm here to tell you this morning! Yes, I am! I'm here to deliver to you *God's* plan!"

He nodded and smiled in recognition of the congregation's shouts.

"You think you're with me. You think you know. But are you ready to hear God's own truth? Because it's just this: 'To everything there is a season. And a time to every purpose under Heaven!' Believe it!"

He moved quickly down to the front, his arm lifted, finger pointing at the people arrayed before him. "*What*ever your circumstance, is yours for a purpose. *Who*ever you are, *what*ever you are, *where*ever you are. It's part of God's purpose. Jesus said, 'I *know* where I came from and where I go.' As Christians, how many of us can say the same?"

He smiled suddenly, a brilliant smile that drew appreciative chuckles as well as a few "You tell them, reverends."

"God knows where you came from and where you go. Let *no* man or woman tell you different. You were *born* in the right place! *Born* at the right time! *Born* in the right race! You are *not* a mistake!"

This time his words struck her with physical force. She felt as if gnats were swarming over her scalp. Her skepticism vanished. The fervor she had so casually dismissed as impossible in this million-dollar sanctuary was now with her, ushered in on the power of his voice.

Perhaps the fame of "X" Savior had seduced the congregation into church, but it was Reverend Thornton who stood before them now, preaching God's word. He held out the promise to them of a glimpse of something greater than the majestic cadence of his powerful voice.

For the next twenty minutes, he was a holy vanguard. God's drum major, striding and strutting, stirring up emotional furor for the Lord. The sleeves of his robe rippled and billowed in emphasis of his every gesture as he paced in impatient, athletic strides. His voice rose and fell in rhythmic intonation until it was as hoarse as a lover in the grip of a passion stronger than his natural caution. By sheer physical will, he dared them to look away, be indifferent or bored.

Halfway through the sermon, Jesse's hand again slipped into hers, and the reflex of emotion was in her grip. She smiled and held on, for she knew then she was not alone in her response.

The organist had begun to play softly in the background, adding musical punctuation to his words. The shouts and amens and hallelujahs increased until the church throbbed with the longing of humanity ready to believe in the power of faith.

Finally, Xavier stood absolutely still at the center of the sanctuary, shoulders heaving from of his exertions but his voice now steady. "Jesus *knew* who He was! He knew that His Father had a *place* for Him. Just as He has set a *place* for every grain of sand and every tiny mustard seed! For *you*!"

As he ended, the choir was on their feet, humming and clapping, ready to lead that wave of fervent believers up to the altar at the Invitation to join the church.

Not too sophisticated to get happy, many younger women rushed forward to reach out and touch the minister who stirred them. Those who pressed his hand too long or flung themselves at his neck were turned quickly away by the phalanx of young men in suits who acted as church ushers and directed toward the pews of sisters in white.

Aunt Della leaned near to whisper in Thea's ear, "The bishop's right. That young man needs to get himself a wife!"

Thea nodded, feeling what they all felt. What the TV screen could never capture was in plain view in person. The smoke from the fire in his eyes had an evangelical source. The man, in this moment, was untouchable . . . and alone.

He needs a wife. Of course he did. Of course!

* * *

AFTER THE SERVICE, Thea and Jesse steered clear of the throng waiting in the vestibule, while Elkeri made it his priority to shake Xavier's hand and Selma kissed his cheek.

"Well, well, this is a surprise!" Aunt Della's voice was suddenly animated as they emerged into sunshine. "Thea, do you know who that is, standing on the sidewalk? No, of course you don't. We must remedy that."

She didn't recognize the middle-aged couple Aunt Della hurried across the grass to greet. She didn't need to. She could feel her pulse edging up as she watched them. A feeling only Jesse had ever before aroused in her jumped to the fore: the mother instinct.

"Who are they?" Jesse questioned in exasperation, for she had made it clear she was ready to roll on away from Saint James's.

"David's parents." Replacements for the ones she and Xavier could never be.

forty-one

SHE HAD MET them at Selma's wedding but didn't remember. This time, they had her full attention. She weighed, judged, and dissected the pair coming toward her as if they were specimens in a biology lab practical.

He was an average-looking man, of average height and form, medium brown color. Pleasant. Aunt Della had told her that he managed a Sears in Biloxi. He looked reliable, the kind to notice a scuff mark on the linoleum or an error in pinning in a window display. Dependable. Earnest. Serious.

Like David.

She was petite. One of those women of middle years who must have been teensy as a girl, for she was enviously slim now. Even in a red chenille sweater coat, she looked fragile. Seemed much too small to house the contralto voice Aunt Della said she possessed and that made her a former voice teacher. The glance she turned on Thea as Aunt Della spoke was thoughtful yet guarded.

Like David's.

They both dressed in off-the-rack clothing. Nothing flashy.

Like David.

Aunt Della swept them before her like the Good Witch ushering Dorothy and Toto along the Yellow Brick Road. "Theadora, dear, this is Lena and Marcus Greer, David's parents. And this is my niece, Theadora Morgan, David's birth mother."

David's birth mother! Just hand me the scarlet "S" for sinner.

She felt Jesse let go of her hand and step back quickly as if she'd been told to butt out. Too late to match that dash for anonymity.

"We've been longing to meet you, Mrs. Morgan." Marcus Greer's handshake was firm, strong without being aggressive. *He's nothing like Xavier.*

"Thea, please." She took Lena's hand in turn and pressed her other on top in a control-the-moment handshake. "So happy to see you both again. David is such a wonderful young man."

Credit where credit is due.

"Thank you, Thea. He is my blessing every morning I wake."

She let go of the smaller woman's hand. *My morning blessing.* This was the mother David had judged her by and found her lacking.

If hostility were spots, I'd be sporting a bad case of the measles.

Marcus pressed in behind his wife and lay a protective hand on her shoulder. That was when she noticed Lena was trembling. "We both want to thank you for giving us such a fine boy."

Della beamed. "I just knew you would get along. A pity it took all these years for it to come to pass. Excuse me, I believe I hear my name being called."

She watched her aunt beat a quick retreat. Was it tact or guile at work?

"You don't know what you've done for David, accepting him into your home as graciously as you did," Marcus continued. "He came home to tell us about it. Talked nonstop the whole time about you and your home."

"You're just as pretty as he said," Lena added, her dark eyes appraising without hostility. David must have mentioned the light, bright, damn near white part.

She knew she was coloring. "Thank you. I like—" *My— your—our?* "David, too. A very well-behaved young man."

"He has your green eyes," Lena said softly. "Looking at you

is almost the same as looking at him. I suppose that's why I feel an instant kinship with you."

"You are very generous to feel that way." Unfortunately, she did not feel as charitable. The poker stuck up her back was threatening spinal injury.

"Now I'd like you meet my daughter, Jesse."

Only, as she turned, the place where Jesse had been standing was vacated. She cast a worried look about the parking lot. Jesse shouldn't be that hard to spot, but her blond head was nowhere to be seen.

"I guess she went with Aunt Della." Too bad Della was standing a few yards away, giving immediate lie to that possibility.

"Only thing left for us to do is to meet Reverend Thornton," Lena said softly. "We were hoping to do that before now. But we were late for church."

"Ain't that something?" Marcus's big grin lifted his features out of the ordinary. "David's got a celebrity for a father. Always told the boy he had a natural talent for sports, but he was more interested in the classroom. Never took sports seriously."

Xavier's prayer answered.

"Where is David?"

"Around here somewhere." Marcus shifted his gaze right and left. "He came to Atlanta a few days early to meet his father's folks. Reverend Thornton flew us in so we could be part of this evening's celebration. That must be why you're here, as well."

"Hm." If only they knew how little information that sound carried.

"I don't know when we'll see him again at home. He's got so much new family to get to know."

"Whose got new family?" Selma had come up behind them.

The sight of Selma widened Marcus's smile to eight lanes of superhighway.

Lena seemed to shrink against her husband. "We're just telling Mrs. Morgan how happy we are to finally know she's family.

Selma frowned. "Thea, what are they talking about?"

"We'll talk later," she answered under her breath. "Lena and Marcus, this is my sister, Selma Yoruba. Selma, these are the Greers from Biloxi." She took Selma by the arm and tried to turn her away. "Why don't you see if you can spot Jesse? I'll meet you by the car in a minute."

"Why?" Selma wriggled free of her sister's strong-arm tactics. "What is it you don't want me to hear?"

She put every ounce of her pent-up annoyance into a quietly spoken, "Selma."

"All right. I don't have to be told twice." Selma turned away but shot suspicious glances over her shoulder several times as she headed for the parking lot.

"Oh now," murmured Lena, "I hope I didn't—"

"No, it's just a matter I've needed to take in hand for a while." She felt every muscle in her face resist the smile she forced on it. "So where were we?"

"Talking about David meeting the Thorntons," Marcus answered. "I suppose you know about Reverend Thornton's press conference?"

"No, I don't." *What now?*

"Reverend Thornton's going to announce his paternity of David," Lena said.

"It's today at four. I suspect only cable news will carry it." Marcus grinned. "The major stations will be covering ball games."

"Imagine, our David's going to be on TV." Lena gave her a coy smile. "It's so exciting. I've never been on TV."

"There's a reason for that. You haven't done anything newsworthy," her husband teased.

Lena swatted her husband affectionately on the arm. "Now, you just take that back, Marcus Greer!"

David had nice parents, loving parents. She could tell the relationship was a happy one. Maybe Aunt Della hadn't done right by giving David away without telling her, but she had chosen well his surrogate parents.

Too bad she couldn't be more gracious about it. Right now, all she wanted to do was to kick something so hard it would land in the middle of next week.

"If you'll excuse me, my sister's waiting for me. A pleasure meeting you." She did a diva pivot on her heel to do Selma proud and headed for the parking lot, but her superheated thoughts were fogging up the view.

Xavier is going to announce David's paternity to the world!

He has no right! No right to make decisions that affect the lives of others without their permission.

Without my permission!

A press conference! Is this Xavier's attempt to make David news before he becomes gossip? Fire with fire.

Born in the right time. Born in the right place. God makes no mistakes.

Was that sermon meant to convey a father's feelings concerning the circumstances of his son's birth? Easy for him to feel magnanimous. He'd lived without the guilt of all the years in between, while she'd served her time for her mistakes and still did.

How could I have missed noticing David in the sanctuary?

All of a sudden, Xavier, big and bad as life, stood on the walkway before her. Pearl and Cerise and Liz, their spouses, and several other family members stamped with the Thornton profile gazed her way as she approached. Only Uncle Way waved, grinning like he held the punch line to a joke that had yet to be told.

"Good morning." She gave a general nod in the direction of the group, which didn't seem particularly happy to acknowledge her, then cut her eyes to Xavier. "May I speak with you?"

He smiled. "Surely. Excuse us."

"Now just a—!" From the corner of her eye, she saw Pearl's husband reach out to stop her from following them.

Xavier tried to take her arm, but she elbowed away his touch. When they were out of earshot, she turned quickly to him. "What's this about a news conference?"

Xavier smiled politely at her and took her hand. "And a very good morning to you, too, Mrs. Morgan. Welcome to Atlanta. Do you come here often?"

Okay, I get the point. They were being watched by more than his family.

"I didn't expect to be here at all."

"Then know you're always welcome in our fair city." He squeezed her hand a little more. "Anytime at all."

"Thank you." She could feel herself flushing as he released her hand, but fifty percent of it was anger. "I enjoyed your sermon, Reverend Thornton. I was quite . . . moved."

He leaned toward her. "You see now why I need you with me?"

The quiet words went through her like lightning. He understood better than she did the effect his sermons had on his congregation. Yet at this moment, the look he offered her was from the man not the messenger. *Remember David!*

"About this news conference?"

"It's for David." He grinned, looking well satisfied with himself. "I want the world to know he's mine."

"Scoop the scoop?"

"That, too. I wanted to ask you to be there with us, but you . . ." He smiled. "You're here now. It would mean a lot if you'd join us. A lot to me."

She was too worked up to be mollified by his charm. She suspected he knew what her response would be and so had tried to avoid it. Too bad. Here she was to deliver it in person. "You seem to think you have all the answers. But how do you know you're right about this? Did you ask me? Did you ask David? Did you consult anyone?"

Long, long pause. "I prayed over it."

The seeming one-upmanship of that statement pushed her into defensive overdrive. "I'm not a righteous, regular, churchgoing body. But I do know the difference between asking God for guidance versus praying for the strength to do what *you* think needs to be done. One is a plea for truth. The other is begging an indulgence for your side to win. This isn't a football game."

His expression emptied of all emotion.

She wasn't supposed to touch, but the moment was no longer about supposed-tos. She reached out in what she hoped would appear to be a straighten-his-tie gesture, but her fingers spread and stilled the moment they touched his shirtfront. "Xavier. You have a gift. A rare and precious gift. People listen when you speak."

"And it's up to me to get the word out." The chill left his gaze. "My tactics may be unorthodox, but the message is sound, Theodora. I've spent my life fronting for one cause or another. I think I know how to attract the right kind of attention to this."

She recoiled from his I-know-best tone. "Maybe that's the

trouble. You haven't let go of your old life because you like the spotlight a little too much."

The look that came into his face this time made her own anger seem like a match struck in a hurricane. "Theadora, you don't know what—"

"Mom?" Arms crossed, a hip jutted out at an angle of aggravation, Jesse stood a few feet away.

Reminded of her transgression, she backpedaled from him as though Jesse was reeling her in. "Coming, Jesse. Good-bye, Reverend Thornton." With Jesse on her left flank, she hurried toward the church parking lot.

Selma stood by the SUV in a pique that soured her supremely feminine face. "Girl, did you see yourself? Flirting with my minister!"

She gave her sister a back-off look. "Your eyesight must be getting bad."

Selma grabbed her husband's arm to pull him up short. "Elkeri, I ask you. Was Thea massaging the reverend's chest, or what?"

Elkeri frowned. *"Aw* now, Selma."

"I know you're not taking her side."

"Selma, baby, don't start . . ."

Thea stepped up into the vehicle. She didn't want to hear an argument. Selma was a fool to flaunt her insecurities before Elkeri.

Jesse scowled at her mother.

"Do you have something you want to say?"

Jesse cut her eyes away. "No."

"Good." *Because your mother's ready to spell out her mood for her family using* all *capital letters, starting with a B.*

forty-two

SELMA EYED THE bracelet Aunt Della had given her for Christmas. "I think platinum is a more true description of my Porsche. Silver's a little too bright. Now this platinum bracelet is just about a perfect match."

The mood of the rest of the gathering in Selma's video room was serious and intense. Thea sat between her aunt and Selma. Jesse preferred a cushion on the floor. The football game had only one spectator. Elkeri stood an arm's length away from the fifty-two-inch screen, watching as though at any second he might be needed to jump into the picture and referee.

Thea glanced at the clock for the third time in as many minutes. "It's time."

Elkeri punched the remote to change the channel.

Xavier looked, as always, as if he had been created for just such photo ops. His suit was deep navy. A bold Kente cloth tie and matching silk handkerchief in the pocket made him look Kwanza festive. Arrayed behind him was his family. She would not have thought Uncle Way could look quite so serious. Had something changed since this morning? Directly behind Xavier stood an elderly couple she had not seen before. David stood to his left.

"I have come here today to announce two matters. The first is of a purely personal nature. The second will be of interest to the public that has supported me in my ministry from its infancy to the present.

"Behind me today are members of my family, including my parents, Reverend and Mrs. Martin G. Thornton of Chicago."

He paused to offer them a smile before he continued. "It is through their support and encouragement and inspiration that I have achieved whatever measure of success I have had in my life. As the touchstone of my ministry, I have exhorted men to take their rightful positions and responsibilities within their own families. I still firmly believe in these tenets and am here today to embrace the consequences of my own stipulations.

"I have for some time prayed that I would be one day blessed with a family of my own. This Christmas, I was gifted with the answer to that prayer."

"Amen!" Uncle Way said loud enough to be picked up by the mike. "God works in mysterious ways."

"Praise His name," Pearl added.

Xavier reached out and pulled David to his side. "I would like to introduce my son, David Darnell Greer."

"Darnell? That's *my* middle name." Indignation spiked Jesse's tone.

"That's right, sugar. D-A-R-N-E-L-L is a family name." Pride swelled Aunt Della's voice. "Searle Prescott Darnell was one of Louisiana's first colored legislators—"

"Isn't anything about me mine alone?" Jesse jumped to her feet and marched out. "I wish he'd never been born!"

Her mother rose, too, but only to move closer to the screen. In oversized image, David looked as if he had been plucked from the spectator section, handed a red cape, and shoved in front of an angry bull.

I knew it. He hates the spotlight. Just like me.

David slipped free of his father's one-arm embrace as Xavier turned back to the mike, beaming with parental pride. "I issued a statement just previous to this interview and will not be answering any questions at this time about my son and our relationship. On to the second matter.

"I was challenged recently by someone whose opinion I respect. The question was: Had I not perhaps brought to my new calling some of the mistakes of my past?"

Now it's my turn!

"At the time, I saw the comment as criticism. Now I see it as a wake-up call."

She felt as if he could see right though the lens into the room where she stood.

"Therefore, I am announcing my sabbatical for the next year. During that time, I plan to study and pray and reflect upon the future course of my ministry as well as get to know my son. Further, I have tendered my resignation as pastor of Saint James's AME church here in Atlanta. Thank you. God bless and keep you during this holy season."

Oh, Xavier! Too much.

Was that what he had been about to tell her when she walked away this morning? *"Theadora, you don't know what—my plans are?"*

"No, man! He can't be allowed to do that." Elkeri danced in place.

A man who identified himself as the bishop for the Atlanta area stepped up to the microphone Xavier abandoned. But not before he had embraced Xavier in an emotional hug that said better than words how he felt about the younger man. "I thank Reverend Thornton for his frankness this afternoon. I am proud to say I've known him . . ."

"Sounds like the bishop is planning to run for office," Selma said.

"That's called good PR," Elkeri answered. "Got to spin this ASAP."

". . . rarely comes along a man of Reverend Thornton's dynamic powers. The church needs him. I will not accept his resignation . . ."

"That's what I'm saying!" Elkeri clapped his hands and nodded. "The bishop knows how popular Reverend Xavier is. All the money he's bringing in—"

"It's nice he has all that family behind him," Della interjected. "That's what family's for. Maybe you can't hardly stand some of them some of the time, but when the chips are down, those are the ones that stick by you."

"Blood is thicker than water," said Elkeri and smiled a happy-man smile.

"Some blood's just harder to take," Selma answered. "Funny thing, Thea. He didn't even mention the mother."

"Can you even believe that? My minister's got a love child." Elkeri was frowning now, as if the main portion of the announcement had just reached his brain.

Selma shifted gears. "You sit on the Thornton Foundation board. How's this going to look? Remember how out of hand things got for Jesse Jackson for a while."

Elkeri was still watching the screen. "That boy doesn't look all that much like his daddy. Too light! And what is he, twenty? Let me guess. The mother's some Ofay heifer from his Hollywood days, holding out for big bucks to tell her side."

"Next thing you know, she'll be spread-eagle in *Playboy*," Selma suggested with a spiteful sideways glance at Thea.

"Selma, that's quite enough." Della's tone was matriarchal. "Your nephew is going to need all our support."

"Nephew?" Elkeri turned from the screen at last. "What's this about a nephew?"

Della smiled serenely. "Selma will explain another time. But first, would you be so kind, sugar, as to fetch your Aunt Della a thimbleful of sherry? Dry Sack, if you have it."

Though the press conference had broken up, Thea continued to watch. Xavier remained behind the reporter who was recapping the story. He was smiling. He was hugging David's shoulders. He was happy. But could he really give up the spotlight? Should he have to? Perhaps she hadn't done right by him, after all.

forty-three

"GOOD MORNING, *MS*. Morgan!"

"Hi." She gave a second glance to the business colleague she passed in the hallway. She wasn't wrong about it. Fredda Nichols was grinning like she knew something Thea didn't.

Like I'm trailing toilet paper from my heel.

"How're you doing, Ms. Morgan?"

"Fine." She drew out the word as Don from Traffic gave her an arch smile. That made the third person she'd passed since entering the building who'd eyed her oddly.

She stopped short at her secretary's desk. "Marcia, is there something going on I should know about?"

Marcia grinned and pointed at her boss's closed door with her pencil. "Why don't you check out your office, Ms. Morgan?"

She drew back. "Who's in there?"

"Not a who, what." She wriggled her brows. "We had no idea you were so popular."

Popular? She sucked in her breath and turned toward her door.

She had a hint before she turned the knob. Through the glass panels on either side of her door, she saw several yellow roses. When she opened the door, she found that vases of more yellow roses occupied every surface in her office.

"Secret admirer or not so secret?"

Marcia had come to stand behind her. "We have an office pool going. They came first thing this morning. Took three deliverymen to bring them up. So, word kind of got around."

Thea hid her inclination to smile. "Since I'm not part of the pool, I don't see why I should make it easy for you."

"Okay. But I say you know exactly who they're from. No one would dare embarrass *you* this way if they didn't think it would be okay."

"That's an interesting point of view."

Marcia's smile drooped. "Can't blame a girl for trying."

She waited until Marcia moved away, then searched among the bouquets for the note. She was pleased to find the envelope still stapled shut.

> *If a potion tastes bitter,*
> *And yet brings relief,*
> *Would you give it up?*

She understood now what he meant by that quote. That he wasn't giving up, despite the bitterness between them. That should have made her happy. Instead, it made her want to weep.

"Well, well. I see I'm a little late with my news."

She looked up at her door, which Marcia hadn't completely shut. "Oh. Hello, Ron. I didn't hear you knock."

"I didn't." He banged two knuckles against the wood. "Mind if I join the party?"

"Not at all." She glanced swiftly at the vases. Six in all. Xavier had deep pockets. "Sorry about all this."

"Don't be. It's worth a celebration. What I want to know is, who leaked it before I had the chance?"

She moved quickly behind her desk to tuck the card out of sight. "I don't think I know what you're talking about. I just got in five minutes ago."

"So this is personal? Excuse me." He wiped his raw nose with a tissue from his pocket. The flu had rebounded on him

during the holidays, and he'd missed the first three days of the
new year's work week.

"Yes, the flowers are personal."

He grinned. "Good. Because I always like to give the good
news myself."

He held out his hand, then thought better of it with a wave
of regret. "Anyway, congratulations, Ms. Morgan. You're the
new comanager of Transportation."

"Comanager? Is that an official title?"

"Sure is." He grinned. "The company's decided on a two-step
approach to the amalgamation of Transportation. For the time
being, we're folding four jobs into two. In addition to your
present responsibilities in Marine and Barge, you'll be adding
Trucking and Special Packages. For the interim, Rail will stay
with Leman. He's made it known he plans to retire next fall and
wouldn't like to see the position yanked out from under him
before then. That should give you enough time to learn his side
of the business."

"Thank you, Ron." *Job safe!* "I didn't . . . thanks."

He nodded. "We all have our missteps. Correcting them,
that's what counts. You're a good manager, Thea. When Leman
retires, we'll see how good you are as a director." He winked.
"Meanwhile, you're going to need someone to fill in as Marine
manager while you reconstruct your new position."

"I think Joe Ortega has proven his worth in the company."

Ron frowned. "Anyone else appeal to you?"

"Joe's the best I've got." *Protect your people, first rule of a
good boss.* "He deserves a promotion if anyone does."

Ron looked around at the flowers. "So all this, you're seeing
someone?"

She almost laughed. Ron never asked about her personal life.
"Why? Are you part of the secret admirer pool?"

He chuckled. "No."

"Then, yes, I'm seeing someone."

*Was seeing. Wish I could see this someone. But a bargain
with Jesse . . .*

"Looks to be serious." He rubbed his whiskerless chin. "I
suspect the other was just so much talk."

"What other?"

Ron hesitated, his gaze going south. A very bad sign. "Personally I think it's nobody's damned business who employees date, but company policy is very strict. Still and all, that's old business."

His aw shucks shuffle didn't fool her. Ron had baited her, and she was hooked. "If this is about Joe and Marcia, they're only friends. I'll vouch for that."

"It's not about them. It's about you." Ron glanced up at her from beneath bunched-up brows. "I figured you'd heard something by now. The talk started a while ago. All the late hours you were working. Weekends at the office. Traveling together."

She didn't have much of a span to cross to connect those thoughts. It was a shocking distance all the same. "You thought Joe and I were having an affair?"

"O' course not." Ron huffed like a bull. "But in a situation like this, I'm not paid to think. I must enforce the company policy that's in every contract. I didn't doubt your professionalism. That's why I spoke with Joe. I was sorry as the dog's dinner to have to put him through that. It was obvious he wasn't having any part of it."

She shoved her brain out of idle. Office gossip. She and Joe. How long? "Is Joe the reason you offered to move me to another department last August?"

Ron looked extremely uncomfortable. "I did wonder if a way out might come in handy. Even I had noticed how much Joe admires you. Short step from that to more personal feelings. Once they get worked up, young men can sometimes be . . . let's say, tenacious."

"Especially those hot-blooded Latinos."

Ron actually blushed to his gray blond roots. He thought she had gotten herself into something she couldn't handle.

Her skin felt clammy, but inside, she was steaming "Why didn't you just ask me, Ron?"

He waved that off. "You were going through hell. With Evan's death. Trying to raise a daughter. I didn't think you needed to know about it."

"So, this started after I became a widow?" She sat down heavily. "That's something in favor of my character."

"Now, don't take it personally, Thea. These things get going of their own accord all the time. Die out quicker than a prairie fire."

"I didn't even suspect." She felt a deep shudder rising.

Ron nodded. "A professional woman like yourself never would. I told Tom Grant he had his hat screwed on too tight."

Her insides locked up. "My favorite person."

"That guy's a real kidder." Ron's snort had a wet snot sound. "Said you were keeping serious company in D.C. last fall. With a black ballplayer!" A case of belated memory sent his gaze skittering toward her. "Not that there'd be anything wrong with that, either."

Too angry to speak, she let that slide. Politically correct had developed a severe case of the runs.

"Anyway, glad to see you back in form, Thea." He tossed her a casual salute and walked out.

Director. Di-rec-tor. It had snap, pop, and sizzle. She could hear the glass ceiling cracking like ice in the Rockies in April.

And it didn't mean a damn thing at the moment.

Don't take it personally.

. . . Just because your young, handsome Hispanic assistant has been called on the carpet on the suspicion of sniffing at your heels.

. . . No sweat off your nose that a business colleague is spreading lascivious stories about your fling with a black jock 'cause, honey child, we all know what oversexed animals them black playas are.

. . . No reason to be offended that your white boss feels he has to preserve your free, just-about-white, and way-past-twenty-one honor against these equal-opportunistic men of color.

Makes me wanna holler!

She thought about the evasive expression so often on Joe's face last August. That must have been about the time Ron spoke with him and then offered her a transfer. Now it all made sense. Perfect sense. Except that it was nonsense!

She stood up suddenly, about to smother in her own anger. But they must never know. Neither Ron nor Joe and Marcia nor Tom Grant, nor any of those who had whispered any vile word against her. They must never suspect how violated or impotent or vulnerable she felt.

She needed this job. Hell, had coveted the position that had just fallen like a ripe peach into her lap. No, she had earned and overearned this promotion as a double minority in what was still a good ole boy field. No one was going to take away the triumph.

She wiped at the dampness running down her cheeks to her chin. It didn't seem that warm. Surely it must be sweat. Directors didn't cry.

THE DAY GOT longer.

"I've been offered a job in Houston. It's a chance to expand my professional portfolio. I've decided to take it."

"I see." She glanced down at her desk. Joe was resigning. Despite the promotion she'd offered him.

She looked up and managed a big smile. "I'm really happy for you, though I can't say that I'm completely happy for me. You've done an excellent job here. Been a real team player. And a friend. I'm going to miss that."

"Thank you." Though he was looking back, his dark eyes had locked her out of his thoughts.

"I didn't know, Joe."

He blinked a couple of times but didn't answer.

"I didn't know a thing until today about the rumors last summer," she said, just in case he could possibly have put any other interpretation on her words.

He dipped his head once in acknowledgment. Too difficult to ask the questions that had to be on his mind because they were on hers.

"Good luck, Joe. If there's ever anything . . ."

He smiled then. "You already have. You gave me a chance. That's all I ever asked of anyone."

She smiled back. "It's why you had this job."

BY THE TIME she walked in her door, she was too tired to eat the steamed dumplings she had stopped to pick up on the way home. Jesse was out at the library cramming. She had three exams to make up on Saturday and two more Wednesday after school. She was trusting that was what Jesse was doing. Just as Jesse was trusting that she wouldn't call Xavier to thank him for the flowers.

She was ten minutes into *Eve's Bayou* on one of the cable stations when the phone rang.

"Hello, Mrs. Morgan. It's David."

"I know your voice, David. Hello."

"Just thought I'd see how you're doing."

"I'm fine. How are you?"

"Okay." He didn't sound sure.

"A lot of excitement in your life lately. Must make pulling a nine-to-five seem like double duty."

"Something like that." A smile was in his voice. "My parents will be in town next weekend to see my new apartment. We'd like you to join us for dinner Saturday night. Jesse, too, of course."

"I'd like that. And I'll ask Jesse."

"Good. And, there's someone I'd like you to meet."

"Lady friend?"

"Oh now, you must have heard something."

"Your parents mentioned it." There, she could say it. His parents. They had earned her respect.

A pause. "I've been thinking. I can't go on calling you Mrs. Morgan."

"Thea?"

"Nawgh. Got to acknowledge the respect."

She smiled. All the time, it was about respect. "Aunt Thea? Mama Thea?"

He chuckled. "Makes you sound about a hundred years old. How about Ma'Thea?"

"Ma'Thea." She tested the word. It had an affectionate quality to it. She could almost envision Jesse's children calling her that. In a few years. *Make that eight or ten years!* "Sounds good to me."

"Okay then, M—Ma'Thea."

David hung up quickly, as if he felt he had thawed out enough for one encounter. Talking with him was still awkward, but it felt good. The one subject he hadn't mentioned was Xavier. She suspected he had marching orders from the source on that one.

Xavier had retracted his resignation from Saint James's. News accounts said his congregation had inundated the bishop with pleas while the Thornton Foundation was being threatened with sudden withdrawls of large donations. His people needed him, and Xavier, she suspected, needed to be be needed.

Don't we all?

She smiled. David was the child she couldn't get her hands on. Would he always be elusive? Ma'Thea. That was something she could get her heart around.

forty-four

THEA EXPELLED AN impatient sigh that disturbed the tendril of steam uncurling from her cup of herbal tea. Seated in Beryl's kitchen, she'd been lured away from her Saturday morning wash load so, *"Grrrl,* I can tell you about some gossip even you need to know." Yet Beryl seemed in no hurry to get on with her news. She kept dodging the purpose of this tête-à-tête.

In so many ways the most practical person she knew, Beryl had one inexplicable vice: a passion for gossip. Not the garden-variety guess-what-the-neighbors-are-doing kind. Her need-to-know taste ran to the details of the often hilariously messy lives of what passes for celebrity in America. She knew about Wesley Snipes's supposed food phobias and the secret ingredient in Vivica Fox's beauty pack treatments, Dr. Dre's philosophy of dressing well, as well as what each of the *Friends* cast had done on their off-season hiatus. Her reading room was stacked with back issues of the *National Enquirer,* the *Star, Entertainment Weekly, Soap Opera Digest, Jet,* the *Sun*, and half a dozen lesser-known mags that only a dedicated celebrity junkie would bother to suss out. Until now they had an understanding. Beryl wouldn't try to involve her in her hobby, and she wouldn't gag and roll her eyes when Beryl occasionally brought up a tidbit in conversation.

Beryl looked good in a blue wide-leg pantsuit that complimented her pale blond Afro. It seemed Harold had grown to like the length—or rather lack of it—and the color. But the look on her face was more serious than most Saturday morning gossipfests were worth.

"So, what's up? Don't tell me. Denzel's left his wife!"

"*Grrrl, please!*" For once Beryl seemed nervous. "Harold says I shouldn't be the one to show you this but, Thea, it'll be on news racks tomorrow. I subscribe, so I get it ahead." She pushed the tabloid lying on the table toward Thea.

"No thanks. That's not really my idea of light reading."

"Oh, you don't have to read much. Just the headline." Beryl picked up the rag sheet and held it chest high. Just below the banner was a full-cover shot, made grainy by a telephoto lens. It was of Xavier and a woman. Below was the caption, " 'X' Black Radical Woos White Mistress."

"Okay, so?" Her gaze lingered on the photo. It wasn't a particularly good picture of Xavier who faced the camera. The woman, whose hand rested so confidently on Xavier's chest, faced three-quarters away. The suit she wore—

". . . Don't know your friend as well as you think."

She blinked. Her eyes felt vacuumed dry. "What?"

Beryl smirked. "A man of his reputation shacks up with a snowflake? You just know that's got to be middle-age crisis time."

"You don't know who that is?" Was that her voice? It sounded pipelined in from the well of chagrin into which she had fallen.

Beryl turned the paper around and gave it a long look. "I read the inside scoop, but it doesn't say. Probably means she's a nobody. They'd name a singer or actress. Too bad you can't see her face. And look at those hips. That's no sweet young thing."

"Maybe he likes mature women." She couldn't believe she was making a joke.

Beryl gave her a funny look. "Tell me you aren't furious?"

"I'm furious all right. For Godssakes, Beryl, that's me!"

Beryl gave the picture another look, this time after she picked up her over-the-counter for-small-print granny glasses. "It doesn't look a bit like you."

"Okay, so it's not a glamour shot, and I didn't know my rear was that big but—"

"Thea, it *is* you!" Beryl's cackle of laughter shattered the shock. "*Grrrl,* what were you doing feeling up the man in public?"

"It wasn't public. Well, it was taken out of doors. But I wasn't coming on to him."

"*Um-hm.* Well, you're shortly to be famous for what it looks like."

She snatched the paper. "I got to go!"

The chill January air seemed to sear her lungs as she walked home. Beryl had had her heat set way up. Why was it snowbirds, transplants from cold climates, cranked the heat up twice as high as Southerners when the temperature dropped below fifty in the South?

Found out! In full color with a screaming headline tailor-made to rack up interest at the front of every grocery checkout counter in every town in America.

She gripped the tabloid so tightly the pages made crunchy noises. It had taken a hint for Beryl to recognize her, but that didn't mean somebody somewhere else might not be swifter to the mark. Like Xavier's bishop or Selma. She had to warn Xavier, had to prevent Jesse—

"Oh God! Jesse!"

She hadn't yet had the talk with Jesse about what they were going to do about their man problems. Nor would Jesse discuss her grandparents. She wouldn't even have known that Jesse had started returning their calls if she hadn't picked up the phone without realizing someone was on the line. She didn't want to speak against Evan's parents, but it was hard.

When a car didn't materialize on the drive within a few days after Christmas, she hoped Jesse, poor baby, would get the picture that her grandparents were as much about getting their own way as generosity.

Had they come up with another scheme? Were they pumping Jesse for details of her mother's life that they might be able to use if it came to a court battle? Regardless of Xavier's reminder that grandparents didn't have rights, the Morgans had money. In America, that often trumped reason or rights.

She closed her front door before she glanced again at the paper. She was now front-page news in a scandal sheet. Scandal wouldn't look good in a civil suit.

Okay, so maybe Beryl had done her a favor. She might not, otherwise, have known about the article until it was too late.

It is too late, Thea! You've been outed!

"HATEFUL! WHAT KIND of adult makes a living nastying up other people's lives? It makes our relationship seem sordid, ugly."

Xavier was quiet a moment. He had stepped out of an important meeting to answer her panic call. When he spoke it was quiet, almost a whisper. That meant he didn't want to be overheard. "Are you certain this isn't about your feelings about us?"

"No! But—"

"No buts, Theadora." His voice continued in a slow, deep cadence. "Either you see this for the tabloid sleaze it is or admit that you care more about what people think than you do our relationship."

The rebuke came through clearly. "You think I'm making too much out of this."

"I think it rattled you. The first invasion of privacy usually does. Still, if Beryl didn't recognize you, there's every chance no one else will." He chuckled. "For one, they're fishing in the wrong ethnic pool. For another, from the way you describe the shot, it was taken from a great distance. Paparazzi do that, blanket a well-known celebrity location with shots. Jerome does the best he can to run interference. But someone must have gotten wind of the reason behind my planned press conference and sent a reporter to the church to snoop around."

"So I'm supposed to ignore this sleaze, even though I'm an innocent party?"

The Thornton hesitation. "Can you?"

"You make it sound like a test I have to pass."

Why are you trying to put this on him? Wasn't that your own happy self in the photo, too?

"You just need to figure out how to live with it, Theadora."

"Why? Are you telling me that there will be more stuff like this?"

"Very likely. David's gotten a few phone calls offering him money for an exclusive on his birth mother. If he found you, you can bet a group of dedicated professional snoops can."

The room took on the queasy pitch of a small boat at sea. "I told you making a media hype of finding David wasn't a wise idea."

"Despite what you think of my wisdom these days, I'm going to offer you another piece of advice. Don't go to the paper for a retraction. It will only make them think there's even more to hide."

"What about Jesse? If they find out about me, it's only a hop to Jesse. What do I tell her?"

"That there's a different set of rules for people who are part of the so-called celebrity life. Things will happen that will make you want to holler, and you can't. Not in public. Once they smell blood, they'll hound you to death."

"That's a pretty cynical and fatalistic point of view."

"You asked my opinion. I gave it."

Now shut up, Thea, before you're sorry.

The truth hit her, as it often did, as humor. This was as close as they ever came to phone sex, sort of. Like high school kids afraid to make that leap into their first sexual encounter, they kept the fires of this not-quite-a-relationship relationship at breathable levels by expending their pent-up heat in verbal combat.

"Xavier." Oh Lord, would he hear the laughter in her voice and think she was amused by his indignation? "Xavier, this has got to stop."

She could feel him nod through the phone. "We need to work this out one-on-one."

One-on-one, not one-to-one. A lot of heat in that allusion. The man had a way of following her thoughts.

"I can't get away right now. Not with my promotion brand new."

Liar. You're this close to saying race you to the first bedroom we can locate. "And I made a promise to Jesse. We swore off men for a month."

He didn't laugh at her. Then she realized she could hear footsteps. He must be seeking a more private place for the rest of their conversation. Finally a door closed, and she heard him take a long breath and release it just as slowly.

"Marry me."

"Don't—"

"I'm serious—"

"It's too soon. Too soon for Jesse, for everybody. For me."

"I'm not giving up."

She felt her smile well up from deep within. "I was counting on you saying that. But I can't hold you to it. You've got things you need and want to do. And I'm not fool enough to hope that someone else won't come along before I'm ready to consider any kind of future with you."

"You doubt me."

"No." Yet she couldn't help remembering the confidence factor in Celeste's boast before church a week earlier. "But I saw how your congregation reacts to you. Your female congregation. And I know your bishop is pressing marriage." He must have Xavier backed into a corner now that the illegitimacy of a son had been confirmed.

"Now, how'd you hear about that?"

"I have my ways."

"Yeah, you heard right. The bishop's about as stuck as a broken record on the subject of me marrying."

What sounded like tapping on a door was followed by Xavier saying in a very annoyed voice, "I know, Jerome. Tell them I'm coming."

She watched the second hand of the kitchen clock sweep past two numerals before he spoke again.

"Theadora, I can't debate this now. Two things. One, I don't date within my congregation, so I hope you didn't fill out the membership form in the church bulletin. Second, I won't marry to please anybody but myself."

"Tough but tender."

His pauses could wear a body out. "I'm past forty, feeling the chill of being alone."

"Loneliness isn't a good reason to marry."

"Sure, it is. All that talk about a well-adjusted man or woman not needing a mate to feel complete is bull. We all have needs. It's built into us. I need a lady who's interested in *all* that I'm about. The whole package. She's got to be able to get past the rep, the money, that whole adoration of the preacher thing."

"That's a lot to get past."

"You do it without trying."

"I knew you before."

"Yeah."

Two . . . three . . . four . . . five.

"But if my liabilities have come to outweigh my usefulness to you, that's how it is. I helped you get over Evan so now you can get on."

She glanced at her bare ring finger. "That's a lousy thing to say."

"I promised you I'd always tell you the truth as I see it."

"Fine. Great. See you around, Reverend."

"Thea, don't—"

How many times can you hang up on a man?

She stared at the tabloid until she noticed the date. Dinner with David and his parents was tonight. How was she going to face them now that she was scandal meat?

forty-five

"DO YOU HAVE expectations for me?"

Jesse had come into her bedroom just as Thea was trying to pull a new pair of control-top panty hose up over her photogenically challenged hips. Children knew when to attack their mothers with issues. Thumbs locked next to her thighs by hosiery, she couldn't really give her whole attention to the topic heading.

"Expectations?" She wriggled until the panty part rose two inches up the moon of her backside. "You mean like things I expect of you?" Wriggle, hop, wriggle, and her generously padded hipbones were encased. "Of course."

Jesse frowned. "What kind of expectations?"

"Let's see." She looked down and noticed the panty crotch had stopped a good six inches below her own. She shoved the hose down to her thighs and gathered up the extra material in her fingers. "I expect you to do your homework, get good grades, graduate, go to college, become a productive citizen." Already having made the journey once, the panty hose cooperated this time when she pulled, and the crotch made it to within an inch. Close enough. "Oh, and brush your teeth before bed and take out the trash on Wednesdays *and* Saturdays."

"Be serious, Mom."

"I'm very serious. You didn't get the trash out in time this morning."

"Okay, so what else? Like, for instance, socially, marriage."

"Well, you are socially adept most times." She reached for her best black slip. "And yes, I want grandchildren with a father to call their own."

"Never mind, I shouldn't have tried to talk to you—"

"Wait—" She pulled her slip over her head. "What's this about, Jesse?"

Jesse heaved a big sigh. "You never asked me why I came home at Christmas."

"No." The gravity of the topic took on new weight. She sat down on the edge of her bed. "It was enough that you did. But I'm not so grateful that I didn't realize you were running back home. Somebody did or said something you didn't like, right?"

"Maybe." When Jesse tossed her head, blond hair rippled and flowed over her shoulders in a way achieved only in shampoo commercials and for some few lucky teenage girls.

"Have they asked you to come back? Offered you things? That car?" Okay, she wanted to know what she was up against before they began negotiations.

Jesse took a few steps into the room and collapsed at her mother's feet, legs folded into a denim-clad pretzel. "It's not about things. It's about what I want."

"What do you want?" The most loaded question a parent could ask a child.

"Gramma and PopPop say I have a legacy to maintain, a social history to uphold. Because I am the last of the line, I have this huge responsibility to see that the Morgan family dynasty continues."

"Makes you want to puke and run in ten different directions at once, right?"

Jesse grimaced but then smiled. "Something like that. They showed me my portfolio. There's the Philly house and a trust fund and all these assets I'll have to one day manage. They have an apartment in Manhattan and one in Antwerp." Jesse's grin flashed through her doubts. "I'd like an apartment in Manhattan."

"After college graduation." Did she dare speak the truth? "With the Morgan fortune, you can hire managers to handle your assets. You'll live extremely well, can travel when and where you want. You could even draw an allowance from that trust fund so you won't have to work, if you're careful."

Jesse shook her head.

"Really?" What could she have left out of that alluring scenario?

"You and Daddy always said that the only things worth having are those that you've earned yourself."

"You were listening to those boring lectures?"

Jesse grinned. "I guess. Anyway, I don't want the burden of expectations. I want to make my own way. Mom, they even have a list of guys they think I should meet."

She smiled. "They had a list for your father, too. He swore he never dated a single one.

"Gramma asked me if I liked anybody. I told her about Keith." She looked away with a shrug.

"What did she say? You can't hurt my feelings."

"She said he sounded like a nice young man, only she wondered if he was the right kind." Jesse colored to the tips of her ears. "You know, like you. So we'd be inconspicuous in public."

Oh, you mean someone who looks white, even if he isn't. She wasn't going to call Jesse's Gramma racist. She wasn't.

"Do you think it's better for people to marry someone like themselves?" Jesse looked so earnest. "Someone they share social and economic values with, as well a certain resemblance?"

"Are you sure you want me to answer that question?"

Jesse shook her head. "You're different."

You're different. The standard rejection of the possibility that what seems the exception to the rule might actually be commonplace.

"So, you agree with your grandparents."

"No I don't. I just—" Jesse made a gesture of helplessness. "Mom, they're prejudiced! I know I shouldn't say that, but I can't stand the idea of them being ashamed of you."

Even if you marched out of here last month mouthing similar feelings? It's hard when someone mirrors our own failings to us.

She smiled at her child. All that brave young idealism under fire. Nowhere to run and nowhere to hide. "When it comes to race, not everybody who talks the talk can walk the walk."

"You're giving me jingoism."

That's my AP English baby! "It's not prejudice. It's self-protection. Your dad's parents taught him to believe that all peoples are equal. He was able and willing to go into the world and experience that truth. But for people who have a lot invested in the status quo, a true change of heart isn't easy."

"You're saying they can't help it?"

"Oh, they can help it." Fine lines, splitting hairs. "Try not to expect too much from them, Jesse, that's all I'm saying. They can leave you all the money in the world, and it won't matter, if you've learned to be yourself."

"What if I mess that up?"

"You can't mess up being you. But you have to be open, take chances." Had to bring it up, even if it met another rejection. "For instance, you could come to David's dinner tonight. Meet his parents."

"I should have known." Jesse rolled her eyes. "You're just like them. Always trying to force what you want on me."

"No, there's a big difference." She waited until Jesse looked directly at her again. "I expect you to become independent. I even tolerate your hostility to my opinions. That's why you came home."

Trying to sound as no big deal as possible, she pointed to the clock. "Now, child of mine, I really do have to finish dressing."

But for a while after Jesse left, she sat on the bed caught in a reverie that had no resolution.

The Morgans took so well the news that their only child was in love with a colored, Negro, black, Afro-American, African American. Too well? she'd asked Evan. Would they have been openly hostile had she shown up on their son's arm in a skin tone to match Beryl's? He said that his folks took her at face value, and that was enough.

Face value. Now there was a loaded metaphor.

Men never probed the surface when they suspect they wouldn't like the answer lying beneath. Women could worry a thing to death, teasing out all the nuances and threads until sometimes the detail was clear but the overall pattern was lost. She would probably never decide which was best. Each way just *was*. Like the Morgans. In this life, one had to learn to deal with the other side.

"THEADORA?" XAVIER SOUNDED hoarse, like he had developed a cold since noon.

"Oh, hi, Xavier." She adjusted the sound level on her cell phone. "Sorry about hanging up on you before. You're right about us needing to talk. But I'm on my way to David's for dinner at the moment."

"He's not there."

"Oh? Where is he?"

"Theadora, pull over and park. I need to talk to you."

"I can talk and drive. I have a hands-free system."

"Just do it, Theadora."

"If this is another ad hoc proposal . . ." She pulled into a service station as she neared the corner. "Okay, pulled over. Do I need to put on the parking brake?"

"Theadora, you've got to be strong now—"

"What's wrong? Oh God, David's been hurt. Xavier? He's hurt bad, right?"

"He's gone, Theadora."

forty-six

BILOXI WAS GRAY. A steady, hissing rain bleached all color from the lush tropical hues one expected of a Southern coastal town. A north wind seeped through coats and scarves, its touch as chilling as the sight of the discreetly covered mound of earth a few yards away.

She resented that fertile earth smell. From bitter experience, she knew that for months afterward, the pungent aroma of soil from a flowerpot or freshly spaded garden would remind her of a grave. And then the memory of this moment, this day, this void would trigger in her the grief gone numb after three days.

"The Lord giveth and the Lord taketh away . . ."

No feeling. She felt nothing as she glanced slowly around the sorrow-filled faces ringing the graveside. They were there for David, and for his parents, and for the young woman beside them who would now never be family. But it was no comfort at all. Couldn't they see that?

Ba'Mama used to say, "There's one God's truth about life, baby. We come into this world alone, and that's surely how we leave it." Her grandmother should have added, "And that's how the living get left. Alone."

She hugged her daughter closer as Jesse began to sob again. Thea had no tears. Tears were for things that could yet be fixed or for regret over what could have been prevented. She had no tears for the unimaginable.

Real enough. The casket at my feet. Real enough.

David was dead.

Three days ago, a pickup truck ran a red light just as he made a left turn onto the street where he lived. One second of difference in either direction, and they might not be here. Full impact on the driver's side. They said he didn't suffer. She prayed to God not. Everyone here today was doing that suffering for him.

At the church service, the Greers' minister spoke about the inexplicable grief when a young life was taken away. Yet there was rejoicing in heaven, for another of the faithful had been borne home to glory. In time, understanding would come, and the grief would depart. But one had to possess in order to let go.

The child I could not get my hands around.

She looked up at Xavier, who stood beside her, tall and dark and still as a monument. Grief was a terrible thing to see on a strong man's face. She wondered if he knew he was crying.

She reached for his hand, but he moved it away. He hadn't said a word to her as they sat together during the church service. Had said little since the call that once more shattered her understanding of how life should be.

He blames me. I cannot blame him for that.

She had kept David a secret from him all these years. Just when he had found his son, he had been snatched away, this time irrevocably.

They didn't stand with the rest of the family. David had grandparents and uncles, aunts, and cousins to occupy the family seats under the canopy. That cocoon of compassion didn't include her. She was not the mother. Just as Xavier was not the father.

Not for the first time she felt like a stranger in her own life.

As she turned at last away from the graveside, her expression must have betrayed her thoughts, because Selma approached and hugged her. She even leaned her head on Thea's shoulder for a moment, uncaring it seemed this once that she squashed the thick collar of her mink.

On the other side of her, Elkeri held an umbrella for Aunt Della while helping her maintain her footing in the slick grass.

Thea hadn't been able to contain her surprise when they appeared at the church. Della explained that without being asked, they had flown to New Orleans and then driven her over for the service. Another time, Selma's sacrifice would have amazed her. Now it only lent another layer of unreality to the day.

When Selma lifted her head, she sucked in the full wedge of her lower lip, her eyes brimming. "You be strong, Big Sis."

Aunt Della gripped Thea's arm with surprising strength. "It's by God's grace. I believe that, Theadora. All things through Christ Jesus." The dusky-pearl skin about Della's eyes and mouth had collapsed, creating fine crepeing in the hollows. Today she looked every one of her seventy-eight years. "But, Lord, Lord," she whispered. "Some things these old eyes don't need to witness."

She bent to hug the older woman. "It's all right, Aunt Della. I'll be all right."

Della nodded. "You're strong, Theadora. The strongest among us." She seemed about to say more but then gave a tiny shake of her head and turned away.

She feels so much. I feel nothing.

She noticed Xavier had disappeared. So had Jesse.

She found him on the far side of the cemetery, standing bare-headed not far from a lone black limo. He was not alone. Jesse was hurrying to catch up to him.

She saw Jesse reach out to him, and Xavier take her hand and hold it in both of his. She couldn't hear what they were saying, but Jesse looked so grown-up, as if she were comforting him.

When Jesse turned away from Xavier, she spied her mother. After a short hesitation, she marched up to her.

"I need to get out of here. Can I have the car keys?"

"It's a rental, and you don't have a full license yet."

"Fine. I'll ride with Aunt Della."

She watched her daughter dart off at an angle back toward the line of cars waiting to depart. What had she said to Xavier or what had he said to Jesse to make her want to run away?

She turned back to find him standing alone. This once, no one else seemed willing to intrude upon his solitude.

She approached slowly, gave him plenty of time to stop her by look or word or action. He said nothing, just stood watching her through raw eyes.

She didn't mean to touch him, but he moved in response to her, and then his arms were about her, holding her.

"It's God's will, Theodora. Inexplicable to us mortals but part of the divine plan."

She pulled back a little. "You still believe that, don't you?"

He nodded slightly. "It's all that sustains me. But today it's a bitter harvest, Theodora. Bitter."

"I wish I had your belief."

"In so many ways you don't credit yourself." He closed his eyes. "You found the courage to go on after Evan died."

She felt a deep tremor in him and backed away, afraid his sorrow would breach the barrier to her own. "That wasn't courage, that was a retreat into the dull routine of life."

"Sometimes that's what grace looks like, the dull routine of life." This time he backed away. "Now I've got to go."

"So soon?"

"As long as I stay, they stay." He nodded grimly in the direction of the two cameramen she had noticed earlier outside the church. Now they hovered under a dripping oak several plots away from the burial site.

"You were right. I couldn't protect him." His expression fractured into new lines of grief. "Mrs. Greer says David was upset about more calls from one of those rags to his place of work. The day before, someone offered coworkers money for leads to finding his birth mother. Maybe that's what he was thinking about when he drove into that intersection. If he'd been paying attention . . ."

She heard his anguish, but it didn't move her. She felt hollow. "You aren't responsible. A driver ran a red light. You couldn't control that."

"I was so full of myself! So prideful! Wanted the world to know. My son." He wagged his head.

She tried to touch his wet cheek, but he again jerked away

from her touch. "Let me be, Theadora. Just walk away, and let me be."

"I can't."

"Then I'll have to do it for both of us."

It took only seconds for him to disappear into the interior of his private limo, and then it drove off, its direction opposite that of the funeral procession.

forty-seven

SHE TOUCHED A finger to the streaming glass patio door of her motel room. The Greers tried to insist that she and Jesse stay with them, but a hotel room seemed a better idea. Other out-of-town friends were staying here as well. An impromptu gathering had begun in the room next door, where visitors continued to eat and drink the remains of the funeral dinner held earlier in the church fellowship hall hosted by the women's auxiliary.

Dozens who had not braved the rain at the burial site had waited in the warmth of the hall to express again their condolences and, of course, eat. The smell of fried chicken, baked ham, and peach cobbler permeated every corner.

After looking over the homemade fare, Aunt Della rallied long enough to remark in her best N'awlins voice, "All those casseroles! I had no idea there were so many uses for cream of mushroom soup and canned onion rings."

How many times this day had Thea pressed a hand, hugged a pair of shoulders, or just smiled tight and hard as the knot in her stomach and said, "Thank you," or "I appreciate your words"? Or just let someone else, someone less affected than her, cry for her benefit? Too many times to recall or want to recount.

The litany of sorrow was always the same, as familiar as a childhood nursery rhyme. That did not dull or lessen the sentiment.

Such a good young man . . . son . . . friend . . . too young . . . such a shock.

The service was . . . lovely . . . beautiful . . . inspiring . . . moving . . . just right.

We . . . love . . . pray for . . . are thinking of . . . you.

You're . . . so brave . . . so calm . . . so strong.

Can I get you . . . coffee . . . tea . . . a drink . . . water . . . anything?

Anything we can do . . . don't hesitate . . . the slightest thing . . . anything at all.

In a few . . . days . . . weeks . . . eventually . . . things will look . . . better . . . brighter . . . up.

"Mommy?"

Still dressed in the new black suit and heels that made her seem a good five years older than her sixteen years, Jesse stood irresolute on the threshold of the motel room, as if she thought she might not be welcome.

"Come in, Jesse."

She moved quickly, shutting the door behind her. Her face was still swollen from weeping, but her expression was one of sullen exasperation. "Mommy, when are they all going home?"

"In a little while." She brushed a strand of hair from her daughter's face, then cupped her suspiciously warm cheek. "Are you all right, baby?"

Jesse shook her head. "It's been a horrible day!" The complaint ended on a wail of primal longing for seclusion that Thea shared.

She hugged her close as Jesse began to sob. *Sweet baby mine.*

After a minute, Thea said calmly. "Why don't you go to the lounge and watch TV for a while?"

Jesse shook her head. "I don't want to go back out there." She leaned down to press her head against her mother's neck. "I want to stay here with you."

"Okay. Then come and get in my bed for a while."

She folded back the coverlet of one of two beds in the room and then the sheet, remembering how often she had done this when Jesse was sick as a child. How easy it had been in those days to delight and comfort her daughter. The privilege of sharing her parents' bed, if only for an afternoon nap, had made her feel safe and a little less ill.

Jesse kicked off her shoes and slipped under the covers.

Though it was cool outside, the room's air conditioner had been running all day to combat the humidity. She pulled the sheet up protectively over her child. "See if you can fall asleep."

Jesse looked up at her. The trusting toddler she had long outgrown peeked out for an instant through the candid gaze of the independent teen she had become. "Don't leave me."

Thea sat down on the edge of the bed and brushed at the tear sliding down her daughter's cheek. "I promise I'll stay right here until you fall sleep."

Out of habit, she punched on the radio, turning the dial in search of something less inappropriate than the plaintive voice of Tyrese singing "Sweet Lady."

She seldom listened to any of the religious stations that had sprung up on the airwaves in recent years. It seemed somehow disrespectful to groove through one's workday to the Lord's music the way one might Take Six or Kenny G.

Yet the first slow cadences of "How Great Thou Art" stilled her hand on the dial.

"*. . . When I in awesome wonder, consider all the things Thy hands have made. I see the dark, I hear the rolling thunder . . .*"

That voice, a black woman's contralto bigger than the mortal body encasing it, embodied a grandeur and pain and majesty seldom heard. It made her scalp tingle and her fingertips itch. It squeezed her heart.

"*Then sings my soul, my Savior God to thee. How great Thou art, how great Thou art . . .*"

She closed her eyes. That voice called to her. It felt good, but it hurt, too, deep down, so deep inside that it bent her over as the melody pulled out of her that fearful neediness she had seen in Xavier's grief but refused to acknowledge in herself.

Finally she understood, in a way no reasoning it out had managed, that this was real. David was gone. Like Evan. Life would ever after be different. But not hopeless, and not lost. But first there was the need to grieve.

"Mom? Are you all right?"

She glanced at her daughter, caught between the rush of feeling sweeping her and the desire to protect. "Yes . . . I . . . Don't be afraid, Jesse. I'm just sad."

"I feel like this is my fault."

"What are you talking about?"

Jesse looked away. "Remember that day at Aunt Selma's when I said I hated David and I wished he'd never been born?" Jesse looked up again, features flattened by shame. "I didn't really mean that I wanted him to die."

"Oh, Jesse, of course you didn't."

"But now, after everything." Her voice shrank to a whisper. "It's like I cursed him."

She looked at Jesse with all the tenderness of which she was capable. "Do you really think your anger is that strong?"

Jesse shrugged. "Maybe."

"What about the other people you've been mad at lately? Me. Your dad."

"I'm not angry with Daddy!" Jesse looked stunned. "I still love him."

"I know you do. But I was angry with him for a while, too. He left us without warning. We didn't have a chance to say good-bye. We felt cheated."

Jesse began twisting her pearl birthday ring around her finger. "I just want things to be the way they were."

"Some changes can't be taken back, Jesse."

Jesse nodded, and she suspected she was thinking about all the ugly things she had said and done while David was alive. "I didn't get a chance to say sorry. That's scary."

"It's very scary. In the days after your dad died, I felt as if I'd been shoved through the door of a plane without instructions for my parachute. I didn't know if I could take care of myself, let alone you. I was terrified every day for months."

Jesse looked at her with a gaze brightened by tears. "You never told me that you were scared."

"That's because I didn't want to frighten you. I needed to be brave for both of us. I didn't even want you to see me cry."

Jesse reached out and touched her hand. "It's okay to cry now, Mommy."

"Yes, it's okay."

She leaned into the arms of her daughter and at last wept for the loss of the son who had never been wholly hers.

forty-eight

"AND A PAIR of those capris cut low so the belly button shows, just like Jada Pinkett Smith wears."

"I don't know. We didn't show our pregnant bellies when Jesse came along."

"You didn't have as cute a belly button as I have!" Selma's throaty chuckle sounded as sassy as ever. "And there's this skin-tight number I bought for the Easter cruise Elkeri's booked. Long sleeves and to the floor but dips so low in back it gives a whole new meaning to cleavage."

"You go, girl!" Thea laughed and shook her head, although Selma couldn't see her through the phone line.

As with all things she put her mind to, Selma was turning expectant motherhood into an event. No other woman ever had been with child quite the way Selma Yoruba was working it. Six months along, she was deep in the launch stage of a new branch of her interior decorating firm called Bashiri Baby. The first showcase, her own nursery, contained commissioned murals by Atlanta artists of the lives of Shaka Zulu, Haile Selassie, and Martin Luther King, Jr., as well as original scenes from *The Lion King*. "Because you know that's an African tale Disney laid claim to."

Furnishings were receiving a similar custom treatment. Selma had faxed her sketches of her ideas for bamboo-finished bassinets and cribs, chests with zebra and leopard finishes, and African animal cutouts for drawer pulls. Mud cloth window treatments, Kente cloth spreads, and fake fur throw rugs would be available for older kids. "Got to plant what you mean to grow," ended Selma's every pitch.

That meant a mini diva or black urban princelet.

The one surprising aspect of her pregnancy? Selma didn't want to know the sex of her child. "I told Elkeri it would disturb my creative flow. This way, I wake up and go with the vibe of the day, boy or girl. Motherhood is powerful, Big Sis. Empowering."

After a few more exchanges, Thea hung up, smiling to herself.

It had come to her a few days after David's death that she and Selma needed a readjustment. Jesse was still getting accustomed to the idea that churchgoing wasn't a phase her mother was going through but was back in the family agenda to stay. She had found an AME church in Plano, and with Jesse driving, headed up there each week. That first Sunday she had given over to a reflection of her relationship with her sister and how it needed to change. Not ought to or might or could but *had to*.

Right in the middle of the sermon the *how to* hit her. She needed to start *acting* like a big sister.

The answer came so swift and hard she jumped in her seat, making the woman next to her shout, "Amen, child!"

That thought led to a lot of others during the next few days, some of them painful to admit. For instance, she was every bit as much to blame as Selma for the split. All these years, she had allowed Selma's sniping and ugly remarks to be her penance, her hair shirt, the thorn in her side that reminded her that no matter how much good she accomplished, she had once done wrong. It didn't take much thought on that topic to grant that the punishment worked both sides of the street. The buildup of hostility and resentment had poisoned every aspect of their relationship. Perhaps after a while, it hurt Selma more than it penalized Thea. After all, she'd moved on to have a happy marriage and daughter to love, while Selma had charge of the shame-on-you department. That left her without a sister she could confide in or feel close to. One who openly loved her.

She patted the frame of the snapshot she'd brought in to work a month ago, one taken the summer she was fifteen and Selma was ten. In it, two skinny girls in pigtails hugged each other's necks, caramel and cream cheeks pressed together, wearing grins as wide as their faces. Hard to remember that time. But not impossible. And getting a little easier each day.

Not that she had simply called Selma with her new attitude. She could imagine the reply. "Oh, so now *you* want to be friends. Now that it's *your* idea!"

Instead, she begun calling once a week just to talk. And then kept it up for the past two months. The first call elicited the news that Selma had decided to keep her child.

"After what you went through with David, I told Elkeri we could start thinking about being parents. Girl, he got shouting-down-the-house happy. So then I said I guess it was all right with him then if he was going to be a daddy a bit sooner than later."

Motherhood was their new link. Sometimes their conversations still walked on the wild side. Fighting back worked better than "Let me explain." And just to keep things on a level Selma felt comfortable with, so it wasn't only about sisterly love, she told her yes, she had an agenda: Great-grandmother Estelle's mango wood armoire.

Last time the subject came up, Selma said, "You'll have to pay for the shipping because I still say it's mine."

Thea chuckled. *Things do improve.* The armoire was on its way.

Other things weren't so easily resolved. But she was on a fast learning curve, inside and outside the office.

She glanced at her handiwork on her office bulletin board. She'd made the scandal rags one more time. A week after the funeral, she was relegated to a small picture on page twenty-eight. "Grieving parents" was the caption of the photo that showed Xavier and her embracing in the rain. The short text below identified her as the natural mother of Reverend Thornton's son. No further reference to mistress or race. Beryl explained that once the illegitimate biracial son angle was gone, the story lacked juice. Misfortune didn't make for sexy copy.

She'd seen Ron's bug-eyed glance the first time he noticed the two tabloid stories pinned next to shipping schedules and in-house notices, but he'd said nothing. She'd offered him the only explanation she offered anyone who dared to comment, a confident smile. Notoriety had its advantages. No one refused or even put off her business calls these days.

Then there was Joe Ortega. The day after he left Petro Chem, he'd sent her a small, wrapped package. Inside was a silk box containing a set of Chinese chiming balls. Not the ordinary silver kind, this was a large pair of brass balls. "Thanks," was all the card said. She still smiled each time she passed them on her office credenza.

Marcia buzzed in. "Are you expecting a personal guest, Ms. Morgan?"

"No, I'm not." She glanced at her schedule to double check.

"Oh. Because there's a Mr. Thornton in the lobby asking for you."

Her heart stumbled. "Thank you. Please send him up."

She didn't realize she was sitting down until her backside hit the seat with a jolt. Xavier hadn't been in touch since the day of David's funeral. Nor had he returned her phone calls or replied to her letters. When the man did not want to be gotten to, he wasn't. Jerome wasn't even responding. She'd been cut off.

Why now? Why here?

She glanced around her new corner office, wishing the paint job was complete. No, stupid thought. Xavier Thornton wasn't going to be impressed by paint.

She quickly cleared her desk and then wondered as she applied fresh lipstick why she cared how she appeared. And why her hands shook. She understood good-bye. This was a formal call. Otherwise, he would have come by the house. Fine. Good. She knew where she stood.

She didn't at first recognize the blurred silhouette of the slight man who passed one of the sand-washed glass panels flanking her door, but she knew before the door opened that this wasn't Xavier.

"Mr. Thornton." She was on her feet in an instant. "Welcome."

"How you doing, Ms. Morgan?" William Thornton's easy smile unclenched the fist of her stomach. "My, my, so this is what an executive's office looks like." He grinned and nodded. "Looks good on you, Ms. Morgan."

"Thank you, Mr. Thornton."

"Thought I was Uncle Way to you?" He took the hand she offered him and held it firmly. "Now, how are you doing, Theadora?"

She met his concerned gaze level with her own. "I'm fine."

He slowly moved his head back and forth. "You lost a son a little while back. No mother would be fine behind that."

So Xavier had told his family. "I'm better. Thank you for asking."

"That's better." He patted her hand before he let it go. "You don't need to be polite with me. But if you'd rather not talk at your place of business—"

"No, no problem." She pushed her door shut. "These days, people have come to understand my personal life is pretty much my own business."

"I hear you." His gaze had lit on her bulletin board, and his grin turned impish. "Can't stop folks talking, but you don't have to give it a hearing."

She indicated a chair for him, but he refused it. "What can I do for you?"

"I'm a old man about to get up in your business. You tell me go, and I'm out that door. But I got a few things I think need saying." He waited a beat then went on. "First off, why weren't you there to stand up with David at the Christmas press conference?"

"Xavier didn't tell me about it." His snow-white brows lifted. "He knew I thought it was a mistake."

He studied her hard, then nodded once. "Told Xavier he was moving too fast. We all did. Especially Pearl. Should've heard her."

She smiled. Strange to think of Xavier's sister and her as being on the same side. "I said at the time it was a mistake. Now, after all that's happened, I'm glad he did it."

He rubbed his chin whiskers. "You know my nephew blames himself for his son's death?"

"Still?"

She didn't know if his head motion was a yes or just a comment on his own bewilderment over Xavier's belief. "Says he pushed the boy into a high-profile world he wasn't prepared for. Said you told him different, and you've never been wrong. Know him better than he knows himself."

She felt herself blushing under that shrewd glance. "I had no idea Xavier talked so much about me."

Uncle Way chuckled. "Now, I didn't say he talked all that much. My nephew's a lot like his uncle. Got words for everything and everybody but himself. Why I'm here." He looked around for the chair he had initially declined. "Can I sit now?"

"Certainly." She took the other chair so that they were seated side by side.

"I ain't got this old being a fool. I know how to hold on to family business. But the way I figure it, you already are family. You talk with my nephew lately?"

"Not since the funeral." She felt funny confessing it. "He won't accept my calls."

"That's what I figured. You heard he took that sabbatical from Saint James's despite the bishop's wishes?"

"My sister told me." She smoothed her skirt, uncertain what was expected of her beyond pleasantness.

His gaze moved away from hers for a moment, peering out the corner set of windows behind her desk. "Nice view. Real nice."

When he turned his head back toward her, she noticed that he had that Thornton serious way of looking at you, as though what he said next might change your life. "My nephew's in deep pain. You know about that kind of pain, don't you?"

"Yes." No need to ask if he knew about Evan or her problems with Jesse or her in-laws. He knew enough.

"All right then." Uncle Way nodded to himself. "Been a while since we've had so dynamic a presence in the pulpit. Someone experienced enough to be respected by our national leaders and young enough to command the respect of the youthful brethren. Xavier's got crossover appeal, too." He sneaked a peek at her, eyes flashing. "That Reverend Billy Graham's an old man. Country's gonna need a new spiritual leader."

"Forgive my smile, Uncle Way, but you make Xavier sound like the next messiah, something that I suspect he would reject."

"No doubt, no doubt." He looked very satisfied with her answer. "But you understand what's at stake. Xavier's future is not just the life of one man. Within his life's work lies the hope of the many. But to do good works, he's got to first find peace within himself. You know anybody could help him with that?"

She placed a protective hand over her heart. "Not me?"

"I expect you're about the only body who could. My nephew's got some good qualities, but he's also got itchy feet. Never stays long doing anything. His son's death together with the circumstances of his birth has him questioning his fitness to preach. Guilt and itchy feet might carry him right out the pulpit. Somebody's got to stop him."

"I tried to talk to him at David's funeral." A shadow of sadness sailed through her thoughts. "He walked away from me."

Uncle Way wagged his head again. "My nephew's too stubborn to ask for help. And he's afraid."

"Afraid of what?"

"He's scared of *you*." Uncle Way's chocolate Santa face wreathed itself in smiles. "You got to know you get to him in places he didn't know he had to be gotten to. You bother and bewilder the boy."

She laughed nervously. "You're giving me way too much credit."

"Oh no. I've seen you handle Pearl and the others." He chuckled. "They didn't like above half the idea of your first marriage. But when they tried to talk to Xavier about it, he forgot he was a child of God for the time it took to put them in their place. When a woman has that kind of power over a man, she can have him any way she wants him, sautéed, broiled, or fried."

Embarrassment popped her out of her chair, and she moved a little away. "You seem to think a lot of my powers of attraction."

He nodded. "You got the boy wide open. You just got to give him a reason to turn around. If you feel the same." He cocked his head to one side. "What I see when I see you two together says you do."

She knew she needed to choose her words carefully. "There's a lot of pain between us. Past mistakes and hurts."

"And I'm not asking the why of any of it." He stood up. "Well, I had my say. Now, I won't be cluttering up your nice office any longer with these old bones."

She tried to keep the question from slipping out. It got the best of her, anyway. "Where is Xavier?"

Uncle Way grinned. "I got it right here, written down on this piece of paper in my pocket." He took it out and handed it to her.

But when she reached for it, he held on to the other end. "You're woman enough to turn him around if you want. But if you do, you gotta come all the way for all time. He needs the kind of love and encouragement only an all-time woman can give."

She held on to the paper when he released it. "I can't promise anything."

"Not asking you to. But if after this, my nappy-headed nephew ain't got sense enough to appreciate you, I'm a come back down here and propose to you myself." He winked. "I got moves that boy ain't ever even thought of."

She laughed.

Uncle Way kissed her cheek and grinned. "You're family, Theadora. Always will be to me."

As he opened the door, she said, "You didn't say what brought you to town."

He stopped at the door and looked back at her. "Sure I did."

For several seconds after the door closed behind him, a sense of absolute desolation washed over her. She had begun to heal, was slowly but steadily reerecting the self-protective walls that had been her security until Xavier reentered her life. For months she'd felt like a raw egg minus its shell. Now she had practically promised to go where and do what for a man who didn't want to know her name? The back of himself was the last thing Xavier had shown her. That might be all he had to offer her.

The palpable beat of fear knocked against her breastbone. She hadn't promised Uncle Way anything. What did she owe herself?

forty-nine

"YOU NEVER JOINED."

Thea opened the refrigerator. "Does this discussion have a subject?"

"Sororities." Jesse leaned against the kitchen counter. "I've been asked to join the Delta Delta Chi little sisters."

"One of those high school grooming groups for college Greek organizations?"

"Only the top one."

"That's nice." She stuck her head in, looking for something quick and appetizing to present itself for dinner.

"Maybe. It's just that they have these rules."

"Most groups, do."

"They have dumb rules. Like restrictions about weight and hair and stuff."

She located a salad in a bag and closed the door. "Hair?"

"They have a Blondes Have More Fun day once a month. Everybody, I mean *everybody* has to be blond, even if it means wearing a wig."

"I see." She kept her eyes on the tossed salad she was unwrapping. She had promised herself to stay out of Jesse's personal decisions as much as possible, but she could feel herself tensing. Farrah Fawcett was still an icon in Texas.

"Do you think I should trade on my looks?"

"I suppose it depends on the purpose."

Choose your battles carefully, Mom.

"If you were a model or a movie star, that would pretty much be your raison d'être. But using beauty as a standard for worthiness in a club . . . What do you think?"

"I think it reeks. There're a lot of pretty girls at school who aren't blonds. Juanita Martinez says it's just a way to keep Latinas and blacks out of Delta Delta Chi. But then she's always accusing someone or something of discrimination. Besides, they asked her."

A car horn blared in the street. She noticed Jesse had a backpack slung across her shoulder. She gave her mother a quick look. "I'm going to the library for an hour. I have this research report to do with my physics lab partner."

"With who?"

"A guy."

"Name, please."

"Etienne Steele. He's a new transfer student. His mother is English and his father's from Trinidad. He wears these amazing little glossy braids all over his head. And, Mom, he's got brown skin, but his eyes are blue, just like mine!"

"Sounds cute."

"He's not *that* cute. He's an inch shorter than me. But he's funny. And smart. He can talk this crazy language that is part French and Spanish and Carrib. Cracks everybody up."

She smiled and nodded. "So you've made a new friend."

"Guess what? He's asked me out. To prom."

"And you said?"

"I'd think about it. It's two months off." Jesse smiled mischievously. "Harper's gonna have a cow! He's *not* Delta Delta Chi boyfriend material."

No need to weigh in on that scale.

Jesse was feeling her way through this just fine. "Tell him your mother doesn't think much of guys who blow their horns instead of using the doorbell."

"Mom!"

"Jesse!"

Jesse giggled. "You're right. I deserve respect."

The world might have to turn about a thousand more times before Jesse had it sorted out for herself. But there was progress being made.

"Oh, Jesse, just a minute." She grabbed a dish towel to dry her hands. "I'm thinking about taking a short trip this weekend. To see Reverend Thornton."

Jesse turned around and leaned back against the doorjamb, speculation in her expression. "You've heard from him?"

"No, and I'm worried about that."

Jesse nodded. "He was kinda freaked at the cemetery. You know what he said? That I didn't need to worry, because he wasn't going to be in your life anymore."

Surprise thumped her in the chest. "And you're just now telling me that?"

Jesse shrugged. "He was upset. I didn't think he meant it."

"He meant it."

Jesse sucked her lower lip a moment. "You still love him, don't you?"

She nodded. "Part of me always will."

"Then you should go after him. A modern woman doesn't take no for an answer."

"Jesse, you can't change your mind again. Not about this."

Jesse shrugged. "I'll be gone in a year, to college or whatever—"

"To college."

"Okay. Then you'll be here all alone in this big house. You're still young. You need a life, and I don't want to have to worry about me not being here for you."

"What about your grandparents?"

Her expression darkened for a moment. "I figure it's about time they got used to things the way they really are."

Thea nodded as the car horn sounded again. "That young man is getting impatient."

Jesse rolled her eyes. "Aunt Selma says a woman should never let a man think he's got it made with a woman."

"When did you talk to your aunt about boys?"

Jesse smirked. "She calls me sometimes. Said that since you hadn't had much experience with men, marrying so young, she thought I should talk to someone who's dated since Carter was president."

"Ow!" Even Selma's helpful hints had a sting.

"But she's so busy being pregnant, I figure the talks won't last that long."

"She loves you."

Jesse shrugged again. "She's okay. And I'm going to finally have a cousin."

This time there was a knock at the garage door. A smile lit up Jesse's face. "Looks like you get to meet Etienne."

She started toward the door but then did a fast break turn that made her the top scorer for her team. "Where are you going? Atlanta?"

She shook her head. "Baja California."

Jesse's right eyebrow arched, just like her father's. "Sweet!"

fifty

"NO, SEÑORA. NO one here by that name."

"Gracias."

She exited the hotel and tilted her head back so that the broad brim of her straw hat no longer obscured her view of the town. Until she arrived on the southern tip of Baja, she hadn't understood how vague Uncle Way's information was. Xavier was in Cabo San Lucas. This area at the tip of the Baja peninsula was a compilation of old fishing villages, secluded villas for the rich, and brand-new hotels with enough international tourists to turn her search in a place where she did not speak the language into a life-size version of *Where's Waldo*.

She stepped out into the square awash in the prickly heat of the desert sun. An old well decorated in brightly colored tiles stood at the center, surrounded by adobe buildings in colors of yellow, soft peach, and orange. Bougainvillea vines bursting with fuchsia and white flowers cascaded from balconies overhung by Spanish tile roofs. In the shade, the air was perceptibly cooler and laced with the fresh smell of sea salt. It was the perfect place for a vacation. For relaxation.

"Muy romantico," the airline attendant had said with a wink when she told him her destination.

But this was not a romance. This was more like *Night of the Iguana*. She had come here to look for a self-defrocked minister who had expatriated himself to the land of sun and surf and . . . sin?

She adjusted the strap of her sundress and headed across the square. It had been building all morning, the feeling that she'd made a mistake in coming to search for Xavier. What if he wasn't only not glad to see her but furious to be disturbed? Worst-case scenario? He wasn't alone.

Would he tell even Uncle Way if he had slipped off for a little solace with a lady friend?

Lawd 'a mercy, Thea! It's too late to second-guess yourself. This hen's flown that coop. The trouble is you're scared. Runnin' scared. Like Xavier.

She paused by the fountain, its single trickle of water coming from a slightly rusty pipe sticking through the Mexican tiles. She stared at the painted designs of birds and flowers and shells until the colors blurred, and she took one of those deep, cleansing breaths that yoga instructors were always rhapsodizing about. This was her day for courage.

SHE NOTICED A cab stand as she walked out of the square and into the main street. Three drivers lounged in the shade of the tin roof shelter and smoked. Who would know the tourists better? They shook their heads after she described Reverend Thornton. "No one by that name, *señora*."

She tried not to let the tang of disappointment defeat her, but the taste of tears was strong in her mouth. Then she remembered what his sisters had said about the family code when they wanted to get through to him.

"How about someone named Javier?"

"*Ah, sí, señora.*" The shortest of the three, a man with an Inca bowl-cut hairstyle, nodded and smiled. "There's a black man here by that name. Reverend Javier. He rents the last cottage in the curve of the bay. That way." He pointed toward the far end of the beach. "You walk. It's faster. The road takes you back through town. More than an hour."

"*Gracias.*" She tipped him and hurried away.

Tourists slathered in suntan lotion filled the near end of the beach, simmering in the sun while a succession of steel drum bands performed on the patios of the resorts she passed. To feel the sun-baked sand, she slipped off her sandals. The stretch was longer than it seemed. After fifteen minutes, her shoulders and the tips of her nose were as pink as boiled shrimp and just as tender.

She saw him long before she could really recognize him. Alone on an empty stretch of beach, he sat on the hull of an overturned dinghy facing the water. One foot plowed into the sand, balancing him on the curving surface. The other bare leg was bent, ankle resting on the opposite knee. Both arms were stretched out, the back of his hands resting on his knees, palms up and fingers gently curled toward the sky. A modified Lotus position for meditation or prayer.

She noticed, as she had at odd moments throughout the last months, that his expression was very serious when he was alone. She paused a little away. He looked complete, peaceful, and she didn't want to break that perfect peace. How near to impossible it was to get down that deep, to become privy to the most intimate of one's own thoughts. How hard-won his peace was. And how beautiful.

Impossible, too, to ignore the feeling that came over her in his presence. That recognition of a need in oneself, not unlike the let-down reflex when a nursing mother hears her child's cry. The physical expression in that flow of love warmed her now. He was someone she could not walk away from. She knew it in her soul. When, after several seconds, he didn't sense her presence, she reached out and touched his shoulder. He turned his head, looking genuinely astonished, but didn't speak. The deep serenity of the previous moment left a residue of tranquillity in his expression, despite his surprise. After a moment, he looked up past her, as if in expectation that she had brought others straggling along behind her. "You alone?"

"Like you."

He looked at her with a slight smile of understanding.

She thought she had a lot more to say, ways to spin the damage of showing up uninvited and making points that could not be denied. Looking at him now, she knew that what they hadn't

said—was there the least possibility there was such a subject?—
wasn't worth the jaw time.

He stood. "Walk with me."

She fell into step beside him, moving without speaking down
to the water's edge and then turning up the beach, following the
gentle curve of the bay. The damp sand squished between her
toes as the surf flooded in around their feet. The salty sting of
the warm breeze lifted her hair back from her face. With every
footstep, the distant music and laughter of others lessened as the
ocean filled in with its *shur-shur* sounds.

When he reached for her hand, she sighed. She had been
dangling hers near his, fingers spread in anticipation of his touch
yet reluctant to initiate it.

They made their way along the full curve of the bay away
from the resorts to where a single cottage stood right on the
beach.

He paused at the entrance and turned to her. In his eyes she
saw a world of hope. "Theadora, I . . ." Two coats of paint could
have dried before he continued. "You don't have to come in."

"I came to be with you."

"Here I am." He wrapped an arm about her shoulders and
pulled her close for a kiss.

epilogue

"MY GRANDMOTHER USED to say that"—an involuntary breath escaped her as Xavier's tongue flicked her fingertips—"kissing a man without a mustache is like eating an egg without salt. The spice is definitely missing."

"Your grandmother was some smart lady," he murmured, proceeding to demonstrate the point thoroughly.

When they finally came up for air, all she could see in his molasses eyes were twin reflections of herself. She looked happy and ready for more. He took his time. When it seemed he would be satisfied simply by staring into her eyes, he took her face in his hands, holding it like a precious object. "Theadora, I want to make love to you."

He took each of her hands in his and turned them over so that his dark fingers were laced with hers. "How does that look to you? My fingers and yours?"

"It looks right."

He released her hands and slid his own up her arms to cup her elbows and massage the crooks with his thumbs. "You're soft as butter. Sweet as a lullaby." His hands slid under her arms to fold gently up over her breasts. "Even softer."

She had a clear view of his body as he led her to the bed. From his muscular neck and football-star shoulders to the intimidating power of his thighs and calves, he was a sold hunk of man.

But when they got into bed, there was a hesitation in his expression.

That made her smile and say, "I promise. I will be gentle."

Grinning, he snagged her by the waist and pulled her hard against him. "You do that!"

SHE WOKE UP laughing.

He opened one sleepy eye. "What's so funny?"

She rolled over to face him. "Why did you go without so long? I'm not complaining. A man who's been saving himself has definite advantages for the female."

He folded his arms behind his head and grinned at her. "I told you how I've been praying for a wife, right? I decided if I was serious, I didn't want certain urges clouding the picture."

She smiled as she sat up cross-legged on the bed, facing his reclining form. He had put a new curl in her hair, that was for sure! Was he wondering, as she was, what to say about what came next for them?

He reached out and laid a hand on her bare breast.

"Theodora?"

"Yes?" *It was as if he'd read her mind.*

"You really are one *white* looking woman."

She threw her head back and laughed out loud. When their eyes met again, he looked more serious. "Do you believe in second chances?"

"Yes."

He nodded and rolled toward the edge of the bed, reaching for a drawer in the nightstand. As he turned back to her, he brushed his fingers over her cheek.

"It's time we get a few things straight between us."

"Okay."

"I know I come on strong, push things. But I have my reasons."

He took her hand and turned it palm up, then placed something hard into it, folding his fingers over her hand so that she couldn't see what it was, though she could tell by its shape. "I've had this since before Christmas. I don't expect you to answer me right away. Just so you know." He slid his hand down her arm and pressed her wrist. "I've found exactly the woman I want." He dipped his head, trying to read every thought in her eyes. "I want to marry you. Think about it. Take your time. But keep the ring, to remind you that I'm serious."

She put a hand on his shoulder to detain him when he would have moved away. "I'm thinking."

He tucked her close to his body. "I need a wife. I don't want less. Does that scare you?"

"In every way possible."

He hugged her tighter. "It scares me, too. But it feels good in here." He thumped his chest over his heart. "It feels so good, Theadora, to say the words at last, and mean them. I love you, Theadora."

"I love you, too."

The happiness in his expression seemed to have no limit. "We can get married whenever you say. I can be patient. But don't make it too long. I mean to start a family."

She chuckled. "I may be a little too old for that hope."

"Maybe." His grinned back. Then he wiggled his brows suggestively. "Maybe not."

As they kissed again and fell back into the pillows, Thea knew she was home, not just for now, but for all time.